Small Sacrifices

L.E. Luttrell

First Published in Great Britain in 2020

Copyright © L.E. Luttrell 2020

A CIP catalogue record for this book is available from the British Library.

ISBN 978-1-9999334-4-9

ISBN 978-1-9999334-5-6 ebook version

Typeset in Great Britain by Set-to-Print Ltd, Lancashire
sandra.stp.ltd@gmail.com

Published by Woolloomooloo

Printed in Great Britain

To Heather with thanks for your support and friendship

Also by **L.E.Luttrell**
DRAWING DANGER
THE BREAKDOWN

FREE BOOK

Sign up to L.E. Luttrell's VIP list to receive your **free book**.

Go to: **lelutrell.com**

1

Windsor, New South Wales
Sunday 6th January 2013

Ellen Gibson knew she would do almost anything to be like one of the celebrities she was reading about in her magazine. She would even be prepared to eat disgusting things which those British contestants who came out to Australia for 'I'm a Celebrity – Get me out of Here' had to do.

She envied the women whose photographs were plastered all over the celebrity pages; their freedom and ability to dress in the latest fashions and be out on the town. Something she hadn't been able to do for some years now, thanks to her husband Max, who was sitting a few feet away from her watching the news. He had curtailed her nights out with friends since the birth of their son Joshie, a little over five years ago.

Max wasn't one for going out for drinks with his mates. In fact, she'd realised at their wedding that he had very few friends, apart from those he worked with – and he only went out with them on odd occasions. They'd met at a club a little over six years ago while he'd been on a rare works outing. His good looks had caught her eye and there had been an instant attraction between them, but never for one moment did she think she would end up married to him.

Max was an only child and his parents and paternal grandmother were the only family members who'd attended their wedding. He'd told her family members on his father's side had been wiped out by the Second World War, The Vietnam War or cancer, which is the way both his grandparents had died; his grandmother only last year. His mother, Pamela, had an elderly father still alive, living in a retirement home suffering from dementia. There was an ex-sister in-law and two nieces, Max's cousins, living in Wellington, New Zealand who they received cards from on birthdays and at Christmas. Pamela's brother remained in New Zealand after his divorce, but she had no contact with him at all.

So when Max said he considered himself to be a 'family man', Ellen suspected it was more to do with the fact he hated spending money, didn't seem to know how to have 'fun', and was anti-social. He was close to his parents, and also his grandmother when she had been alive. It was clear he adored Josh. In some ways she was thankful; a couple of her friends had ended up with heavy boozing and irresponsible gambling types. But she missed having a laugh with her friends. She missed 'fun'. If things had been different she might have been … but she didn't want to think about that now.

Ellen sighed and looked at her watch. Only a few minutes to go. One of her favourite programmes, *Sixty*

Minutes, was due to come on soon. Tonight the show was featuring an enquiry into the death of a glamorous young Sydney model and the man suspected of killing her; her husband. She wanted to see what kind of man would do that. She didn't think Max ever would.

Max had refused to buy a new digital recorder when his old video machine had finally packed in a few years back and now she had to watch everything live. It was such a pain that most of the live shows she watched included advertisements. With the ads stretching across a good five minutes, she always kept a magazine handy to read. If Max was watching the show as well, she'd be unable to do this as he insisted she turn the overhead light off. There was a low level lamp sitting on a side table near where she sat on the couch, but with its large shade, it gave off insufficient light for reading. The lamp had been a present from Max's mother, and her suggestions that it be moved somewhere else and be replaced with a 'reading lamp' had met with steely glares.

While Max sat staring into space during the ads, thinking God knows what, she might nip off to the loo, pop outside for a quick ciggie (because Max wouldn't let her smoke in the house), or make a cup of tea – so the ads had their advantages. If they had a recorder she could always pause it anytime she wanted and do all the same things. Thankfully Max wasn't interested in too many of the shows she liked to watch and he'd often leave her to it while he retired to the kitchen to read where the lighting was better. He didn't read novels, just boring things like history, politics – nothing upbeat. But she didn't read novels either, unless it was a romantic one she'd been given by one of her friends.

This evening she'd put the overhead light on before sitting down, knowing Max would be leaving as soon as the news was over, and he hadn't challenged her. He'd told her earlier that he was planning to look at their finances tonight to see if there was anything else they had to cut back on before his next pay day. No doubt he'd suggest expensive cuts of meat, or her cosmetics.

Max's tight reins on the purse strings infuriated her so much. He'd placed a ban on all things he considered to be luxury items while he saved money towards building their new house. He'd once suggested her magazines came under the heading of luxury items, but as she pointed out to him, he had his papers and books, so why shouldn't she have her magazines? He'd restricted her magazine purchases to two a week though.

Ellen's attention was drawn back to the closing item of the news; the newsreader was announcing a big Powerball win. She snapped her head up to listen.

'As yet no-one has come forward to collect the fifty-five million dollar win in last week's Powerball draw, so you never know, your unregistered ticket might be the winning one.'

'Did you buy a ticket in last week's draw?' she turned to ask Max. He wasn't a registered ticket holder like her, but he did buy the odd Lotto or Powerball ticket on impulse. He'd rationed her ticket purchases, categorising them amongst *small sacrifices* she needed to make and so limiting their chances of winning. He'd also banned her from playing the poker machines on the odd occasions they drove over to their club in Richmond for a meal. Max didn't seem to understand you had to speculate to have a chance of winning big.

'Hmm?'

'Powerball. Did you buy lines in last week's draw? Someone won fifty-five million dollars and hasn't come forward to claim it yet.'

'Yes, I did as it happens.'

'Have you checked the ticket?'

She'd bet that Max had only bought a quick pick ticket with the minimum number of lines. Four she thought it was. The one she'd bought had sixteen lines and she hadn't won a cent.

'No, I haven't yet. I'm not sure where it is. I'll look for it when I come back from my trip.'

'*Max*! We could be sitting on the winning ticket!'

He laughed. 'Fat chance of that I'd say.'

'Well *someone* has won fifty-five million dollars. It could be us. Can't you look for it tonight?'

'I've got paperwork to do tonight. And if we've won, it's not like there's any urgent rush to collect it. It'll still be there when I come back.'

'Can you at least check your wallet? *Now*?' she asked in exasperation.

With some reluctance Max stood and walked through to pick up his wallet from the dining table where he'd left it earlier. After he methodically checked through everything, he shook his head.

'It's not there.'

'Oh, you're so infuriating Max Gibson! Where is it likely to be? I'll look for it.'

'I don't know Ellen. It could be in one of my trouser or suit jacket pockets.'

She flounced out of the living room and headed off to the spare bedroom where Max kept his clothes.

'I thought you wanted to watch your programme. If you don't want to see it, I'll turn the television off,' he called after her.

She didn't deign to reply. As if she could concentrate on watching anything with the thought that Max might be holding the winning ticket for fifty-five million dollars!

When Max was preparing for bed several hours later, she was re-hanging the last of his suits back in the wardrobe of the spare room. She'd been through them all twice checking and re-checking every pocket. The old house had no built-in wardrobes and the freestanding one in their bedroom was too small for her clothes, let alone Max's. His suits had been relegated to the tallboy which had once belonged to his grandfather and was in the spare room.

'Any luck in finding it?' Max asked popping his head around the door.

'No. I can't find it anywhere.'

'Leave it for tonight Ellen and I'll think about it on my drive up to Grafton tomorrow.'

'But you won't be home for another *two* days Max. I can't wait until then.'

'Of course you can. Don't be silly. There's no point in getting worked up over it. It'll be somewhere. I'll ring you from Grafton if I recall where I might have put it. Come on, time we went to bed.'

Ellen could tell by the sound of his breathing that Max was asleep. She was still feeling agitated at the thought of the missing Powerball ticket. If they had the unclaimed winning ticket it could change their lives dramatically. They could get out of this dump for starters and move anywhere they wanted to.

Max had inherited the ramshackle old house they lived in from his grandmother, triggering a move from their old rental in Rhodes to this dump out in the sticks. She hated it out here, isolated from all her friends and with no interesting places to go to. No amount of her pleading and cajoling could persuade him to sell the dump and buy a house in a better area.

'I grew up around Windsor. It's a great place to live,' he'd told her. 'I want Josh, and any other children we might have, to experience the wonders of semi-rural living.'

She knew Max wanted them to have at least one more child. They'd talked about it, but it was out of the question for her. She didn't think she could cope with carrying a young baby around the house – not after her accident. Joshie was more than enough for her to handle.

As for the local town. It was quaint, but it held little appeal for her and there were no shops anywhere near their house. They didn't even have close neighbours. She often wondered if that was part of the appeal for Max, with the added bonus of keeping her isolated from friends and family. There was no-one close by she could develop a friendship with. It had suited his grandparents because they reared animals, but their land was sold off long ago. It made no sense for her and Max to be living in such a remote place with a small family like theirs.

On one side of their place was open farm land. The house on the other side was falling into disrepair after the owners had died some years back in a road traffic accident. Max often talked about how he'd like to purchase that old house and its adjoining land to add to their property, some of which had once belonged to his grandparents, but unless they won big money that wouldn't be happening any time soon. And if money wasn't an issue, there's no way she'd want to stay in the area.

The one concession Max had made when they moved to Windsor was to admit that his grandparents' old house either needed a complete renovation or to be replaced. She'd told him unless he agreed to a new build she wouldn't move there. He'd had plans drawn up for the new house which was to be located behind the current one so they could remain living on the site while the build was done. Old outbuildings and the barn had been demolished to make way for it.

'We can start building when we've saved a good portion of the building costs,' Max had said. They had no mortgage so she didn't understand why Max couldn't just borrow *all* the money they needed for the new house. When she'd complained again the other week, he'd suggested she could perhaps find part time work once Josh started school which would enable them to save more.

'What if Josh is sick? What if he needs to go to the dentist or the doctor? I need to be available for him,' she'd told Max. She always used *Josh* when talking about their son to anyone, especially Max, who hated her calling him Joshie. He'd just nodded when she put forward her excuses, so hopefully she'd won that argument.

A job was out of the question – for a good while at least. She wanted to take advantage of the little bit of freedom she'd be afforded once Joshie started school, visiting shopping malls further afield without having to think about anyone else. She'd seldom had that opportunity since Josh's birth. It would be mainly window shopping apart from the odd bottle of perfume, make-up or skin cream which she bought out of the housekeeping, contraband items that had been on Max's 'luxury' hit list.

'We all have to make *small sacrifices* Ellen,' he'd said when she'd told him she couldn't do without her cosmetics. 'I've given up buying *daily* newspapers and only buy them on weekends now.'

As if newspapers compared to cosmetics. What he didn't know wouldn't hurt him. She'd managed to continue buying these items without his knowledge, claiming she was rationing use of her supply to when they went anywhere special. She didn't like to leave the house without her make-up on though. He'd never understand that these were *essential* items, not luxuries. She wouldn't be taking Joshie to school without any make-up on either. Having caught sight of the other mothers, it was out of the question. And she needed to look after her skin.

In the meantime, she had to go almost make-up free while at home and put up with the old house with its hideous seventies style kitchen and bathroom.

The rental they'd had in Rhodes before moving

to Windsor hadn't been a palace, but it seemed like it compared to what they had now. She wasn't used to living so far inland. She'd thought Rhodes had been bad enough and so different to what she was used to, but at least that had been near water. She'd grown up on the Central Coast and the family house was only a fifteen-minute walk to the beach. It would be great to move back to the coast where temperatures were more balanced all year round.

Wide awake still, her mind started whirling. Imagining they'd won the fifty five million, she started designing an amazing new house. She could just picture it, set up high to catch sea breezes with fantastic views. She could have a large walk-in wardrobe and whole set of new clothes, a new car and … *Stop!* She had to stop wishing for things she couldn't have. It would only make her unhappy. It was all just a pipe dream anyway. Her mind snapped back with *but you never know....* If only she could find that damn ticket. Where could it be?

While she was in middle of fantasising a scene of her watching Joshie splashing about in their new swimming pool, it suddenly came to her. Max might have been at a suburban newsagent when he bought the ticket and walked back to his car with it in his hand. It could be sitting on the passenger seat or somewhere else in the car. She needed to check. He was driving up to Grafton tomorrow for a meeting. If the ticket was on the passenger seat and he gave anyone up there a lift they could throw it out or pocket it themselves.

She eased out of bed, and tiptoed out to the hallway. Max's car keys were sitting on the hall stand. Another piece of antique furniture that had once belonged to his grandparents. She'd be so pleased when she could get shot of all the old stuff. She knew Max would want to hang on to some things out of sentiment, but they could all go into a spare room – not taking up pride of place amongst the modern furniture she wanted.

Taking the key, Ellen slipped her feet into her Crocks, opened the door as quietly as she could and stepped out onto the veranda. The crickets were still in full flow and they masked the sound of her movements as she walked down the steps and turned left towards the side of the house. As she rounded the corner she pressed the button to release the locks. Their bedroom was at the front of the house on the opposite side to where she stood now, and Max's car, standing on the concrete driveway in front of the old garage, was out of sight. He had the latest model Holden, provided courtesy of his company. It was hypocritical of him to say her rusty old car was more than adequate while he drove around in his smart vehicle. She checked the door pockets on the driver's side first. Nothing. Looking across she couldn't see anything on the passenger seat either. Max liked to keep his car clean. She walked around to the passenger side and found nothing in the door pockets there either. As she expected, there was nothing on the floor or under the seats. When she opened the glove box she was greeted by a pile of receipts sitting on top of the car service log. There were other sundry items in there as well, but it was the paper work that she needed to look through. She removed the pile of receipts setting them on the passenger seat, and with care lifted each one placing them face down in a new pile. It was as she was almost a third of the way through the pile that she found it. Eureka! She shoved the receipts back into the glove compartment and clutching the ticket, she closed the car door, reset the locks and retraced her steps. She walked through to the kitchen, sat at the small breakfast table and examined the ticket. Eight lines Max had bought. Eight chances of winning. She had no idea what the winning numbers were, she'd had hers checked while she was out shopping on Friday, but she was certainly going to find out tomorrow. She opened one of the kitchen drawers, took out the recipe book which sat on top and placed the ticket inside the front cover. It would be safe there. She was the only one who ever looked at recipes. Knowing the ticket was now safely in her possession, she returned to the bedroom hoping she might now be able to get some sleep.

2

Monday

Max snapped awake on the first ring of his phone alarm at four am and reached out to turn it off before it disturbed Ellen. He heard her groan before turning over; her breathing returning to a steady rhythm. He slipped out of bed, taking the phone with him and after washing and dressing walked over to the partially closed door of Josh's bedroom to listen; he was still sound asleep. Max continued on to the kitchen where he prepared and ate a bowl of cereal, then made a flask of coffee for the road. He noticed the kitchen bin was overflowing so he pulled out the liner, tied it up and took it out the back door to the rubbish bin. At the front door he sat on a stool while he put on his shoes and then, taking care to be quiet, he left the house. He had a long drive ahead of him this morning and hoped to arrive in South Grafton by lunch time. His meeting was scheduled for three this afternoon. Unless there were any major hold-ups, he anticipated that with minimal stops he'd make it in plenty of time.

It was as he was driving up the freeway later that he

remembered he might have shoved the Powerball ticket into the glove compartment. If so, it would be sitting among the pile of receipts he kept in there, waiting to be sorted and submitted to his employer for re-imbursement.

He worked as the Sales Director for a large logistics company. The meeting today was with his company's regional manager and a firm who manufactured tools. They hoped to obtain a lucrative new contract with the tool firm for transporting their goods to customers across the country.

If successful, they would suggest the tool company directors dined with them this evening. If not, it'd just be him and the regional manager. He had to make the long drive back tomorrow so he'd have to remember not to drink too much alcohol tonight – in case he was pulled over for a random police breathalyser.

He would check for the Powerball ticket after the meeting and then phone Ellen.

Ellen woke to sound of Josh's cries. She could tell by the volume level that he was in her bedroom. She turned over to see him standing at the side of the bed.

'What's up hon?' she asked him, hoping it was just something like a bad dream where he would snuggle up to her in bed and drop off to sleep again. She was desperate for more sleep herself.

'I have that itchy thing again and it hurts,' Josh said, scratching his arms and then legs to make the point. 'I've been calling out to you for *ages.*'

Last summer he'd broken out in a rash which her mother had insisted was a heat rash and didn't warrant a trip to the doctor's.

'You used to get them all the time when you were about Josh's age. It'll go in a day or so,' her mother had said.

Sure enough the rash had vanished within a few days, but Josh had been grizzly with constant moaning throughout its duration.

Resigned to having no further rest, Ellen sat up and rubbed the sleep out of her eyes. After dragging herself out of bed, she drew the curtains back to have a closer look at Josh's arms and legs. She could see large angry red marks which looked quite different to last year's rash. She definitely needed to take him to see a doctor this time.

'Let's go and have some breakfast,' she suggested in the hope of distracting him. He sniffled as she held his hand and walked through to the kitchen.

Looking up at the clock in the kitchen she was surprised to see it was just after nine. Josh seldom let her sleep in this late. He said he'd been calling her for ages. Had he come into the bedroom earlier? She'd obviously been dead to the world as she'd not heard a thing. It was a good thing it wasn't a school day, she wouldn't be able to do this once he started. It would be back to setting alarm clocks when he started school in a few weeks. Something she had always hated when she worked. Especially after a late night.

She prepared a quick bowl of cereal and a glass of milk for him which she placed on the table.

'Sit at the table Joshie and eat your breakfast while mummy makes a call to the doctor.'

She picked up her mobile, found the doctor's surgery listing in her contacts and dialled the number on the land line. Max only allowed her to have limited credit on her pay-as-you-go mobile and she didn't want to waste a call using it. The signal was dodgy at their house anyway. After explaining Josh's rash, she was given an appointment for eleven am.

Catching sight of herself in the hall mirror, she realised she'd have to get her skates on. She needed to shower, consider what to wear today, do her hair and put her make up on. There'd be no time for breakfast. She turned and headed off to the bathroom, forgetting Joshie for a few seconds. He wasn't about to let her get away with that though and his loud wails followed her down the hallway. She turned back towards the kitchen, stopping in the doorway.

'I've made an appointment to take you to the doctor's this morning, so mummy has to have a shower and get ready. Be a good boy Joshie and finish your breakfast, then find some clothes to wear. By the time I'm finished I *will* expect you to be dressed. In sensible, going out clothes. Not in any of your superhero costumes. A pair of shorts and a t-shirt. Clean ones from your shelves. And don't forget to put on underpants. Okay?'

His mouth took a downward turn and his forehead creased in a scowl, before he nodded and started eating. She'd given him one of her steely glares, he knew better than to defy her when she showed him that face. She knew he preferred her to dress him, and he sometimes threw a tantrum if she wouldn't, but he was quite capable of doing it himself and she had no time for any of his nonsense today. She couldn't help but smile as she turned away from him. He was so cute when he scowled.

'Your son has eczema, Mrs. Gibson,' the doctor told Ellen after examining Josh.

'What's caused that then and what does it mean? Is it contagious? Will he be able to start school next month if he still has it then? What can we do to get rid of it?'

Ellen saw her opportunity for some freedom slipping away; she felt quite breathless and panicky.

'The exact cause of eczema is not known. It's a form of dermatitis which is a reactionary skin condition linked to the immune system. It is commonly found in families who have a history of other allergies. Do you or anyone else in your family suffer from any allergies?'

She thought about it for a few seconds. 'No, no allergies as far as I know. My mother told me I used to break out in heat rashes during the summer when I was little. Do you mean something like that? Josh had a heat rash last year.'

'Yes that's the kind of thing I mean. It's not contagious and there's no need to keep Joshua away from school. It may be that he has become overheated in this weather and has had an adverse reaction. You'll need to stop scratching yourself young man, you'll only make it worse,' the doctor said turning to Josh who was dragging his short nails across the inflamed spots. Thankfully she'd cut them on Saturday.

'I'll prescribe some corticosteroid cream which you need to apply twice a day.'

The doctor went on to give a list of other natural products and items she should buy and how she should use them which left her head spinning.

'And make sure all his clothes are made of natural fibres like cotton, like he's wearing today. Man-made fibres can cause further irritation to the skin. If you don't have any at home, I would suggest you buy some baking soda to add to his bath. His bath water needs to be warm, not hot, and don't allow him to spend any longer than ten to fifteen minutes in there. Whichever moisturiser you decide to buy will need to be applied to his skin immediately after bathing, plus several other times a day. There are a number of other things you could add to the bath as well. If you ask on your way out, the receptionist can give you a leaflet. None of these things will cure eczema but they will calm the condition.'

'That's such a lot to remember and change,' she said with concern. 'Josh was wearing his Spider Man suit yesterday afternoon and charging around the place. It's made of some horrible man-made fabric and I kept telling him he'd be too hot in it. Could that have caused this eczema thing to break out?'

'It may well have.'

'Do you hear that Josh? You can't wear your Spider Man suit anymore. Or have long plays in the bath.'

Josh had been sitting quietly on his chair, his hands clasped in his lap since the doctor told him to stop scratching. Silent tears now fell down his face. At least he wasn't crying loudly as he had been this morning.

'Thank you, doctor,' she said standing after he printed out the prescription for Josh's cream. 'Come on Joshie, we've got to go shopping to get you some of these special things.'

She suspected everything the doctor had suggested was going to cost a fortune. That would scupper her intention to buy moisturising cream for herself today. On the other hand, perhaps she could add at least one jar of cream and tell Max it was all the stuff she'd had to buy for Josh. It wasn't until she walked into the pharmacy that she realised she hadn't mentioned Josh's asthma attacks. He hadn't had one for almost a year now, but their old doctor in Rhodes had thought they might have been triggered by pollution from building work. Would that be considered an allergic reaction? She wasn't sure. Anyway, he seemed to be over them now and hadn't had to use his inhaler for some time.

While waiting for Josh's prescription she looked around the pharmacy and picked up some Aloe Vera gel, some Tea Tree oil for Josh and a night cream for herself. She'd have to buy some special washing powder too and on the way to the tills spotted that Lux was on special offer. That would do for now she decided, grabbing it. She intended to go around to the newsagents after to check the Powerball ticket but it was then she remembered that she'd left it at home in the drawer. Damn! That meant she'd have to come back to the shops. What a pain!

Josh was still whining about his rash when Ellen pulled the car into the driveway.

'Have you been scratching it again?' she asked him. He went quiet and didn't respond as she climbed out of the car. Josh had released himself from his car seat and was attempting to scamper out of the car without her noticing him but when she opened the back door to collect the shopping, she could see all the indications that he'd been scratching his right arm and leg. The eczema was an angry red colour.

'You have been, haven't you? Remember what the doctor said Joshie. It will only make it worse. We have to go out again, but I'll put some of this cream on you before we go. Perhaps that will help.'

Josh followed her into the house and sat quietly on a kitchen chair while she rubbed the cream onto the rash patches.

'Better?'

He nodded.

Turning to the kitchen drawer, she retrieved the Powerball ticket and put it into her bag.

'Come on then Joshie, let's go and see if we've won any money.'

At the newsagents in the Penrith mall, Ellen picked up a print-out of the winning numbers that the newsagent put out for customers to check their own tickets. She scanned down the eight lines of the ticket, disappointment setting in as the numbers didn't match. She finally reached the last line and saw that some did. She looked at the winning sequence and compared it to her ticket. Every single number matched. Could that be right? She looked again and had the same results.

'Oh my God!' She screeched. 'OH MY GOD!' She screeched even louder. 'I've won the Powerball jackpot!'

Other customers paused in their business and looked at her. With a wide grin she scanned the crowd, waving her ticket before rushing up to the counter.

'I've got the winning Powerball ticket. Can you check it on your system, just to make sure?'

She passed the ticket to the young woman behind the counter who was giving her a sceptical look. The woman scanned the ticket and her face registered shock.

'It's true isn't it?' Ellen said jumping up and down.

Greg Walton, the owner of the newsagents, had been working on orders further down the counter when he heard the commotion. He rushed over to join his employee.

'Let me see,' he said taking over.

He scanned it again and realised it *was* the missing ticket that had been announced on the news. This was going to be fantastic for his business. Although the ticket wasn't bought on his premises, registering the win through him was going to bring a spate of publicity. Personally, he thought the woman was mad for announcing to all and sundry that she had won. A large crowd had gathered around the woman and many people were snapping photographs of her and her little boy on their phones.

He cleared his throat and spoke to the woman. 'It seems you do have the winning ticket madam and I can help you with the claim,' he said with a generous grin for the crowd who were now taking photos of him holding the ticket.

Josh was confused. His mother said she wanted to check and see if they had won some money. She was jumping around and squealing so he thought she must have. Normally when she won money, she smiled and bought him a little treat like a toy car, a hot doughnut or an ice cream. He'd never seen her like this. And she seemed to have forgotten all about him, talking to a bunch of strangers over near the counter. He wriggled through the crowd and tugged on his mother's dress.

'Mummy, what's going on?' he asked her.

She looked down at him as though surprised to see him. He was right, she had forgotten he was with her.

'Oh Joshie, I'm sorry. Mummy's just so excited. We won! We *won*,' she repeated grabbing his hands and pulling him around in a little dance. He felt silly with her doing this in front of all these people.

'Does that mean you can have a new spider man costume made for me that doesn't hurt my skin?' he asked her when she stopped dancing.

'You can have anything you want from now on Joshie,' she said with a big smile.

Anything? Wow. He'd have to think about it and ask Daddy to help him make a list. But for now he was going to ask for some treats.

'So can I have a milk shake and an ice cream now?'

'Not now Joshie, mummy has some important things

to arrange.'

He knew it was too good to be true. Adults told fibs all the time.

One man in the crowd watched the little display the mother was putting on for her audience. He took an instant dislike to the woman. What a fool she was. If he discovered he'd won fifty-five million dollars he certainly wouldn't be advertising the fact to a crowd of perfect strangers. And telling a little kid he could have anything he wanted was so wrong. Judging by the look of the woman, he'd bet she'd spend the money creating an obscene fancy lifestyle. He hovered around the display pretending to look at cards, listening to everything she told the newsagent owner before snorting in disgust and leaving the shop.

After his successful meeting Max spent some time looking through the paperwork from his glove box. He had a few hours before he was due to meet up with his new clients and the regional sales manager again. His search proved fruitless. The Powerball ticket was not amongst the receipts. What could he have done with it? Ellen would go mad if he couldn't find it and he'd have to face her nagging questions of exactly what he'd done after he'd bought it. He could have sworn he put the receipt from the newsagent straight into the glove box, so the ticket must have been with it. He hoped he hadn't accidentally thrown it out. There had been instances of winners claiming they had lost a winning ticket and a thorough investigation had to be made to prove their purchase. The machines at outlets who sold the tickets recorded the exact time and location any winning tickets were sold. He had the receipt for other things he'd bought at the same time. A new pen and a notepad. The shop would surely have security footage as well. He might be able to salvage things if he couldn't find it. He'd telephone Ellen later and explain that they could easily check if they'd won even without the ticket. Hopefully that would appease her.

Ellen had been busy all afternoon making arrangements for the press to visit their property for an interview the following day. They'd wanted to come that day, but she needed time to prepare for it. She'd organised for her hairdresser to come to the house in the morning first thing and do her hair. Her hairdresser had put her in touch with a make-up specialist who was coming to do her make-up after her hair had been done. Although they didn't have the money in the bank yet, she'd treated herself to a new dress and shoes for the interview, using the credit card that was supposed to be used for emergency purposes only. She considered this an emergency. She was so excited. Now was her chance to become famous. Something she'd dreamed about since she was a little girl.

When she ten years old, she'd been chosen for the lead in the school musical that year, but one of the school bullies, jealous at how good she'd been in rehearsals, had deliberately tripped her as she'd been running towards the main school entrance, the day before the scheduled performance. She'd landed on a sharp jagged rock that formed part of the border around a small garden bed. Instead of being able to do the show, she'd ended up in hospital with a serious leg injury which required an operation – and a broken heart.

The father of one of the other girls in her class was in charge of a children's television programme and she'd told Ellen her dad was coming to see the production. Ellen had dreams of him choosing her to appear on the show which she watched with great envy every week. She could sing and dance as well as any of the kids on that show and her starring role in the musical would have shown off her skills.

The break on her leg was so serious that even after it healed, she had to give up her dance classes. She could no longer bear weight on it for pirouettes or balances. And she walked with a slight limp, even after it had healed. Her dream of being a stage performer was crushed. Her mother had attempted to persuade her to turn to acting or singing instead, but perversely she'd refused. Dancing had been her true love.

Shaking off all thoughts of her past shattered dreams Ellen focused her attention on what she still had to do. Everything for the interview seemed sorted, but she hadn't bought Joshie his promised milk shake and ice cream. She'd told him earlier that she'd take him out for a McDonalds. Looking at the kitchen clock, she saw it was about time they left. The McDonalds would also serve as their evening meal tonight. Joshie loved McDonalds and rarely had the chance to sample their treats because Max disapproved of going to places like that. Well he wouldn't be home tonight so she'd ask Joshie to keep it as their little secret.

Max made several attempts to reach Ellen before he headed off for the celebratory meal. There had been no answer on the land line or her mobile, with both going to voicemail. He'd left her a couple of messages saying he'd call her later. He couldn't help but worry about where she could be at six pm which was roughly Josh's bath time. He hoped she wasn't out wasting money on junk food.

Ellen had been busy on the phone to friends and family since putting Joshie to bed. When she realised it was almost eleven she made excuses and rang off. She needed her beauty sleep. She just hoped Joshie would sleep well and not wake her too early. With all the excitement of the win she'd forgotten about his eczema treatment in the afternoon, but remembered to apply the prescribed ointment to his skin before bed. He'd moaned when she'd said he could skip his usual bath when they returned from McDonalds, but she had so many calls to make. If the eczema was still showing so prominently tomorrow, she'd have to dress him in long trousers and a long sleeve shirt for the cameras.

3

Tuesday

The motel bed was not particularly comfortable and Max decided the booking his secretary had made had been a mistake. It hadn't been the cheapest one in town, but nor could it be called luxurious by any stretch of the imagination. He woke at three, tossing and turning for a while. When he couldn't get back to sleep he thought he may as well get up and set off for home. He hadn't been able to get through to Ellen the previous night despite many further attempts. The land line had been constantly engaged and Ellen's mobile had been switched off. Was everything alright? He couldn't help but worry.

'Can you tell us what first went through your mind when you discovered you had won fifty-five million dollars on Powerball?' the news journalist asked Ellen.

She'd rehearsed this type of question as she lay in bed last night, trying to decide what would be the best thing to say to show her in a good light.

'Well to start with I was just overwhelmed with shock and delight. Then I thought of all the things we could do for our family and friends.'

Ellen made sure she said "we" and "our", not wanting the press to think she intended to take all the glory for being generous. She did plan to persuade Max that they should help family and friends. She suspected Max would be furious with her for arranging to meet the press, which is why she'd arranged the interviews to take place long before he was due to return home. This was her opportunity to become famous and nothing and no one was going to stop her.

'Of course, my husband and I can now build the dream home we've been saving so hard for and send Joshua to the best schools. We'll never have to worry about money again,' she told the cameras. And her dream home was not going to be in Windsor, she'd make sure of that. If Max objected, she'd be packing her bags and leaving with Joshie. She wanted a beautiful, custom built large modern house near the coast and not far from a decent shopping complex.

The cameras continued flashing and more questions were fired at Ellen. She became a bit flustered at one point when a journalist asked her what her husband thought of their win. She didn't want to tell them that Max knew nothing about it. She'd sent him a message saying she had wonderful news, but hadn't told him what that news was. She turned the reporter's attention to Joshie, referring to him as Joshua.

'Joshua's going to sit down with his father and compile a list of all the things he wants aren't you darling?' she asked pulling Joshie in front of the cameras.

Joshie looked at her before turning back to the cameras and nodding.

She had dressed Joshie in his best clothes making use of the long trousers and long sleeves to cover his eczema, because, as she suspected, it was still showing this morning. Although the colour had faded to a lighter pink rather than the angry red it was yesterday. She'd applied two lots of the prescribed cream already today to ensure he didn't start scratching himself in front of the cameras.

It was while she and Joshie were posing for still shots for the newspapers that she heard another car pull into the driveway and realised it was Max.

'Well I think that just about covers everything I have to say. Thank you all for coming,' she said hoping they'd all beat a hasty retreat. 'I have to take Joshua in now to make him his lunch.'

She took Joshie's hand and began walking towards the front door. She heard Max's voice calling out to her but she kept walking until she felt Joshie pull his hand free and move away from her.

'Daddy,' he cried out and she could hear the sound of his running footsteps.

Max was shocked to see a range of media vehicles both parked out on the grass verge in front of their house and on the driveway. He wasn't able to pull his car up to the front of the garage as he normally did with so many cars blocking him.

His first thoughts were that something terrible had happened to Ellen or Josh, but then he spotted them walking towards the front veranda. What the hell was going on?

'Ellen,' he called as he stepped out of the car. Within seconds he was surrounded by flashing cameras and reporters firing questions at him. One of them asked him what he thought of their big win. *Big win?*

The next minute Josh was calling his name and running towards him. He kneeled down to welcome his son who flew into his arms.

'What's going on buddy?' he asked Josh in a whisper.

'We had the big win daddy. Mummy can tell you all about it.'

'What on earth were you thinking?' Max shouted at Ellen once the last of the media vehicles had driven off. 'And is that a new dress?'

'I'm sorry Max. I knew you wouldn't want to speak to the television or newspaper press so I deliberately arranged for them to come while you were still away. I don't see why I shouldn't have my moment in the limelight just because you wouldn't want to.'

'Your moment in the limelight? Have you realised what you've done Ellen? We'll probably have every man and his dog around here invading our privacy once your interview is shown on the news tonight and appears in the papers tomorrow.'

'Well we don't have to stay here. We could go and stay in a luxury hotel. That's what I'd like to do anyway,'

Ellen said pouting. 'It's not like we can't afford it now.'

'And what have you done with the ticket? I thought you said you couldn't find it?'

'It was in your car. I found it in the glove compartment on Sunday night. You were in a deep sleep when I found it and I didn't want to disturb you because you had to get up so early in the morning. I didn't hear you get up otherwise I would have told you I'd found it.'

He thought that unlikely. 'But you could have phoned me. Why didn't you?' he asked, working hard to control his rising anger.

'I knew you would be driving and then had a meeting. I had other things to think about anyway. I had to take Josh to the see a doctor on Monday morning. He woke up covered in a nasty rash which was causing him a lot of pain. The doctor said he has eczema. Then I had to go and buy all this special stuff the doctor told me to get and put some cream on him when we got home. It wasn't until later in the day that I remembered about the ticket and went to check it. My phone needed charging last night, I forgot about it in all the excitement. I sent you a message this morning.'

Hearing that Ellen had looked to Josh's needs before doing anything with the ticket, caused his anger to recede. And she had sent him a message.

'I was probably driving. I left the motel in the middle of the night and haven't looked at my phone since I stopped at about six am. I'm going to check on Josh.'

He left Ellen in the kitchen and walked into his son's bedroom. Josh had removed his trousers and shirt, replacing them with a t-shirt and a pair of shorts.

'Let's see your rash buddy,' he said. Josh turned around allowing him to see the marks on his legs then thrust his arms out. Max could also see a range of large pink marks on his arms.

'I've got a big one at the top of my right leg as well,' Josh said rolling up his shorts for Max to see.

'Is it very painful?'

'It felt very hot and itchy Daddy, and made me cry. But it feels better now mummy has rubbed some cream over the marks. The doctor told her to use it.'

'I'm sorry you have this Josh, but we'll make it better soon I promise. Daddy still has to talk to mummy for a bit, can you carry on playing in your room? I just wanted to see you were alright.'

Josh nodded and Max rubbed his blonde hair affectionately before leaving him to return to the kitchen.

'So Ellen what have you done with the ticket?'

'I've submitted it for a claim. The owner of the newsagent helped me and he phoned into the office that deals with it in Sydney. It's been sent there by a special courier.'

'I hope you've put both our names on it?'

'Of course. I realise you bought the ticket Max, but it's *our* ticket.'

That made him hesitate for a second, realising that if he had put in a claim he would have only put *his* name on it to ensure he had control of the funds. Perhaps he was judging Ellen too harshly.

'I know. I was just making sure you weren't claiming it as *your* ticket.'

'I wouldn't do that.'

'Good. So fifty-five million dollars we've won? It's all a bit much to take in at the moment. It doesn't seem real.'

'Oh it's real alright. Just think Max, we can build the house of our dreams now.'

He nodded. 'I could ask the architect to come out and draw us up new plans. I'm sure your vision will have changed and you'll want a bigger house. I can also look into buying that land next door.'

'What *here* you mean?'

'Yes. It was what we planned.'

'It was what we planned because you inherited this house from your grandmother and we didn't have much money. We don't have to stay here now. We can build a dream house *anywhere* we want. I would rather it was near the sea where it's cooler in the summer and warmer in the winter. If you don't want us to bring Josh up in a crowded suburb we could look further out of Sydney so you have your wish of a semi-rural area. Just so long as it's near the sea and close to some shops I don't mind where we go.'

Max was unsure how to answer Ellen. He would prefer to stay in the Windsor area but he could understand her wish to be closer to the sea. It was where she grew up after all. It was an argument he was not going to win if money was not going to be an issue.

'Okay, I won't contact the architect,' he said. 'We can talk about it and consider other areas. Have you told your family about the win?'

'Of course. I phoned them last night. Mum is thrilled for us. We'll have to help them out a bit. And your parents of course. Are you going to phone them now?'

'I'll do it later. Now tell me what we need to do to treat Josh's eczema.'

4

The man slowed as he drove past the Gibson house.

'That's where they live,' he said to his companion. 'She gave me her address and I followed her about thirty minutes after she left the mall yesterday just so I'd know where it was. I came past earlier and she seemed to be giving interviews with the press. There were loads of cars here. Looks like they've all gone now.'

'Yeah, but how are we gunna do it? Are we gunna break into the house in the middle of the night or somethin'?'

'Nah, her husband might be a big bastard. There's two cars there. The old Holden is her one. Best if we come back early in the morning. We can hide the car in the garage of that old wreck of a house next door, keep watch and see if any opportunities arise,' he said before accelerating and driving off.

'Josh is asleep. He dozed off the middle of the story,' Max told Ellen as he entered the living room. 'I suspect as he's in bed so early he'll be getting us up at the crack of dawn.'

'I hope not. He's tired because he's had a long day.

Shh. I'm waiting to see how much of the filming they did today they're going to show on the news.'

Ellen had been glued to the television since the news started, flicking between channels. More than one television station had interviewed her she'd told him and unfortunately a couple of them ran the news at the same time. She was hoping to catch other channels later.

He really couldn't bear to watch it, but thought he should to be aware of what Ellen had said. He was still furious with her for contacting the press. What was she thinking? Her desire to always look glamorous and be a celebrity had reached new heights and was an unbecoming side of her character. It was an obsession she'd developed since she'd been watching all these reality TV shows.

If he'd been able to see into the future and how their marriage might pan out he doubted he would have proposed to her. He had initially considered his affair with Ellen as just that. An affair that was not serious. He had been attracted to her beauty and shapely body and had taken full advantage of what was on offer. But after announcing she was pregnant with his child, he'd made a half-hearted proposal. Her eager response should have sounded warning bells. She'd always said it was an accident. The coil she'd had fitted had supposedly slipped out of place, resulting in the pregnancy. He hadn't taken additional precautions after their first night of intimacy because she'd told him it wasn't necessary; coils were fail-safe. The doctor recommended that she have the coil removed with immediate effect once her pregnancy was discovered. Or so she'd told him. He'd always believed her, but in recent years he'd wondered whether she'd told him the truth. She didn't seem too keen to have any other children and a couple of times had claimed her body wouldn't be able to cope with carrying a young child around. He was sure she was playing on the injuries she'd received in the accident some years back. It was an argument they'd had many times. Since Josh's birth she'd had another coil fitted – or possibly her first – to ensure she didn't fall pregnant. Sometimes he thought she'd deliberately fallen pregnant with Josh so she could give up work. Many of his colleagues had working wives, and complained about them being home so little. They said he was a "lucky bugger". Despite discovering that one of the lines in the Powerball ticket he'd bought had won fifty-five million dollars he didn't feel so lucky tonight. In fact, as he waited for Ellen and Josh to appear on the news, he had a sense of impending doom. Would this win spell the end of his marriage? He dreaded to think of the obscene amounts of money Ellen would want to spend once the money dropped into their bank account. He should make an appointment with the bank for some financial advice.

The announcement that a local Windsor family had won a massive fifty-five million on Powerball caught the attention of Detective Inspector India Hargreaves as she prepared the evening meal. She stopped and watched a blonde woman posturing and gushing in front of the cameras. She had her small son with her but no sign of her husband. The woman was wearing a deep red dress with white polka dots. The dress flared out from the waist to calf length and the overall image reminded India of shots of Marilyn Monroe she'd seen in magazines. All she needed was a hat and white gloves to complete the fifties look.

'Lucky buggers,' her husband Rob commented as he set the table.

'I think she's very foolish to give interviews like that. It's almost asking for trouble,' she said.

'Some people just love the attention. I suspect she's one of those.'

'Hmm. Mum and Dad always said they'd never allow their names to become public if they won the lotto. There was that famous case back in the sixties of a child being kidnapped whose parents had won the lottery. It didn't have a happy ending.'

'Yeah I remember learning about it during my training,' Rob said. Like her, Rob was in the police force, having now risen to the rank of Detective Superintendent and was based down in Penrith at Nepean Police Area Command.

'And that woman has just paraded her young child in front of the cameras. Bloody stupid if you ask me,' she said.

'I'm sure they'll be fine. She was talking about them building their dream home. I don't imagine they'll be doing that in Windsor.'

'No I imagine she's the type who'd want to build in some swanky suburb on the coast somewhere.'

'Would you want to stay in Windsor if we won fifty-five million dollars Mrs. Ellis? I know I wouldn't. I'd want to see some of the world.'

She'd kept her maiden name at work, but at home and in all other places, she was Mrs. Ellis, as Rob liked to remind her on a regular basis. She loved him calling her that. It was kind of sexy.

'Mmm. I wouldn't mind travelling for a bit. But I've never thought about where I'd want to live if money was no object. I'll think about it and let you know Rob. Just so we're ready when we have that big win,' she said winking at him before she turned back to strain the rice.

5

Wednesday

Max rose at his usual time and showered before preparing to head off to the office.

'You're not going into work today are you?' Ellen asked, following him into the kitchen.

'Of course I am. Why wouldn't I?'

'I hope it's just to hand your notice in. We've just won fifty-five million dollars Max. We have a lot to talk about and there's so much to do. One of the first things I want to do is buy a brand new car. A four wheel drive. I thought we could go and look at some today.'

'We don't have the money yet and we don't know when they'll be presenting it to us. Until we have that money we can't buy anything. I'm not sure I want to stop working just yet anyway.'

'I was thinking of *planning* ahead. You won't have time to work Max. We'll be busy looking for land for sale in an area we both like, then planning the build. And why would you want to work when we'll have all that money. We could invest it in something that would bring a return for us. Like rental properties.'

'I don't know Ellen. It's something we need to talk about.'

The idea of spending twenty four hours a day with Ellen wasn't appealing. Not the way she was now. He could imagine her telling everyone, everywhere they went, about their big win. He couldn't bear the idea. Josh was another matter. He could spend all day with him, but he'd be starting school in another month and it would be just the two of them while Josh was there during the day.

'Work will keep me level-headed. We need to take care with the money we've won and invest it wisely,' he said. 'One step at a time.'

'I refuse to live like a pauper while you consider whether we're spending the money *wisely*. I want to be able to buy things as I need them. Like my make-up and beauty products. And any clothes I fancy.'

'Those kinds of things are okay Ellen. I just mean we have to make sensible decisions about bigger items.'

'I hope you're not suggesting that buying myself a new car is not a *"sensible decision"*,' Ellen said, making inverted commas in the air.

'No, a new car for you is also fine. I know you've been wanting one for a long time.'

'Then what are you talking about?' she asked him seeming to brighten up a little.

'The decision on where we live. Where we might stay while we make that happen. I don't want to be forking out money for luxury hotels. There's no need. I want to be able to help myself to anything in my kitchen when

I want. Not to have to ring some bloody room service and pay a fortune for it. Once we decide on where we're going to build, we can rent an apartment or house.'

Ellen's face took on that disappointed look again. 'I was rather looking forward to decamping to a hotel. Oh Max, come on, I've never stayed in a luxury hotel. Why not let other people wait on us hand and foot for a little while? I thought you were worried about the press coming around here again.'

'I am. But I'd rather rent an apartment somewhere. We can talk about it later. I have several meetings and other things to tie up at work, then I'll ask for some time off. Maybe come home a bit earlier. We could spend the rest of the week driving around looking at places.'

'That sounds good to me,' Ellen said smiling and looking happy. She looked beautiful when she smiled. Maybe things would be okay.

'Anyway look, I'd better get off. See you later. I'll get home as early as I can,' he said leaning over to give Ellen a peck on the forehead. 'No more interviews. I don't want our son exposed publicly again like you did yesterday.'

She nodded at him before he left by the back door.

Ellen had considered telling Max that she'd be prepared to have another child now if he gave up work and helped look after it. Now money wasn't an issue. They could even hire a day nanny to help out. She thought that might make him look at everything she wanted more favourably. But something had made her hold back. She wanted to enjoy spending some money first. Also finding a suitable site and building their new house was going to take at least another year, so it would be better to wait as she wanted to be actively involved in that process. There was plenty of time for her to have another child.

'Has Daddy gone to work?' a sleepy Josh asked her as he stumbled into the kitchen. He looked so cute Ellen wanted to hug him to death. She pulled him onto her lap, wrapped her arms around him and gave him several kisses before answering him.

'Yes, just a few minutes ago Mr. Sleepy Head. He did pop his head into your room on the way to the kitchen earlier but you were sound asleep.'

'You said Daddy wouldn't need to go to work anymore.'

'I know. He doesn't, but Daddy had to go into work today. Tomorrow we're going to drive around looking at new places we might move to. Won't that be exciting?

'You mean we won't stay here?'

'Probably not Joshie. I want to live by the sea-side and we can afford to now. Wouldn't you like to as well?'

He shrugged, not looking too keen. 'What about my school? Will I be starting there if we are going to move so far away? And what about Nana and Pop Gibson? Will we still see them?'

'Of course we'll see them. Just as we did when we lived in Rhodes. They'll either come over to our new house or we'll go to their place. I don't know what we're going to do about your school Joshie. We'll have to wait and see what happens.'

She could see he wasn't happy with this news. His mouth took on a downward shape reminding her of the unhappy faces she inserted into her text messages to friends when she hadn't been out anywhere for weeks, or hadn't been able to buy any new treats.

'Come and have some breakfast and don't look so glum. Everything is going to be exciting from now on.'

Ellen was washing up the breakfast dishes at ten when there was a knock at the front door. She'd had more important things to do before cleaning up the kitchen (like dressing smartly and applying make-up in case any more reporters came around). She'd also been interrupted by a phone call from the company that dealt with the Powerball. They were going to present a huge cheque to them the following afternoon. Max would no doubt say no photographs were to be taken. He could be really miserable sometimes. She hoped she wouldn't have to do these boring hand washes for much longer. Her new house had to have a dishwasher. She removed her washing up gloves, walked through the hall and opened the front door.

'Good morning Mrs. Gibson. My name is Jude Ronson from the Windsor Chronicle,' a man greeted her, holding up his identification. 'I saw the feature on your Powerball win on the news last night and wondered whether you'd be willing to give me an interview that we could feature in next week's edition.'

She hadn't contacted any of the local press, considering them too small fry. She'd sort of agreed to no more interviews in response to Max's statement this morning but he'd been talking about ones that included Josh. She didn't see what the harm would be if she gave this man an interview with only a picture of herself.

'How did you find out where we live?' she asked him.

'One of my friends was here interviewing you yesterday.'

'Okay, I'll give you an interview, come in to the dining room,' she said opening the fly screen door for him. 'You'll have to excuse the mess in there, I had maps out last night looking at different places we might consider moving to.'

'So you won't stay in the Windsor area now you've had this big win?' Ronson asked her as he followed her down the hall to the dining room.

She was about to say *not on your life* but thought that might offend him as he was representing a local paper.

'I was brought up by the sea side and would prefer to move back to somewhere like that. Don't get me wrong, I love Windsor, but it's just so hot in the summer and cold in the winter. Something I'm not used to,' she said, hoping that he'd find her statement satisfactory.

'I know what you mean,' Ronson said. 'My cousins lived down on the south coast and when I was a kid I stayed with them during both summer and winter holidays. I found the temperatures much easier to cope with.'

She nodded. 'Would you like a tea or coffee?' she asked him.

'A coffee would be great thanks. With milk and one sugar.'

'Mummy who's that man?' Joshie asked her. He was standing near the entrance to the kitchen and staring at the stranger sitting at the dining room table.

'My name's Jude Ronson. I work for the local paper. Your mother is going to give me an interview. You must be Joshua, right?'

Josh nodded.

'My husband doesn't want Josh to be included in any more interviews so you can't take any pictures of him or quote anything he says. You also can't print our address or take any pictures of the house.'

'I understand,' Ronson said.

'Josh why don't you go outside and play. I won't be too long with Mr. Ronson. Put your hat on first and don't run around too much and get hot. Stay away from next door and keep a sharp eye out for snakes. If you see one – even if it's in a tree, run back inside straight away.'

'I will,' Josh said his face lighting up.

Ellen knew he liked going outside to play on his own, exploring all the different corners of the large yard. She'd been reluctant to let him do that since she'd spotted a snake basking in a tree over the fence in the neighbouring yard. She didn't take him outside often as she was afraid of snakes. Sometimes she'd take him out to the front which somehow felt safer, but usually she took him to a local park to play. It was Max's job to play with Joshie outdoors at weekends.

'I'll just make those coffees and be right with you,' she told Ronson.

From a back room of the house in the property next door to Ellen and Max's, the two men watched out of the side window as the young boy came charging outside and ran up the back yard.

They'd set up their observation post at six that morning and had seen a man leaving about seven thirty who they surmised was the husband. There'd been no sign of the mother and the boy. They'd seen another man arrive in a car a short time ago. He hadn't reappeared so they believed the woman had let him into the house.

'You think that's her fancy man?' the large man asked his companion.

'I don't know. It might be another reporter.' He'd witnessed the media circus the previous afternoon.

'Are we gunna go and get him now?'

'Not just yet. We need to wait a bit longer.'

He knew he'd have to repeat the instructions to his large companion who would be doing most of the work.

They waited a further ten minutes and when the coast seemed clear, he said, 'Right, let's do it. Now remember what I said. You speak quietly to the boy as you approach him. Tell him his mother wants to see him. When he comes closer you grab him and put this cloth over the boy's face. Then lift and carry him over to the fence. Don't hold the cloth to his face for too long for Christ's sake or you'll smother him. Just for a few seconds like I told you. Count to five. You got that?'

'Got it.'

He doused the cloth in liquid before they crept out the back of the house and moved towards the boundary fence. The grass and weeds were almost up to his head, but his larger companion towered above them. The vegetation, which was dry, crackled as they made their way through it.

'Crouch down a bit,' he hissed. His oversized companion was a lumbering fool and he was worried they might be spotted. When they reached the fence he looked across at the yard next door. The boy was right up the back.

'We should move up closer, but this bloody grass is so noisy I'm worried it will alert him. Climb over here and move carefully up the yard. When you've got him run back down here and hand him to me. Then you can climb back over. Okay?'

The big man nodded and jumped over the low wire fence that separated the yards. He watched as his companion lumbered up towards the boy. About halfway up, he heard a twig snap. The fool had trodden on something lying in the grass and stopped to look down. He held his breath waiting to see if the boy had heard or turned around, but he seemed oblivious. His companion moved forward again and he could tell that he'd spoken to the boy as the kid had turned with a startled expression. A few words were exchanged – the kid was no doubt asking who the man in his yard was. Kids were so trusting though and as the boy moved towards the house his companion pounced. The boy struggled for a few seconds before his body went slack. Still holding the cloth to the boy's face, his companion ran down the yard.

'Take the cloth away you fool,' he hissed as they got nearer.

'I only just reached five like you said,' the big man protested as he handed the boy across before climbing back over himself. He passed the boy back to his companion and before they retreated through the grass he wiped the fence down with the cloth to obliterate any sign of fingerprints the larger man had left. They'd both been wearing gloves when they arrived at the house, but the larger man had taken them off moaning they were too hot. Although he'd told the fool not to touch anything he couldn't help himself and he'd had to constantly tell the idiot off and wipe any surfaces he'd touched.

They moved back through the long grass and into the garage where the ute had been parked, hidden from view. Opening the back door he placed the young boy down onto the seats then felt for a pulse. There was a steady beat so the kid was still alive – thank goodness. He plunged the needle he had prepared into the boy's arm. That should keep him unconscious for a good few hours.

'You stand at the back and push the ute towards the gate like we said. I don't want to start the engine yet,' he said. He stood with the driver's door open to help with the pushing. Once they reached the front gates he signalled to the other to stop and reached into the ute and pulled the handbrake on. Speaking quietly to the larger man he said, 'Now close the garage doors while I open the gates. Make sure you brush away our footprints and the tyre tracks like I showed you. I'll roll the ute out and wait for you. Close the gates behind you. Put your gloves back on before touching anything though.'

'It's too hot for gloves,' the larger man complained.

'It will only be for a minute. I told you, you can't leave your fingerprints on anything.'

With some reluctance the larger man pulled his gloves out of his pocket and after wriggling his hands into them, walked back to the garage. After rolling the ute out of the gates he nipped along to the Gibson house and popped a letter into their post box. Once they were both safely back in the vehicle, he started the engine and they sped off.

'Did you hear something?' Ellen asked the reporter. The interview was over, and she'd had enough. She wasn't too happy with the shots he'd taken of her at the table and had suggested he take more outside, showing her standing on the veranda without revealing the appearance of the house. Loads of old houses in Windsor had verandas. The sun wouldn't be in her eyes there and he could take a full body shot of her. That would be much better.

'It sounded like a car to me,' the reporter said.

'I hope it's not more reporters. I'm planning to go out soon,' she said getting up, walking through to the lounge and looking out of front window. She was relieved to see there was no sign of a car.

'Shall we take those shots of you out on the veranda then?' the reporter called out from the dining room.

'Sure,' she said. She watched from the hallway while the reporter packed up his things and joined her.

'I can't be too long though as I need to get Josh washed and changed.'

They moved out onto the veranda and she called out to Josh. She wanted him to come and see her posing for these pictures. He didn't appear.

She started posing but was distracted. Something didn't feel right.

'Can you stop a minute,' she said to the reporter. 'I just want to check on my son.'

'I think that's all I'll need anyway,' he said. 'Thanks …'

She called out to Josh again, but when he didn't reply, she kicked off her heels, jumped down off the veranda and ran down the side of the house calling out loudly to him. She couldn't see him anywhere.

'Josh. Josh where are you? JOSH!' she screamed.

She circled around to the other side of the house, stepping inside the back door first and calling out to Josh. The house was silent. She moved back outside and around to the garage, opening the door. 'Joshie, are you in there?' There was no response. 'If you're in there Josh I need you to come out now. I'm not angry. I'm just worried.'

She wouldn't step inside the garage as it gave her the creeps. It was full of Max's grandfather's old rusty tools and there were cobwebs everywhere. She didn't like Josh to go in there unless he was with Max. She looked around worried about where he might have gone. She could see the reporter packing his car. He looked up as Ellen approached him.

'Is something wrong Mrs. Gibson?'

'I can't find my son. He's not in the yard anywhere – or the house, I think he's wandered off somewhere,' she said, feeling close to screaming. 'Can you help me look for him?'

6

Detective Inspector India Hargreaves received the call about the missing boy at twelve forty-five, just as she was about to pop out to buy a sandwich. She stepped out of her office to speak to Detective Senior Constable Aaron Jacko, the single remaining detective left in her department. Their Detective Senior Sergeant had just been promoted to a Detective Inspector and moved up to Broken Hill, a place which she wouldn't dream of relocating to. The silver city as it was known, was a trouble hotspot. He'd be kept very busy there. She'd been told by her superiors she'd have to manage as things were.

'Lunch is on hold Jacko, we have a missing five-year-old.'

'Oh cripes. Not near the river?'

'No, from his home.'

'What's the kid's name?'

'I don't know, I've only been given the address. Sergeant Morrison is waiting there for us. We need to head out there now.'

India passed the address to Jacko once they were seated in the car.

'It think it's one of those smallholdings,' he said. 'There's a few of them out that way. There'll be dams on the property. Let's hope the kid hasn't fallen into one.'

'With the dry weather we've been having, I doubt there'd be much water in any of the dams,' she said.

'It only takes a couple of inches for someone to drown.'

'True.'

They drove in silence until they reached the address she'd been given. There were already a couple of patrol cars there as she pulled into the driveway.

Spotting her old friend Sergeant Morrison, she climbed out the car and walked over to him, with Jacko two steps behind.

'Sergeant Morrison,' she said nodding her greeting, 'What have you got for us?'

'A five year old boy. One Joshua Gibson,' he said passing her what looked like a studio photograph of the boy. He looked younger than five.

'His mother discovered he was missing shortly before eleven this morning, but as he was playing outside while she was inside the house, the boy could have gone missing almost an hour prior to that. She didn't report him missing straight away. She thought he was hiding on the property somewhere.'

'Joshua Gibson, isn't he the one whose parents—'

'Yes. They're the ones,' Morrison confirmed, anticipating her question. 'The mother, Ellen Gibson, was giving yet another interview, for the Chronicle this time, to a reporter named Jude Ronson, while she sent the boy out to play. After the interview she was posing for photographs out here on the veranda. She called out to her son to join her but there was no answer. She then ran off to search for him.'

India looked up on the veranda and could see a discarded pair of red heels lying there as though someone had kicked them off in a panic.

'The mother and the reporter searched the property, but found no sign of him. The reporter also did a quick check on the empty property next door, but he couldn't find him there either. They then phoned it in to us.'

'Is the reporter still here?'

'Yes. He's still helping with the search. Apparently next door's property extends into many paddocks surrounding the Gibsons' place. The paddocks are all rented out so will make for an easy search. The land surrounding the house next door has been a nightmare. No-one has been in there to cut down the grass behind the house for some time.'

Looking across to her right, she could see what he meant. 'Can you tell the reporter to stay behind? We'll need to speak to him. I take it you've done a thorough search of the boy's own house.'

'Of course.'

'So the father wasn't at home?'

'No, he went to work as usual this morning. Left around seven thirty. He's on his way home now.'

'You wouldn't catch me going into work if I'd just won fifty-five million dollars,' Jacko said.

'I don't believe you Jacko,' Morrison said. 'You'd swan into work late, boast about your winnings and then depart.'

'Why Sergeant Morrison, you think so little of me. I'd never boast about winning so much money. Not like this one has done,' he said thumbing in the direction of the house.

At that moment a distraught looking Ellen Gibson came out of the house. She was wearing a smart cream dress with red beads around her neck. Simple, but elegant India noted. The dress came in at her slim waist and accentuated the woman's shapely figure. It was a style India had never been able to wear and for a second she was envious.

'I heard a new car arrive. Have you found him?'

'No, I'm afraid not Mrs. Gibson. This is Detective Inspector Hargreaves and Detective Senior Constable Jacko. They will want to ask you a few questions.'

'I've already told you everything that happened. Why aren't you looking for my boy instead?'

'We are looking for your son Mrs. Gibson,' said Sergeant Morrison. 'But for us to begin a thorough investigation, the detectives need to ask you some questions.'

'You'd better come in then,' she said, turning back to the house.

India raised her eyebrows at Morrison before indicating to Jacko that they should follow Ellen Gibson. She suspected this was not going to be an easy interview.

A female police constable brought drinks and biscuits into the living room where India, Jacko and Ellen Gibson were sitting. India dived in the biscuits with gratitude having missed lunch, nodding at Jacko to start the questioning.

'Can you take us through your movements this morning and tell us when you last saw Joshua?'

'I've already done all this,' Ellen Gibson said with irritation, waving her right arm around in the air as though she was warding off flies.

'I appreciate that Mrs. Gibson, but in each telling there might be something else you recall. Every single little detail might be able to help us.'

'Alright,' she said and launched into a recount of her movements during the morning up to the point of Joshua disappearing.

'One thing I didn't tell your police sergeant was that I'm sure I heard something just before we went out to the veranda. I asked that reporter whether he heard anything, and he said he thought it sounded like a car. I looked out of the window but didn't see one. I thought the noise was coming from next door. That reporter searched over there but didn't find anything. He didn't go through all that long grass though, just a bit of it calling out to Josh. What if he's lying in there somewhere having been bitten by a snake? I've seen snakes next door. I couldn't go in there and that reporter wouldn't go in far either. He muttered something about he might destroy evidence. I think he's afraid of snakes – the same as I am. You need to look in there. It's wrong that property owners let their grass grow that high. They shouldn't be allowed to.'

'You're right,' Jacko said nodding as though he agreed with her. 'We have people searching there now. If Joshua is there we'll find him,' he assured her.

'You didn't see any other cars outside your house this morning?' India asked.

'No. Once I got up I was at the back of the house most of the time. In the kitchen with Max, my husband, with Josh in his bedroom or in the bathroom tending to Josh or doing things for myself. I was in my bedroom for a short time to dress and put on some make up, but I didn't see or hear anything.'

Judging by the amount of make-up Ellen Gibson had on, India suspected she'd been in her bedroom for more than a "short time". The eye make-up was smudged now through crying but she could see the layers on Ellen's face and eyes would have taken more than the two minutes she usually spent applying her own 'make-up', which tended to be just a little mascara on odd occasions.

'This is because I did those interviews yesterday isn't it?'

'We don't know that for sure Mrs. Gibson,' she said.

'Someone's taken Josh and they're going to ask us to pay out all of our winnings to get him back. How did they know where we lived though? On the news they just said we were from "the Windsor area". I asked them not to show a picture of the house or give out our address and they didn't.'

'That's what we're going to need to find out,' India said. 'Which television channels did you invite here yesterday?'

'All of them. The ABC, Channel 7, Channel 9, Channel 10 and SBS.'

'What about newspapers?'

'All the dailies. Not the local. He just turned up this morning.'

'And how did you find out that you'd won the money. Where were you at the time?'

'I was at the newsagents in Penrith shopping mall with Josh. I asked the owner Greg to check the ticket and tell me how I could make the claim. I knew they wouldn't be dealing with the payment there like they do on small wins.'

'You would have given him your address for that claim wouldn't you?' Jacko asked her.

'Yes. You don't think he was anything to do with Josh disappearing, do you? He seemed like such a nice man.'

'We don't think anything at the moment Mrs. Gibson. We just need to follow up on all the information you give us,' Jacko told her.

'Can you describe what Josh was wearing this morning?' India asked. 'We'll need that information if we decide to release a statement to the press.'

Ellen Gibson didn't hesitate for a moment before she replied.

'Yes,' she said nodding. 'He had on a blue checked short-sleeve shirt and a pair of navy-blue shorts. He put his red baseball style cap on to go out to play. I won't let him play out in the sun without a hat.'

'What kind of shoes was he wearing?'

'Um … he wasn't wearing socks, I know that. Oh, I remember now – he was wearing his sandals.'

India was making notes when she heard the front fly screen door slam and an angry looking man, who she assumed was Max Gibson, stomped into the room. He was tall, well built, had light brown hair and had what would be considered a handsome face if he wasn't scowling so much. He was wearing a smart tailored navy-blue suit with a white shirt and loosened red tie. He wasn't the type that she would have ever gone for, but she knew from experience that many women would.

'What have you done Ellen? We agreed this morning that you'd do no more interviews. The sergeant out there has just told me you were giving another interview when Josh went missing.'

'You said no more interviews that included Josh. I told the reporter he couldn't take Josh's picture or use anything he said.'

'That's stretching things a bit Ellen – you know damn well the agreement meant you as well. You sent Josh out to play on his own while you gave this interview and weren't keeping an eye on him.'

'Well you could have stayed home from work,' Ellen said bursting into tears.

India and Jacko watched the exchange between husband and wife with interest. *Some matrimonial issues there*, India thought. She stood and introduced herself and Jacko to Max Gibson.

'We're investigating your son's disappearance and we'll need a few words with you as well,' she added.

7

'Can you tell us what time you left for work this morning Mr. Gibson?' India asked. They'd moved into the kitchen to question Max Gibson, leaving his wife with the female police officer in the lounge room.

'It was around seven-thirty. The usual time that I leave.'

'And what time did you arrive at your place of employment?'

'Why would you want to know that? Josh didn't come to work with me. It's what happened here you need to be focusing on,' Gibson said frowning.

'It's routine Mr. Gibson. We need to account for your movements today.'

'Alright,' he said raising both hands as though conceding the point. 'Sometime between eight-fifteen and eight twenty. It was a good run this morning.'

'Did you leave work at any time?'

'No, I had back-to-back meetings from nine to eleven and then a short report to write.'

'So, if we were to approach your employers this could all be confirmed?'

'Yes, of course. I only left work after receiving a call from your lot about Josh.'

'What time was that?'

'Just after I'd returned from buying my sandwich. Someone from the Windsor Police called me. I assume Ellen gave them my contact details.'

'You said "after I returned from buying my sandwich" Mr. Gibson. Returned from where?' Jacko asked.

'The local café.'

'So you *did* leave your place of employment?'

'What? No. The café is on the industrial estate. Just a few minutes' walk from our building. I meant I didn't leave the industrial estate until I drove home after receiving the call.'

'We need you to be very precise in the information you give us Mr. Gibson,' Jacko said. 'We'll need to have the details of both your company's name and the café details to verify what you have told us.'

'You don't suspect me of taking Josh, do you?' Gibson snorted.

'As I said Mr. Gibson. It's routine. I'm sure you'll appreciate, we have to consider everything. We need to confirm your movements in order to eliminate you.'

Gibson nodded and sighed. He dug his wallet out of his pocket, opening it to remove a business card which he passed to Jacko.

'I don't know the name of the café. Someone from my work might be able to tell you.'

'Do you have any close relatives living nearby who might have picked up Joshua?'

'My parents don't live far away, but they'd both be

at work right now. I'll give you their details, so you can eliminate them, shall I?'

Gibson said this with a hint of sarcasm, which she and Jacko ignored. 'Yes, we will need their details,' Jacko said. 'What about your wife's family? Do they live in the area?'

'No, they're up on the Central Coast. Ellen can give you the information. I know how to drive there, but I couldn't tell you their exact address. So, can you tell me what has been done so far to find my son?'

'We have a team of uniformed constables checking through the long grass next door and others out scouring the surrounding paddocks. Do any of the paddocks belong to your property?' she asked him.

'No. My grandfather sold them off when he became too unwell to continue working. My grandmother continued to live here alone after he died and then I inherited the house last year when she passed on. Ellen, Josh and I have only lived here for four months. The next-door neighbour bought the land off my grandparents some years ago and then soon after he and his wife died in a road traffic accident. Their only son lives in Hong Kong and rents the land out now. I don't know why he didn't sell the property. The house is falling apart and no-one deals with the yard. I've complained to the council about it numerous times. I often cut the grass at the front and the side of their house when I'm doing my own, but I haven't ever done the back. I almost went in to cut it all down last weekend. I wish I had now.'

'If your grandparents once owned the land, I take it you would be familiar with any possible hidey holes or dangerous spots where Joshua could be?'

'Yes. There isn't much really, now we've demolished the outbuildings that stood at the back of our yard. There's the dam over in the far paddock, but I can't imagine Josh would wander over there. I've taught him to swim – at the swimming pool. He's not very proficient yet though. I can't see Josh going into the dam. He'd be afraid of it. I've told him over and over not to wander out of our yard and I didn't think he would. Not on his own anyway. He's a cautious child. Do you think he's lying out there somewhere?'

'He might be. We don't know Mr. Gibson, but we'll soon have the answer to that,' she said, standing. They needed to go and check on the search progress. If Joshua Gibson was not found anywhere on the surrounding land, it indicated that he'd been taken away – either forcibly or willingly. They could be looking at a kidnap scenario. With Ellen Gibson's interviews all over the television and newspapers, someone might have decided to take advantage of their Powerball win to kidnap Joshua and demand a ransom.

'Ellen is right. I shouldn't have gone into work today,' Gibson said shaking his head. 'I should have stayed at home and then Josh would still be here. I need to get out there and help in the search for him.' He stood to follow her.

'It might be better if you spent a little time with your wife Mr. Gibson – without blaming each other. It won't help anyone. We have plenty of officers out there searching. We'll let you know how the search has gone,' she said walking out of the kitchen with Jacko on her heels.

'Any news?' India asked Sergeant Morrison.

'He's not visible out in any of the paddocks. Water in the dam is quite low so, contrary to protocol, one of the boys stripped off and took a quick look. He's not there.'

'Well that's a relief.'

'The search in next door's jungle of a yard is slow going. Until we finish that I can't tell you with any certainty that the boy's not there. But I suspect that's going to be the answer. Our men found what looked like fresh flattening of the grass and weeds there, creating a pathway which led to the Gibsons' boundary.'

'Ahh. That's not good news. Has the house itself been checked?'

'Yes. There were indications of recent entry. The back door had been forced. It looks like someone has been in there and was clued up enough to wipe away any footprints made on the dusty floor.'

'More bad news. Have shots been taken of everything?'

'Yes, I've got forensics on it. I hope you don't mind, but when I realised who the missing child was, I thought it best to get them in right away. I'll get them to report back to you as soon as possible. You're not going to go over there?'

'No, not right now. We have lots to follow up on and only Jacko and I to do it at the moment. Where's the Chronicle reporter?'

'He's on his way back from next door – in fact that's him walking along the road now.'

She looked across to where Morrison was pointing and spotted a dishevelled looking young man trudging across the grass verge at the front of the house.

'I hope he hasn't rung into his office or to anyone else, otherwise the press will be descending on us.'

'I took his phone and camera off him when I arrived and switched the phone off. They're still here on the veranda couch,' Morrison said pointing to the items in question behind her. 'He might have called someone before we arrived though. I didn't check his phone before turning it off.'

'Right, well, we'll take those and him back to the station with us for questioning now. Jacko before we leave, could you pop in and ask Max Gibson for their telephone numbers? Both the land line and their mobiles. And ask them whether the land line number is available for anyone to obtain on directory enquiries.'

'Yeah sure,' Jacko said, pulling out his notebook before turning back into the house.

'I'll go and break the good news to Mr. Ronson. I'm sure he's going to love me,' she said with a grimace. 'Keep us posted on the search would you Sergeant Morrison.'

'Will do.'

'Can you tell us Mr. Ronson, how you knew which address to go to this morning when the Gibsons' address was not released in the interviews yesterday?' India asked the reporter once they were settled in an interview room back at the station. She was expecting him to say he'd picked up their information from the electoral register or the telephone directory, but she knew they weren't on either. Jacko had checked.

Ronson was sitting opposite them with a sulky look on his face.

'I have a contact at the Sydney Morning Herald. He gave me the details last night.'

'We will need the name of your contact there Mr. Ronson. Did you mention to your contact that you were intending to visit the Gibson house today?'

'Yes. Why? My paper wasn't invited to the party yesterday and I thought it only fair that we should have the opportunity to interview the family.'

'Did you pass the address on to anyone else?'

'No.'

'Not even to anyone back at your office?'

'No. I called into the office this morning saying I was going to approach the family, but I didn't pass the address on to anyone else. Reporters like me aren't in the habit of sharing information about a potential story until it's done and dusted.'

'Right,' she said nodding. That made sense – unless Ronson had another agenda for withholding information from his colleagues. Local reporters didn't earn a huge wage.

'When you arrived at the property this morning did you see any other vehicles in the vicinity? Either parked along the road or in the driveway next door?'

'No. None. There could have been a car next door though. Driving in from Windsor I couldn't see down the side of that house if they parked it further back or even in the garage there. The garage doors were closed when

I went looking for the boy.'

'Did you open them and look in the garage?'

'Yes, briefly. I thought it unlikely he was in there. The kid was only little and the garage doors were those old fashioned types that opened from the middle, rather than a roller. The closing bolt was quite high and I would've thought it was out of his reach.'

She nodded. She'd also thought that when she'd had a quick look at the property.

'Mrs. Gibson mentioned she thought she'd heard a car out on the road. Did you hear it?'

'Yes. Just as I'd finished interviewing Mrs. Gibson I thought I heard the sound of an engine starting up and a car driving away. She looked out of the lounge window but didn't see one. If it was a car it was long gone when we went outside.'

'And that's the only vehicle you heard?'

'Yes. They haven't found the boy, have they? It's a kidnapping isn't it?'

'Why would you say that Mr. Ronson?' Jacko asked, jumping in.

'If you can't find him anywhere near the property it makes sense, doesn't it? I also saw the flattened grass in next door's yard.'

'You didn't flatten it yourself when you assisted Mrs. Gibson in looking for Joshua?' Jacko continued.

'No, it was like that when I went over there.'

India sat back and let Jacko carry on with the questioning.

'Did you enter the house next door at all?'

'I discovered the back door was unlocked. It looked

like it had been broken into. So yes, I put my head in there and called out to the boy. I didn't enter any of the rooms though in case it was dangerous. The place looks like it's falling apart.'

'I assume you touched the door handle when you opened the door, so, with the garage doors that makes two things we'll need to eliminate you from. We'll need to take your fingerprints,' Jacko said.

'Sure. Then can I go? I need to go back to the office to write up Mrs. Gibson's interview and this latest development. And I'd like my things back,' he said pointing to the items which were lying on the table in a clear plastic bag.

'In good time,' India said. In truth, unless he was to be detained as a suspect, they had no justifiable reason to hang on to him or his possessions. Right now though everyone was a suspect – until eliminated. It was mighty convenient that Ronson was at the property at the time Joshua disappeared. He might have been there to divert Ellen Gibson's attention while someone else grabbed the boy.

'Did you phone anyone before we arrived?'

Ronson went quiet and she suspected the answer was yes. They'd attempted to look at his phone before starting the interview, but it was password protected. They'd looked at his digital camera and it only showed pictures of Ellen Gibson posing indoors and on the front veranda.

'I left a message with my editor to tell her that the boy was missing and that I'd be delayed. I haven't been in touch for hours, so they're probably wondering what's happened.'

'Would you be willing to let us look at your phone log?'

Ronson shrugged. 'Yeah. Okay.'

She reached for the bag, pulled out Ronson's mobile phone and passed it to him.

After switching it back on, he tapped in the code to unlock it and passed it back to her. She noticed he had four missed calls from the same number. Trawling through the log she saw only one call Ronson had made last night, but had received a call from the same number thirty-three minutes later.

'Is this the number of your contact at the Sydney Morning Herald?'

'Yes. After speaking to him, he phoned me back with the details. It was his colleague, one of the female reporters, who interviewed Ellen Gibson yesterday.'

This confirmed her concern that members of the press had passed the Gibsons' address on to others. They would have to track down every single person who was at the house yesterday and find out if they'd given the details to anyone else.

'We need his full name.'

'He's not going to get into trouble is he?'

'We just need to talk to him Mr. Ronson, to confirm the information you've given us.'

'Right. Well his name is Jeff Brody.'

Jacko made a note of Brody's name and number.

Ronson had made a call at twelve minutes past eleven to the person who had been attempting to call him.

'Is this the phone number for someone from your

office?'

'Yes, my editor. Jane Hollis.'

India knew who Hollis was, having come across the woman while working on other cases. A prickly ruthless kind of journalist.

Jacko made a further note of the editor's name and number. Everything that Ronson had told them seemed to be corroborated by his phone log. So, if he made contact with anyone else about his visit to the Gibsons', it wasn't done on this phone.

'Do you have any other mobile phones?'

'No.'

'What about a land line at home?'

'No. I don't have a land line any more. Just this phone.'

'We will need to verify that Mr. Ronson,' she told him. 'Do you have your driver's licence on you?'

'Yes,' Ronson said sighing. He reached around to his lightweight jacket which was hanging over the back of the chair he was sitting on, pulled out his wallet and after a few seconds of flicking through a mass of cards, he passed his driver's licence to them.

'We're going to photocopy your licence Mr. Ronson and then after you've given us your fingerprints, you will be free to go,' she said passing the licence to Jacko.

'Can I take my phone and camera now?'

'Detective Jacko will pass them back to you when you're ready to leave.'

'Well, can I phone my editor then and let her know what's happening?'

'I will be phoning her to verify the information you have given us, so I'll let her know you'll be returning soon. If you'd like to follow Detective Jacko, he'll ensure you're processed as quickly as possible.'

With weary resignation Ronson stood and followed Jacko. She waited until they were out of earshot before using her mobile to call Morrison for an update. He told her there was still no sign of the boy. Not good news. She hoped not, but all indications were pointing to a kidnapping. She then returned to their squad room upstairs to make the call to Ronson's editor from the land line. She didn't want to call Hollis on her mobile as then she would have her number and would probably start hounding her for information.

'*Hollis,*' came the swift reply.

'Good afternoon. It's Detective Inspector Hargreaves from Windsor Police Station. I just need to verify some facts about your reporter Jude Ronson.'

'*Why, what's the problem? He left a message with me to say the son of the woman he'd been interviewing this morning was missing and he was staying to help look for him. Did they find the boy?*'

'Mr. Ronson took part in the initial search and has been helping us with our enquiries.'

'*What does that mean?*'

'We needed to verify how he obtained the Gibsons' address and who he might have passed it on to.'

'*He didn't give it to anyone here in the office if that's what you're asking. I saw him briefly this morning before he left and he told me he'd picked up their details from a contact whose paper had been there yesterday. I couldn't tell you which one. He didn't say.*'

'He has given us that information.'

'So where is he now? Why hasn't he returned to our offices and you haven't answered me about whether you've found the boy.'

'I can't tell you anything else at the moment Ms. Hollis, except to say that Mr. Ronson will be with you shortly,' she said before thanking Hollis for her help and ringing off. It looked like Ronson had been telling the truth. One down, but goodness knows how many more they had to clear. With a sigh she dialled through to Richmond to speak to Superintendent Havering, the Commander of her region. Tracking all the media and making other relevant enquiries would be an impossible task with just her, Jacko and their admin person Dale. They were going to need more staff, especially as it looked as though they might have a kidnapping on their hands.

8

Superintendent Havering agreed that India could have a detective sergeant, a detective constable, a couple of uniformed officers and a further support officer attached to her team until they found the boy. He was also prepared to make the search for Joshua Gibson a priority amongst all uniformed officers from Windsor, Richmond and Wiseman Ferry Stations. He had seen Ellen Gibson's appearance on the news last night and told India he'd been concerned about how foolish the woman had been to have her five-year-old son with her.

'It was just asking for trouble,' he said. *'So you think we might have a kidnapping on our hands?'*

'It's starting to look that way, sir. I think you'll need to give a press conference and get it out to the public. We need to know if anyone saw or heard anything. The problem is the Gibsons' house is isolated. Both Ellen Gibson and the reporter thought they heard a car, but saw nothing. There might have been a car parked in next door's driveway – or the garage. Forensics are checking the place over. Sergeant Morrison also has the sniffer dog team out there at the moment. I'll head back to the house and pick up a recent photograph of Joshua Gibson and have it sent over to you for release to the press.'

'Okay. Make sure you keep me in the loop with the latest developments. I'll get your back-ups over to you as soon as possible. In the meantime, I'll draw up a press release statement. We need this on this evening's news.'

Back at the Gibsons' house India asked Sergeant Morrison to get his men to set up a cordon on the road. With Jude Ronson's release he was bound to make contact with other members of the press and they could descend on the house at any time.

'Ideally I'd like a large section of the road down here completely closed,' she said. 'Would that be possible?'

'There are a couple of other properties further down this road. Access for them could be a problem. They'd have to detour several kilometres.'

'That wouldn't be any great hardship would it? We want to avoid having nosy parkers and millions of press vehicles turning up here. I want them kept at a distance.'

'Okay, leave it with me; I'll see to it.'

'From what I've been told the photograph you gave us is about a year old. Do you have more recent photographs of your son?' she asked Ellen and Max Gibson when she joined them in the house. They had both changed into casual clothes now. Ellen Gibson was wearing cream linen trousers, a tangerine vest top and sandals. She was hugging herself as though she was cold.

'I took some digital photos of Josh last week that I've put onto my laptop,' Gibson said.

'Are you on the internet here?'

'Yes, why?'

'I'd like to send one of the pictures to my Superintendent. He is calling a press conference and will need a good image of Joshua to release to them.'

'I see. So you think someone's taken Josh?'

'We can't say for sure, but it's looking increasingly likely. The sniffer dogs traced Joshua to the garage next door. We believe there was a vehicle hidden in there that he was put into.'

'Oh God,' Gibson moaned, collapsing into a chair, and dropping his head. Ellen had silent tears streaking down her face, but India noticed she was carefully wiping underneath her eyelashes in case more of her mascara smudged. She'd had to deal with distraught parents and families many times in the past, but never connected to such a young child. This was a new experience for her and she was surprising herself at how calm she felt. Was it because it didn't seem real yet?

'What can we do?' Gibson asked her after he composed himself. 'Should we do an appeal?'

'Yes, that's what we should do,' Ellen said nodding and brightening up. Even with the potential kidnapping of her son, the woman still seemed keen on the idea of appearing in front of the cameras.

'If you could let me have access to those pictures first, we can talk about next steps later,' she said, her eyes fixed on Max Gibson in an effort not to react to Ellen.

After forwarding the photo to Superintendent Havering India returned to the living room to join the couple.

'If, by tomorrow we've heard nothing, we can look at you doing an appeal,' she told them.

'When you say "heard nothing", are you talking about a ransom demand?' Gibson asked.

'Yes. That is what we will be expecting. How the demand will be made we have no idea. With your telephone number not being available to the general public, it's unlikely it will be by phone. I noticed that your mail box is locked. Have you checked your mail today?'

The couple looked at each other. 'I haven't,' Ellen said.

'I never gave it a thought,' Gibson added.

'Would you mind giving me the key, I'll check it. What time does your mail usually arrive?'

'Anytime between ten-thirty and eleven-thirty as a rule,' Ellen said.

Gibson returned from the kitchen a minute later and handed a small key to India. She gestured for Jacko to join her.

Donning a pair of gloves, she unlocked the box. Inside she found two white envelopes. One was a business letter addressed to Max Gibson. The other had the name Ellen on it, cobbled together from letters cut out of a magazine and had been hand delivered.

'Aha!' Jacko exclaimed in an exaggerated tone.

'Call the forensic techies over here will you Jacko. They're still finishing up next door as far as I know. We need to have them fingerprint the letter box and this letter will need to be looked at in a sanitized environment. Ask one of them to go in and take fingerprints from the Gibsons as well. I'll go and speak to the couple.'

'Righto. You're going to wait for the techies to open it?'

'Yes.'

She turned and walked back into the house, joining the couple in the living room.

'There was a hand-delivered letter in the box addressed to you Mrs. Gibson. From the appearance of it, it could be a ransom demand.'

Ellen's face turned pale; she held a hand over her gaping mouth and started snivelling again.

'What do you mean by the appearance of it?' Gibson asked.

'The envelope spelling out Ellen's name was created using letters cut out of a magazine. I've asked forensics to come over before we open it. We're going to need to take fingerprints from both of you to eliminate your prints from the letter-box. Are you both alright with that?'

'Of course,' Gibson said, answering for both him and his wife. 'Can we be there when they open the letter?'

'I'd rather you weren't at the moment. I'll see what it says in the first instance. I'll send a member of the team in to take your prints,' she said before moving back outside.

One of the forensic technicians had set up a portable station with her kit. On her nod the technician sliced open the envelope and drew out the contents. It was a single white A4 page with yet more letters cut out of a magazine saying:

We have your **son** if you want **him back** it **will** cost **you two** million *dollars* in **used** notes **have the** money ready to deliver **Saturday night** *we* will phone you with **details**

'They claim they're going to phone, so the kidnappers must have one of their mobile numbers or the land line number. That indicates it could be someone they know, not a stranger,' India said.

'It looks like they're demanding Ellen Gibson delivers the money, not her husband,' Jacko noted.

'Mm. It could be that they watched her interviews on television and have little idea about her husband. She did make reference to him, but it was Ellen Gibson who was featured. And Joshua of course. We have three days. In the meantime, we need to be checking out everyone who was connected to those interviews.'

Turning to the technician she said, 'Once you've checked this letter for fingerprints can you put it into a transparent plastic sleeve for me? I need to show this to the Gibsons. Jacko, can you go and find Sergeant Morrison and tell him to put a stop to the search out in the paddocks. We need the door to door along this road to be implemented. Then come back for the ransom demand and bring it in to us. I'm going to go and talk to the Gibsons again.'

'It *is* a ransom demand,' India told the couple. The technician had just completed taking their fingerprints and was leaving to join his colleague.

'What did it say?' Max Gibson asked leaping to his feet.

'They're demanding two million dollars and want you to deliver it Saturday night Mrs. Gibson.'

'They want *me* to deliver it? Why me?'

'I suspect they watched your television interviews and have just latched onto you in particular.'

'Where do they want Ellen to deliver it?' Gibson asked.

'They haven't said. The note said they would phone with further instructions. That means the kidnappers have one of your numbers.'

'Only my friends and family have my mobile number,' Ellen said.

India nodded. She was sure Ellen Gibson would have been on the phone to many of them in the past few days. 'We'll need to know the names of *anyone* you made contact with following discovery of your win. Did you give a phone number to the newsagent?'

'Yes, but only the land line.'

'What about you Mr. Gibson? Who would have your mobile number?'

'Family, work colleagues or work contacts. My mobile is supplied by my employers.'

'Who have you spoken to since learning of your Powerball win?' she asked him.

'Only my parents last night. And I told my boss this morning. He didn't know about it before I mentioned it to him. I haven't spoken to anyone else.'

'We'll need his name, nevertheless.'

Gibson shrugged. 'Did the note say *who* they were going to call?'

'It was addressed to Ellen and indicated they were going to call her.'

'Did they say when they were going to call?'

'No.'

'I don't think Ellen should be delivering the money alone. I should go with her,' Gibson said.

'You mean we're just going to pay them this money? What if they don't give Josh back? What if they try to take me as well? I don't think I could do it. And if we pay out this money, who's to say there won't be hundreds more lining up to do the same thing next week. We'll have to move away and change our name Max.'

'The problem is everyone would recognise you Ellen, even if we did change our name. Because you did those interviews. I told you it was foolish.'

'This hasn't happened because I did those interviews. It's because these people are criminals, isn't that right detective?'

India was not prepared to be drawn into the rights and wrongs of Ellen Gibson doing the interviews.

'They are demanding you deliver the money on Saturday night Mrs. Gibson. That's all I can tell you,' she said.

'So, you want us to give them the money? Give away two million dollars just like that with no guarantee they'll release Josh?'

'Ellen, stop. If we want to see Josh again we have no choice at this point. We need to give them the money and trust that the police will catch the kidnappers.'

'How are you going to do that? How are you going to catch them?' Ellen turned to ask her.

India sighed. 'We have many more enquiries to make Mrs. Gibson. With any luck we might track the kidnappers before the ransom deadline. Can you give Detective Jacko the names of all those you called Mrs. Gibson? Ideally with their phone numbers.'

'Yes, of course, but I can tell you none of my friends would have been involved in taking Josh. As I told you, they don't have this address. Only my family has it. My parents and my sister.'

Jacko came into the house just then and passed the ransom demand to her. She handed it on to Gibson. Ellen moved to stand beside him to read it, her eyes full of concern. Gibson shook his head and didn't speak. Ellen put a hand to her mouth as though to stifle a scream.

'You might notice they say "we", indicating more than one person is involved,' India said.

They both nodded.

'Have you received the winnings yet?' she asked them.

'No. Ellen told me they rang this morning. They—'

'We're supposed to go to a presentation ceremony tomorrow. I was really looking forward to it,' Ellen said cutting her husband off.

Where there'd be more cameras, photographs and interviews no doubt, India thought.

'We haven't got time for that nonsense now,' Gibson said. 'I'll phone them right away and ask them to put the money straight into our account. It won't be clear for some days though. I'll have to arrange an express clearance on it. What do I tell them?'

'Say something unforeseen has arisen and you are unable to attend the ceremony. Refer them to me if they start asking too many questions,' she said.

'Right. I'll do that now,' he said, jumping up and moving swiftly into the hallway where she had noticed there was a hands-free set on a small side table. There was probably a matching one in one of the other rooms.

She asked Jacko to sit with Ellen Gibson and take the names and numbers of anyone she called.

India then followed Gibson out to the hallway and watched as he dialled a number listed on a notepad sitting on the hall table.

'Can you put the phone on loudspeaker,' she asked him.

Gibson nodded and pressed a button, enabling her to hear both sides of the conversation. An operator answered and he asked to be put through to whoever was dealing with the presentation tomorrow.

'Rae Barrett deals with these matters. I'll put you through'

After a few short rings another female voice came onto the phone stating, *'Rae Barrett speaking.'*

India could see Max was momentarily surprised by this response. Like her, he'd obviously been expecting a male voice. Wasn't there an actor called Ray Barrett? She listened as he made his request.

'I'm afraid that won't be possible Mr. Gibson. In order

to ensure you are the rightful ticket holders, we need to see you in person, view your identification and verify where you purchased the ticket,' Rae Barrett said.

'My wife told me she did all that with your agent in Penrith,' he argued. 'Why do we have to do it again?'

'As you might appreciate Mr. Gibson, we are talking about a very large sum of money. When the claim was submitted your wife was unable to tell the agent where the ticket was purchased.'

'I can tell you now if you hang on a minute. I have receipts in my car from other purchases I made at the same time I bought the ticket. I can get them and give you that information.'

'Nevertheless, I would rather you visited us in person,' the woman insisted.

'Alright. I need to come into your office now then and get this sorted.'

'It will have to wait until tomorrow.'

'I've told you we can't come tomorrow and I need the money deposited in the bank today.'

India could hear the woman sighing. *'That won't be possible. I'm not going to be available later this afternoon. I won't be in the office.'*

'Look Miss Barrett—' Gibson started.

'It's Mrs Barrett,' she said cutting him off.

'Right,' he said, with a painful expression on his face. India thought he looked like he was about to explode. Antagonising the woman was not going to help anyone. She made hand signals to him to indicate he keep his frustrations down. At least she hoped he understood that was what she was attempting to convey. Taking a deep breath, he started again.

'Mrs. Barrett, it's imperative that I am able to bank the money today.'

'Like I said Mr. Gibson, I won't be in the office this afternoon. I am happy to meet you tomorrow afternoon as planned.'

'Surely there is someone else who can deal with it?'

'I'm responsible for dealing with this matter.'

She signalled for Max to pass her the phone, which he did without hesitation.

'Mrs. Barrett, my name is Detective Inspector Hargreaves from the Windsor Police. A statement to the press will be given by my Superintendent this afternoon regarding a matter involving Mr. and Mrs. Gibson. In the meantime I have to insist that you cancel whatever you had planned this afternoon, or make arrangements for someone else to take charge of dealing with your legal issues and ensure the payment is made to Mr. and Mrs. Gibson. A strict code of silence will need to be adhered to, and I don't want to hear of any publicity about the Gibson win, or anything related to it, leaking from your offices. One of our detectives will accompany Mr. Gibson to your office and you, or someone else in authority there, needs to be available to deal with this matter. I don't know how you normally make payments to winners, but this money needs to be sent by a bank transfer to Mr. Gibson's account. They will be leaving shortly and, traffic permitting, should be with you within the hour. You are not to ask them any questions when they arrive. Is that clear?'

Barret made a loud squawking noise, followed by stony silence for a few seconds before she responded.

'*Crystal clear,*' she said.

Within minutes of disconnecting the call, India sent Jacko off with Max Gibson, armed with the relevant documentation and paperwork required. Time was tight if any money was going to be available for withdrawal on Friday. On the way there Gibson was going to call his bank requesting that the manager remain available for them to visit once the payment was sorted. Jacko would also speak to the manager to verify it was a police matter. Fingers crossed it would all go smoothly.

She was still standing outside when a couple of other cars pulled up. She recognised Detective Sergeant Jun Li, who'd once told her he was from a third-generation Chinese family who'd settled in Australia. He was taller than most Chinese men she'd met in the past, and he always dressed in smart mid-grey suits which matched his thick greying hair to perfection. She knew that in the Chinese culture he would be called Li Jun, with his surname first, but here in Australia he was known as Jun Li. She'd worked with him a few times and he was a very able detective. He preferred people he was working closely with to call him 'Jun Li'. That would be the equivalent of everyone calling her 'India Hargreaves', which would sound ridiculous, but with his short name it rolled off the tongue with ease.

India didn't recognise the young woman who stepped out of the other car, but she'd heard a new female detective constable had started at Richmond. She watched as Li waited for his colleague before joining her on the veranda.

'Inspector Hargreaves,' Jun Li nodded his greetings. 'This is my new colleague, Detective Constable Marlee Kuri.'

She could see that Marlee Kuri was, like Jacko, of mixed aboriginal and European blood. She wondered where Marlee's family was originally from. Being a local herself, she knew many of the indigenous population had inter-married with the European settlers around the Windsor and Hawkesbury region over generations.

'Call me Marlee,' the detective constable said breaking into a huge grin to exhibit a set of perfect white teeth. India was instantly envious. Why couldn't the dentist ever get her teeth to look like that?

Marlee had dark brown curls cut into a shape that reminded India of a nineteen twenties style and she had the most beautiful smile that lit up her light-brown eyes. She was wearing camel coloured trousers, a green top, and brown shoes, colours that complemented her appearance perfectly. She suspected Marlee, in a similar way to Ellen Gibson, had the knack of wearing clothes that enhanced her appearance. Unlike her. Since working for the police she had never taken the time to give any serious attention to her wardrobe. She tended to wear clothes that she liked and were comfortable without worrying whether they suited her. Perhaps she should look into one of those colour consultants. Rob claimed she looked beautiful in everything she wore – saying she looked like a more attractive Cate Blanchett – with a few freckles and nicer ears he often added. But she knew he was biased and there was a lot more she could do if she had the time and a greater understanding of what might suit her better.

'Hi. I can't tell you how happy I am to see you both,' she said nodding a greeting to the new arrivals.

'We have a potential kidnapping on our hands from what the Super told us,' Jun Li said.

'No longer potential. It's definite. We've received the ransom demand.'

'Ah, that's a bummer. The kid's only five years old, isn't he?' Marlee asked.

'That's right. Joshua Gibson.'

'I saw his mother on television last night. Crikey that was quick work. How much are they demanding?' Marlee asked.

'Two million. We need to look into everyone who had knowledge of the Gibson win and their address. Our admin person Dale, back at the station, is compiling a list of everyone who was here yesterday. There's also the newsagent down at Penrith where Ellen Gibson registered the win on Monday. The owner's first name is Greg. That's all Mrs. Gibson knows about him. We also need to check with the post office and find out who delivers the mail here. The ransom demand was placed in the letter-box. There was other mail in the box so we need to find out if the postie saw anyone in the area.'

Jun Li and Marlee nodded. Marlee already had her note-book out and had been jotting down things as India spoke.

'Maybe the postie put the ransom note in there when he or she was delivering the mail,' Marlee suggested.

'It's a line of enquiry we need to pursue,' she agreed.

'Considering their win was fifty-five million, why do you think they've asked for such a small sum of money? Why not five, ten or twenty million?' Marlee asked.

'It could be that they're worried about moving and using a larger sum of money. Or perhaps they're just testing the water, and this is their *first* demand.'

'Would you like us to follow up on all the names Dale has compiled?' Jun Li asked.

'Yes – thanks. I think the newsagent in Penrith should be your first port of call – in person, not as a phone enquiry. We need to check his security cameras and I'd like you to ascertain the newsagent owner's movements, and those of any staff he had working in the shop – from the point of Ellen Gibson's visit there, up until now.'

'Do you want us to do that together or make separate enquiries?' Jun Li asked.

She thought for a moment. 'I think you need to go together to the newsagent – but take both cars. One of you could stay on to look at any security footage they have while the other returns to start following up on Dale's media list. We don't have time to visit *everyone* on the list. We might get away with some phone calls to press members. Personal visits to everyone would be best where we can gauge their reactions to our questions, but we simply don't have time. The ransom has to be delivered on Saturday night.'

'We'll get straight onto it,' Jun Li said, using his hand to usher detective Kuri off the veranda and return to their cars. She watched as they huddled together for a few minutes before climbing into their respective vehicles and driving off.

She was about to go back into the house when the senior forensic technician approached.

'We have a problem Inspector Hargreaves.'

9

India sat facing Ellen Gibson who had some explaining to do. Was the woman a complete fraud? Was that why the ransom had been addressed to her and she'd been asked to deliver the money?

'Mrs. Gibson,' India started. 'Could you explain why your fingerprints are all over the ransom demand?'

'What? What are you talking about? I haven't touched it. You handed it to Max to read inside that plastic sleeve. I only read it while standing beside him. I didn't touch it.'

'We have picked up partial fingerprints of yours from the pasted lettering on the demand.'

'I don't understand. How could that be?' Ellen asked.

She scrutinised Ellen's face. She certainly looked surprised and confused. Was it an act?

'I can see from the coffee table here in the lounge that you are a magazine reader. Do you keep all your magazines?'

'I usually keep them for about a year. Max made me throw out the old ones I had before we moved here. So the ones I have now I've only collected since we moved here four months ago.'

'Where do you keep them?'

'On the top shelf of a bookcase in the spare bedroom. I have them in date order in piles of each magazine.'

'Can you show me please?'

Ellen stood and walked through to the spare bedroom with India following. She could see the piles of magazines on the shelf as Ellen described.

'These are the weeklies and these are the monthlies,' Ellen said, pointing to different piles.

It was the monthly magazines, *Hello* and *Ok* that she was more interested in. They weren't magazines she had ever personally bought, but she had skimmed through some out of date copies that were available to read at the doctor's and dentist's surgeries, plus at her hairdresser's. She knew from her mother's subscription to Woman's Weekly that the thickness and appearance of those pages would not match the ransom letter page cut-outs.

She looked through the piles. The December copies of *Hello* and *OK*, which should have been at the top of the piles, were missing.

'Do you still have the December copies of both these magazines lying around the house somewhere?'

'No, I put them both in here. Weeks back,' Ellen said. 'Are they not there?'

'No, they're not.'

'That's really strange. I know they were there last week because I wanted to look something up. I couldn't remember if it was *Hello* or *OK* it was in, so I checked through both. I didn't take them out of the room.'

'Would Joshua or your husband have touched them?'

'Certainly not Max,' Ellen said, shaking her head. 'He keeps his clothes in here, so he's in here every day, but I've never known him to touch my magazines, except to maybe clear them off the table when we're about to eat. Josh sometimes asks me for pages from the magazines for his little craft creations, but I usually give him the magazines from the Sunday paper Max buys. Not from my magazines. Josh would never touch anything without asking. He's a good kid like that.'

She considered other possibilities for a minute. Ellen Gibson seemed genuinely surprised that the magazines were missing.

'When the press was here yesterday morning, did any of them come into the house for any reason?'

'Yes, a couple of them came in to use the bathroom, much to my embarrassment. It's not exactly a show bathroom. I think Max's grandparents last updated it back in the seventies.'

'Can you remember exactly who entered the house?'

'There was one woman and definitely one man. He was the last to use it and he left the toilet seat up in typical male fashion.'

'Do you remember who they were representing?'

'I think the man was from Channel ten. I can't remember where the woman was from. Do you think one of them took my magazines?' Ellen asked with a shocked expression. 'Why would they do that?'

'I think someone took the magazines to create the ransom note. That would explain how we found your partial fingerprints on them. Can you tell me, did you go out at all after the press left?'

'No, because Max had arrived home. I did go out the previous evening though. I was so excited after arranging all the interviews that I couldn't be bothered to cook. I decided to treat Josh and myself to a McDonald's. Max doesn't approve of places like McDonalds or Hungry Jacks, but Josh and I have a sneaky one every now and then.'

'Do you always lock the house up when you go out?'

'I didn't check it that evening before we went to McDonalds. When I was going to bed, I discovered that the back door was unlocked. I rushed Josh off to the doctor's that morning and then I had to come back and pick up the Powerball ticket to take it in for checking. I only used the front door and it never occurred to me to check and see if the back door was locked. It might have been unlocked since the night before because we didn't go out the back that day – unless Josh went out without me noticing while I was on the phone. Max usually checks it every night before we go to bed – he might have forgotten on Sunday.'

'So someone could have entered the house while you were out at McDonald's? Did you notice anything out of the ordinary or whether anything was moved when you returned?'

It was unlikely someone would have removed the magazines prior to Ellen Gibson registering the win. There would have been no reason to. So it would have been either while she was out in the evening or during the press interviews.

'No. I was too busy to notice anything anyway. After rubbing some cream on Josh's rash and putting him to bed, I was on the phone all night, telling everyone my good news.'

India could just picture it. Another thought just occurred to her.

'The bill for your land line – do you receive a paper copy or digital copy?'

'A paper copy. It comes monthly. Max likes to check through it to make sure I haven't been making any expensive calls during peak times.'

'What about your mobile phones?'

'Mine's a 'pay as you go', and the bill for Max's would go to his firm, not us.'

'Where do you keep the copies of your land line bill?'

'Max keeps them in a file here on the shelves,' she said pointing to a range of files on a separate free-standing shelf unit.

'Can you show me which one?'

'I don't really know. It's one of those files. Max deals with all that kind of thing,' Ellen said waving her right hand dismissively. 'Knowing Max, he probably has them all labelled.'

'Do you mind if I have a look.'

'Help yourself.'

India put on a pair of gloves she pulled from her pocket and looked across the file headings. There was a 'household bills' file and when she looked, the lever file was divided into sections labelled: electricity, rates, telephone, water. Alphabetical even. Much more organised than her and Rob. She opened the telephone section and noticed the last bill filed was for October, last year. No November or December statements – although the December one might not have been sent out yet. She checked all the ones underneath, but they were all in monthly order. That could mean the person who removed the magazines took a phone bill as well and would therefore have the land line number. She needed to check with Max Gibson to clarify that he had filed the November bill and whether the December one had arrived. She was pretty sure she knew what the answer would be though. He was not the kind of man to leave bills lying around like her and Rob.

'Okay, well I'd like you to return to the living room for now. I'm going to need forensics to check this room, the bathroom and the back door.'

'I found only Max Gibson's prints on the file you asked me to look at. I've picked up multiple prints from the back door handles. Both inside and out. The same with the bathroom door, the toilet flush, the taps and the sink. Many of them are smudged, or partials, so it will be difficult to pin-point precise prints,' the technician told her.

'Well do the best you can. I'd like you to separate out any that don't match Ellen and Max Gibson – or their son. You should be able to pick up Joshua Gibson's prints from his bedroom. What did you find over at the garage?'

'There was definitely a vehicle in there recently. There's a fresh oil spot on the garage floor. Plus a boot imprint up near the back of the garage. Size twelve I'd say. It looks like they swept across any tyre tracks that would have been in there or on the gravel leading to the gate. No clear fingerprints on the garage door handle or the gates. Only smudges.'

'Hmm. Not so amateurish then. Can you check what shoe size Max Gibson wears? There's some shoes just inside the front door and there'll be more in the back bedroom where he keeps his things. Check in both locations. See if you can find a match to your boot print. He might have gone in there for something.'

'Right. Will do.'

India spotted Sergeant Morrison heading towards the house. She stepped off the veranda and walked to meet him.

'I called off the search of surrounding paddocks as you suggested. We didn't find anything anyway. Some of the team are doing a door to door along this road in both directions. The press have arrived in force, but we're not letting any of them through.'

She nodded and looked at her watch. It was just after five-thirty pm. So Superintendent Havering must have met with the press.

'How far do you want us to go in this door to door? Do you want us to extend it all the way into Windsor? If so, it would take a fair old time.'

'Yes, I think we need to. And going in the other direction.'

'Righto then. I've got some more uniforms on the way over from Richmond apparently. I'll get them onto it.'

'Thanks.'

Ellen Gibson stepped out onto the veranda and lit

up a cigarette. From her spot at least ten feet away India could see the woman was shaking. After a few puffs she seemed to relax.

'Mrs. Gibson I'm heading back to the station now. We have many lines of enquiry to follow up. Someone will remain here at the house with you.'

She didn't wait for a response from the woman but turned to Morrison. 'Can you make sure someone stays with her?'

'Of course.'

'Okay, I'm off. Let me know if anything crops up.'

Morrison nodded before she turned and walked to her car.

10

Josh woke confused and feeling a little strange. Where was he? And what was this smelly, itchy thing over his head? He went to move his arms to pull at the thing on his head but they seemed to be tied behind him. He tried moving his legs, but they were tied as well.

He had no idea where he was. It took him a while to clear his head and his thoughts. He remembered walking towards the house. He'd been out playing in the yard when he'd heard someone call his name. He'd turned to find a very large man standing near him who said his mother wanted him back inside. What had happened?

He could hear a man's voice close by – he was talking to someone so Josh called out.

'Hello? Mummy? Daddy? Are you there?'

A dog barked and he heard the voice say, 'Quiet Queenie, it's only Joshua. Come inside and meet him.'

A door squeaked and Josh heard footsteps on bare boards. He recognised the sound from his house where they had rugs on bare boards in every room except in his parent's bedroom. If he was wearing his shoes he couldn't sneak past his mother in the dining room where she sat reading her magazines or playing with her phone. At first she'd been happy to let him play outside at the new house, something he'd never been able to do at their old flat – as long as he wore a hat. But *ages* ago now she'd seen a snake next door and so had forbidden him to go outside alone anymore. She'd made him promise and he'd kept that promise ever since. The trouble was she hardly ever came outside with him, so he'd been really excited when she'd said he could play outside today.

Someone pulled the thing off his head and he was propped up into a sitting position. He had to blink a few times until he could see everything properly.

'Hi Joshua. My name is Billy. We met earlier today at ya house. This is Queenie, my dog.'

Josh looked at the dog which was looking at him and wagging its tail madly. It was brown, but a bit red as well and looked like dogs he'd seen before.

'Hello Queenie,' Josh said and the dog immediately moved over towards him and put its head in his lap. He wasn't afraid of dogs like his mother. His grandparents in Windsor had a dog and he played with it at their house. Their dog wasn't allowed inside though and slept outside under the house.

'Where are we and why am I tied up?'

'It's part of a game we're playin', ya see. Your mummy asked us to look after ya while she gets some money to pay us. So you'll be stayin' here with Queenie and me until then. For a few days.'

'Why is my mummy giving you some money? And why would she ask you to look after me?'

'Ya know she won a lot of money?'

Josh nodded. He'd heard her talk about nothing else since she'd found out about their "big win".

'Well she wants to get on the news and television so we said we'd hang on to ya for a few days.'

Josh was puzzled by what the man was saying. Mummy had already been on the news. A lot of people had come to the house and asked them questions which she said would be in the papers and on the television. And another man had come to their house this morning. So why would mummy want this man to look after him? He looked around him. They were in some really old wooden and stone cabin that was falling apart. He was sitting on a strange skinny bed with no mattress or sheets. On the other side of the room was a chair with a cloth over it and next to it was a sort of kitchen. There was a sink, with no taps, and he could see what looked like the camp stove his daddy used when they went camping on a table near it.

'Are we camping here then?'

'Yes, we are.'

'I need to do a pee,' he said. 'Where's the bathroom?'

The man laughed. 'There's no bathroom here Joshua. Ya don't have bathrooms when you're camping. This is a cabin.'

'But aren't there showers and toilets nearby?'

'No mate. There's nuthin' here. We're campin' in the bush.'

'Well I still need to do a pee.'

'Alrightie. Let's take you outside then. I'll release ya feet and hands, but ya must promise not to try and run away Joshua. Do you promise? It's dangerous out there in the bush.'

'I promise. But stop calling me Joshua. No-one calls me that. It's Josh.'

'Okay Josh. Whatever ya like.'

The man undid the rope around his hands and feet and walked him out of the cabin. It was in a small open space but there was bush around them everywhere and all he could hear were bird sounds in the distance. It was a bit creepy and he didn't like it. The place his daddy took him to the other week was much better. They'd spent a night camping somewhere out west just after Christmas. Mummy hadn't come with them as she was having one of her *pain* days. She used to have them a lot when he was younger, but not so much now.

'Where are we?'

'Way out in the bush mate. Just do ya pee over there,' the man said pushing Josh towards the edge of the open space.

He turned his back to the man and pulled his shorts and underpants down. His mother still made him wear shorts and underpants without the front opening like his daddy had. He'd told her she had to buy him 'big boy' shorts and undies for when he started school. So far she hadn't. It was embarrassing to pull his shorts down exposing his bottom, but unless he wanted to wet himself he had no choice.

When he finished he asked the man where he could wash his hands.

'Ya can't wash ya hands Josh. We only have enough water for drinkin', not washin.'

'Mummy will be angry with me if I don't wash my

hands.'

'Well what she don't know ain't gunna hurt her. Now come back inside.'

'Can't we play out here for a bit?'

'Not now Josh. I gotta go somewhere. Queenie and I have some work to do.'

He followed the man back into the cabin where he was ordered to sit down on the bed again.

'Can I have a drink please? I'm thirsty.'

'I'll give ya a small drink of water, but we're on rations. That's what it's like when ya camp in the bush.'

Josh nodded. The man picked up a plastic bottle of water and poured a small amount into a tin cup before passing it to him. He quickly gulped it down.

'Can I have some more please? My mouth feels all funny.'

'No. Not until later,' the man said taking the cup from him and putting it on the floor. 'Now put ya hands out in front of ya. I'll tie them at the front this time.'

'I don't want my hands tied.'

'No choice mate. Ya have to be tied up. I'll fix the rope to the hook over there and leave ya legs free so you can move about a bit, but I'm afraid ya have to be tied up. For ya own safety. And I'm gunna have to gag ya before I leave.'

As well as tying his hands, the man looped the rope around his stomach before tying it off on a hook on the wall. He felt like crying. He didn't want to be here.

'I don't think I like this game. I want my mummy.'

'Oh Joshie,' Ellen cried holding Josh's favourite toy donkey to her face. It was Eeyore from Winnie the Pooh. She hoped he was safe, wherever he was.

'Mummy and Daddy will have you home real soon,' she whispered to Eeyore. She had to cling to that belief otherwise she'd go mad. Max wasn't helping, he was just angry with her all the time. And she was angry with him too.

She'd been furious with him for agreeing that she should deliver the ransom money as the note demanded. Why had they asked *her* to deliver it? They should have asked Max to do it. She didn't have a lot of faith in the detective who seemed to be in charge. The woman had almost accused *her* of cutting up her own magazines to make the ransom note. She was sure she'd seen the detective somewhere before, but couldn't place her. Maybe she'd seen her while shopping somewhere, because the only police she'd encountered before had all been males.

Poor Joshie, wherever he was, he must be terrified. She thought winning this money was going to give her everything she wanted, but nothing seemed to be going right. She threw herself on Joshie's bed and wept.

Max slowed at the police barricade and waited for Detective Jacko to show his identification. One of the police officers on duty created an opening and waved them through. There seemed to be hundreds of media people hanging around the barricade. They swarmed towards his vehicle.

'Mr. Gibson?' he heard one of them shout. 'Mr. Gibson, can you tell us what the police are doing to help rescue your son? Has a ransom demand been received?'

'Ignore them and drive on,' Detective Jacko told him.

After they'd cleared the throng of reporters he glanced at the detective and asked, 'Have you heard anything further from your colleague as to what is happening?'

'Not since we left the bank. I told you the latest then.'

The newsagent, who had processed the claim Ellen had made had been ruled out as a suspect, he'd been told. The same applied to the staff who worked there. The detectives were now questioning members of the media who had attended the interview with Ellen.

'Do you think any of that lot we just passed were at the interview with Ellen?' he asked.

'As far as I know uniforms took all their names earlier to see if they were on the list. If they were they would have been taken back to the station for further questioning.'

'Right.' The detectives seemed to be quite thorough, but he wondered how many kidnappings they'd dealt with.

He was dreading being at home again. He'd phoned work while they'd been out to tell them he wouldn't be able to work for the foreseeable future. The CEO had seen the press release since his call and had sent a message on his mobile with his condolences and wishes for a speedy resolution.

He couldn't stop worrying about Josh. Was he being treated alright? Where were they keeping him? Were they giving him enough food and liquids? It was the height of summer and if he was being held in an isolated place alone he could become severely dehydrated. He'd also be terrified. When Josh came back to them he was sure he was going to need some form of counselling. A severe trauma like that could lead to serious emotional problems his mother had told him.

On their way back to the house Detective Jacko had suggested they stop and buy a take away. 'I can't see either you or your wife wanting to cook a meal tonight,' he'd said. 'I could do with something to eat as well. I suspect I'm going to be in for a long night.'

He'd waited in the car while the detective had gone into a Chinese take-away. Loaded with the bags now, he and Detective Jacko entered the house. Ellen was nowhere to be seen.

He felt a bit guilty that he'd had another go at Ellen earlier. When they learned that someone had entered the house and taken Ellen's magazines and the phone bill, he'd laid all the blame on her, believing it was someone who had attended the press conference. Then he discovered that she'd been out the night before and it was possible someone had come into the house while she was out. By then she'd given their address to all the papers and TV channels so they knew where they lived. There was no sign of a break-in and Ellen confessed to finding the back door unlocked when she'd gone to bed on Monday night. He had a go at her for not checking it when she'd gone out that evening. Sneaking off to MacDonald's he'd learned. But as she said, neither she nor Josh had gone out the back that day and instead accused him of leaving it unlocked on Sunday night. He knew he'd locked it. He checked it every night as a last ritual before he went to bed. And reminded her of this. However since he'd been out with the detective this afternoon, he remembered taking the rubbish out before he left for Grafton. Had he left it unlocked then? Ellen should have checked it anyway.

'Where's my wife?' he asked the female constable who had been with them since he'd arrived home from work.

'She's asleep on your son's bed.'

He wandered into Josh's room to check on Ellen. She was sound asleep, clutching one of Josh's cuddly toys. Her mascara was streaked, indicating she'd been crying again. He decided not to wake her. He'd save her some of the meal to be heated up later.

Back at the station India had just completed a round of interviews with two further press members from Channel Seven. They'd been picked up at the road block near the Gibsons' house and had both attended the interview with Ellen Gibson the day before. A female reporter and a cameraman. Neither of them had used the bathroom in the house but their alibis still had to be checked. It was proving a long and arduous task going through all the press names and she silently cursed Ellen Gibson and her vanity.

She'd spoken to Detective Li who'd confirmed the alibis for the newsagent owner and his staff. They were in the clear, but Greg Walton had told Li a large crowd had gathered in the shop after Ellen Gibson made a loud announcement about her win. He had recognised a few regular, elderly customers, but most were strangers. As

Li said, someone in the crowd could have followed her home. She had made a call to Rob, who was based down in Penrith and he'd sent a couple of uniforms to look at the security cameras in the parking lot to see if they could track Ellen Gibson's car to check if she'd been followed. So far she'd heard nothing back.

Jun Li was now on his way to interview a Channel Ten reporter at his home. The one who'd used the bathroom. Marlee Kuri was on her way to visit the female SBS reporter who had also entered the house. These two were their priority, but they still had a long list of reporters to speak to.

She'd obtained the name of the Herald reporter who'd been at the interview and dialled her number. She was next on her list. When the woman answered India introduced herself and asked if she would come in to speak to her.

'I've heard about the kid. Why are you ringing me? I flew up to Brisbane last night,' she told her. *'It's my mother's fiftieth birthday today and I've booked some time off.'*

'We are speaking to all the reporters who were at the Gibsons' house. I've also been told you passed their address to one of your colleagues. A Jeff Brody?'

'Yes, that's right. He said his mate, who worked on a local paper in Windsor wanted to see if Ellen Gibson would give him an interview for their weekly. I didn't think there was any harm in giving Jeff the address to pass on to his friend. His friend would have tracked Ellen Gibson down sooner or later anyway, being local. You can't keep news like that quiet for long.'

'Did you pass the address on to anyone else?'

'No.'

'Not even back at your paper's headquarters when you returned after the interview?'

'I didn't go back to the office. I filed my story from home. I had to pack for my trip up to Queensland.'

'And you didn't give the address to any of your friends, or other colleagues?'

'No. Look, I know Joshua Gibson is missing. I've seen the newsflash. I'm sorry to hear that and that I'm not there to cover the story. But his disappearance is nothing to do with me. Now if you don't mind I need to go. I have a party to help prepare.'

With that the reporter disconnected their call. India was annoyed at her rudeness and was tempted to call her back and launch into a lecture about respect, for Joshua Gibson and the enquiry, but she didn't have time.

Jeff Brody swore he'd only passed the address to Jude Ronson. The Herald editor confirmed Brody had been working on another story that day and couldn't have been anywhere near Windsor. It didn't rule out accomplices, although she thought it unlikely. Two more excluded. For now. Her rumbling stomach reminded her she hadn't eaten anything but a couple of biscuits since breakfast. Jacko should be back soon and then she'd order them some pizzas.

'I managed to grab a Chinese take away for me and the Gibsons on our way back,' Jacko told her when he arrived just after she'd finished talking to another reporter she'd cleared. 'Didn't think they'd feel like cooking tonight,' he added.

'So you've already eaten?' She felt envious at the thought of a Chinese.

'Yeah, but I'm sure I could manage a slice or two of pizza later. Especially if we're here till all hours.'

'I can guarantee we will be. Right, well I'll order half a dozen then, so there'll be plenty for others as they drop in. Our two colleagues from Richmond will no doubt be here later. I've also asked Dale to work late tonight.'

11

Josh heard a rustling sound and loud thumping noises outside the cabin and froze. Was it Billy and Queenie returning? It didn't sound like footsteps. He couldn't see much at all, now that it was dark. Billy had stuck some grey tape over his mouth so he couldn't scream or call out, but with some practise he'd discovered he could make some muffled noises. Should he try? He'd already had to have another pee which he'd managed with some difficulty. He'd had to empty his bladder near him on the cabin floor. The smell of it was making him feel a bit sick. He remained still and waited. The thumping noise continued every few minutes followed by a munching sound. He believed it was some kind of animal but what type and was it dangerous? Suddenly the cabin door swung open and he could just make out the shape of a large monster leaping into the cabin. His heart started pounding really fast and he was having to take quick short breaths. He felt the trickle of liquid warming his shorts before giving a final muffled shriek and passing out with shock.

Max Gibson thought he heard the sound of a child's cry outside the house. *Josh* was his immediate thought and, grabbing his torch from the kitchen, he rushed out of the back door.

'JOSH!' he called out, frantically charging around the back yard sweeping the beam of his torch over the ground. The light caught the shape of some kind of small animal scampering towards the back fence.

The young policewoman who had made endless pots of tea for them rushed out to join him. The last he'd seen of her she seemed to have dozed off on the couch.

'What is it?' she called. 'Did you see something?'

'I think it was just an animal,' Max said, feeling deflated. 'I thought I heard a child calling out.'

'Why don't you come back inside Mr. Gibson? Would you like another cup of tea?'

'No, I don't want any more bloody tea!'

'I'm sorry,' the young constable said. 'I know you must be feeling—'

'YOU HAVE NO IDEA HOW I'M FEELING!' he shouted at her, his anger and frustration boiling over.

The male police officer who had been standing guard on the front veranda appeared around the side of the house.

'Is everything alright?' he called out.

'Yes,' Max sighed, feeling guilty now. It wasn't the young woman's fault. 'I'm sorry for being so rude,' he said to her.

'That's quite alright. I understand.'

She didn't understand though. None of them did.

Maybe Ellen did; she seemed to be going through it. And so she should. If she hadn't been so stupid, wanting to become an overnight celebrity, like those brainless idiots she admired so much in her stupid magazines, then his son would be sleeping soundly in his own bed. Not being held a prisoner in god knows what conditions.

Ignoring the police officers who were huddled together whispering, he trudged back into the house. Maybe he should try to get some sleep. Ellen seemed to be managing it. She'd woken up earlier, eaten a few mouthfuls of the Chinese meal he'd brought home, and was now crashed out on Josh's bed again. He was sure she was taking some of her tablets again.

His parents had turned up around seven, the police allowing them through the road block after checking with him. They'd offered to stay and keep him company, but he didn't feel like talking to anyone so had insisted they go home to rest.

'You both have to go to work tomorrow,' he'd said.

'There's no way we'll be able to work with all this happening Max,' his mother had said. 'I've handed in my notice anyway, just like you told me to.'

'Nevertheless, you'd just be sitting around here, unable to do anything. At least at home, you'd have a bed. I promise I'll phone you if we hear anything.'

Ellen's mother had also wanted to come down from the Central Coast, but he'd put her off, promising to contact her the minute they heard anything.

Max didn't think he'd sleep much. Not without aid of some sort like Ellen and he didn't want that. He felt so helpless, unable to do anything that might lead to the release of his son. There was almost another three days until the money handover. Anything could happen in that time and he was powerless to do anything about it.

'I think we should call it a night,' India told the small team who were assembled at the station. 'There's still about eight media personnel to track down and follow up on their alibis. We can deal with them in the morning. We won't get anywhere calling at people's houses, either in person or by phone at this time of night.'

The three detectives, plus Jacko once he'd re-joined them, had been rushing around all over Sydney for the past six hours, establishing contact with newspaper and television personnel who had attended the interview with Ellen Gibson. It didn't look as though any of them were involved in the abduction of Joshua Gibson. So far.

'Dale, have you and Sue finished checking all Ellen Gibson's friends out?'

'Yes. None of them have the Windsor address. And they only spoke to Ellen Gibson *after* she returned from her meal.'

'So it wouldn't have been possible for any of them to have entered the house. It has to be one of the media team or someone linked to the newsagent who picked up the address,' India said.

They'd interviewed and eliminated the postal worker who had delivered the mail that morning. He had no idea that the Gibson family had won Powerball and he hadn't seen any vehicles in the area. His time had been accounted for and there were many witnesses who had either seen or spoken to him on his round and after returning to the depot.

Rob's officers had tracked Ellen Gibson's car as it left the car park. A white Toyota, the only other car which left the car park at the same time, turned right taking the opposite direction to her. They'd picked her car up at various CCTV points on her way out of Penrith and no-one seemed to be following her. So that was a dead end. India had imparted the news to the team about an hour prior.

'I'd like to go back to the shopping mall first thing tomorrow,' Marlee said. She'd looked at the security footage at the newsagent. Cameras in the shop were limited and showed a crowd of people milling about at the entrance, as Greg Walton had said. Marlee had spotted one man who'd made his way through the crowd to leave the shop, but there was no clear image of him.

'I still think it strange that everyone else hung around to talk about Ellen Gibson's news and this one man left,' Marlee added.

'He might have been in a hurry,' Jacko suggested. 'Or pissed off that it wasn't him who'd won any money.'

'I showed the image of the man to Greg Walton and his assistant. Neither of them remembered serving him.'

'It would have been difficult for anyone to be served with the fuss that was going on around Ellen Gibson,' Jacko reminded her.

'I suppose. I'd still like to follow it up though. I'll go first thing in the morning if you don't mind,' Marlee said, addressing India.

'Fine,' India said nodding. 'I think everyone should

head off now. With any luck we might manage a few hours' sleep. Make sure you have a big breakfast before you come in. It's going to be a long day.'

At home Rob was waiting up for her. 'I'm sorry I couldn't give you good news,' he said taking her into his arms. 'You must be absolutely exhausted. Do you want anything to eat or drink before you crash out?'

'No, thanks. I had endless cups of coffee at the station earlier and quite a few slices of pizza. I am tired but I'm worried I won't be able to sleep now with so much caffeine in my system.'

'I could think of a few things to wear you out. Why don't you take a relaxing bath first? I can run you one if you want.'

'I might just do that. Thanks Rob.'

Several hours later India was still tossing and turning. The bath had helped but Rob's promise to wear her out in other ways had not exactly gone to plan. By the time she was ready for bed he was sound asleep. Ever the optimist, she hoped tomorrow would bring in new leads. The door to door enquiries would be continuing first thing. Sergeant Morrison had reported back that they'd been unable to speak to everyone whose houses they'd approached. There'd been no answer at quite a few of them – the residents no doubt not home from work yet. She couldn't bear to think about that sweet little boy being held captive by strangers and just hoped the kidnappers were treating Joshua well.

He lit the camp lamps and shook the boy awake. 'What the hell's happened here?' he asked.

He'd forgotten Josh couldn't answer with tape over his mouth so ripped it off, causing the boy to squeal.

'Sorry Josh. So what happened?' he asked the boy again.

'A big monster came into the cabin,' Josh said. 'Where were you Billy? I was frightened.'

'I told ya Queenie and I had things to do. I needed to get some more food and water as well. Ya've wet yourself haven't you?' he asked looking at the wet stain on the boy's shorts.

'I … I couldn't help it. The monster scared me so much.'

He looked around and could see no sign of human entry. 'It was probably a nosey roo,' he said. 'There's a few of them about in the bush here.'

'Did you bring any of my clothes? I want to get changed.'

'Yeah, I've got a small bag of ya stuff here, but ya should wash first. Ya can't put clean clothes on, over a pissy body. You'll have to stay in them things until tomorra. There's a little stream not far away. I can get some water for ya to wash tomorra. I'm not doin' it now. It's too dark.'

'Did mummy pack my special cream? My legs are itchy.'

'I doan know what ya talkin' bout.'

'I have something called ex … exma the doctor said. I have to put special cream on it.'

'Well she didn't pack any of that. Now do ya want something to eat?'

'What have you got?'

'Bread, jam, vegemite and cheese slices.'

'Don't you have anything sweet? I'd like some lollies, and I need a drink. I'm really, really, thirsty.'

'Nope. No lollies and they're not good for ya. They'll rot ya teeth.'

'Can I have a vegemite and cheese sandwich then please? And a drink.'

'Okey doke. Comin right up,' he said rising to prepare the kid's food and pour him a small cup of water. He'd been into a pub and had steak and chips himself, plus he'd bought a steak for Queenie. He had meant to buy some more bottles of water, but he'd forgotten. If there'd been a McDonald's nearby he would've brought one back for the kid, but there was none around here. The kid would have to put up with snacks, like he was going to have to for the next few days. Unless he managed to sneak off again.

12

Thursday

India was in the process of putting a line through yet another name on the white board when DC Marlee Kuri burst into the squad room at nine-fifty. Although it was another elimination and reduced their list of suspects, she wasn't optimistic they were on the right track. All the media staff they'd interviewed or spoken to were able to account for their time which had been verified. Including the two who had gone into the house. One look at Marlee's excited face and she could tell the DC had had some kind of result. At least she hoped so.

'I have a lead,' Marlee announced. 'The man I spotted leaving the newsagents – I picked him up on other security cameras in the mall and in the car park. I managed to get a good visual of his car, so I have a name and address. His name is Roger Lansford and he lives near Richmond.'

'What type of car does he drive?'

'A white Ford ute.'

'Ah. Uniforms ascertained that a white ute was seen driving past one of the neighbour's houses around the time the kidnap might have occurred. Well done Marlee,' she said, smiling. At last a glimmer of hope. 'Roger Lansford you said?'

Marlee nodded. 'Do you want me—?'

'Well I think the two of us should pay a little visit to Mr. Lansford. Jacko has gone to collect Max Gibson, and Jun Li is interviewing another media suspect. I've just returned from checking out another one on the list. Shall we go?'

'You betcha!' Marlee said full of enthusiasm.

At the Lansford home, an old neglected looking weatherboard, there was no answer. They'd tried knocking on the front and back doors. The garage doors down the side were open a little and India and Marlee wandered in to take a look. The garage floor was strewn with what looked like engine parts.

'Can you hear that?' she asked Marlee. The sound of 'Catch a Falling Star', an old popular classic that she thought was a Perry Como song was wafting out of a window from the property next door. She'd heard it played many times at her grandparent's house when she was little.

'It seems likely that someone is at home next door. Let's try knocking,' she said. 'They might know where Mr. Lansford works.'

An elderly woman answered their knock. She appeared to be bending over looking at her shoes. India took out her identification and introduced herself. The woman shuffled her body around, still bent in that awkward position to look at the identification. It was then that she realised that the woman was not bending over, this was her natural posture. She felt a desperate impulse to take hold of the woman and pull her into an upright position.

'I'm looking for your neighbour, Mr. Lansford,' she said, trying her best not be distracted by the appearance of the woman. 'I wondered if you might know where he works.'

'He's a mechanic,' she answered. 'Runs a repair place on Macquarie Street in Richmond. What do you want him for? He's not dealing in dodgy cars is he? Only my husband bought one off him a few months back.'

'No, nothing like that. We're hoping he might be able to help us with another matter.'

'Right. Well you'll find him there I imagine.'

'Thanks for your help,' she said turning away.

'Does Mr. Lansford have a family?' Marlee asked. 'Any children?'

'No. There's no children there. Only him and his cousin Jimmy.'

'No visiting family with children?'

'No. I don't think they have any other family.'

'Thanks again. Sorry to have troubled you,' Marlee said.

'You didn't mind me asking whether Roger Lansford had a family, did you?' Marlee asked her as they were walking away. 'Only I thought if he didn't, and a child suddenly appeared the neighbours might notice.'

'No, it was a good question. I should have thought of it.'

Beaming, Marlee almost bounced back to their car.

'How does someone end up like that?' Marlee asked once they drove away. 'What kind of condition do you think she has?'

'I don't know,' India said, shuddering.

'God, I'd hate to end up like that. I wanted to ask her to straighten up, and had an urge to make her do it.'

'Yeah, me too.'

'How do you think she manages to sit in the car her husband drives?'

'Perhaps she doesn't go out much. It would be very difficult for her. Can you keep an eye out for Lansford's place?' she said, wanting to change the subject.

'There it is! Over there on the right.'

She shot past the place, did a quick U-turn pulling up outside a motor repair garage that had the name 'Lansford's Motor Repairs' emblazoned across a sign.

'It must be his own business,' Marlee said as they climbed out of the car.

The entrance led them into a deceptively spacious workshop where a couple of young men were working on cars. One of them looked up with raised eyebrows.

'We're looking for Mr. Roger Lansford,' India told him.

Using a tool he was holding, the young man pointed towards the front of the workshop. They'd passed a closed door without noticing. Retracing their steps India knocked on the door, receiving a rather grumpy 'come in' as a reply.

She had a gut feeling as she opened the door that this was the breakthrough they'd been looking for. She'd felt it at the house as well. She noted that the premises had security cameras. That would be handy – if they were real.

Roger Lansford looked to be about forty years old. A thin wiry looking character with an unattractive sharp pointy nose and pock scarred face which was smeared with grease stains. His close-cropped hair was beginning to thin and he had the look of a man who was disappointed with life.

'Mr. Roger Lansford?'

'That's me.'

'I'm Detective Inspector Hargreaves and this is Detective Constable Kuri,' she said flashing her identification. 'I'm from Windsor Police and would like to ask you a few questions.'

'Yeah? What about?'

'You were at a newsagent in Penrith earlier this week when a customer announced she had the winning Powerball ticket.'

'That's right. The stupid woman was making such a song and dance about it, I wasn't able to pay for my paper and left the shop. I didn't want to stand around listening to her for hours. I didn't believe her anyway, thought she was just an attention-seeking nutter, but I saw in the paper a few days later that she had won it. If I'd won that money, I wouldn't be announcing it to the whole world. Why are you asking me about her?' Lansford asked looking a little irritated and nervous. He moved his chair back a fraction. The office was so small, there was little room for movement and she was blocking the doorway. There'd been no room for Marlee to follow her in, but Lansford must have been able to see that Marlee was right behind her. Was he feeling cornered and panicky because he had something to hide?

'Have you not seen the papers or the news today?'

'No. I was out until late last night and came in here early this morning. I had a repair to do and then a lot of paperwork to catch up on – as you can see,' Lansford said pointing to the pile on his desk. 'Why what's happened to her? And why have you come to speak to me?'

'Joshua Gibson, the woman's five-year-old son, was taken from his home yesterday. We're treating it as a kidnapping and are questioning anyone who came into contact with her, either at the newsagent shop, or during the press conferences she gave.'

Lansford looked shocked, which she judged to be genuine. Was he shocked that they'd caught up with him so soon, or because he was innocent?

'I'm sorry to hear that,' Lansford said, 'but I don't understand what that has to do with me. I didn't even speak to the woman, and there were loads of other people in the shop.'

'Can you tell me your movements, from the point of leaving the newsagent's up until today?'

Lansford sighed. 'That was Monday, right?'

'Yes.'

'After I left the shopping mall, I went to the Panther's Club in Penrith. I'm a member there. I had a sandwich and a beer, then I came back here, did a bit of paperwork before going to my local club. The RSL in Richmond. I eat there most evenings as I can't be bothered to cook for myself.'

'Why were you in Penrith that day?'

'I had a dentist's appointment, my six- monthly check-up.'

'We'll need the name of your dentist to verify that.'

Lansford pulled an appointment card from a small tray on his desk and handed it to her. She could see Lansford's appointment time on the card, so he was telling the truth. They needed to check that he'd attended. She passed the card to Marlee asking her to go out and phone the dentist for confirmation.

'You live with your cousin Jimmy, don't you? What does he do? Don't you share meals with him?'

'How do you know about Jimmy? And how come you knew I was at the newsagent?' Lansford asked, his face screwed up with a look of suspicion.

'We were able to track you to your car on security cameras,' she said. 'And we questioned your neighbour briefly.'

Lansford swore under his breath, mumbling something about 'big brother.'

'Your cousin Jimmy?' she reminded him.

'I don't see Jimmy all that much. He works away a lot. He has some problems – mentally that is, and has the age of an eleven/twelve-year-old. He's a big, strong bugger though and is in demand for manual work. He gets jobs all over the place and often stays over wherever he's working. He uses my place as a base more than anything. He's not capable of living independently. He can make snacks but he'd never be able to cook proper meals – I wouldn't trust to him to anyway. I took him in after his parents died. If he's around I will cook for us both occasionally.'

'Where is Jimmy now?'

'I've no idea. He came to see me here Tuesday afternoon saying he wouldn't be back until next week and that he was staying at the place where he'll be working. Jimmy doesn't have a driving licence you see, so if he's working a distance away it's not easy for him to travel back and forth.'

'Does he have a mobile phone?'

'He did have but he lost it a couple of weeks ago and couldn't remember where he left it. It's the third one he's lost. Memory like a sieve.'

'How old is Jimmy?'

'He's thirty-four.'

Cousin Jimmy might be the kind of handy person who could assist a kidnapper. From Lansford's description of him, he wouldn't be the brains behind it though. It would have to be someone with more organisational skills. Someone capable of planning and executing a kidnap. Someone like Lansford? At last it looked like they might be getting somewhere. After a few seconds she looked up at Lansford and said, 'We'll need the numbers of your mobile and Jimmy's. Also your land line number at home and here at work.'

'I don't have a landline at home. Only here at the office. Why would you want our numbers?'

'It's just routine Mr. Lansford. We need to eliminate you and your cousin from our enquiries.'

'You can't think Jimmy had anything to do with

kidnapping a kid do you? I can assure you he wouldn't have the mental capacity to do anything like that. He's all brawn, no brains. And he wouldn't hurt a fly.'

'He could be assisting someone though.'

'Nah,' Lansford said, shaking his head. 'Not Jimmy. He's a hard worker and a good person. He can be annoying and irritating at times, but no-one would be able to convince him to commit a crime. Especially one that involved a little kid.'

She ignored Lansford's description of his cousin. He might be spouting it to deflect attention away from himself.

'If Jimmy lost his phone weeks ago, how would he have been hired for this latest job?' she asked him.

'I don't know. He often has a meal in the Colonial Arms a few blocks in from my place. It's not a place I go to myself very often. Maybe he picked up the work from someone there.'

She pulled out a card and gave it to Lansford. 'If Jimmy returns home or you hear from him, I'd like you to call me immediately.'

He nodded.

'What is your shoe size?' she asked him.

'My shoe size?' Lansford asked looking puzzled.

'Could you just answer the question Mr. Lansford?'

'Size ten.'

She looked down at his shoes. Size ten seemed about right. He looked as if his feet were the same size as Rob's.

'And your cousin, Jimmy?'

'I don't know. Eleven I think.'

'Ok. Thank You. You've told me what you did on

Monday. Now can you tell me your movements on Tuesday and Wednesday, and do you have film in your security cameras that we can check?'

'What do you think boss?' Marlee asked as they drove away from Lansford's workshop.

'Don't know. I'd say Lansford would be capable of the planning needed to carry out a kidnap. But as you verified, his staff claim he was in the workshop all day yesterday. His cousin Jimmy doesn't sound like he'd be capable of taking Joshua on his own. That would mean a third person would need to be involved if Lansford and his cousin are in on it. We've got lots to look into, but let's check out this Colonial Arms first.'

13

India called a team briefing at two pm.

'Jacko has to leave soon to collect Max Gibson to head to the bank and finalise details for the collection of the money tomorrow morning,' she told them. 'Can you explain what's happening with that Jacko?'

He nodded. 'Yeah, we're going to bring the money back here to be locked up overnight as Max Gibson said he doesn't want that much cash hanging around his house. The boss agrees with him. The kidnappers might have said the money had to be delivered on Saturday night knowing the cash would have to have been collected prior to that. A raid on Gibson's house could be planned for either Friday or Saturday night before they phone with instructions. They wouldn't be able to enter the house by road as it's securely blocked off. But they could approach the house from the rear paddocks,' he said looking back to her.

'So I've organised extra uniforms to be on duty in case,' India said. 'I've also organised for a technician to be stationed at the house with recording equipment that can be linked to the phone. I made a quick call to the house a few minutes ago which confirmed that nothing has been heard from the kidnappers. Before we move onto other things I'd like to know the latest situation on the interviews? Jacko, you got anything?'

'The one I interviewed this morning has been cleared. And he didn't see anyone, other than the two we know about, going into the house.'

'The same with me,' Jun Li said.

'How many more are there to do?'

'Three. That's all,' Jacko said. 'One journo, one photographer and one cameraman.'

'Well we need to divide them up between us. I'll sort that once Jacko's gone. We had a bit of a breakthrough this morning,' she said. 'Marlee's research at Penrith mall led us to a man called Roger Lansford. He was the man captured on camera leaving the newsagent after Ellen Gibson made her big scene. We paid him a visit this morning. He owns and runs a motor repair workshop in Richmond. He drives a white ute, similar to one that was seen driving down the Gibsons' road. He claims he went to the Panther's club after leaving the mall, before returning to work. I checked out footage at the Panther's and he was there as he said. Dale has checked the security footage Lansford gave us from his workshop. Did you find anything Dale?'

'No, the footage tallies with his claims of leaving work Monday, Tuesday and Wednesday evenings. The problem is that we only see him leaving or arriving at the premises on Tuesday and Wednesday. They don't keep the camera running during opening hours.'

'Okay. Thanks. Marlee also checked with Richmond

RSL. What have you got for us Marlee?'

'Lansford was there every night as he claimed. Eating a meal, drinking at the bar, and playing the poker machines. It looks as though he walks there from work and according to the two club receptionists I interviewed, he orders a cab to take him home if he's had too much to drink. Otherwise he walks back to his repair shop to pick up his car before driving home. Dale spotted him collecting his car on Tuesday night on his security footage. He was at the club again last night and went back to a friend's house for more drinks. I've checked with Rafe and Connie Barton, the couple whose number Lansford gave us and they confirm that. The cab driver who brought him home later confirmed the time he picked him up and dropped him off. It looks like he was telling us the truth.'

'I'd like to have his ute and house checked over, but there's no way I'd be granted a warrant. There's no evidence indicating that Lansford is involved in the kidnapping at all. But there's something not quite right there, I'm sure.'

'One of your gut feelings?' Jacko asked.

'Yes. I don't know if it's linked to Lansford himself or his mentally disabled cousin. According to Lansford he doesn't know where his cousin is working at the moment. We went to the Colonial Arms, a pub that Jimmy Lansford goes to for meals some nights. He was last in there on Monday and they haven't seen him since. Lansford and his cousin Jimmy could be working with someone else. We know that someone must have entered the Gibsons' house to take the magazines and compile the ransom demand. The only time that could have been was when Ellen Gibson took Joshua out for a meal on Monday night, or at the press conference. We've ruled out the two members of the press who went into the house. That means someone else did. Jimmy Lansford has a mental age of about eleven or twelve according to Roger Lansford, so I can't see him doing it – or putting together that ransom demand. It has to be someone else.'

'Have you had Lansford's phone checked out?' Jun Li asked.

'We're waiting on information to come in from his provider. I was able to obtain a warrant for that before other information came to light. Lansford also gave us the number of the phone his cousin supposedly lost and we're having that checked out.'

She noticed Jacko checking his watch. He then stood and nodded.

'I need to be heading off,' he said. 'I'll see you later.'

They watched in silence as Jacko walked out the door.

'What about having Lansford followed?' June Li suggested after a pause. 'You could get a couple of the uniforms attached to go out in an unmarked car. I'm sure they'd appreciate the overtime.'

India nodded. She'd been thinking along the same lines.

'I would like a couple staked out at his work and another at his house. In case the cousin comes home. I'll need to speak to Superintendent Havering first to see that he'll okay the extra hours. I tell you budgets are a pain in the butt!'

14

Ellen watched as Max left the house with the male detective. She felt sick at the thought of the two million dollars that they were going to give away on Saturday night. She had a bad feeling about all of this. The kidnappers had not contacted them and both Max and the police said she couldn't go out anywhere because they were waiting for the call. She'd said she wanted to go to the supermarket this morning – they were running out of milk and other fresh food.

'You're not going anywhere,' Max had said. 'The kidnappers could call any minute.'

'But we need shopping,' she had protested. She felt like she was going crazy just sitting around at home doing nothing. She wanted to go out and do some shopping to take her mind off things.

'We'll organise anything you need to be brought in,' the new policewoman who was with them today said. The one who'd been with them yesterday had been sent home.

She'd managed to sleep through the night with the aid of a sleeping tablet. She had a stash of them she kept in reserve, in case she wanted to escape Max's demands – not that that had been a problem lately. She couldn't remember the last time he'd initiated any sex.

The tablet she'd taken last night were left over from the days when she used to suffer terrible pain following a car crash she was involved in when Josh was one. She had strong painkillers and sleeping tablets. After they'd moved into a ground floor flat and she no longer had to carry Josh up so many stairs, her pains had lessened. Her condition still flared up occasionally; she had days when she was crippled with severe head and back ache but nothing like as often as she used to have – or made out. She sometimes used it as an excuse to avoid things she didn't want to do – like visiting her in-laws. No-one needed to know that though and she always managed to persuade male doctors to give her any medication she wanted. The tablets were proving handy for her now so that she could block out everything.

It was going to be another couple of days before she was supposed to deliver the ransom. She didn't think she could stand to be cooped up in the house until then. It wasn't fair. Max was going out. Why shouldn't she? It was unlikely the kidnappers would phone her today and give a location. They weren't going to be that stupid surely? They would know the police would surround the drop-off place if they gave advance notice. So why shouldn't she go out?

Despite protests from the police on duty at the house, Ellen managed to escape. She changed into smarter clothes and insisted she needed to go for a drive. As she headed towards town she could see the road was cordoned off with a couple of police officers guarding it. Apart from a small section in the middle, they had cars parked at angles across the road as well. She hoped they weren't going to stop her going through. She could see a range of press vehicles and a crowd on the other side of the cordon. Her pulse quickened. They were going to fire lots of questions at her. What should she say?

'I just received a call from one of the constables on duty at the Gibsons' house,' India announced to Jun and Marlee who, like her had been on the phone attempting to track down the last three media personnel they needed to clear. 'Ellen Gibson has taken off. She told them she just wanted to go for a drive. I hope she's not going to talk to the press.'

'I'd bet on her doing exactly that,' Marlee said.

'Hmm. So would I. I've asked for patrol cars to keep an eye out for her.'

'What if the kidnappers call?' Jun Li asked.

'I've told the female police constable there to pretend she's Ellen Gibson if they call. Apparently Mrs. Gibson told her that the kidnappers wouldn't call today, so there was no reason for her not to go out.'

'She can't possibly know that they won't call today, unless she has inside information,' Marlee said.

'Her reasoning, and I have to say I'm inclined to agree with her, was that the kidnappers won't tell her in advance where to deliver the money because they know we'd stake the place out. She believes they'll call at the last minute.'

'Makes sense I suppose. But still, she shouldn't be out gallivanting about while her son is being held by kidnappers,' Marlee said. 'What if someone recognises her, gets the bright idea of kidnapping her as well, and makes a second ransom demand?'

'Let's hope that doesn't happen,' India said turning back to her office.

'I'm bored,' Josh told Billy while scratching his arm. The rash bits on his arms and legs were really itchy. Billy told him his mother forgot to pack his special cream. She'd also forgotten Eeyore and sent Ted instead, but he wondered whether it was because she didn't want him to get Eeyore dirty. She was fussy about things like that.

'I gave ya a couple of ya things to play with. What's wrong with ya?'

'But you only brought a couple of my small toy cars. At home I have lots more toys. So I can switch to doing different things when I'm fed up.'

'Well that's too bad. Read ya book then.'

'I've already read it twice today and I've read it loads of times before.'

'Do ya know all the words then?'

'Not really. I know the story off by heart from when my mother reads it to me. I can recognise quite a few of the words. But I'm starting school in a few weeks, so soon I'll be able to read all the words.'

'Ya lucky you have a mum that reads to ya.'

'My daddy reads to me as well.'

'My ol man never read anythin' to me when I was a kid. All he did was bash me about.'

'Your father hit you?'

'Yeah, belted me all the time. Cracked me skull a couple of times and then lied to the hospital sayin' I had a fall. Claimed I was always climbin' things. I was, but he was lyin'.'

'You didn't tell on him?'

'Nah, I was too scared.'

'My daddy has never hit me. Mummy has a couple of times. Just a little slap that didn't hurt, but I pretended it did so she'd feel bad. She did and told me she was sorry after.'

'What do ya parents do to punish ya then?'

'I have to sit on the naughty chair in the kitchen. But that hasn't happened a lot. A few times in our old flat and just one time in the new house.'

'Yer spoilt then.'

'I don't know what spoilt means.'

'It means yer given everythin' ya want and don't get punished for doin things you shouldn't.'

'I don't get everything I want. We don't have enough money mummy and daddy tells me.'

'Well that's gunna change isn't it? They've got loads of money now.'

Josh sighed. He preferred it when they didn't have loads of money. Then he'd be at home feeling safe with his mummy and daddy, not sitting in this smelly horrible place.

'How are you feeling about your son being kidnapped, Mrs. Gibson?' one reporter asked her sticking a microphone right in her face.

'I'm devastated. Josh is only five years old. He must be truly terrified without his mummy and daddy with him. I—'

'Have the kidnappers asked for a ransom?' another voice cut in.

'Yes, they've asked for two million dollars.'

'How do you feel about that?' the first reporter asked.

'It's a small sacrifice to pay to get my darling boy back. Now if you'll excuse me, I need to get on.'

'Where are you going Mrs. Gibson?'

'I just need a drive to clear my head. I've been going crazy waiting for the kidnappers to phone.'

'When are they going to phone you?'

'I don't know. I'm sorry but I need to go.'

'Shouldn't you be in the house waiting—'

Ellen wound up her window cutting off the reporter's question. She didn't want to talk to them anymore. They had swarmed around her car like vultures, snapping their pictures and honing the cameras in on her. It wasn't like the press conference she gave earlier in the week and she didn't like it.

She decided she wouldn't go to the shops after all and instead turned the car around and headed back to the house. Perhaps she shouldn't have spoken to them.

Max was furious with her when he discovered what

she'd done.

'How could you leave the house?' he yelled at her. 'What if the kidnappers had phoned?'

'They're not going to phone today Max. Stop fussing. They'll phone at the last minute on Saturday.'

'You don't know that. If you've done anything to jeopardise Josh ...'

'I haven't done anything.'

'You spoke to reporters! That was a bloody stupid thing to do.'

She refused to answer him and walked into Josh's room and slammed the door. She wanted to read his favourite book and pretend he was lying there listening to her. She searched the room but couldn't find it anywhere. Where had Josh put it? She was sure it was here a few days ago.

Ellen Gibson made headline news that evening with her statement about the ransom demand and it being a "small sacrifice". Watching it in the squad room with some of the team, India cursed the woman's foolishness. What were the press thinking broadcasting her making that statement? It was just asking for trouble.

Sure enough she received a call from the family liaison officer who was in the house with the Gibson couple telling her a call had just come in from the kidnappers. Jacko's phone had rung at the same time as hers. He was still talking as she hung up with a sinking heart. She waited until he terminated his call before speaking.

'You've heard?'

'Yep. That was Max Gibson. He's contacted his bank

manager, who gave us a direct contact number, to tell him the ransom's been increased.'

Turning to the others in the room she said, 'Listen up everyone. The kidnappers have reacted to Ellen Gibson's statement. A call was made to the Gibsons from one of the kidnappers who has said they want four million now, as two million was such a *small sacrifice.*'

'It was probably their plan all along to increase the ransom,' Marlee said. 'They've just used Ellen's statement as an excuse.'

'Maybe. Do you know how the bank manager responded to Max Gibson's call Jacko?'

'Yeah. He's going to arrange for Head Office to put together another two million. They may not be able do it all in used notes though. We have to meet the manager at Sydney's Head Office tomorrow around midday. I'm picking up Max around ten forty-five. He's headed out now to buy another large holdall before the shops shut. The one he bought the other day won't fit the extra money that has to be handed over.'

She noticed Jacko was now using Gibson's first name. Clearly on their excursion to the bank, they'd become matey.

'Okay. Why don't you head home Jacko. Grab a decent night's sleep. Tomorrow is going to be a long day.'

'Yeah. If you're okay about me leaving, I'll pop downstairs now and confirm tomorrow's escort and make sure there's plenty of uniforms on guard duty tonight.'

'Yes, go for it.'

The team members watched Jacko grab his keys and

head out the door. She could see their faces matched hers. A look of envy.

'Right,' she said turning to the others. 'The technician had no luck in tracing the call. It was from a blocked number and only lasted a few seconds. The kidnapper said he'd phone on Saturday with instructions and they want Ellen Gibson to answer the phone next time. Max Gibson answered it this evening.'

'Did the technician record the call?' Jun Li asked.

'Yes.'

'It was a *he*?' Marlee asked.

'The caller was using one of those voice distorters, but it sounded like a male.'

'Organised then,' Jun Li commented.

'Mmm. Jun Li can you get onto our colleagues who are watching Lansford's house and workplace? See if there's been any movement there and if they know where Lansford was when this call came in?

'Ok, I'll do that now,' Jun Li said turning away.

'Have you finished checking Roger and Jimmy Lansford's phones?' she asked Marlee.

'Yes. Roger Lansford's seems innocuous. He mainly uses his mobile to call taxis or the landline at his workplace. There's been no activity on his mobile today. I've called the few numbers which made calls to Jimmy Lansford – apart from his cousin Roger. There was nothing recent and they were all people he'd worked for at some point or another. None of them had seen him for months.'

'I'd love to know how he picked up his current job without his phone. He must have bought another one without his cousin knowing.'

'Despite the bar staff at the Colonial Arms claiming it was unlikely, I wouldn't be surprised if it was someone he met there. That's what Roger Lansford thought,' Marlee said.

'If someone at the Colonial Arms offered him a job, it would be more likely to be local work and he'd return home of a night. When I spoke to the manager he said their customers were mainly locals. It's not on a main road, so they don't get much passing trade, he claimed. I can't imagine customers who were passing through stopping to talk to Jimmy and then offering him a job. Why would they?'

'Because they needed some muscle for a particular job and he fitted the bill?'

'Maybe. But no-one we spoke to had seen Jimmy talking to any strangers, just some of the locals like he normally does. He sat with them for his meal on Monday.'

'Yeah, but would the staff have had their eyes on him the whole time?'

'I don't know Marlee. From what I picked up he's a bit of a loud character and you can't miss him. But also if you remember, he never stays long at the pub.'

Jun Li returned at that point and they looked up at him waiting for his update.

'Roger Lansford has been at the RSL since shortly after five this evening. He played the poker machines for a bit, had a drink at the bar and now he's eating a meal. According to his tail, Lansford hasn't made any calls.'

'Well that rules him out as being our mystery caller then,' India said. 'What about back at the house.'

'No activity there. The cousin hasn't returned.'

'Okay, thanks Jun Li. Now we've ruled out all the members of the press who were at the Gibson's, we're running out of options,' she said. They were looking at her for guidance, but she wasn't sure what their next move should be. The only thing she could think of was to go over everything they'd already covered to see if they'd missed anything and interview ones they'd eliminated through phone calls.

While everyone was on a tea break, she grabbed a quiet moment to nip off to the bathroom. There was something important she'd been meaning to do for days.

15

Friday

The following morning India and Rob met over breakfast. It had been a late night for her and Rob hadn't stirred when she crawled into bed. As she'd closed her eyes, she realised she hadn't told him her news. In fact, she'd forgotten about it as she'd been so preoccupied with Joshua Gibson.

'I did a pregnancy test at work last night. It was positive,' she blurted out to Rob.

'Oh my God. You never mentioned that you suspected you were pregnant, or were planning on doing a test. Why didn't you wake me last night when you got in?'

Rob looked shocked. Wasn't he pleased with the news?

'I didn't remember until I was about to drift off to sleep and the next thing I knew it was morning. You were already in the shower when I woke up.'

They'd been trying for a child for the past nine years. Ideally she would have preferred to have children while she was still young. There'd been a couple of miscarriages in the early years of trying and a few false hopes. Yesterday's test was the first positive one she'd had for several years. Rob claimed it didn't matter if they didn't have children, but she knew he wanted them as much as she did. She would be thirty eight later this year. Time was running out for her.

'How far gone are you? I didn't notice that you ...'

'About seven weeks. It was when I missed my second cycle that it occurred to me. That and the fact that I've been off certain foods. I thought it was just the heat at first and recovering from that stomach bug I had over Christmas. I must have already been pregnant then without realising.'

Rob's face finally broke out in a smile and he moved off his breakfast stool to give her a big hug.

'Are you pleased with the news?' she asked him.

'Of course I am,' he said before stepping back. 'But India, I think you need to cut back on your hours. Not take any chances this time.'

'I'm pregnant Rob. Not sick.'

'I still believe that first miscarriage was because of your physical interaction with that suspect.'

She had tackled a suspect in an armed robbery during his attempt to flee. The miscarriage had come on a week later, just as she approached fifteen weeks. She wasn't so sure the miscarriage was down to the tackle. Her doctor told her she would have miscarried much sooner if her physical actions had caused problems and that it was very common for women to miscarry their first child. She'd also miscarried her second child at four months and hadn't been doing anything physical then.

'I promise I'll keep physical actions to a minimum, but we have a five-year-old child who's been kidnapped Rob. I can't just stay in the office and put my feet up.'

'I know, but you can avoid working long hours like you did yesterday. Delegate more.'

'We're not exactly bursting at the seams with feet on the ground. Jacko, Jun Li, Marlee, Dale and Sue, the other part time admin person we have on loan, are doing a great job, but we simply don't have enough manpower for this case. Havering was talking about bringing in some big guns from Headquarters. In some ways that would be a relief. I promise to do my best though.'

They made little progress on the case that day. Every member of the media who'd been present at the interviews on Tuesday had been eliminated and they'd gone over some of them again. Roger Lansford, and possibly his cousin Jimmy were the only ones who remained on their radar and observation of Lansford hadn't produced anything concrete.

'We need to double check *everything*,' she told the team. 'We also need someone to go back to the newsagent and see if the owner has remembered the names of any of the other witnesses.'

'I'll go boss,' Marlee said.

Jacko returned by mid-afternoon confirming they'd collected the ransom money. It was safely tucked away and she ordered an increase in the number of armed uniformed constables to be stationed outside the Gibsons' home that night in case the kidnappers planned a raid on the house.

At seven that evening India told everyone to go home. They'd tracked a couple of more witnesses. A few who had been in the newsagents on Monday had come into the shop again and the owner had taken down their names and addresses to pass onto the police. Visits to the witnesses' homes hadn't given them any new information. All eyes had been on Ellen Gibson and no-one had noticed anything else.

'We'll just have to wait for the kidnapper's phone call,' India said as they packed up.

16

Saturday

The call came in a few minutes before nine pm. India watched as Ellen Gibson reluctantly answered it. The phone was on loudspeaker so everyone could hear. The caller was once again using a voice distorter.

'Bring the money in large holdalls with handles as we said in our last call. Drive in your own car. Pull into the layby at Colo Heights on the Putty Road and drop it off at the back of the layby there at ten pm. Then leave. Make sure you come alone. We'll be watching you. If we see any sign of anyone else, you won't see your son again. Once we've checked the money we'll release your boy.'

The call was then terminated.

'Again he wasn't on long enough to work out where the call was coming from. And the number was blocked,' the technician told them.

It had been agreed that Jacko would be travelling in the back of the car and would hide as they approached the drop-off point. Ellen Gibson was not happy about one policeman being with her.

'I can't do this,' she told the group who were watching her.

'You have to Ellen,' Gibson said. 'And you need to leave soon. We agreed. It's the only chance we have of getting Joshua back.'

'I *can't* do it. I won't,' Ellen repeated shaking. 'How can I drive in this state? Look at me!' she said holding out her shaking arms.

'I'll go in your place,' India volunteered. 'The only problem will be if they realise I'm not you, seeing as I'm several inches taller. Although I suppose it will be okay as it will be dark.'

Ellen was only about five foot three. She was five foot seven.

They'd discussed the option of India acting as a substitute for Ellen the day before. Suspecting it would be her delivering the money, she had gone shopping on her way in that morning. She'd bought a short blonde wig with a similar hair style as Ellen's. Her own hair was past her shoulders and she'd worn it up today in preparation for wearing the wig. She'd also bought an outfit that was the type of thing she thought Ellen might wear. Something she wouldn't be seen dead in. A short grey skirt, a smart sleeveless red top and red low-slung heels. Rob would not be happy with her being the one delivering the money, which was why she hadn't told him. He'd say she was putting herself and the baby at too much risk.

'I'll just go and get changed, then we need to head off,' she said. 'Jun Li can you notify the back-up team about the location so they can move into position. Then you need to head back to base.'

'If I can't be with you for the money drop, I'd like to be at your police headquarters to know what's going on,' Gibson said.

India started to shake her head to say no.

'I have a right to be there,' he said.

Jun Li shrugged and eventually India agreed. 'But you cannot interfere with anything Detective Li is doing,' she stressed.

Gibson nodded. 'I'll take my own car,' he said.

They already had the money at the house in a guarded vehicle, which would now have to be switched into Ellen's car. The armed back-up team from headquarters were on standby waiting to hear from them.

Jun Li nodded and moved out onto the front porch to make the call. Marlee and Jacko spread maps out on the kitchen table to examine the area around the drop-off point.

'You may as well pack up your gear now,' Jacko told the technician. 'They won't be phoning again and you haven't been able to trace them anyway.'

India had proposed a plan which the Super had organised for her. Two vans of armed officers would follow them at a distance then make the final approach on foot to the designated drop-off zone. They would be equipped with special night-vision glasses, as they'd suspected an isolated venue would be selected. Other unmarked cars would be lying in wait, hidden, on all roads leading out of the area with officers keeping tabs on any passing traffic. As soon as a vehicle passed, it was to be radioed in to the next point and monitored. Any vehicle stopping would be followed even if it didn't give off signals from the trackers they'd placed in the bags. In this way they hoped they'd covered all scenarios and that the kidnappers would lead them back to their base. And hopefully Joshua. It wasn't an area that would be busy with traffic.

'I know that lay-by at Colo Heights. Heading towards Singleton, it's on the right past the Public School and a short distance beyond Colo Heights Road. There's no street light there, and no mobile phone coverage,' Jacko said from the back seat as they headed off with the money. 'There's very little around there. Just the one main road passing through. If the kidnappers come and pick the money up in a car we'll see them.'

'Let's hope so. How many trackers did you put in each bag?' she asked him.

'Three – in case they looked for, and picked up any. They wouldn't think we'd put three in the bags. They won't get away with this. We'll have them soon enough – once they lead us back to their base.'

She hoped so, and if somehow the kidnappers eluded them and escaped with the money that they'd keep their word and release Joshua. They hadn't said where they'd drop him and it could be anywhere. She didn't have a good feeling about this though. Kidnappings didn't always have a happy ending.

'Okay, I'm not far from the lay-by, you'd better get down,' she told Jacko. She'd seen the vans pull over a short distance back. Once dropping their cargo, the vans would leave. She indicated right and turned into the lay-by. There were no other cars there, but the kidnappers said they'd be watching her so she suspected they were nearby somewhere.

India sat in the car for a few minutes with the engine running, to give the armed officers time to get into position. She then stepped out of the car, opened the boot and grabbed the first holdall. It was enormous and seemed to weigh a ton. She was sweating and shaking a little as she hefted it across to the back of the lay-by as instructed, dropping it close to the dense bushland. She then attempted to repeat it with the second one, but it was too much for her. She dropped the bag, let out an expletive and stopped to look around. Were they watching her? Listening to her? Rather than attempting to lift it again, she dragged the bag across the loose and stony ground, praying that her actions wouldn't rip the fabric and cause the money to spill out everywhere. She was used to hearing crickets and other creatures making a loud racket once it was dark, but apart from the noise she'd made with the bag and her grunts, it was eerily silent. It gave her the creeps. She turned and hurried back to the car, hopped in, did a U-turn and drove off, pulling over a hundred yards down the road. Sweat was pouring down her face and she was still shaking.

'I couldn't see anyone,' she told Jacko, doing her best to make her voice sound calm.

'No, I didn't see anyone either.'

Picking up his radio set Jacko called up the head of the foot team.

'Can you unplug your earphone so I can hear him as well?'

He nodded, removed his one earplug and pressed a

button on the handset.

'Jacko here,' he said. 'Any sign of anyone?'

'Not yet. The bag is still in position. No wait, we have movement. Ah, it's only an animal.'

'What kind of animal?'

'Can't really tell. Could be a fox. No, it's too big to be a fox. Looks like a dingo. Are there dingoes around here?"

'No.' Jacko cut the radio. 'Obviously he's a city boy. Bloody idiot thinks there's dingoes here!' her told her and snorted.

'Could be a dog,' the voice cut back in. *'The second bag is moving now. Do you want us to move in?'*

'No. Tell them to stay put for now. We need to follow the money to wherever they take it,' she said. Jun Li was tracking the signals and she trusted he was watching the movements.

'That's a negative,' Jacko said. 'Wait for further instructions.'

'Hang on. Did he just say "the second bag is moving"?' she asked. 'Did they see the first bag move? Can you check that with him?'

'Can you confirm you've seen two bags moving?' Jacko asked.

'Negative, We only saw the second bag – which is now gone. They must have moved the first one while you were still there with the car blocking our view.'

'How the bloody hell have they managed that? And where the hell would they be going?' Jacko said sounding frustrated and confused at the same time.

'Hm. Maybe he's right. The kidnappers must have moved one of the bags before I turned the car around.

I wasn't looking and thought the armed unit would be able to see. Bloody hell. They were taking a risk doing that. I could have jumped back out of the car, but then I suppose they thought I was Ellen Gibson. Okay, let's head back down towards Wilberforce where we'll pick up mobile phone signals,' she said starting the car. The shaking had stopped and now she felt angry. Angry with herself for being such a wimp and not keeping her eyes on the bags. . 'I want to be able to have phone contact with Jun Li to know what's happening. I can then get one of the uniforms to take Ellen's car back to their house.'

'Don't tell me you're having withdrawal symptoms without your phone,' Jacko said sarcastically.

'I don't like using these radios. There's too much distortion and if the kidnappers are hiding in the bush, they're likely to hear that someone is out there talking, even though it sounded as though he was whispering. It's eerily quiet and any noise would carry.'

'Well back in the good old days, radios are all that would have been available.'

'I know. You don't need to remind me. We didn't have mobiles issued to us when I first joined the force. We only had our radios.'

'Oh I forgot you're an old timer.'

'Look who's talking. You're only two years younger than me.'

'But I joined up later than you and it wasn't that long after that we were issued with phones.'

'Okay, okay, don't rub it in. Now can you give me a few minutes privacy, I want to change out of these bloody awful clothes.'

'The signals moved about half a kilometre north-east then stopped. There's been no movement since,' Jun Li told India.

'There aren't any properties there. Perhaps they've set up a camp of some sort,' she said.

'Do you want the team to follow them?' Jacko asked.

'Not yet. Wait another twenty minutes and see what happens. If they're camping, they won't be staying there overnight with the money. They'll want to move it somewhere else and try and make their escape under the cover of darkness.'

'They might be counting it,' Jun Li suggested.

She and Jacko were sitting in a squad car they'd requisitioned from uniforms and which was hidden on a residential driveway. They had Jun Li on loudspeaker.

'I don't think we should wait twenty minutes,' Jacko said. 'If they're camping, they'll probably have the kid with them.'

'Maybe. Call me back in ten minutes,' India instructed Jun Li before disconnecting the call.

Ten minutes later Jun Li called to report there'd been no movement.

'Ok. Thanks. I'm going to send the squad in,' she said. 'Send me the co-ordinates and call me if you see any activity.'

'Will do.'

A few seconds later her phoned pinged. She passed the phone to Jacko and said, 'Here's the co-ordinates. Tell them to move in.'

She then phoned Jun Li back. 'We need to set up the

road blocks and get squad cars despatched to every residence or business in the area. Sergeant Morrison has the list. Give him the go ahead.'

He made it back to the cabin in good time with a large, long duffel bag draped over his shoulder which he plonked down onto the floor. Untying Josh he said, 'we're gunna move off now, you've gotta be real quiet.'

'Are we going to meet my mummy? Did she bring you the money?'

'Yeah, she did. We're gunna meet her real soon.'

Picking up the duffel bag again, he grabbed Josh's arm and pulled him out of the cabin.

There was a crackling of twigs over to their right, which made him freeze.

'Stop,' he whispered.

'Is that my mummy?' Josh asked, his voice rising in excitement. 'MUMMY, I'M HERE,' he shouted out.

'I told ya to be quiet,' he hissed dropping the duffel bag and placing his hand over Josh's mouth. Josh struggled against his hand, 'stop wriggling will ya.'

Queenie started growling, let out a single bark and took off.

'*Queenie*,' he hissed. 'Come back here!' Queenie ignored him

In the torchlight he saw a large dark shape emerge from the bush. 'Ah, it's only that bloody roo again Josh, no need to be frightened. If we just keep real still he'll move off. Don't want him attackin' us – or Queenie,' he said.

Queenie was circling the animal and growling. Before he could call out to her again he heard Queenie let out a squeal of pain and saw her body go flying across the clearing. He let go of Josh and ran over to Queenie.

'Queenie,' he cried, dropping to the ground and placing a hand on her body. 'I'll kill ya, if you've bloody hurt her,' he turned to say to the roo. But it had gone from sight.

'Queenie,' he whispered, but there was no response. Shining the torch on Queenie he could see her head had smashed against a rock. Tears trickled down his face. Queenie was the only person in the world who loved him and now it looked like she was hurt bad. He picked her up and hugged her to his body rocking and crying.

'It's alright Queenie, I'll take you ...' He didn't know where he could take Queenie. He'd only ever taken her to a vet for her jabs when she was a puppy. Where was that? He had to think quickly and act or Queenie could die.

'Billy? Is ... is Queenie ...' a breathless voice sounded behind him. He'd forgotten all about Josh. But he couldn't just leave Queenie. The kid was making funny noises. He was obviously upset about Queenie as well.

'Get up Josh. I can't carry ya, Queenie and the bag all the way to the car.'

Josh didn't get up. Still holding Queenie, and with some awkwardness, he shone the torch on the boy to see him curled up lying on his side holding his chest. He prodded Josh with his foot and the boy rolled over onto his back, one arm reaching out for him. Josh was still making funny sounds and was shuddering and shaking.

'Ya can stand up yerself. I'm sorry if yer upset about Queenie. I am as well – I need to get her some help,' he whispered. 'Come on now, stop messin' about and makin' those stupid noises. We've gotta get movin'. Do ya hear me Josh?'

17

Sunday

It was three am before India made it home to bed early Sunday morning. She'd decided they all needed to go home and grab a few hours' sleep before the big search tomorrow.

'How did it go?' a sleepy Rob asked her as she crawled into bed.

'A total disaster. They emptied the money into something else, dumped the bags and the trackers, leaving them in the bush. There was no sign of them anywhere.'

'You had all the roads leading out of the area blocked off, didn't you?'

'Not immediately. We were planning to follow them. But no vehicles drove through the area while we waited. Once we discovered they'd switched the money I implemented the road blocks and blocked all property entrances. There was no sign of them or of a car taking off anywhere.'

'They must be still in the area then.'

'I hope so. Havering is furious with me. He said I should have sent the team in as soon as they saw the bag moving. I left it for about fifteen minutes as the signal stopped moving. We were waiting for them to leave and hopefully lead us to Joshua.'

'I would have done the same, if it's any consolation.'

'Havering said he's bringing in the big guns now. Someone from Headquarters, muttering that he should have done it days ago.'

Rob turned over and switched on the bedside light, turned back and took her into his arms, kissing her forehead a few times.

'I'm sorry it didn't work out for you. What's the plan for tomorrow?' he asked releasing her.

'Searching all the properties in the area. Combing the bush beyond where the bags were found.'

'I imagine they always planned to switch bags and must have assumed there'd be trackers.'

'Probably. Jacko swears he tucked two of the trackers in amongst the notes, so that even if they did move the money into other containers or bags, it would still be there. But they were sitting in the bottom of the bag. The third tracker was in a side pocket.'

'Either they did a very thorough search or just got lucky.'

'Who knows? I do know we have no leads now and it's my fault. I should have had the team move in sooner.'

'It's not your fault India. You did what you thought was right for the safety of the boy. I would have done the same. It was important to follow the money to lead you to the boy.'

'I know, but we weren't able to do that.'

'They're releasing him today you said?'

'Supposed to be. I'm worried that as they got their hands on this money so easily, they might make a second demand.'

'Well let's hope not and that the boy will be home safely with his family tonight. There's nothing more you can do about it now. You need to get some sleep. I'm concerned about you working such long hours. You have someone else to think about now.'

'I know. I know.'

Rob switched the light off again and kissed her.

'Night, darling. Try to get some sleep.'

Fat chance of that. She felt dreadful and was convinced she'd mismanaged everything. Now a small child could be at risk because of her. She lay on her back and placed her hands on her stomach, imagining the life that was growing in there to distract her thoughts.

In the squad room early the next morning India gave out instructions for the search. She'd managed an hour or so of sleep before her alarm went off at six-thirty. She was at the station by seven-fifteen and was surprised to see Jacko, Marlee and Jun-Li walk in a few minutes later. Like herself, Marlee and Jacko were dressed in clothing suitable for bush-walking. Jun-Li was in his usual smart attire.

'What can we do boss?' Marlee asked her.

'We need the uniforms who have been covering the property entrances in Colo Heights to start knocking on doors now. Jun Li can you call Sergeant Morrison and get onto that? Make sure that they've had the road blocks going on all night as well, checking any vehicles that came through the Putty Road or Colo Heights Road. Jacko, find out whether the team on the ground has returned to the site. I asked them to return at daylight and start searching.'

'Already done it and they're there. I detoured on my way here and drove over to Colo Heights. They have a makeshift post and a control van set up at the layby. I think Havering organised it. I've asked them to spread out and search for a couple of kilometres from the layby. Is there anything else you'd like me to get them to do?'

'No that's it for now. Well done – thanks for doing that. I'm going to call the Super.'

'Superintendent Havering has insisted I remove the surveillance guys from Lansford and his house. Says there's no justification for having them there and we need every body we can for this search. I've sent them over to join Morrison's lot now,' she told the team.

'Is Superintendent Havering bringing in specialist investigators from headquarters?' Marlee asked.

'He's in the process of organising them he said, but will wait to see if Joshua is released today. He's managed to get a helicopter – they're doing an aerial search as we speak.'

'We could have done with that last night,' Jacko said.

'I know, I did ask for one to be on standby, but apparently nothing was available. They're all busy tracking criminals in the city on a Saturday night.'

'What do you want us to do now?' Jacko asked.

'Jun Li you can stay here and man the phones and the radios. Jacko, you and Marlee can join in the search. Make sure you take plenty of water and I hope you brought some snacks for yourselves. It could be a long day. I'll join you in a little while. I'm just going to go over to see Max and Ellen Gibson first.'

'I'm very sorry, but so far we've found no trace of the kidnappers – or Joshua,' India told the Gibsons.

'Detective Li told me that the kidnappers switched the money into another bag after they collected it. Is that right?' Gibson asked.

'Yes, that's correct,' she said nodding. Jun shouldn't have told him about the bag switch.

'Why the hell didn't you follow them as soon as soon as you saw they'd taken the bag?' he asked in a somewhat hostile tone.

'We were monitoring movement of the bags. I told the team to hold off because they seemed to have stopped. We were hoping to follow them and that they'd lead us to Joshua as I told you yesterday. If we had apprehended them too soon, there was a risk that they wouldn't tell us where Joshua was being held. That could have proved dangerous if he was left alone in an isolated place without food or water.'

'I understand that, but why didn't you follow them once they were on the move?'

'I don't know if you are aware of what it's like in

the bush in complete darkness. Any sound echoes and reverberates. If they had heard us and taken off, we might never have found Joshua. It's unfortunate that they switched bags and dumped the trackers.'

Gibson waved his arms in the air in exasperation. 'So, what's happening now?'

'We have a large search team out combing the area and a helicopter doing an aerial search. We're searching every property in the area. Extra officers have been drafted in. All the roads around the area were sealed off since last night, so they wouldn't have been able to escape that way.'

'They could have escaped on foot though, couldn't they?'

'I suppose, but it would have been dangerous and they'd have to travel a long way to clear our blocks.'

She had been wondering about a foot hike, but didn't think it feasible with so much weight to carry. The kidnappers would also have to know the area well to risk that. Heading off into the bush from the layby wouldn't have led them to any other road for many miles. They'd looked at the terrain last night and decided they must have holed up in a property somewhere nearby.

'Can I help take part in the search?' Gibson asked.

'I think it would be better if you remained here. The kidnappers said they'd release Joshua this morning. Superintendent Havering is going to give a statement to the press this morning asking the public to be on the lookout for him.'

'Are you sure the kidnappers haven't phoned the police to say they've released Josh and where they've left him?' Ellen asked.

'No,' she said. 'Definitely not.'

'What if they've released Josh and someone else has picked him up and will now make a new demand for money? The man on the phone didn't say exactly where they were going to release him,' Ellen said. 'This could go on forever.'

India sighed. There was always a risk that could happen. But she had faith in the public being empathetic to the family's fears for their son.

'If you hadn't made our win public, this would never have happened,' Max said turning on his wife.

'But you could've—'

'You need to support each other now. Not churn out the same old arguments,' India said cutting Ellen off. When Joshua first disappeared, Ellen had questioned whether her actions in giving the press conference might have contributed to her son's disappearance. Now she was blaming her husband. Max Gibson kept blaming his wife and didn't see how his actions could have played any part in events. As his wife had said some days ago, if he hadn't gone to work on the day Joshua was taken, it was unlikely the kidnapping could have occurred. Not then anyway.

'I'm sorry. You're right,' Gibson said. He seemed to cave in and collapsed onto one of the dining chairs.

'Fingers crossed the kidnappers will keep their word and release Joshua today. I'll come back to see you later, let you know how we've got on.'

The couple nodded, without speaking. She signalled to the duty officer that she wanted a word with her.

The woman followed her outside to the front veranda.

'What's your name?'

'Cheryl,' the young officer said.

'Have they been sniping at each other like that regularly Cheryl?'

'I was here on Friday night and there was a bit of unpleasantness between them after the ransom was increased, but otherwise it's not been too bad. They've been avoiding each other. Ellen has been either crying or sleeping in her son's room much of the time. It's been hard to get her to eat anything. Max is not helping matters, he's not giving her any comfort.'

'Okay. Keep an eye on them. If they start arguing, intervene, making it clear it's not helping matters. Perhaps you could give her some support.'

Cheryl looked up startled. 'How do you mean?'

'Give her some kind words. Maybe put your arm around her. Give her some reassurance – without making any promises.'

'But I—'

'I know she's not the most likeable character, but she clearly loves her son. She is upset and worried. Her husband isn't helping. Think of the boy.'

'Right. Okay,' Cheryl nodded.

'I doubt they will, but call me if the kidnappers phone and say where they've dropped Joshua.'

18

India took a bite of her soggy peanut butter sandwich. After a few chews she wanted to spit it out. The last time she'd been pregnant, she'd craved peanut butter and even sat eating it by the spoonful. The smell of it now was a bit of a turn off. Eating sandwiches in the sweltering heat, hours after they'd been made, was difficult. She'd chosen peanut butter thinking it was safe and had even packed it in a small cooler bag. It had made the sandwich soggy, but she knew she needed to eat – she hadn't eaten anything since her cereal at breakfast. She managed to finish half of it and put the remaining half back in the cooler bag. She had some potato chips. They'd be easier to eat, but then she'd have to guzzle much of her water supply as they always made her thirsty. She sighed and looked at the map spread out in front of her. They'd covered a vast area of bushland behind the layby with no success. There was no sign of the kidnappers or any indication of where they'd gone. They'd found a couple of snapped branches off low lying bushes in different directions that had proved useless in tracking them. Property searches had brought no results either. They'd come across a few white utes at some of the properties, but none that they could link to the kidnappers. The problem was that white utes were so commonplace in Australia. They'd brought in a dog team, using some of Joshua's belongings as scent, in case the kidnappers had had him with them. That had proved useless as well.

'I'd kill someone for a cup of tea, I'm sick to death of water,' Marlee said walking up behind her. Marlee looked hot, sweaty and dirty. She'd been traipsing through the bush with the rest of the search team.

'They've got facilities in that van over there,' India said. 'I was brought one earlier.'

'Cool. Would you like a cuppa?'

'Yes, I wouldn't mind one, thanks. A little bit of milk, no sugar. Not too strong.'

Marlee returned a few minutes later with two steaming cardboard mugs balanced on a little tray.

'They didn't run to china. They're too hot to hold at the moment so I'll put them on this table,' Marlee said, placing the tray down beside the map and moving closer to her. The areas that had been searched were marked. It was only a fraction of the bushland in the area. They were in the middle of a National Park.

'Any word from the kidnappers?'

'No. They've got a satellite phone in the van. I called about thirty minutes ago. Still nothing.'

'The kidnappers said they'd release Joshua this morning, didn't they?'

'Yes, but it doesn't look like they've kept their word. It's not looking good.'

'Perhaps they're still holed up somewhere that's not

easy for them to move from with our search going on.'

'Hmm. Maybe.'

'What's your thinking boss? Do you want us to search further afield?'

'We've assumed the kidnappers took off into the bush behind the layby, heading to a property nearby or doubled back to a property on the other side of the road. What if they doubled back to the *bush* on the other side of the road? I think that's where we should be searching next.'

'They'd have to travel a hell of a long way to reach a road there.'

'Not as far as on this side. They could have done that and joined Colo Heights Road beyond our road blocks, which are about here,' she said pointing to the map. 'That would be an easier route than where we've been searching. I think we should move the search team.'

'It'll take a long time for them to all come back. We've only got about four hours of daylight left.'

'Yes, but we can make a start. I'll radio it through to everyone.'

The search team eventually all made their way back to Putty Road and moved into the bush on the other side. They'd found nothing when the search was called off for the day, to be resumed at first light.

India made the journey back to the Gibsons' house to break the bad news to them. She was dreading facing Max Gibson's anger and Ellen's distress.

'I'm sorry, we've had no success today and had to call

the search off until tomorrow morning,' she told them once she'd entered the house.

'They can't have just disappeared into thin air!' Gibson protested. 'Someone must be hiding them.'

'We've done a search of all properties in the area.'

'A thorough search? Surely you'd need warrants for that.'

'We did have warrants for business premises and the school, but householders were very willing to let us search their homes and outbuildings in case anyone was using their properties to hide. The community has been very co-operative and many have taken part in the search,' she told him.

'I know you're doing your best Detective Hargreaves, but isn't it time that someone more experienced in kidnappings was brought in?'

'We are expecting a specialist team from Sydney to join us tomorrow.'

'About time.'

She had received word from Superintendent Havering that this was happening. They'd done their best he told her and said they should continue with the search they'd started today. A team with experience might be able to bring new thinking into the investigation. In her previous posting in homicide, she'd taken part in an investigation of a young twelve year old who had disappeared and later turned up dead. But they'd been working in a built up residential area. Not a national park covered in dense bushland. She wondered if the specialist team would have any experience of searching in the bush. What they really needed were experienced bush trackers. She'd told

Havering that yesterday morning, but he seemed to think they needed specialists with kidnapping experience instead. She wondered if it was a financial issue. If Havering was to hire a bush tracker as she wanted, it would mean paying a private individual – most likely an indigenous person. He'd have to gain clearance for the cost from Headquarters and perhaps it was not something they'd be willing to fork out for. The big guns at Headquarters, being unfamiliar with dense bushland, wouldn't understand their need.

'One of the specialist team will no doubt pay a call on you tomorrow,' she told the Gibsons. 'So I'll say goodnight then, and once again I'm sorry that I don't have better news for you.'

She turned to leave; anxious to get home. Rob had a meal waiting for her. She was longing for a cool shower to clear off today's dust and dirt. She was looking forward to putting her feet up as well. She'd spent much of the day standing.

'Thank you for everything you've done,' Ellen called out to her. That was unexpected. She turned to look at the woman. Ellen's face was all red and blotchy. She'd clearly been crying again. Gone was the aspiring beauty queen she'd first encountered when she'd met Ellen Gibson. She knew it was a little skewed, but she thought Ellen looked more real and beautiful like this. Without all the gloss and glamour. It was just a shame it was due to tragic circumstances. She nodded at Ellen and continued walking out to her car.

19

Monday

Two detectives were waiting for India when she arrived at the station at seven the following morning. Two men. Was this the specialist team she'd been sent?'

'Morning,' the elder man said standing. She judged him to be around fifty. He was solidly built and had brown hair streaked with grey at the sides. He was only a few inches taller than her, but had an imposing presence. The taller, slimmer and younger man standing beside him looked to be in his thirties with black hair and smoky-looking grey eyes. 'I'm Detective Inspector Brian Talbot and this is Detective Sergeant Marcus Penn. You must be India Hargreaves?'

She noticed he hadn't used her title. 'Yes, I'm *Detective Inspector* India Hargreaves,' she said just to make the point.

'Of course, apologies.'

'If you'd like to follow me, I'll take you up to our squad room, but I have to warn you it's probably nothing like you're used to.'

'Oh, we've worked in some pretty basic places, so it won't be a problem.'

'It's not that basic,' she shot back, leading the way upstairs.

'You're right,' Talbot said when they entered the room. 'It's not that basic and it has a familiar air to it. Reminds me of squad rooms I worked in when I first became a detective. It's a characterful old building. It's a bit small though. Isn't this building the Headquarters for the Hawkesbury Area Command?'

'It was, but that's now been transferred to a new building in Richmond. Some of us remained here.'

'Ah so that's why Superintendent Havering said he would be in Richmond today. He's not based here anymore?'

'He keeps an office here up on the next floor, but no, you will usually find him at Richmond. So, what have you been told and what do you need to know?'

'We'd like to see all the files. All we know is that five-year-old Joshua Gibson was kidnapped five days ago and that you delivered a ransom on Saturday night which the kidnappers collected, but the boy has not been released. And that you've been searching in dense bushland near the ransom drop site.'

'All of that is correct, but very simplistic. Your summary cannot describe the long sweltering hours our small team has spent in the bush with a team of uniformed officers – or back here, investigating and interviewing large numbers of people to exclude them from our enquiries. I have all the files out here for you to look at,' India said pointing to a pile of folders on the table.

'Mm. I see you have been busy. Do you have an office we can use for privacy? What about that one over there?' he said pointing to her office.

'That's my office. We do have a larger, spare office that once belonged to our Detective Chief Inspector. The office has been sitting empty since he left and wasn't replaced. You're welcome to use that. It's just around the corner here.'

'I'd rather one that had clear eyes onto the squad room,' Talbot said.

'As I said, you're welcome to use our old Chief's office. It is a much bigger space and would accommodate the two of you better,' she said staring at Talbot. *Bloody cheek.*

Talbot looked as though he was prepared to challenge her, but didn't. She led him and Penn around to Rob's old office. You could see into the squad room from one corner of it where the desk was placed. 'I'm sure you'll find this quite comfortable,' she said. 'We plan to continue our search in the bush today, so if you'll excuse me, I'd like to get going on that and leave you to it. Detective Sergeant Jun Li should be here shortly. He can answer any further questions you might have. The remainder of my team will be out in the field today.'

'I think you're wasting your time searching through the bush. They've clearly long gone from there, and wouldn't have been holding the kid anywhere near it. I think you'd be better off concentrating on family and friends. It's usually someone the family knows who is involved in kidnappings.'

'We've looked at family and friends and dismissed them as options. We concentrated mainly on the media who were at the house the day before the kidnapping occurred and those who we were able to trace from the newsagent where Ellen Gibson made her big announcement.'

'Well we'd like to re-interview the parents, and interview all other members of the family. We could do with the help of your team in doing that,' Talbot said.

'Detective Sergeant Jun Li could help you. As I said, the other three of us will be out in the field today,' she said, looking Talbot squarely in the eye. He was now the senior investigating officer and if he insisted, she'd have to cancel today's plans for Jacko, Marlee and herself.

'Fine,' Talbot said waving a hand dismissively at her.

She turned, moved back to grab her bag and rushed out of the building before he changed his mind. This morning she'd been optimistic that the *experts* might bring fresh eyes to the investigation. Now she wasn't so sure. She'd been tempted to ask them for details of kidnappings they'd been involved with in the past when Talbot had said it was usually family members or friends involved. The only one that sprang to mind was the billionaire Henry Carlton whose daughter had been kidnapped a few years ago. She was a sixteen-year-old girl and it had turned out to be friends of Carlton who had taken the girl. Was Talbot involved in that? She couldn't remember. Rob might know. She hadn't asked Talbot because she didn't want to waste valuable daylight hours and she wasn't sure she wanted to hear him boast about his achievements. He seemed a little too arrogant for her liking. When Havering had said a specialist team was taking over, she'd expected at least half a dozen bodies to appear. Still two fresh pair of eyes were better than none. Maybe. At least he hadn't stopped her carrying on with the search.

Three hours into the search they struck lucky. India received a radio call to say they'd found some sort of semi-derelict cabin and it looked as if a child had been kept there. Jacko and Marlee confirmed they were on their way to the site.

'Don't touch anything,' she told the officer who'd radioed it in. 'I'll call forensics and get a team down there. Give me the co-ordinates.'

She made her way back to the comms vehicle to contact forensics. She'd been called to an area just off the road heading out of Colo Heights towards Singleton where a bunch of cigarette butts and empty bottles of beer had been found. She'd thought it was more likely to be a place local teenagers used, but had asked the officers to bag everything up.

As she stepped in the van, the officer in there said, 'Oh Inspector Hargreaves, I was just going to try and reach you on the radio. I've received a call from an officer called Rhona Mitchell. She's been at the Gibson's house this morning. She said to tell you that Mr. and Mrs. Gibson were picked up by two detectives and have been taken into Windsor for questioning. Mitchell said the couple became very upset about it.'

'Right.' That'd be Talbot and his sidekick. Presumably

he wanted to isolate the couple and hoped to bully a confession out of one of them. She was convinced he was barking up the wrong tree. But Talbot and Penn hadn't been working on the case since day one and so had little idea of what the couple were like. She supposed that, based on their past experience, it was the right direction from which to start their enquiry – even if it was insensitive. Should she phone in to Talbot to let him know their latest findings? She decided she'd let the woman in charge of comms in the van deal with it after she called the forensic technicians. Talbot would be busy with the interviews right now and probably wouldn't want to be interrupted.

Answering to Marlee's 'Coo-ee' calls, India met with her on the way down to the cabin site. The ground was rough going and several times she was worried about slipping and falling. *The baby* were her first thoughts after a few near misses. Rob would be furious with her if he knew she was trekking through dangerous bushland.

'Thought it'd be best to come and meet you to show you the easiest route,' Marlee said.

'Thanks, I've had a few near falls, it's not the easiest of places to get to is it?'

'No.'

'So what's been found at this cabin? It's strange that it isn't marked on any of the maps we have – even if it's semi-derelict.'

'It looks pretty old. The base is made of stone and the rest timber. It looks as though it's had some makeshift repairs in more recent years. I can't imagine what it was built for, except maybe as a place to shelter from poor weather. Or maybe an escaped convict built it to hide in – back in the days when the Windsor area was first settled by the Europeans.'

'You don't think it's that old, do you?'

'It could be. One of the floor boards is rotten and you can see underneath it that there's a packed earth floor. I imagine that's how it would have been when it was first built. Anyway at a first glance from the door I could see there's some children's clothing and a child's story book that could have been left there recently.'

She stopped and looked at Marlee, her eyes widening. She'd registered that the officer who'd radioed it in had said it looked like a child had been at the cabin, but he could have been mistaken – or it could have been from a family camp-out from many years in the past.

'I know,' Marlee said nodding. 'I was shocked with what I saw. It looks like it might be the place where they held the boy.'

'I hope no-one has been trampling over the scene.'

'I don't know about the first officers who arrived there. They claimed they didn't go into the cabin. Just stood at the entrance, realised it was significant and stepped out again. I have to tell you there's something else there that doesn't look good.'

'What's that?'

'We found some blood and there's some freshly turned soil just outside the cabin. It looks like something small – the size of a young child, was buried there and dug up recently.'

20

India squatted down and looked across at the area around the freshly turned soil. It and the cabin had been cordoned off with tape. They were still waiting for the technicians to arrive. From her position she couldn't judge accurately whether it would be big enough for the size of a small child, but it certainly looked like it. Whatever had been there hadn't been buried very deep. She'd examined the blood the team had found on the edge of the clearing, next to another small area that had been freshly dug. There were a couple of large pieces of rock which were covered in blood. It wasn't looking good. She'd radioed in to ask comms to contact Talbot with the news. They wouldn't know what had been buried until forensics checked it out. So far, she'd heard nothing back from Talbot.

The sound of a loud gunshot rang out, echoing across the valley. It sounded as if it was nearby.

'What the bloody hell was that?' India shouted to no-one in particular. Taking her radio set out of her pocket she called into it: 'It's Detective Inspector Hargreaves here. Who fired that shot? And what were you shooting at?' She hoped it wasn't one of the kidnappers.

'Sorry Inspector, a giant bloody roo leapt out of the bushes and attacked one of the men knocking him flying with a hefty kick,' a voice came back. *'I had to shoot it. I think we might need an ambo.'*

'How badly injured is he?'

'Hang on a minute.'

A few seconds later the voice came back on the radio. *'He says he's okay to make his way across to Colo Heights Road, but he might have broken ribs or something. I still think we should get an ambo.'*

'Okay I'll send for one. Make sure someone goes with him. Radio your position when you reach the road.'

'No worries.'

'What happened?' Marlee asked when she turned back to the cabin site.

'A kangaroo kicked one of the team. We need to call for an ambulance. He's going to make his way across to Colo Heights Road. Can you see to that Marlee?'

'Righto. I noticed there was quite a lot of roo poo around the cabin clearing. I suspect it's been munching on the grass here. Lean pickings though. I wouldn't have thought you'd see many roos in this dense bush. Must have strayed from its normal feeding grounds. Apart from grass at the edge of Putty Road, there wouldn't be a lot for it to eat in here. It'd have to go onto private properties to find juicier pickings.'

'What have you found?' India asked the forensic technicians when she stepped into the cabin. They'd had to wait a further hour before they'd arrived, moaning about the trek. One of the techies had given her a crime scene suit to put on so she could enter the cabin. She'd waited a short time before following them in. One techie was still taking photographs and another held up a couple of plastic bags for her to look at.

'So far we have a couple of small toy cars, a child's story book entitled *Willy the Wimp* by Anthony Brown. Clothes and a red baseball cap that I'd say belong to a young child—'

'That looks like the shirt Ellen Gibson said her son was wearing the day he disappeared,' she said. 'He was also wearing a red baseball cap. So, the boy was definitely held here.'

'Looks like it,' the techie said, nodding. 'There's a couple of enamel mugs and empty plastic bottles – plus the remains of a loaf of sliced bread, a jar of strawberry jam plus one of Vegemite, some spread, an empty packet of sliced cheese and a couple of knives we're bagging up. The food items are recent additions judging by the sell-by date. There's some very old empty tins that were lying around and there's also an old kettle and a camping stove here. The kettle's rusty, and it doesn't look as though it's been used in a while.'

'Bag it all up,' India said. 'And check the place thoroughly for fingerprints. 'What about this bed and blanket? And these,' she added, pointing to pieces of nylon rope that had been fixed to the wall. 'They look like ties that might have been used to restrain the boy.'

'I'd say so. We'll cut the hessian off the bed base for checking. Looks as though there might be urine stains on it. We'd struggle to take the chair through the bush though. We'll check the wooden arms for fingerprints and take the old bedspread covering it.'

India shuddered at the thought of Joshua Gibson being tied to the cabin wall while the kidnappers sat guard over him. Or left him alone while they collected the money. The poor kid must have been terrified. The place was filthy and stunk of piss. Was Joshua forced to relieve himself inside the cabin? The pungent smell was making her feel sick, so she stepped back outside to gulp in some fresh air and walked over to the techies who were sifting through the shallow grave.

'Have you found anything here?' she asked them. She hoped they were going to say they'd found animal hairs, not anything that indicated a child had been buried there.

'Nothing yet. We're bagging up soil samples to take back to the lab.'

'What about the freshly dug area over there and the blood on that rock.'

'Looks like animal blood. There's some animal hairs attached to the rock. We'll check the turned earth there as well.'

She was relieved to hear it was probably animal blood, giving her renewed hope that Joshua was still alive.

Back at the station, India filled Talbot and Penn in on the team's find. She was dying to say that her decision to search the bush was not such a stupid idea after all, but didn't.

'We'll know more when the labs get back to us,' she

added.

'So it looks like the kid is still alive,' Talbot said rubbing his hand across his chin. He had a thick stubble growth and could do with a shave.

'I'm hoping so. There's still no word from the kidnappers though, which is worrying.'

'They might be about to make another ransom demand seeing as they got away with the last lot of cash so *easily*,' Penn said, making an obvious dig at her which she ignored.

'So how did things go for you two today?' she asked with an innocent looking expression on her face. She'd heard from the desk sergeant that the family had been outraged and were threatening to make a complaint.

'We've interviewed the boy's parents and Max Gibson's parents. We'll interview the other grandparents later up on the central coast,' Talbot said.

'But we established alibis for all of them,' she reminded him.

'Doesn't mean they didn't have accomplices acting on their behalf.'

That was a possibility. But she doubted it was the case.

'Did you learn anything new from them then?'

'No. Although Ellen Gibson was acting a bit strange – we think she was holding something back. We plan to have another go at her tomorrow.'

'Really? Do you think that's necessary? She might have acted foolishly when she discovered they'd won the money, but our judgement on her actions was that it was simply down to her need to be in the limelight. She's a wannabe celebrity.'

'That's may be the case, but I reckon she knows something she's not telling us,' Penn said.

'Such as?'

'That she knows where her son is and who has him.'

'I beg to differ. Why would she arrange to have her son kidnapped when they'd just won all that money?'

'As you said. Fame, media attention.'

'That's what all the interviews were about,' India said shaking her head. 'She might have acted thoughtlessly on the spur of the moment, but she doesn't seem the type of person who would become involved in having her son kidnapped. She barely knows anyone in the Windsor area. All her old friends live in other parts of Sydney or up on the central coast. We checked out anyone Ellen had been in contact with following her win.'

'We'll be looking closely at all of them as well,' Talbot said.

'Ellen told us that none of her friends had been to see her at their current address. Only her family. We confirmed that with the friends she'd been in contact with. She hasn't given the address out to anyone because she's so ashamed of it.'

'That's what she told us, but winning this money might have changed all that.'

'I can't see it, but I guess you need to look at all possible options. Forensics have given me a couple of things to take to the parents for identification. It needs to be done soon and taken back to the labs. Do you want to do it or shall I?'

'Probably best if you do it,' Talbot said, 'but I'd like to look at them first.'

21

When India and Jacko turned up at the Gibsons' house, the family, including Max's parents, launched into lengthy complaints about the way they'd been treated by Talbot and Penn.

'They questioned us as if we were *suspects*,' Gibson said, clearly feeling outraged.

'Well the first thing we did was question both of you,' she reminded him.

'Yes, but that was here in our house, and you explained why you were doing it. They took us down to the *police* station. The press saw us being taken off in a police car and there was more press waiting outside the station. I can imagine the headlines tomorrow will be something like "Parents questioned in son's kidnapping".'

He was probably right. The press would have seen it as an opportunity to make up sensational headlines and point the finger at them. She felt sorry for the couple. They were fodder for the press in this whole situation.

'I know you haven't been around much today to be informed of the latest developments. We have some news and some things we'd like you to look at. If you don't mind, I'd rather it was just Max and Ellen we spoke to,' she said turning to the senior Gibson couple.

'Right, well, we'll wait outside on the veranda then,' Pamela Gibson said, nodding at her husband.

India waited until they'd closed the front door behind them and turned to look at the young couple who had worried expressions on their faces.

'Let's sit at the dining table and I'll go over everything,' she suggested.

The couple sat down – she noted at different ends of the table. Were these their normal eating seats or were they attempting to sit as far apart as possible?

She explained the discovery of the old cabin in the bush.

'Would either of you be familiar with the location of such a cabin?' she asked them.

'I don't know anything in this area, apart from some of the shops in Windsor,' Ellen said.

India could believe that was true, making it highly unlikely that Ellen would be working with kidnappers who had knowledge of a remote cabin in the region.

'I grew up in Windsor, but I don't know the area around Colo or Colo Heights. It's only a place I've passed through,' Gibson said.

India nodded. It was what she'd thought.

'Why are you asking about this cabin? Do you think the kidnappers used it? Surely they wouldn't have kept Josh there?' Gibson asked.

India grimaced. 'We think they did have Joshua there. I'd like to show you a couple of things. See if you recognise them.' She opened the small rucksack she had with her and took out a see through evidence bag that held the child's shirt.

'That's Josh's shirt!' Ellen squealed. 'The one he was wearing the day he disappeared.'

'Are you sure?'

'Positive. I bought him that shirt. I know my son's clothes.'

She passed the bag up to Max Gibson who had gone a deathly pale colour.

'What about this?' India asked placing another see-through bag on the table which contained the red baseball cap.

'That's Josh's cap as well,' Ellen said, looking worried.

India held up another bag containing the toy cars. The cars were a bit rusted and didn't look new. She wasn't sure if they would've belonged to Joshua. 'We also found these in the cabin.'

'They look like some of my old car collection that I gave to Josh,' Gibson said. 'There's a whole box of them in his room.'

'What about this story book?' she added pulling out another bag and placing it on the table with its cover face down.

'That looks like Josh's favourite book. It's usually on his bedside cabinet. I've been looking everywhere for it. I thought Josh must have hidden it somewhere. He said he was beginning to get fed up with it. I didn't say anything because I didn't think it was relevant, but I've been worried about where it was,' Ellen said.

'Do you remember what it was called?'

'*Willy the Wimp*', the couple shouted out in unison.

Obviously they were both familiar with their son's favourite book. So the kidnappers had removed the book from the bedside cabinet – or it had been passed on to them by someone else. This confirmed once and for all that Joshua Gibson had been held in the cabin.

'Did you find these things in the cabin you mentioned?' Gibson asked.

'Yes, I'm afraid we did. Confirming that this was where Joshua was held.'

'But there's no sign of Josh or them there now?'

'No.' She decided she wouldn't mention the empty shallow grave they'd found.

'That means the kidnappers must have come into the house to take the book – unless Josh had it outside with him the day he was taken. I can't imagine he'd do that. I didn't see anything in his hands except a ball when he went out to play,' Ellen said, tears starting to run down her face.

'Have you noticed whether there's anything else missing from Joshua's bedroom?'

Ellen sniffed and was silent for a moment before saying, 'Ted is missing as well.'

'Ted?'

'Josh's teddy bear. Not that he plays with it any more – he hasn't for some time. It used to sit on top of a trunk with other toys, but I noticed it's no longer there. Do you think the kidnappers took that as well?'

'Why didn't you say anything about the book and the bear?' Gibson asked Ellen in a hostile tone.

'I ... I wasn't sure if I'd put them somewhere else while cleaning up – or whether Josh threw them out. You know he was fed up with the book and he hasn't liked Ted since I put him through the washing machine.'

'You still should have said something.'

Ellen ignored him. 'Why haven't the kidnappers released Josh?' she asked turning to India. 'He said they would.'

'He?'

'The kidnapper. The one who phoned.'

'I don't know Ellen.'

'Do you think they're going to ask for more money? Or do you think something has gone wrong? They have the money so why aren't they releasing him? Are you *sure* they haven't phoned you with any information on Josh's whereabouts?'

Ellen's voice was beginning to rise in pitch and she had tears streaking down her face again. India wasn't sure what to tell her.

'We've heard nothing from the kidnappers. We don't know what has happened or why they haven't released Josh. It could be something simple like their car broke down,' she said in an attempt to make plausible excuses.

'What are you planning to do next?' Gibson asked.

'We have quite a lot of evidence we've collected from the cabin. Our labs are processing it at the moment. It might give us some leads on where to look,' Jacko interjected.

'Can I ask whether you've ever taken Josh to see a dentist?' India asked.

'Yes, I took him for a check-up a few weeks back. We both had check-ups the same day at a new dentist in Penrith,' Ellen said wiping her face.

'Can you give me the name of that dentist? We'll want to have access to his records.'

Ellen looked horrified. 'Are you wanting those in case …?'

'It's just a routine measure,' she reassured Ellen. 'Nothing to be worried about. Do you have the contact details of the dentist?'

Ellen left them and walked off to the kitchen. Gibson watched her for a second before turning back to her and Jacko.

'Where do you think they've taken Josh now? Do you think they'll return to the cabin?'

'We think it's unlikely. There's so many police in the area. We've left some constables on duty there in case though.'

'We think the kidnappers have taken Josh to one of their houses. We're pretty sure there's more than one person involved,' Jacko added.

'We'll be making a public appeal – asking people to keep an eye out for Joshua,' India said.

'Do you want us to be involved in the appeal?' Gibson asked.

Ellen, who had just returned and passed a card to India with the dentist's name on it, lifted her head, her eyes sparkling with interest. The idea of being filmed seemed attractive to her, but then she lowered her shaking head and said, 'No, I can't do it. Not after … not after the horrible things they've said about me in the papers.'

'I'm no longer the senior investigating officer on Josh's kidnapping. I'll confer with Superintendent Havering – he did the last press conference, and see if he thinks a personal appeal by you would be a good idea. Now we need to get this evidence over to the labs,' she said standing. 'I'm sorry we don't have better news for you.'

22

The labs confirmed the blood found at the cabin site was from an animal. It was fresh blood though which suggested there had been an animal at the scene. Searches of the surrounding bush had brought nothing to light. Forensics found nothing in the shallow grave. Recent human faeces had been found in the other turned soil at the clearing and some dog faeces in other sections. They were waiting on DNA results. A number of fingerprints were collected from the cabin, but none that matched anyone in their system. Superintendent Havering decided to go ahead with a personal appeal, but he wanted both of Joshua's parents to be present. He had asked India to attend and Talbot had been placed in charge of overseeing things.

The press conference was held in a room at the Richmond station. Ellen had cleaned herself up for the session, wearing a long summer dress, but sat quietly while Max Gibson did the speaking. The press wasn't having that though and many questions were fired at Ellen.

'Mrs. Gibson, do you think the fact that you held a

press conference about your win led to your son being kidnapped?' one reporter asked.

'We heard that the kidnappers doubled the ransom demand after you claimed two million was a *small sacrifice* to pay to get your son back. Is that correct?' another reporter asked.

'Why were the police questioning you both on Monday?'

'Do you blame yourself Mrs. Gibson?'

'Did you do all this as a publicity stunt Mrs. Gibson?'

The final question caused Ellen to look up with a horrified expression on her face. Up until this point she'd been sitting with her head down.

'No!' she shouted, shaking her head vigorously.

Talbot allowed the questions to be fired at Ellen Gibson until Superintendent Havering stepped in.

'Thank you all for coming. We are *not* taking questions,' he said firmly.

'How could you let the press ask me those questions,' Ellen shouted at Talbot when they retreated to another room.

Ellen was shaking, much like India had seen her do on other occasions. The woman was a nervous wreck. She could see Talbot was about to hit back at Ellen with a smart comment so she intervened.

'I'm sorry you had to go through that Ellen. Let's get you both home, shall we? Detective Jacko and I'll see to that,' she told Talbot as she brushed past him, daring him to make an objection. Jacko was waiting outside for them.

She knew Talbot wanted to ask Ellen more questions. Shortly before the press conference she'd persuaded him not to have another go at her for the time being.

'I think the thing Ellen Gibson was holding back from you was about the story book and Joshua's teddy bear,' she told Talbot. 'She'd been looking for them everywhere – she thought Josh might have hidden them, but was worried about them.'

He'd accepted that might be part of it and agreed to hold off interviewing her again until after the press conference. Now wasn't the appropriate time either. Ellen was visibly shaken by the press's questions.

India thought it was interesting that the press had not levelled any of their accusations of blame at Max Gibson. She suspected Ellen had become the target because of her initial press conference – which of course they'd all lapped up.

There had been no word from the kidnappers. The phone remained silent. She did not have a good feeling about it. Why would they still be hanging onto Joshua?

When she and Jacko dropped the couple back at their house, she thought they looked like lonely, sorry figures as they climbed the veranda steps without touching each other.

India had just finished putting away the pots from the meal she'd cooked that evening when her mobile phone rang. It was Jun Li calling.

'Evening Detective Sergeant, what can I do for you?'

she asked.

'We have a body over at Richmond I think you ought to come and see,' he said.

'It's not Joshua Gibson is it?' she asked, her stomach lurching.

'No, It's Jimmy Lansford, but he's left a note saying Joshua Gibson is dead. I'll text you the address, but I think you already know it, don't you?'

India's stomach cramped – she felt like someone had punched her in the gut. A moment later she felt a wetness between her legs. *Oh no! The baby!*

'Yes, I'll … I'll be… be with you as soon as I can,' she stuttered. After ending the call she rushed to the bathroom. Tell-tale signs of blood were visible on her underwear. Her stomach cramped again and she felt a gushing of fresh liquid.

She put her hands over her face and heaved with sobs. She was losing another baby and Rob wasn't home. He'd gone off to Sydney for a two day conference and was staying at a hotel in the city. What was she going to do? Jun Li was expecting her and had said something about Joshua Gibson being dead. Should she call Talbot and tell him to go over there? She couldn't. It was something *she* needed to do.

Her suspicions about Roger and Jimmy Lansford being involved had been right. And they'd cancelled her surveillance of the pair. If they hadn't, they might have saved Joshua. She couldn't bear the idea that that little boy was dead. And her baby gone.

The bleeding seemed to have eased off. She cleaned herself up, added protection and changed into a navy blue linen dress, conscious that she might need a dark colour in case of further problems. She felt a bit faint and wasn't sure if she was up to this.

She phoned Jacko to see if he'd heard the news. He hadn't.

'Could you come and pick me up, I'm not sure I should be driving. I've had a glass of wine,' she said as a cover. She hadn't had any wine but didn't want to say what the problem really was. She didn't think to ask Jacko if he'd been drinking tonight. He didn't as a rule – he'd mentioned in the past he "avoided grog" because of his father. He'd never elaborated and she hadn't probed. 'We'll need a couple of scene of crime suits. If you don't have any in your car, I've got a couple in mine.'

Ten minutes later Jacko pulled up and she climbed into his car. She hated driving with him, he was a bit of a maniac on the road and she was a terrible passenger. But needs must. She closed her eyes so she didn't see the things he almost hit on the way over to the Lansford house.

'Who rang it in?' she asked Jun Li when they walked in to see Jimmy Lansford lying in the back bedroom with his head half blown off.

'His cousin, Roger Lansford. He came home from his club just before nine, saw the ute parked in the driveway and found his cousin like this. There's a note.'

She picked it up and read:

*I'm sorry Josh and Queenie are ded   It
was all my folt becos I new he was
fritened of the roo The roo kilt Queenie
Josh had a fit and dide   He wasn't
ment to di and shood have gone home
to his mummy I put them together in*

The writing was set out in large, neat, print on a lined notebook page where Lansford had used every second line.

'It looks like this note has been ripped in half. Have you found the other half?'

'No, there was no sign of it. We found it like that. Lansford claims not to have read it. After he found his cousin, he phoned us and didn't go any further into the room.'

'Who's Queenie? A pet or something?'

'Yes, Queenie was Jimmy's dog according to Roger Lansford. A red kelpie. Jimmy was very attached to her.'

A dog. The team at Colo Heights had reported sighting a dog.

'We also found this bag with loads of new bank notes in it,' Jun said opening a small rucksack.

'That doesn't look like an equal split of four millions dollars.'

'No. We've spoken with a neighbour; a Mrs. Kerr, who suffers from arthritis and Parkinson's disease. She told us she heard a loud bang at about three this afternoon. She was out the back at the time. She thought it sounded like a gunshot, but wasn't sure if it was a car backfiring.

She came through to the front, although she said that took her some time, and saw a man climbing into a dark car and driving off. She couldn't tell me the exact colour or the model.'

'I've spoken to Mrs. Kerr so I know who you mean. Her husband wasn't at home?'

'No, he was at the supermarket, picking up a few things they needed.'

'Right. And where was Roger Lansford?'

'At work. He said he then went to his club for his evening meal and decided to come home earlier than normal. Marlee has gone to the club to confirm what he's told us. We'll have to check where he was this afternoon with his employees tomorrow.'

'You mentioned Lansford found the ute in the driveway. There's two of them out there. One I presume is his. Who owns the other one?

'It was a ute he had in his garage last week. They were due to carry out some checks on it. Apparently it had been leaking oil.'

'Ah. That might tie in with what the techies found in the garage next door to the Gibson house.'

'Yes, I thought that. Lansford claims the ute disappeared from the street outside the workshop last Tuesday. He rang the owner to check whether he'd collected it without telling anyone and claims that's when he realised it must have been stolen. Lansford and the owner reported it. I've checked and it was logged as stolen on Tuesday night. The keys had been removed from a hook where they kept them in the workshop.'

'That all sounds like a very convenient story

Lansford's concocted. He said his cousin Jimmy didn't have a driving licence.'

'He doesn't, but he said Jimmy knew *how* to drive. Some of the people he'd worked for allowed him to drive vehicles around their property. He didn't normally drive on the road.'

'Right. I assume the techies are on their way?'

Jun Li nodded. 'They'll be here any minute.'

'Get them to take Jimmy Lansford's fingerprints. See if they match the ones that were found at the cabin. And ask them to check for fingerprints on the banknotes. Jacko, you said the people who handled it wore gloves, isn't that right?'

'Yeah they did. They were in sealed packs before that. And there was only $500,000 in new notes. It looks like the main person behind the kidnapping palmed them all off to his accomplice. We have a record of the serial numbers of the new notes. So they can also be checked.'

'Right. That's great. Everything here needs a thorough checking over – including both utes. I think we need to take Roger Lansford in for further questioning and see what else he has to say.'

23

'For the recording could you please state your name?'

'Roger Lansford.'

India had read him his rights and informed Lansford their interview would be recorded. He'd readily consented to being fingerprinted and so far seemed co-operative. In fact, he seemed to be suffering from shock and not fully aware of what was going on. He hadn't asked for a lawyer although they'd offered him one.

'Can you tell us more about this ute that you claim was stolen from your workshop last week?'

'As I told your other detective at the house, it was stolen from outside my workshop last week. It now looks like Jimmy stole it.'

'How do you think that could have happened? You claim that Jimmy didn't drive on public roads and didn't have a licence.'

'He doesn't have a licence. I've never known him to drive on public roads. I know he can drive. I've let him drive my ute when we've been off-road. He's very capable, but he'd never be able to pass the theory, so he's never applied for a licence.'

'So why do you think it was Jimmy who stole the ute?'

'I didn't think so at the time. Jimmy came to the workshop to tell me he had a new job and would be away for a while. He asked me who owned the ute out front and I told him whose it was. He'd seen one of the mechanics reverse it out of the workshop, park it down the road and then put the key on the hook. It would have gone back in the workshop that night once we'd finished work on other cars we had there. We hadn't had time to look at it. Jimmy wondered if I'd bought it as it's the same model as mine. I didn't think anything of his questions – it was the kind of thing he'd ask. I had to go into the office then to answer a call. Jimmy stuck his head in and waved goodbye. That was the last time I saw him until tonight when …'

She waited for a moment and when it didn't look like Lansford was going to speak again she said, 'You still haven't convinced me that it was Jimmy who stole the ute. Yes, he had opportunity, but how do you know it was him and not some other person Jimmy was working with?'

'There was no-one else around the workshop except me and a couple of employees – and Jimmy. None of my boys left the garage before I discovered it was missing. A stranger wouldn't have been able to walk in and take the keys. When I returned home tonight I immediately phoned one of my mechanics to see if he knew anything about the ute being in my driveway. He didn't. I was about to phone the owner when I looked inside it. There were loads of sweet wrappers – small bars of Cherryripes, you know, the ones you get in a big packet at the supermarket. They're Jimmy's favourites and it struck me then that he'd been in it. The wrappers were down on the floor on the driver's side, on the driver's seat, in the pockets of the driver's door and on the passenger seat. I went into the house and from the mess I could see in the living room I knew he was home. I went to his bedroom to question him and found him … like that. I can't understand why Jimmy would blow his head off over stealing a car,' he said shaking his head. 'We could have sorted something out. He … he might have done it over Queenie though. She wasn't in the house with him. Queenie's his dog and he's very attached to her. Do you think something has happened to Queenie?'

'You didn't read the note?' she asked him.

Lansford's head snapped up. 'No, what note?'

'Jimmy left a note on the small side table beside his bed. Are you saying you didn't touch it?'

'No. I didn't see a note. Once I saw him in that room, I had to rush out to the toilet to be sick – but I didn't make it and puked on the floor in the hallway outside the bathroom. I didn't go back into the room then. I couldn't face it and I knew from shows I've seen on television that you're not supposed to – in case you contaminate the scene. I dialled triple zero immediately. What did the note say?'

She looked closely at Roger Lansford. Either he was a good actor or he genuinely didn't have any idea of what his cousin had been involved in.

'I'll come to that in a moment. First of all, I'd like to ask how Jimmy got his hands on a loaded rifle. I can't imagine he held a licence for one. Was it yours?'

'Yes,' he said nodding. 'It was my rifle. I have two that both belonged to my father. I keep them locked in a cabinet in the back sunroom. Jimmy knew where I kept the keys. The ammunition is also kept in the cupboard. The rifle wouldn't have been loaded. He or someone else must have loaded it.'

'Would Jimmy know how to load a rifle?'

'Yes, I think so. Years back I used to take Jimmy out to a friend's property in the country where we'd shoot at tinnies. I say country – it *used* to be countryside. A mate of mine had a pretty large farm out there at the time. I mainly loaded the rifles because I didn't trust Jimmy, but he's seen me doing it many times.'

'When was the last time you took him shooting?'

Lansford puckered up his face, as though thinking. 'Must be about six years ago now. My friend retired, sold the property and moved up to Queensland, so it was no longer an option. When I was out that way not long ago, I realised much of his old farm had been subdivided and new houses built.'

She knew what that was like. She'd seen the areas around Windsor and Richmond change beyond recognition since she was a kid, with much of the farm land disappearing for new housing developments. Richmond and Windsor were once considered country towns – they were now part of the Greater Sydney region. Her parents claimed that was nothing – even Penrith had been considered a country town out in the sticks when India's grandparents were young. Now Penrith was called a city, which spread out in all directions.

'I checked the cupboard with Detective Li who came

to the house,' Lansford continued. 'Jimmy had locked it up again and put the keys back in the sideboard drawer. When we opened it, there was only one rifle in there. I still can't …'

Lansford just kept shaking his head, looking bewildered.

'Do you recognise this rucksack Mr. Lansford?' she asked placing an image of the rucksack they'd found in Jimmy Lansford's room down on the table in front of him.

Lansford looked at it and shrugged. 'It could be Jimmy's. I'm not sure. I don't make an inventory of all his belongings. Why, what is the significance of the rucksack?'

'It contained five hundred thousand dollars.'

'Five hundred thousand?' Lansford asked looking astonished. 'I know he doesn't use banks and keeps all his money hidden around his room, but *five hundred thousand*? I can't believe he's saved that much since he's been working.'

She noted that Lansford kept referring to Jimmy and his actions in the present tense. This was common with family members who had difficulty coming to terms with the fact that their relatives were gone.

'We don't believe it's savings from his earnings. Quite a few more thousand was found hidden, as you say, in various parts of his room. This was all in the rucksack.'

'What? No. It can't be Jimmy's then. Do you think he *stole* it?'

'That's one way of putting it. We believe Jimmy took part in the kidnapping of five-year-old Joshua Gibson and was paid the five hundred thousand dollars for his part in it.'

'That kid you mentioned when you came to see me the other day?' Lansford asked looking shocked.

'Yes.'

'No, I can't believe that. I told you then, Jimmy wouldn't have the brains to do anything like that.'

'His note says otherwise.'

Lansford eyes nearly popped out of his head then. Was it because Jimmy had more or less confessed to his part in the crime and Lansford was shocked that his cover had been blown – or that he knew nothing about the kidnapping at all?

'What did the note say?' Lansford asked, speaking almost in a whisper.

'He said Queenie and the boy were dead and it was all his fault.'

'Dead? … How? I can assure you Jimmy would never hurt a fly. He wouldn't have had anything to do with killing either his dog or a child. If both of them are dead, then someone else must be responsible – not Jimmy. Maybe Queenie's death sent him over the edge.'

'We are still investigating the circumstances. Jimmy didn't say he killed them. He said it was his *fault* they were dead. What can *you* tell us about that Mr. Lansford?'

'What can *I* tell you? I don't know anything about it. I have no idea where Jimmy's been since I last saw him.'

'What can you tell me about a cabin in the bush up in the Colo Heights area?'

Lansford remained silent for a while before asking 'You think that's where Jimmy's been? That old place?'

'You're familiar with the cabin then?'

'Yes, we used to go there when we were kids. My father used to take us up there camping occasionally. It was built by our great, great, great grandfather. Apparently he lived there for a while and put a claim in for the land. He was on one of the last transport ships that came out to New South Wales when he was little more than a boy and was a ticket of leave man when he built it. You know what that is don't you?'

'A convict who has served his time and been given his freedom under licence.'

'Yeah, something like that. My grandfather looked into it in the sixties and the government claimed they could find no ownership rights to it. He always said they swindled our family out of their heritage. Once upon a time there was a decent track leading up to it, and a much larger clearing, but not anymore.'

So Marlee was right; the cabin had dated from the early settler days. She looked at Jacko and suspected she knew what he was thinking. It wasn't Lansford's family heritage. The whole region had been populated with indigenous people long before the European settlers arrived.

'When was the last time you were up there?'

Lansford leaned back in his chair and let out a long breath.

'Phew. Must be twenty years or more. I know Jimmy's been up there a few times since with one of his mates, but not for *years* as far as I know.'

'I can tell you he was there recently. Do you know the name of this mate Jimmy might have gone there with?'

'No, I have no idea. It was long before he came to live with me. Jimmy told me when his father was going through one of his drunken violent rampages, he'd take off up there and hide out. He didn't have it easy as a kid – or as an adult, until his father died. His mother died when he was still quite young and Jimmy's older sister had long flown the nest to get away from the old bastard. She's dead now as well. There was another child between Jimmy and his sister – another boy who died in an accident. Or so we were told. Jimmy and his older brother used to have lots of accidents.'

India wondered if that's why Jimmy had some learning difficulties. His note had been full of spelling mistakes, but was still clearly readable, so he wasn't too impaired.

'Is your father still alive? Would he be able to tell us who Jimmy might have gone up to the cabin with?'

'No. I'm afraid not. My father died fifteen years ago. My mother a year later. They both had the big C. The house I live in was theirs and where I grew up.'

She nodded. The elderly neighbour had said they had no other relatives. It didn't feel appropriate to say, 'sorry for your loss.'

'We found an old half shovel up at the cabin. Can you tell us what that might have been used for?'

'Yeah, it was to bury our waste if you know what I mean. Any leftover food or—'

'We get the picture.' Jacko said.

'Jimmy probably didn't stick to the rules though. I wouldn't be surprised if he left scraps of food and his rubbish lying around the cabin like he does in my place.'

'There were a few *old* opened cans there, but not too much apart from items he'd taken there more recently,' Jacko added.

Lansford's statement about the shovel tallied with what the techies had found at the cabin.

'Right. I think it's time we took a break now,' she said. 'I'm afraid we're going to have to ask you to remain with us for the time being. You can't return to your home anyway; we're still examining it. One thing before we break, I need the address of the property where you used to take Jimmy shooting.'

'Why would you want that?'

'We're trying to piece together Jimmy's movements. We need to look into whether that was a place he might have travelled to in the past few days. We also need to know your movements since Saturday.'

Saturday was when the surveillance on Lansford had been called off.

'Before you tell us that, or write it down for us, are you sure you don't want us to call a lawyer in for you?'

'I think I probably should if what you're saying about Jimmy is true. I still can't believe it though.'

'Right. We'll organise a duty lawyer for you and in the meantime, someone will bring you some refreshments. Do you need anything to eat and what would you like to drink?'

'I may as well have a coffee – if you're going to expect me to stay awake. And I wouldn't mind something sweet – like a couple of biscuits if you have them.'

24

India looked at her watch. It was ten forty-two – too late really to be calling on the Gibsons, but she'd phoned the duty officer before she'd started the interview with Lansford to say she'd be calling in later with some news. She didn't feel up to going, but also didn't think it was something she should dump on Jacko's shoulders. Superintendent Havering had asked her to go anyway. She'd called him from the Lansford house to pass on the news about Jimmy Lansford and ask whether Talbot should be called in to interview Roger Lansford.

He'd instructed her to start the interview process and said he'd inform Talbot. He also wanted her to be the one to call on the Gibson family. Not Talbot. Max Gibson had lodged a complaint about Talbot and Penn with him.

After another trip to the bathroom, she met Jacko downstairs. She'd asked Jacko to drive them over to the couple's house. That meant she'd have to face yet another journey with her eyes closed.

'Has a duty lawyer been arranged for Lansford?'

'Yep. All taken care of. Might be some time before one arrives though. I think we're in for a late night.'

She sighed. It was the last thing she wanted. She saw she had several missed calls from Rob, but had sent him a quick message saying there had been developments on the case and she'd been called back in. She didn't mention the miscarriage. At least tonight's events had created a distraction from her own problems, but she'd have to face them sooner, rather than later.

The Gibsons were waiting up for them when they arrived. They looked as sleep deprived as her and Jacko. Rhona Mitchell was on duty again and organised drinks for them all, before leaving them alone in the dining room with the doors closed.

'I'm sorry, but we have received some unsettling news tonight,' India started.

She didn't really want to say another word. The couple were looking pale and shocked with her opening statement. She clenched her fists together in her lap and continued. 'Tonight we were called to the scene of a suicide at a house in Richmond. The man in question left a note saying Joshua had died from some sort of fit and he was really sorry.'

'Joshie's *dead*?' Ellen asked.

'I'm so sorry. We have no definite confirmation of it, but that's what his note said. We have confirmed that the man in question was most likely the one who was holding Joshua in the cabin I told you about.'

'He *killed* Josh? Why? We paid the money they asked for,' Ellen moaned. 'We did *everything* they said.'

'He didn't say he killed him. He said Josh died from

some sort of fit. Did Joshua suffer from epilepsy?' she asked them.

Gibson had not spoken a word up to this point. He shook his head, cleared his throat and said, 'No, but he used to have asthma attacks. He hasn't had one in over a year and the doctor where we used to live believed they were brought on by high levels of pollution. We were surrounded by large scale building sites. Even the kindergarten he attended had lots of building work going on around it. Once that all stopped he had no further attacks. Perhaps that was what he was talking about.'

Ellen stood up and walked out of the room in silence. A few minutes later they heard her screaming and wailing from Joshua's room. India felt her stomach contract at the sound. It took all her willpower to not run in and join Ellen. Taking some deep breaths she looked at Max Gibson. He should be the one to go and comfort his wife, but he didn't move. He just sat there in stony silence, looking dazed and pale.

Rhona Mitchell popped her head inside the dining room door with raised eyebrows. India nodded at her, and picking up the message the constable went after Ellen.

'What else did the note say?' Gibson eventually asked after a minute without speaking. Ellen's wails had subsided into loud heart wrenching sobs. He seemed indifferent to his wife's misery, but India noticed a quiver in his voice as he spoke.

'The man in question said his dog was killed by a kangaroo. Our search team encountered a large kangaroo not far from the cabin which attacked one of the men.

We found animal blood near the cabin, which probably belonged to the dog.'

'Josh was frightened of large kangaroos. He had an asthma attack when some came near him at Koala Park just before his fourth birthday. He didn't mind the wallabies, but he was terrified of the kangaroos. If he saw this kangaroo then maybe it brought on an attack. So where is Josh? What did he do with him?'

She looked at Jacko and nodded. She really didn't want to continue this conversation so getting the message he stepped in.

'Well that's what we don't know. Part of the suicide note appears to have been ripped off which might have provided us with that information. A man was seen leaving the house shortly after the sound of a gunshot. We think he might have been the dead man's accomplice, and we think he took those details with him.'

'The man who wrote the note shot himself?'

'Yes,' Jacko said.

'So unless you find his accomplice you won't know where Josh is?'

'We are questioning a man at the moment who may be able to provide us with information.'

'Do you believe he is the accomplice?'

'He's not the man who was seen leaving the house after the gunshot, but he may be able to help us with our enquiries,' Jacko said.

Gibson nodded and stood. 'If you would excuse me, I need to be alone now. Thank you for letting us know.'

No mention of comforting his wife. He wanted to be alone.

'I need to tell you that our Superintendent is planning to make a statement to the press in the morning, so perhaps you could let family members know before then,' India said.

'I will.'

She and Jacko sat in silence for a moment. She could feel the weight of the news she'd just imparted to the couple pressing in on her stomach.

'Time for us to go I think,' she said. 'I just need to visit the bathroom first.'

'I'm sorry Jacko, do you think you could take over the rest of the interview with Lansford?' India asked him once they set off back towards Windsor. 'You could call in Jun or Marlee if you don't want to do it alone. I need to go to Hawkesbury Hospital. Can you drop me there before you go back to the station?' she asked pressing a hand onto her stomach.

'Why do you want me to drop you at the hospital? Is something wrong?'

'I had a miscarriage tonight and I think I need sorting out. At least I think that's what happened. I thought things might settle down, but they seem to have become worse.'

'What? You're kidding me? What on earth are you doing here then?'

'When Jun Li phoned I couldn't not go. I was hoping I was wrong, but I've been through this before.'

'Crikey boss, you didn't say you were pregnant. Is that why you wanted me to pick you up? You hadn't had a drink had you?'

'No. I just didn't feel up to driving.'

'Are you alright?'

'Not really, which is why I think I need to go to the hospital.' Her stomach had started cramping and from her previous miscarriage experience, she suspected she needed medical attention.

'Have you told Rob?'

'Not yet. I'll tell him once I get to the hospital. Keep me updated, won't you?

25

Tuesday

Rob withdrew from the conference and raced back to join India at the Hawkesbury Hospital. After waiting in accident and emergency for six hours, she was taken down to be prepped for a D & C and a blood transfusion. She was sure the wait would have been longer except that Rob pointed out her condition had become an emergency. He'd been with her during four of her waiting hours and they'd cried and talked about what had happened. She'd also filled Rob in on the latest with the case to distract them from their own tragedy. Rob hadn't said anything but she suspected he thought working on the case had triggered the miscarriage. She thought there might have been a connection, it was when she heard the news about Jimmy Lansford's suicide and Joshua's death that her stomach had cramped (which she didn't tell Rob). But it might have all been co-incidental. She had been in the job long enough and witnessed many horrors, so why would this news cause her problems? It was more likely that she had some kind of weakness in her reproductive organs that caused her to lose another baby. After her previous miscarriage doctors claimed they could find nothing wrong with her, but she wasn't sure she believed them.

When India came around Rob was at her bedside holding her hand.

'How are you feeling?'

'Groggy at the moment. And thirsty.' While she'd been waiting to go down to surgery, she'd not been allowed to have anything to eat or drink. 'Have they left any water?'

'Yes, there a jug full of water here. Take small sips, no guzzling,' Rob said, filling a glass for her.

'When I went down for the D & C they said I could be discharged this morning if all was well. I need to get back on the case Rob. We need to find Jimmy Lansford's accomplice before he disappears.'

'You're not going back to work today. You need to spend at least a day at home recovering. You've just come out of a general anaesthetic. Your brains would be mush anyway.'

'I guess so. Okay today I'll rest, but tomorrow if I'm up for it, I'll need to get back onto the case. Are you going into work today?'

'Not on your life. I have a beautiful woman who needs waiting on hand and foot,' he said leaning over to kiss her forehead.

India was discharged once the doctor and his cohort of

students had been to see her. She convinced them she was fine, but she felt quite wobbly when she stood to get changed. After they arrived home Rob tried to prevent her from communicating with Jacko, but she wasn't having it.

'I'm resting on the couch, it's not as if I'm doing anything exerting,' she told him, so he eventually conceded.

She'd spoken to Jacko while she'd been waiting to be dealt with at the hospital. Lansford's lawyer had arrived and Lansford had given Jacko details of his movements since Saturday as requested.

Marlee and Jun Li were scheduled to verify Lansford's movements this morning and she'd had just heard back in a message from Jacko, that Lansford's alibis were solid. So either Roger Lansford knew nothing or had been party to events at a distance with Jimmy and another person involved in the actual kidnapping, holding of Joshua and the collection of the money.

Jacko arrived in the evening laden down with flowers, chocolates and a card signed by people from work. Some of the messages were almost indecipherable. Rob made them coffee and left them to it, retreating to the study.

'So, what's the latest?' she asked him.

'We've had to let Lansford go,' he said. 'We've got nothing on him. We've carried out thorough searches of his house and business premises and found nothing. I just heard back from uniforms before I left the station that Lansford is complaining about the mess we made in his house.'

'It wasn't exactly pristine when we arrived there last night.'

'No, but Lansford claimed that was down to Jimmy. To be fair to him, I had a quick look in his bedroom last night before forensics had a go at it and it was pretty clean and tidy. The clothes and mess lying around the living room was Jimmy's stuff apparently.'

'Which had been sitting there for a week?'

'No, since he'd come home.'

'Right. Lansford did say when we interviewed him that he could tell Jimmy was home because of the mess in the living room.'

Judging by the state of Jimmy Lansford's bedroom, he *was* a bit of a slob. If Roger Lansford was a neat freak, she thought Jimmy's messy habits must have driven him crazy.

'By the way, the techos confirmed that the handwriting in the suicide note was Jimmy's. They found other samples of writing in his room that matched.'

'They didn't find the other bit of the note?

'No. So... Roger Lansford. We've looked into his finances as well. His business has a steady income, but no large sums of money have been deposited into any of his accounts. His withdrawals are modest and are amounts you'd expect him to take out to cover his living costs. There's nothing suspicious there.'

'Has he told you anything new?'

'No. Talbot and Penn took over questioning Lansford this morning, but they didn't discover anything that could take us forward in the investigation.'

'That doesn't surprise me. They probably asked him all the same things we'd already raised with him.'

'They did, I was listening in on the interview. Lansford's lawyer kept butting in saying he'd already answered those questions. One piece of information *they* had that we didn't though, was that the techos picked up partial fingerprints belonging to Roger Lansford and full fingerprints for Jimmy Lansford at the cabin. There are other unknown partial prints there as well as Joshua Gibson's prints.'

'How did Lansford account for his prints being found?'

'He claims they must have been from when he was last there.'

'Where were the fingerprints found?'

'On the kettle. On old gas cylinders – which were all empty by the way, and on the controls of the small gas ring they had there.'

'Did the techies say whether they could have been very old prints?'

'Yes – and that's the problem. They could be.'

'What about the utes?'

'Roger Lansford prints were on the driver's door handle of both utes. On the one that was stolen – other prints were also found in different places – probably the owner's and a mechanic from the garage. The techos will take their prints to eliminate them. Only Jimmy Lansford's prints were on the steering wheel and gear change column, so if his accomplice drove it, it was wiped clean. Jimmy Lansford's prints were all over the stolen ute. They also found dog hairs, pale blond hairs which could be Joshua Gibson's and various DNAs in the back. Again, one which we suspect will be Joshua Gibson's, but we'll have to wait for the results to confirm that. Then there was the duffel bag they found in the back ...'

'Joshua had definitely been in the ute Jimmy drove then?'

'Yep, it's looking like it. In Roger Lansford's ute, they found his and Jimmy Lansford's prints. Jimmy Lansford's prints were only on the passenger side. No-one else's. No sign that Joshua Gibson has ever been in his vehicle.'

'If Roger Lansford is involved, he wouldn't have been stupid enough to have Joshua anywhere near his vehicle. What about the property where they used to go shooting?'

Lansford had given them details of the place. It was in Agnes Banks, an area not far from Richmond along the Nepean River. India was familiar with Agnes Banks – there were great swimming and picnic spots along the river there that she'd been taken to by her family as a child. In the past year she'd heard that a lot of new homes were being built in the area.

'Marlee and Jun Li have headed out there this afternoon. They haven't reported back in yet.'

She wished she was joining Marlee and Jun Li, she'd love to see the area again. It was so frustrating being forced to rest.

'If that doesn't bring us any results where do you think we should look next? Jimmy's note said he "put them together". Do you think he meant he buried them or left them lying somewhere where they'd be found?' Jacko asked.

'I don't know. But if Jimmy was as fond of his dog as Lansford claims, he wouldn't have left it lying around for vermin or other scavengers to attack the body. He'd *bury* it. If he buried them together, we'll have a difficult task ahead of us. I think we need to widen the search around the cabin to see if we can find signs of a grave. It looked as though Jimmy was beginning to dig one there. Maybe that had been for the dog and when Joshua died, he decided to take them somewhere else. Either somewhere up at Colo Heights or goodness knows where. It would have to be a place he was familiar with. Somewhere he'd either worked, or went to for other purposes – like the shooting expeditions.'

'That's going to be a major search,' Jacko moaned. 'How are we going to do that?'

'Roger Lansford might know some of the places where Jimmy has worked. We've got a few contacts from Jimmy's old phone that Marlee has already spoken to. We can start with them. Also check with the techies to see if they found any pay slips in his room. Otherwise we're going to have to do a public appeal and/or contact every household in the region with land attached to its property.'

'You're kidding – and who's going to do that?'

'We will, I can't see Talbot doing it. And I'm sure I could get Superintendent Havering to assign a uniform team as well. We can't abandon the search for Joshua. Talking of press appeals, the news is about to come on, shall we see what Havering has to say?' she said using the remote control to switch the television on.

The story was the first headline item. It started with the newsreader sitting at her desk in the studio.

'Following the death of thirty-four-year-old Jimmy Lansford in Richmond last night, police have discovered that Mr. Lansford was involved in the kidnapping of five-year-old Joshua Gibson. We're crossing now to Richmond for Superintendent Havering's statement.'

The cameras then switched to Havering who was speaking to the press outside Richmond Headquarters.

'We were called to the scene of a shooting at approximately eight pm last night to discover the body of thirty-four-year-old Jimmy Lansford. Mr. Lansford had taken his own life and left a note indicating that he had been involved in the kidnapping of five-year-old Joshua Gibson. On Saturday night a ransom was paid, according to the kidnapper's demands, and we believe Mr. Lansford collected that ransom. Joshua was due to be released the following day. Sadly, that did not happen. We have reason to believe that Joshua tragically died – possibly of natural causes, before the kidnappers were able to release him. Yesterday morning we discovered the location where Joshua Gibson was held. Through forensic evidence we've gathered, we have now ascertained that Jimmy Lansford was with Joshua at those premises. We have also examined the vehicle young Joshua was transported in – a vehicle driven by Jimmy Lansford. Evidence in the vehicle indicates that Joshua Gibson is in fact dead as Mr. Lansford's note stated.'

India turned to look at Jacko. 'What's he talking about? You didn't mention anything about evidence being found that confirmed his death.'

'Hang on, let's see what else he says.'

There was a buzz of chatter from the media before the questions started flying.

'Did you find Joshua's body in the car?'

'No. And we are seeking the identity of a man seen leaving the house in Richmond shortly after the shotgun blast that killed Mr. Lansford. We believe that man may hold the answer to the question of where Joshua's body is. The man had dark hair and drove a medium sized, dark vehicle. We would ask that if anyone has any information regarding this tragic incident to please contact our team in Windsor who have been investigating the case.'

'We've heard you've been interviewing a suspect in Joshua Gibson's kidnapping. Is that correct?' one of the reporters asked Havering.

'We have interviewed someone in connection with this investigation, but he is not the man we are seeking,' Havering said.

'Are you talking about Roger Lansford, the deceased's cousin?'

'I am not at liberty to discuss an on-going investigation.'

'Are Joshua Gibson's parents suspects in the kidnapping?'

'No. They are parents grieving the loss of their son,' Havering said.

'Why didn't you follow the kidnappers when they collected the ransom?'

'We had installed trackers with the ransom notes and planned to follow them in the hope that they would lead us to where they were holding Joshua. However, they found the trackers and switched bags. We did follow them, but they had

already disappeared by then. We found their hideout yesterday as I told you. Now that is all I am able to tell you at present. Thank you.'

Reporters continued firing questions at Havering, but he left them and walked inside the station. Uniformed officers prevented the reporters from following him.

The camera then turned to a reporter who continued speaking.

'We know from what Superintendent Havering has told us that Joshua Gibson, and one of his kidnappers, is dead. Two tragic, and some people would say, unnecessary deaths. If the police had moved in on the kidnappers as they collected the ransom would Joshua Gibson and Jimmy Lansford still be alive? If Ellen Gibson hadn't given her press interviews about their big win on Powerball, would Joshua still be alive? Was Jimmy Lansford's death really a suicide or was he murdered? We've been told Joshua probably died of natural causes, but how can they know that for certain when there is no body? Was Joshua Gibson brutally murdered as well? We know Lansford had learning difficulties. He could not have masterminded the kidnap of a child on his own. The mystery man the police are looking for could be the mastermind behind the kidnapping – and a sadistic killer. These are some of the many questions raised in these tragic events. This is Rebecca Hurley reporting from outside Richmond police headquarters.'

'She's got a point, how can you know Joshua wasn't murdered?' Rob asked from the dining area. India had been so absorbed in the television that she hadn't noticed him come in.

'We don't. Not one hundred percent. We've only got Jimmy's note to go on, which seems genuine,' Jacko said.

'We do know for sure that the kid is dead though.'

'How?' India asked.

'I started to tell you earlier about the duffel bag we found in the back of the ute – but somehow we went off in a different direction and then started watching the news. Anyway, we found a large long grey duffel bag – similar to the type used to transport naval linen according to the techos. Well after we left the scene the other night, Rick was brought in with his cadaver dog – you know who I mean?'

She nodded.

'The dog went straight for the duffel bag in the back. It was buried under a pile of other stuff. The techies have examined it and believe both Joshua and the dead dog had been placed in there.'

'But can we be sure it was Joshua's *body*? Maybe some of his *things* were in the bag along with the dead dog. If it's a cadaver dog – perhaps it was the dog it was smelling.'

'The techos had brought some of Joshua's clothing with them. Ones that were found at the cabin. After the dog smelled them it went straight for the duffel.'

'Why would forensics bring some of Joshua's clothes to Lansford's house?'

'They'd been told a cadaver dog was being called in. Joshua could have been at the house – either dead or alive.'

'Okay – if both Joshua and the dog died up at the cabin, Jimmy must have put them in the bag to transport them somewhere else. Where is the question? Was there only one duffel bag in the ute?' she asked.

'Yes. We're thinking Jimmy might have had a couple of duffels with him and put the ransom money into one. It would have fitted,' Jacko said.

'Makes sense. But would Jimmy have been strong enough to carry two heavy duffel bags all the way out to wherever he'd parked the ute up at Colo Heights. It would have been a long trek. Maybe his accomplice joined him there,' she said.

'A five-year-old child and a dead kelpie probably would have weighed less than the money,' Rob said.

'I received word from Rick about the bag before I resumed the interview with Roger Lansford, so I asked him whether Jimmy would have had the strength to carry two large heavy duffel bags – without telling him that there might have been two dead bodies in one of the bags. He reckoned Jimmy would have managed to carry two bags without any difficulty.'

'Was there any kind of marking on the duffel bag?'

'There were no external markings on it. When I called the labs they were still examining it – but they told me that much. They said it looked like there had once been labels sewn onto the bags which had been removed.'

'Have you told the parents about the find?' Rob asked.

'Yes, I went to see them first thing this morning. I told them we now have concrete evidence that their son is dead.'

'How were they?' she asked, her voice wobbling a little. Losing a baby through a miscarriage was bad enough, but it must have been horrendous for the couple to hear confirmation that their five-year-old was dead. She felt her eyes watering up and tucked her head down so Jacko wouldn't see.

'The mother was pretty cut up. They'd had to call in a doctor the night before to sedate her – after we'd gone. Max Gibson seemed angry. He kept pressing me for details. I told him, when his wife left the room, that a cadaver dog had found where they'd kept Joshua's body. I didn't give him the details about the duffel bag.'

'I hope they weren't watching the news this evening. The question that reporter raised about Ellen would devastate her,' she said.

'I suspect the media – and the public – are going to vilify Ellen Gibson over the next little while, now they've been told the boy is dead. If you still have a family liaison officer at their house, it might be wise to suggest the couple avoid watching any news programs and don't read any papers,' Rob said.

'They'll still have their laptop and could pick up the news on it. They're bound to find out anyway. They can't stay cooped up there forever,' Jacko said. 'And I don't think Talbot will be happy with Havering's announcement that Ellen Gibson is a grieving parent. He's got it into his head that Jimmy Lansford's suicide note implicates her in the kidnapping.'

'What?' India felt her emotions swing from sadness to anger.

'That bit where Jimmy wrote "he should have gone home to his mummy" – or something like that.'

'I can understand why Talbot might think that,' Rob said. 'But from everything you've told me India, I doubt very much that the mother was involved.'

'No, I'd stake everything I own that she wasn't

involved. I think Jimmy Lansford was trying to say that the boy was supposed to go home to his parents, but something terrible happened and he couldn't live with Joshua's death and the death of his dog.'

'On that unhappy note, I'll say hooroo to you two,' Jacko said standing. He looked uncomfortable shifting from one leg to another. 'And once again I'm sorry about *your* loss. Do you think you'll be in tomorrow?'

'If I feel up to it. I'll let you know in the morning,' she said without looking at Rob. At least one good thing had come out of Jacko's visit. She'd stopped thinking about the miscarriage.

26

Ellen and Max were watching Superintendent Havering's press conference. Silent tears trickled down her face throughout it. When she looked at Max she could see he was sitting in stony silence – again. He'd not shed a tear – not that she was aware of anyway. They weren't sleeping in the same room anymore. She was sleeping in Josh's bed, staying close to him. She had left the same sheets on the bed from when Josh had last slept there and she could still smell him. Normally she was fussy about sleeping in clean sheets, but she couldn't bear to wash them, wanting to hold on to anything she could of her son.

They'd had little to say to each other for the past few days and Max had not spoken a word to her since the detectives had called to see them on Monday night to tell them Josh was dead. She thought it was probably a good thing as he would only start blaming her again. He couldn't see that he was to blame as well. When the reporter asked whether Josh would still be alive if she hadn't done the press conferences, she stood and rushed out of the room. This was too much. The press had already attacked her over her 'small sacrifice' comment. She wished now she'd never said it, but she had been nervous and it just slipped out. It was something Max had said to her over and over.

She threw herself on Josh's bed and began sobbing. The policewoman, the nice one, Cheryl, followed her into the room and sat on the edge of the bed.

'They're going to blame me for everything aren't they?' she asked Cheryl.

'You know how the press like to sensationalise things. It's all about headlines. You need to ignore them,' Cheryl said.

'But it's not just my fault. I wanted to go and stay in a luxury hotel when we learnt about the win. Max wouldn't do it. I asked him to stay home from work the day Josh was taken, but he insisted on going in. If he'd done both those things Josh would still be with us. He's just as much to blame,' Ellen sobbed.

When Cheryl had first met Ellen Gibson, she'd felt a deep-seated loathing for the woman. How could she have been so stupid to expose her son like that was her first reaction? She thought Ellen was a brainless and thoughtless dumb blonde. Over the days she'd spent with the family her attitude towards the woman had shifted. When Inspector Hargreaves had asked her to give some support to the woman, she didn't think she could do it. If she'd been asked to comfort Max Gibson, that would have been a different matter. With his looks she'd have been happy to take him in her arms any day.

Ellen was shutting herself away in her son's room much of the time, but when they did speak, Cheryl began to see the woman's real character. Ellen might have been a bit thoughtless and carried away with their big win, but she really loved her son and was heartbroken by the news of his death. She had started taking responsibility for her part in everything and this evening she'd learned some new facts. Ellen was right, her husband was just as much to blame in all this. It was a shame the media didn't have all the details. She suspected Ellen was going to cop all the blame. One thing that seemed to have been forgotten in all this were the kidnappers. Weren't they the ones who were really at fault here? They chose to kidnap the boy. A vulnerable little boy who was now *dead* because of *them*. No-one else.

Her attitude towards Max Gibson had changed over the days she been in the house as well. She no longer saw him as the poor man whose stupid wife had caused this tragedy. She'd witnessed him being downright cruel towards his wife. When they should have been comforting and supporting each other – and she'd seen Ellen both seeking and offering him comfort; he'd pushed her away with aggressive hostility. Perhaps it was a good thing they were no longer speaking. He couldn't utter a civil word to her. You could cut the atmosphere with a knife any time they were in the same room together.

Cheryl wished they'd hurry up and find that poor little kid's body so she could go back to her normal duties.

Max couldn't move. He sat staring at the television screen long after the news item about Josh had finished. It was a good thing Ellen was no longer in the room. He'd felt like strangling her. In fact, he'd felt like that for days now. Every time he saw her he wanted to put his hands around her throat and squeeze the life out of her. They'd argued endlessly over events, throwing damning words at each other. But Ellen had started all this with her obsession about being in the limelight. She was right though – he should have checked his ticket after the draw. Then he could have handled their win with discretion. He still couldn't get over how she'd *sneaked* out to the car, found the ticket and hidden it away without saying a word to him. Then organised that ridiculous press conference where Josh was put on show. The money they'd won was meaningless now without Josh – although he was sure Ellen would enjoy spending it when she stopped feeling sorry for herself. And that's what all the tears were about he was sure. Not Josh. He could see no future for him and Ellen. He'd be asking her for a divorce as soon as they found Josh and buried him. Then she could go off and spend to her heart's content with her share of the money. What would he do with his share? He'd already told his parents he planned to pay off their mortgage and give them money – he wanted to give them enough money to live comfortably for the rest of their lives. With thoughts of helping his parents, he started to relax and feel a little better; his murderous thoughts receding.

27

Wednesday

India returned to work on Wednesday, promising Rob she'd take things easy. She didn't have much choice. She was still feeling a little wobbly, but wasn't about to admit that to anyone. They needed to trace Jimmy Lansford's accomplice and find Joshua's body. She intended to spend most of the day at the station, directing events, apart from a visit to Roger Lansford.

Marlee and Jun Li had had no joy out at Agnes Bank. The original homestead was there with a small acreage of land surrounding it. The new owners had not seen anyone entering their property and a search of the grounds had brought no results. There was a vegetable garden with recently turned soil, but on close inspection it was obvious that the soil had only been weeded. The plants there had been undisturbed.

The rest of the old farm had been split into generous plots where new houses had been built. An inspection of these also brought negative results.

A couple of pay slips detailing a handful of Jimmy's

employers had been found in his bedroom and small uniform teams despatched to investigate. Phone calls to companies Marlee had previously been in touch with from Lansford's call log on his old mobile brought no results either. They were mainly small businesses on trading estates and not places where Jimmy Lansford could bury his dog or Joshua. They would be followed up in time though to complete thorough checks. Lansford's tax records were also being looked at to discover whether they could find out other employer's details, but she suspected much of the work Lansford had done was cash in hand and undeclared.

When she and Jacko left for Richmond to call on Roger Lansford as she'd arranged in a phone call, she insisted on driving. She felt wobbly enough, she didn't need to add to her discomfort by being a passenger to Jacko's crazy driving antics.

Press vehicles from all the papers and television stations were parked along Lansford's street near the house. Jacko had organised a couple of officers to keep the press at bay and to clear a space on the street which enabled them to pull into the driveway. Both of the white utes had been removed for forensic testing.

Lansford answered the door and ushered them into the lounge. She could see it was now all clean and tidy. He was a neat freak!

'You've told me I don't need my lawyer here. Are you sure? Because if this is going to be an interrogation, I would want her to be present.'

The duty lawyer Lansford had been assigned was a young indigenous woman who India had come across before. She knew the lawyer to be a sharp and savvy woman and probably wouldn't approve of this visit without her being present.

'No, as I mentioned on the phone, we're here simply to ask for your help Mr. Lansford.'

There was no offer of a tea or coffee. Given the circumstances she was not surprised. Lansford had not had an easy time with them. Especially after Talbot and Penn had a go at him.

'How can I help you then?'

'We are aware of a few large property owners who Jimmy has worked for over the past few years from pay slips with details of the employers which were found in his room. But he must have worked for a countless number of people. We wondered if you could point us in the direction of any you are aware of. We need to find where he buried Joshua Gibson and his dog.'

'Ah. Well he worked out at my mate's place in Agnes Banks for a start.'

'We've checked there.'

'I know once a year he worked for a bloke in Kurrajong who operates a big apple orchard business. He has a shop on the main road there. Then there were properties around Castlereagh, Londonderry, Yarramundi and Grose Vale Area. He's worked all over. Jimmy didn't just work on large properties. He worked for small businesses in Windsor, Richmond and Penrith when they wanted heavy items moved. But they wouldn't be the kind of places where he'd look to bury Queenie. He'd want a quiet peaceful place for that.'

'I would have thought he'd want his dog – Queenie

was it – buried close to him. Why do you think he didn't bury Queenie in your back garden here?'

Lansford shrugged. 'I don't know. I imagine that's what he might have done if it had just been Queenie. But if, as you say, he had a dead child as well, Jimmy might have been told by whoever he was working for to put them in an out of the way place.'

'Do you know the names of any of the properties he worked on, or the names of any of the owners?'

'No. The only ones I know about I've mentioned. I do know one of the families he worked for were Italian. Jimmy used to stay over wherever it was – out Castlereagh way. I think they're veg growers. The grandmother of the family used to cook him huge meals. When he came home from there he'd always put on a load of weight. Sorry I can't help you more than that.'

'Well that's been a big help, thank you,' she said. They were already checking out properties in some of the places he'd described, but they now had some new ones to look at.

'Before you go I'd like to talk to you about how you can help me,' Lansford said. 'I know you have a couple of blokes out there keeping the press from entering my property, but it's not just here that's the problem. I've had to shut down my business for the moment because they were hounding us there. Not only that, the papers and television news have all suggested I am a *suspect* in Joshua Gibson's kidnapping.'

'You were a suspect,' Jacko said.

'But I've been completely cleared,' Lansford protested. 'It was nothing to do with me.'

Not completely cleared, India thought, noting that Jacko had said "were" rather than "are". Clever. As far as they were concerned, Lansford was still on their radar. One of the reasons they had a couple of uniforms outside the house was to keep an eye on him, under the guise of protecting him from the press.

'I thought your lawyer gave a statement to the press,' India said.

'She did, but they're suggesting that it was only her word on the matter. It would be better coming from you lot.'

'Our Superintendent made it clear you weren't the person we were seeking in this investigation.'

'Yeah, but he didn't say I was innocent, did he? Some of my customers have cancelled work with me. If it goes on like this my business is going to go broke. I can't go out anywhere without the press following me. I'm like a prisoner in my own home.'

'What are you expecting us to do?' Jacko asked him.

'You need to give a statement to the press saying I was not involved in the kid's kidnapping or death.'

'I'm afraid we would be unable to do that,' India said. 'We could tell them you've been helping us out with matters relating to your cousin – providing Superintendent Havering agrees. That's about all we could do for you.'

'I suppose it's a start,' Lansford muttered.

India phoned Havering before they left Lansford's house. She knew the press would be shouting out questions at them as they left. Havering agreed she could give a brief statement along the lines that she'd suggested. There was no way they were going to say he was innocent. He might well be, but they didn't know that. Not yet anyway.

Sure enough the press surged forward as a frantic mob as she and Jacko walked towards their car.

'Inspector Hargreaves, can you tell us whether Roger Lansford is still a suspect in Joshua Gibson's kidnapping?' one reporter shouted out. She looked up and saw it was Jude Ronson, the local reporter who'd asked the question. A man who had been questioned as a potential suspect himself.

'Mr. Lansford has been helping us out with matters relating to his cousin, that's all,' she said in reply.

'But is he still a suspect?' Ronson persisted.

'I'm afraid that is all I can tell you at the moment,' she said opening the car door and climbing in.

'They're like vultures, aren't they?' Jacko commented as she reversed the car out with reporters shouting questions through the windows.

'Hmm. That apple place Lansford mentioned. The one up in Kurrajong. I know it. It's called *All Things Apple*. How about we head up there while we're over this way? It won't take long.'

She paused at the T-junction. 'Left to Kurrajong or right to go back to Windsor?' she asked Jacko.

'May as well go to Kurrajong seeing as we're almost halfway there.'

She agreed and turned left onto the main road.

'Have you ever been to *All Things Apple*?'

'No. Can't say I'm all that fond of apples,' Jacko said. 'I know the place you're talking about though. I've driven past it lots of times.'

'They do fantastic apple cakes, apple and cinnamon buns, apple pies, different apple crumbles – either plain or mixed with other fruit, apple ice cream, smoothies with apples and other ingredients. You name it – they sell it.'

'Apple Ice Cream? I can't imagine what that would be like.'

'It's yummy – so are their apple pies. One of my favourite smoothies is apple and carrot juice.'

'Urgh. You do have peculiar tastes. Can't beat a good old meat pie I say. Do they sell those?'

28

The car park at *All Things Apple* was packed and India had to drive around a couple of times to grab a spot as someone pulled out.

'School holidays,' she said.

Jacko nodded. 'I hope we won't have to talk to the owner over a load of screaming kids.'

'We can always ask him to take us somewhere quieter.'

'Mm. Don't forget your hat,' Jacko said popping his own on his head.

'Really?'

'Don't look at me like that. You know we are supposed to protect ourselves when we're walking in harsh sun. This is the hottest time of the day.'

'We're not exactly out walking, Jacko. We're only in a car park.'

'Yeah, at the far end of a bloody big car park. It was fine at Lansford's – it was only a few steps to the door. This is different.'

'Alright. You win,' she said opening the rear door and reaching in for her hat.

The noise hit them when they opened the doors. The place was packed with hundreds of school children with their mothers. She spotted a handful of men which suggested that either all the fathers were out at work or couldn't face coming with their little darlings. Both options infuriated her. As someone who enjoyed her work, she didn't see why it wasn't more common for men to stay at home with the children, rather than the mothers. That wasn't ever going to happen with Rob if they eventually had their own. She'd have to find a childminder or full-time kindergarten, because *she* wasn't staying at home for years on end.

She walked up to the front of the queue and approached an older woman who was serving behind the counter. After flashing her identification she explained that they needed to speak to the owner.

'He was here earlier, but he's gone back up to the main house now. I can contact him for you and see if he's available.'

After giving the woman their names and titles India watched her retreat to what was presumably the main kitchen. Jacko was prowling along the counter looking at all the goodies on offer.

When the woman came back a few minutes later, she said the owner would see them. 'It's best if I let you into the property grounds through our back entrance. The main gates are closed during our busy season in the café.' She opened a section of the counter and beckoned them through.

'What's your boss's name?'

'Aaron Jenson.'

'Right thanks,' India said. They followed the woman through to a hallway that led to a small enclosed courtyard where she pointed to a gate.

'That'll take you onto the footpath which runs alongside the main driveway. It's about a ten minute walk up to the house.'

'Thanks.'

India led the way walking at a quick pace. She was feeling much better now and perhaps a short walk in the fresh air would do her good. She was grateful that Jacko had reminded her to wear her hat. Although the path they were walking along was largely shaded by a long line of trees, it was still very hot when the sun peeked through.

'I don't know if you heard, but the owner's name is Aaron Jenson,' she said to Jacko.

'Mm. It's not often I come across someone with the same first name as me.'

'Not that you use yours.'

'As you know, I feel more comfortable with Jacko.'

'But then people think your name is Jack, and that in typically Australian fashion you just add an 'o' on the end of it.'

'My grandfather told me that we had a completely different family name at one time. A name that's been lost over the generations. It was my grandfather's grandfather who was first called Jack apparently – by his European boss I might add. That was four generations back at the beginning of the 20th century. At some point it changed into Jacko.'

'It's a shame no-one knows your family's indigenous name. Marlee told me her family's name has always been Kurri.'

'According to my grandfather, who was told by his grandfather, he had a long name that Europeans couldn't pronounce; that's why it was changed. Many indigenous people were given the surname of their employers back in the early settler days. At least that didn't happen to our family.'

'I always think it's sad when families lose their heritage like that. It was the same for the African slaves that were taken across to America and the West Indies. They ended up with the surnames of the plantation owners.'

'Changing the subject, did you see they sell pork and apple pasties back there in the café? If they'd been just pork pasties, I might have bought one, but the idea of apple with pork doesn't appeal to me. I'm hungry. It's past my lunch time.'

'We can stop at Brown's Bakery in Richmond on the way back and pick up some pies.'

'Don't tell me you're going to eat an unhealthy pie?'

'I like pies as well Jacko. I just don't eat them that often. Especially in hot weather. I prefer them in the winter months.'

'I can eat them all year round.'

'I've noticed.'

She stopped and looked at their surroundings. As far as the eye could see down on their left were hundreds of apple trees.

'Isn't it a beautiful spot?'

'Mm. It is, but I'm not sure I'd want to live here though.

If a bit of a breeze blew up, there'd be an overwhelming smell of bloody apples! You'd soon get sick of it.'

A few minutes later they arrived at a large two storey house that was built of sandstone with a long veranda running across the first floor. Painted on the glass above the door was *Orchard House*. A wide front door lay open in the middle of the house with no fly screen protection. That wouldn't suit her, although she could understand why one hadn't been fitted. It would spoil the grand look of the house. She could see there was a small lobby with an inner door that was closed. Perhaps that kept the flies out.

India pressed the doorbell, an old-fashioned metal one, fixed on a panel beside the front door. A few seconds later a man, who looked to be in his late fifties, approached them.

'Inspector Hargraves I assume?' he asked reaching out to shake her hand.

The café employee must have told Jensen she was a woman. Normally new people they met assumed any man who was accompanying her held the higher rank.

'Yes. And this is Detective Senior Constable Jacko,' she added turning to Jacko.

'G'day.' Jacko said reciprocating the man's offer of his hand.

'Come in,' he said. 'We can go into the front sitting room.'

They followed him into a spacious room where he indicated they should sit on a sprawling comfortable looking couch. India sank into it and thought she could happily doze off there. Two large ceiling fans were whirling above them.

'Your house is wonderful,' she said. 'When was it built?'

'Around eighteen hundred and forty. Not by my family. My grandfather bought it back in the early nineteen-thirties. From what I was told the previous owner, whose family had owned it since it was built, had lost a load of money in the crash and struggled for a couple of years to keep the place afloat. My grandfather, who had wisely stashed his money in bricks and mortar and cash, rather than banks, bought it for a song. My father opened the shop and café in the late sixties when more people started to own cars. My sister and our families have carried on with it.'

A young woman came into the lounge then, asking if they'd like refreshments, running through a range of options.

'This is my daughter Felicity,' Jensen told them. They nodded greetings at her.

'Just a cool glass of water for me thanks,' Jacko said.

'Same for me,' India added. Carrot and apple juice hadn't been on offer.

'So, how can I help you?' Jensen asked them.

'We understand you have had a man called Jimmy Lansford working here for you on and off over the years.'

'Ah. I saw an article in the Sydney Morning Herald about Jimmy. I can't believe he would have been involved in that business. He looked like a large brute, but he was a gentle soul. Someone must have coerced him into it. Yes, Jimmy used to work for us at harvest time, but not for the past couple of years. He'd acquired a dog and I couldn't allow him to bring a dog with him.'

'You haven't seen him on or around the property recently?'

'No. He wouldn't be able to gain access without coming through the main gates. We do have a couple of other exits, but they are always locked. We've had security issues over the years and crop thefts, so we keep the main gates locked near harvest time and during our busy season in the café – otherwise families just wander in with their kids thinking they can use it as picnic grounds.'

Jensen's daughter returned with their drinks which she put on a small coffee table in front of them. India thanked her and picked up her glass to take a few sips.

'People break in to steal *apples*?' Jacko asked.

'Yes, they usually go after some of the variety of eaters we have, the cooking apples and the ones we use for making cider.'

'What do you think they do with them?'

India could see that Jacko couldn't imagine why *anyone* would want to steal apples.

Jensen shrugged. 'Sell some of them on or make their own cider I suppose. They've never taken the juicers – I imagine they'd be harder to shift and you'd need the right equipment to make juice.'

Jacko shook his head and pulled a face as though he found the whole idea preposterous. She felt an urge to laugh, but smiled instead at his naivety.

'Security aside, is there anywhere Jimmy Lansford could have climbed onto the property?' Jacko asked Jensen.

'Once upon a time he could have, but because of the thefts we've had over the years, we've had to comply with demands from our insurers. Unfortunately, we had to enlarge our perimeter walls and add barbed wire.'

She'd noticed the barbed wire on top on the stone walls as they approached the café. It made the lovely stone walls look ugly.

'If Jimmy had found his way onto your property, say in the middle of the night, would you have noticed?' she asked.

'We have security cameras dotted around the place, and a couple of security guards who patrol with dogs – another costly demand from our insurers. I am sure if he had done, his presence would have been picked up. Are you thinking that Jimmy might have come here looking for a place to bury that poor child?'

'Yes,' she said.

'He wouldn't have managed to do that here. And I can't see Jimmy coming to Orchard House to do it either. He knows how secure the place is. No, I think you're looking for a more remote location.'

'Right. Well thanks for your time Mr. Jensen. We'd better be getting back now and we'd appreciate it if you didn't speak to the press about our visit,' she said standing, with Jacko following suit.

'Rest assured we won't be speaking to the press. On another note – have you tried any of our products up at the café?' he asked as he walked them out.

'Many times,' India said. 'It's one of my favourite places to come for treats.'

'Well that's good to hear. Nice to meet you both. I

hope you find that boy soon.'

'Thanks,' she said as they walked away.

'That's two down, we've only got another few hundred to go,' Jacko said.

'Oh I don't know, we might find Jun Li and Marlee have ruled out other properties by the time we return.'

29

Ellen sat at the kitchen table drinking her tea and watching an army of ants march across the floor carrying biscuit crumbs larger than their own bodies. The table and the floor were strewn with crumbs thanks to the number of people who had been in and out of the kitchen. There were several packets of opened and unopened biscuits on the table. They never had biscuits in the house because she had been worried Josh would want to eat them too often and rot his teeth. She didn't eat them because she wanted to keep her figure trim. The visitors washed their mugs and plates, and occasionally wiped the table but no-one thought to sweep the floor. It was something she normally did but since Josh's disappearance she hadn't done anything. If she was honest with herself, she didn't care anymore. She helped herself to a chocolate mint slice and added to the crumbs on the table. The other packs were Arnott's 'Nice' biscuits which she couldn't stand and a packet of chocolate chip cookies. Her grandmother had always eaten the 'Nice' biscuits – they were very sugary, but boring. One or more of the police who'd been in the house obviously had a sweet tooth.

She was still watching the ants when that nice policewoman, Cheryl, appeared.

'Good morning Ellen. How are you today?'

That was a stupid bloody question. How did Cheryl think she was? Her son was dead. 'I'm not great, and I really would like to go out for a bit. Have a change of scenery.'

'Do you think that's wise Ellen and where were you thinking of going?'

'Into Penrith maybe. To the supermarket to pick up some things. I fancy some fresh slices of meat to make sandwiches. I also fancy a steak for tonight.'

She hadn't felt much like eating, but maybe if she bought food she liked she might be motivated to eat. Max's mother had dropped in pre-cooked meals, but they were things Max liked. Not what she liked. They'd had some take-away Chinese and pizzas brought in by the police, but she hadn't felt like eating them much either. She'd only nibbled at small helpings of food for days now.

There was one loaf of bread left in the freezer, but it was Josh's favourite bread and she couldn't face touching it. She didn't eat a lot of bread (worried about her weight again), but she really felt like making herself a sandwich with some fresh multi-grain bread.

'We could pick those things up for you,' Cheryl said.

'I want to buy them *myself*,' she insisted.

'I don't think you should be doing that on your own.'

'You could come with me then,' she said. 'But not dressed like that in your uniform. Otherwise people might realise who I was and want to have a go at me after what they said on the news. Do you have any normal clothes with you? I saw that you got changed before you left the other day.'

'I have some clothes in the car.'

'Then why don't you get changed and we can head off. I'll smarten myself up a bit as well and find something to put over my hair.'

'If you're sure?'

'I am.'

With renewed vigour, Ellen stood, pushed her chair back and headed off to the bedroom she shared with Max. The only time she'd been in there since Josh had gone was to pick up some clean clothes. The bedclothes were all scrunched up – Max hadn't even bothered to straighten them out this morning. But that was nothing new. She'd taken care of all those things since they married. Well not any more. He could deal with his own mess.

With her headscarf and sunglasses no-one seemed to notice who she was. Unlike at the barricade up the road from their house. The press were still out there, although Ellen had noticed there were less of them now.

She finished her shopping and Cheryl helped her load it into the car.

'I just want to pop into the newsagent's now.'

'I don't think you should do that.'

'I want to see what they're saying about Josh in the papers,' she said marching off towards the newsagents.

Cheryl ran after her and grabbed her arm. 'Ellen, stop.

You really don't want to see what the papers are saying.'

'I do,' she said shrugging Cheryl off.

She charged into the newsagents and grabbed a copy of each daily paper, not stopping to look at what the headlines said. She was paying at the counter when a woman approached her.

'You're Joshua's whore of a mother aren't you?' the woman said in a venomous tone.

'What did you say?' Ellen said turning to look at the woman whose face was screwed up in a look of disgust.

The woman leaned back, made strange noises in her throat, then lurched forward and spat. A large glob of phlegm landed squarely on Ellen's left cheek before starting to dribble down her face.

'Argh,' she squealed with disgust.

'THIS IS JOSHUA GIBSON'S MOTHER,' the woman shouted out for everyone to hear.

Cheryl rushed over to intervene. 'That's enough! Now leave the shop before I arrest you for assault,' she said, flashing her identification.

The woman grunted, but turned on her heels and marched out. Ellen was still standing at the counter with her mouth open in shock. Cheryl pulled a clean tissue out of her pocket, handed it to her and said, 'Wipe your face. Come on, we're leaving.'

A crowd had gathered in the shop and were murmuring quietly amongst themselves.

'You ought to be ashamed of yourself,' one woman called out to Ellen as they left, the papers clutched under her arms.

As soon as she returned to the house Ellen rushed into the bathroom and scrubbed her face. She'd never experienced anything so disgusting in her life and even after cleaning it she could still feel the woman's spit there. She knew it wasn't and it was all in her mind, but it made her shudder.

She moved into the kitchen to see Cheryl closing the fridge door and was just about to pick up the papers.

'Thanks for putting the shopping away,' she said, 'but I'll take the papers now thank you. I want to go off and read them.'

'I thought you were going to make yourself a sandwich?'

'I was, but I think I'll read these papers first.'

'I could make you a sandwich. You've barely eaten anything for days Ellen. Why don't you let me make you a sandwich and a nice cup of tea, then you can go off and read the papers after you've eaten.'

'Okay. I am feeling a bit hungry. I haven't had much of an appetite and I can only eat so many fast food take-away meals before they make me feel sick.'

'I know what you mean. With some of the hours we work, take-away food often becomes our staple diet. I get sick of them as well. So what would you like?'

'A silverside, tomato and lettuce sandwich would be great thanks. But instead of tea I think I'll make myself a chocolate milk shake. I make them all the time for Josh and I – we love them and I couldn't afford to go out and buy him one too often. Would you like me to make you one?'

'No thanks, Ellen. I'll stick with tea.'

'Right well I'll do that while you make the sandwiches. Make one for yourself.'

She'd had bought some more chocolate sauce at the supermarket this morning and plenty of milk. There was still cartons of vanilla and chocolate ice-cream in the freezer. She liked to use two scoops of vanilla and two scoops of chocolate ice-cream with loads of chocolate sauce.

When she suggested she could take her food and drink into the bedroom so she could start reading the papers, Cheryl once again persuaded her to eat in the kitchen first. They made small talk while she ate her sandwich and drank all of the milk shake. She had to admit she was feeling much better, if not a little full. She thanked Cheryl and leaving her to clean up, retreated to Josh's room, shut the door and spent the next hour reading and re-reading everything the papers had written about her and Josh, plus the kidnapper who'd shot himself. She squealed in outrage at the things the papers were saying about her, throwing one paper down and picking up another in anger. They'd even interviewed people who lived in Windsor for their opinion. Every single one of them blamed her. It wasn't fair.

Max had been out mowing the lawn when they'd arrived back at the house. The mower was silent now, he'd obviously finished. She heard the back-door slam and a few minutes later she stomped out to find Max standing at the dining room table.

'Have you seen these?' she asked him, slamming the papers down on the table. 'The papers are saying the most horrible things about me. Blaming me for what happened. They say *nothing* bad about the kidnappers who took our son.'

'Well it's what you wanted isn't it?' Max threw at her with hostility.

'What do you mean, it's what I wanted?'

'You wanted to be famous. Now you are. You know the old saying Ellen, "be careful what you wish for".'

'I didn't want to be famous like *this* Max. Not with anything that involved our son. They're even accusing me of having something to do with Josh's kidnapping. Just like that horrible detective who interviewed us.'

'And did you have anything to do with it?'

'*What*? How can you even ask me that Max? I am your *wife*! You should be just as outraged as me with what they are printing. You were outraged enough to phone the big chief when they accused *you*. I am Josh's *mother*. He is *our* son and those people took him.'

'You *were* his mother.'

'What?'

'You were his mother. Josh is dead Ellen, so stop talking about him as though he's not. He. Is. Never. Coming. Home. Again.'

'I know that,' she said in a quiet voice, 'but I'm still his mother whether he's alive or dead. And he's still our son.'

The look of hostility on Max's face faded and his shoulders slumped.

'I'm sorry,' he said. 'You're right.' He walked over to her, put an arm around her and pulled her close to him.

'I can't stand it Max. Our little boy, gone just like that.

I can't believe I'm never going to hear his voice or see his sweet little face again.'

She began sobbing.

'I know,' Max said. He released her and walked away without another word.

Ellen felt more alone than ever. She needed her mum and couldn't understand why she hadn't phoned her back. She'd left a message with her mother the other day and then tried again the next day but the phone had been constantly engaged. They hadn't spoken for days now. Looking at the clock on the mantle Ellen saw that it was too early to phone. Her mother would still be at work. She'd phone later and ask her and dad to come over. She could send her a message though. But where had she put her mobile phone? She hadn't looked at it for days and didn't have a clue where it was. She wouldn't be surprised if Max had hidden it in case she tried to talk to anyone in the press. She'd heard nothing from her sister or any of her friends either. Had they all abandoned her or was it that she just hadn't picked up their messages? The battery would be flat by now. She couldn't remember the last time she'd charged it.

She found Max in their bedroom and she walked in to speak to him.

'Have you seen my mobile phone Max?'

'No. I've no idea where it is. Why do you want it?'

'I want to send my mother a message. I'd like to see my parents and I want to ask them to come over today. You've had your parents here a few times. Now I'd like mine to come over if they can make it.'

Max nodded. 'I can understand that. Your phone isn't

in here. You must have taken it into Josh's room.'

Twenty minutes later she located her phone under Josh's bed. It was dead. She'd need to charge it and then she could see if any of her friends and family had been in touch. She was about to tell Max she'd found the phone when she realised he was talking to someone on the landline. His mother probably. She waited until he finished his call and popped her head around their bedroom door where he'd retreated to and was in the process of getting changed.

'I found my phone, but the battery is dead. I'm going to charge it now.'

'Right, well I'm heading off to mum and dads.'

'Won't they be at work?'

'Dad will be. Not mum. I told them to hand in their notice once it was confirmed we'd won the money. Mum's not returning to work and she didn't have to give much notice anyway. Dad still has another couple of weeks to go. I plan to pay off their mortgage, and give them some money, just so you know.'

'Of course. I'd like to do that for my parents as well.'

'Yes, fine. What about your sister? Won't she be expecting the same?'

'I don't know if she would be expecting it, but I'd like to do something for her and her family.'

Max nodded.

'What time will you be back from your parents?'

'I'll eat with them, so probably about eight.'

'Okay, mum and dad should be here by then if they're able to come. Do you mind if they have our bed for the night? I'll sleep in Josh's bed and you could sleep on the couch.'

'What about the policewomen? They usually doze a bit on the couch.'

'I'll tell them we won't need them tonight. Not if my parents are here.'

'Okay. I'll see you later then.'

Cheryl had watched and listened to the earlier exchange between the couple from the living room. The double doors that led from the dining room to the living room had been left open and she couldn't help but hear what was said.

She'd seen some of the papers' headlines before she'd come on duty and had read the comments made about Ellen on her phone. Ellen was right, she hadn't read one derogatory comment about the kidnappers. Only Ellen. What was wrong with these people? The woman had just lost her son. There wasn't one scrap of empathy for her. She found it hard to believe the public could be so brutal as well. They were obviously influenced by what the papers were printing. The vitriol directed at Ellen from on-line comments on social media was horrific as well. From total strangers.

She thought Max Gibson's words to Ellen about wanting to be famous was another example of the cruelty he'd directed at her. When he apologised and put his arm around her she thought finally, he's going to stop this. But then in the next minute he walked away without a word. She didn't think the couple were going to survive this tragedy. She wasn't sure how much more she could take of being in this house either. She walked outside to get some fresh air, pulled out her mobile and tapped on to the number of a friend. She wanted to talk to someone about anything other than her work for a short time.

30

When India and Jacko walked into the squad room Talbot and Penn were pouring over maps. Talbot looked up and she could see he was angry. *What now?*

'Where have you two been?' he asked.

'We went to gather information from Roger Lansford—'

'Yes, yes I know that. But that was more than two hours ago.'

So he was keeping tabs on them.

'Lansford gave us information about a large apple orchard business up in Kurrajong. Jimmy worked on the property every year at harvest time. We've been up there to interview the owner of the business.' She didn't mention that they'd stopped at the bakery on the way back and sat in the car eating their pies.

'Did you learn anything useful?'

'We've ruled it out as a possible burial site.'

'I think trailing around to all these properties is a total waste of police time and resources.'

'I don't agree. We've compiled a list of properties and the owner's names; some—'

'Are you really expecting me to approve you visiting every single property in the area?'

'As I was attempting to tell you, we can eliminate some from their size and with a simple phone call. Others we'll need to visit.'

'You don't really think that any householder is going to admit to being associated with Jimmy Lansford do you? They'd be worried about being hauled in as suspects. No, it's a waste of time and I won't agree to it.'

'You don't have to. Superintendent Havering has already given us the go ahead on it. He is my area Commander and the person I answer to. And some of Lansford's employers will be listed in his tax records. They won't be able to deny employing him. What are *you* proposing to do instead?'

'I want to bring in Ellen Gibson for questioning again. I'm sure I can make her give up the name of her accomplice. She must have been working with someone other than Jimmy Lansford. He'll be the brains behind it all.'

'I'm sure the person working with Jimmy Lansford *was* the brains behind the kidnapping, but you can't seriously still think Ellen Gibson had anything to do with it. And it was only a couple of days ago that she learned of her son's death.'

'That's exactly why I think she'll cough up a name. She wasn't expecting that. She was expecting her son to return home alive and well.'

'No,' India said shaking her head. 'You can't do it.'

'You're stepping out of line here Ms. Hargreaves. *I* am the Senior Investigating Officer on this case.'

'It's *Detective Inspector* Hargreaves, and nothing you've done so far has taken the investigation forward. It was *our* team who found the cabin. It was *our* team who made the connection to Jimmy Lansford and were called to the scene after his death.'

'Enough!' Talbot shouted at her. 'We are going to bring Ellen Gibson in again whether you like it or not.'

'We'll see about that,' she said walking into her office and closing the door. She'd really wanted to slam it, but that would have just given Talbot more ammunition to suggest she was just an emotional woman. Bloody chauvinist!

She put a call through to the Super and told him of Talbot's intentions. In view of the complaint made by Max Gibson and his parents, he was equally horrified at the prospect. After hanging up the phone she sat staring at it for a minute, feeling uncomfortable. Running to the boss telling tales on a colleague was not something she would normally do. But there was no reasoning with Talbot. She'd attempted to talk him through everything the other day before he'd brought Max and Ellen Gibson in for questioning. She was sure he hadn't looked at the reports she and Jacko had written after interviewing the couple. Talbot hadn't spent any time in their company and hadn't been able to form a picture of them. He'd insisted that he wanted to speak to them separately in a more formal environment. As Rob pointed out, that was standard procedure. Okay, but he'd done that and had since honed in on Ellen Gibson, convinced she was involved. When India had spoken to him again after the interviews he was even more convinced that Ellen had been involved in her son's kidnapping, but couldn't justify his reasons for thinking this other than he thought she was withholding information. Jacko had played back the interviews and he'd told her that the two detectives had been quite easy going on Max Gibson, but had given Ellen a really hard time, attempting to trick and confuse her. She wasn't surprised to hear that. Perhaps Talbot was a misogynist and hated all women for some personal reason. He certainly hadn't shown her a great deal of respect. He'd virtually ignored Marlee and had spoken abruptly to Dale, the department's admin assistant. That was probably it. She wasn't sure whether Talbot was being swayed by what the press was saying or whether the press were printing theories Talbot or Penn had fed to them. She'd seen the papers today and Rob was right. They were crucifying that poor woman.

'*Leave it with me,*' Havering had said before disconnecting the call.

She wasn't sure if she'd done the right thing, but from what she'd last seen of Ellen Gibson and from the feedback Jacko had given her, Ellen seemed on the verge of a nervous breakdown. Being hauled in by Talbot again might just tip her over the edge.

She picked up the duty chart to see who would be at the Gibson house right now. It was Cheryl Comer. Good. She phoned Cheryl's mobile to get an update on how things were at the house. As the listened to Cheryl she was horrified to hear about the incident at the shopping mall. She considered phoning Havering back to ask him to get onto the press about the issue. It was largely the papers who were creating the public's reaction to Ellen.

Cheryl also went on to tell her about the unpleasant words Max had thrown at Ellen. She could understand that Max Gibson was a grieving father, but it sounded like he had been unnecessarily cruel to Ellen.

'I'll pop over and see Ellen in a bit,' she told Cheryl. After hanging up she looked out into the squad room to see Talbot disconnecting a call. He looked furious and stormed out. He must have been talking to Havering. She placed another call to Marlee's mobile to find out where she and Jun were.

'We're just on our way back. No joy at the three places we've been to.'

'Okay. Look I don't know if you've seen the papers today. Ellen Gibson went out shopping with the duty officer this morning and there was a nasty incident. She's now read everything the papers are saying about her. I want to call in to see her and would like you to come with me.'

'Okay, no worries, I'd be happy to come with you. I've read it all on my phone. They've made some pretty harsh allegations about her. See you in a bit.'

India forgot that young people didn't read newspapers. They used their phones for everything.

31

Ellen dialled her mother's house at 4pm thinking she should be home by now. Her mother answered after two rings.

'Hello Mum, it's Ellen.'

'*Oh, darling we've been so worried about you.*'

'Why didn't you call me then? I've needed you. Have you seen what they've been writing about me in the paper? It's all lies!'

'*Of course they're lies darling. We know that and we've been calling every day. I've spoken to Max quite a few times. Hasn't he told you?*'

'No, Max and I haven't been speaking much.'

'*Each time I phoned he said you were sleeping and he didn't want to disturb you. I was beginning to think something awful had happened and then I spoke to a nice policewoman who was at your house and she told me the doctor had been to see you and you'd been sedated. I spoke to Max again this morning and he told me you'd gone shopping. Shopping? What were you thinking Ellen? Why on earth would you go shopping?*'

'We had no food in the house mum. The police have been bringing in take away meals, but you know what

I'm like. I can't eat too many of those kinds of things. I wanted some *real* food.'

'*Max said his parents had been bringing around cooked meals for you both.*'

'Yes, Pamela has been bringing meals for Max. Not me. She's brought things she knows I won't eat. I'm sure it's deliberate.'

'*I'm sure it's not. She's just probably thinking of providing her son with some comforts.*'

'Exactly. Her *son*. No-one else. Anyway, why haven't you and dad come over?'

'*I've offered to a couple of times but Max said there was nowhere to accommodate us and the place was full of police who stayed overnight. He said we'd be in the way.*'

'It was selfish and wrong of him to say that. You'd *never* be in the way. *One* policewoman we've had staying each night. They did have others on duty here as well at first, but now just one officer has been staying over. You could come and stay. You and Dad could sleep in our room. I can sleep in Josh's room. I've been sleeping in his bed anyway. Max has agreed to sleep on the couch. Can you come over today? Like now?'

'*We were planning to drive down today anyway and were not going to take no for answer from Max this time. We've been so worried about you. I tried to phone you back earlier but the phone was constantly engaged.*'

'Max was talking to his mother.'

'*Okay. Your father and I have taken some time off work. We looked at booking into the Motel in Windsor yesterday, but it's full they told us and is booked out for the next week. Your father thinks that's where the press will be staying, so it's probably a good thing we're not going to be staying there. We found another one in Richmond that has a vacancy and decided that's where we'd go tonight if we need to.'*

'You don't need to. You can stay here. When are you coming then?'

'Dad's just gone to the garage to fill up with petrol, check the oil, water and tyres etc. When he comes back, we can set off. Is there anything you'd like us to bring?'

'No, we're fine now. I did a big shop this morning. I bought a load of steaks hoping you might come and haven't put them in the freezer yet. We can have them for dinner tonight with some fresh salad. Dad could barbeque them. Look, there's a road block down from our house because of the reporters. The police are there to stop them coming up to the house. I'll make sure they have your names so they'll let you through.'

'Okay darling, we'll be with you real soon. We'll be hitting peak hour traffic as we approach Sydney so it might take a while, but we'll be with you as soon as we can.'

Ellen hung up feeling much better now her parents were coming to stay. Max had had loads of comfort and support from his parents, while she'd felt totally alone. The only comforting words she'd had were from that nice policewoman Cheryl. Now it was her turn to be looked after. She went in search of Cheryl to tell her to cancel her colleague coming tonight and make sure the police at the road block had her parent's names.

India and Marlee arrived at the house at five pm. Cheryl let them into the house and took them through to the kitchen. India heard the sound of a vacuum cleaner coming from the front bedroom.

'Ellen's preparing the large front bedroom for her parents. Changing the linen, vacuuming it and tidying it up. They're on their way from the Central Coast to come and stay with her.'

'Will this be the first time they've visited the house since Joshua's disappearance?'

'Yes. Ellen said that Max had told them not to come. I've heard him speak to them on the phone, but I've not heard the full conversations of course. It was always when Ellen was asleep. She hadn't spoken to them for days until earlier and he hadn't even told her that they'd phoned. She was worried they'd abandoned her as well.'

'As well? Who else has abandoned her?'

'Max's parents. They've been cold shouldering her.'

'Ah right.'

'Ellen's asked me to cancel Rhona coming tonight. I've spoken to Sergeant Morrison and he said he'd check with you. Has he done that yet?'

'No, but I noticed I'd missed a call from him when I was out of the office. I meant to phone him back, but forgot. Why does Ellen want to cancel Rhona?'

'Because her parents will be staying. Ellen will sleep in Josh's bed. She said Max will need the couch and with her parents here there's no room, or any need for the police to be here.'

'Okay, that's fair enough I suppose. Have you checked that the parents are definitely coming?'

'Not yet. Her mother said they'd phone when they were well on their way. I'll speak to her then.'

Ellen walked into the kitchen then with the vacuum cleaner which she carried through to the laundry, waving a greeting to them on the way. A few minutes later she returned with a big smile on her face.

'Hello Detectives. Have you heard my parents are coming to stay?' she said joining them at the table.

'Yes, and I'm pleased to hear that. I'm sure it will be a comfort for you. I'm so sorry about everything that has been printed in the papers Ellen. It's not right and is so unfair,' India said.

Cheryl had told her that Ellen had been in a terrible state. She certainly looked much happier now.

'Thank you. It makes a change to not hear someone blaming me for everything. I can't believe the papers think I was involved in the kidnapping of my own son! Even Max asked me if I had been.'

'I know. I'm sorry.'

'I think it's that detective. What was his name? The one who questioned Max and me?'

'Detective Inspector Talbot.'

'Yes him. I'm sure he's been giving these ridiculous ideas to the press. Otherwise why on earth would they think like that?'

'I don't know Ellen.' She was not about to mention that she had a similar theory about Talbot.

'When he interviewed me he said he *knew* I was involved and kept bullying me to confess.'

'You know what the press are like,' Marlee chipped in, 'they make up stories just to create sensational headlines.'

'That's what Cheryl said, but I'm not so sure. Someone must be feeding them with the idea. How can I stop them saying such things? Max isn't prepared to do anything.'

'I will ask Superintendent Havering to give another statement to the press. He did say at the last press conference that you and Max weren't suspects. But in view of today's stories, I'll have another word with him.'

India felt guilty that she hadn't brought it up in today's conversation with the Super, but she'd been so intent on stopping Talbot, it hadn't crossed her mind until later. She should have phoned Havering again.

'I heard what happened at the newsagent's this morning,' India said. 'It must have been unpleasant for you.'

'It was. I've never experienced anything so revolting in my whole life,' Ellen said, her face screwing up in disgust. 'I would never have imagined a total stranger could do such a thing.'

'There's all sorts out there. Suspects spit at us quite often. Especially at female indigenous ones,' Marlee said pointing to herself.

'Oh, that's so gross! How do you stand it?'

'It's nothing to do with us – or me as an individual. It says more about the person who does the spitting. Like the woman who spat at you this morning. It was about her. Not you,' Marlee said.

'It's good of you to say so, but it felt very personal at the time.'

'I'm sure it did,' India said. 'While we're here – although I should be telling both you and your husband together, I'd like to fill you in on what's happening in the investigation. We've been looking at a range of properties where Jimmy Lansford worked. He's the man who was involved in Joshua's kidnapping. We found nothing at his home so we think he might have buried Joshua and his dog at one of the places he is familiar with. So far we've found nothing, but we're not going to give up. We'll keep looking. We'll find Joshua eventually.'

Ellen sniffed. 'Thank you. We need to bury Josh in a proper grave. One where we can visit him. I can't bear the idea that he's lying out there all alone somewhere. I still can't believe he's gone and keep expecting him to call out for me all the time. I keep getting this tight pain in my chest as though my heart is breaking and sometimes I feel like someone has punched me in the stomach,' Ellen said, tears beginning to streak down her face.

'It's hard to lose a loved one. You'll need time and support to get through it,' India said.

'I know. That's why I need my parents here. I'm certainly not getting any support from Max and he doesn't want it from me. He's got his parents – I've had no-one and I've felt so alone. He didn't even tell me my mother has spoken to him every day.'

Cheryl had just told them about Max not relaying details of the calls from Ellen's parents to her. India was finding it difficult to remain neutral listening to how things had been for Ellen, but it was not her place to speak out against her husband. She just nodded at Ellen without speaking.

'Have you ever lost someone you really love detective?' Ellen asked her.

Ellen's question took her by surprise. She hesitated before replying. 'I've lost people I care about – like my paternal grandparents, but I didn't see them all that often as they lived so far away, so no, no-one that I was very close to. I've had a few miscarriages which I found very distressing, including one last week. That was pretty heart-breaking,' she blurted out without thinking. She struggled to prevent tears forming in her eyes.

Although India was looking at Ellen, she could sense the surprised eyes of Cheryl and Marlee boring into her. The only people she'd told about the miscarriage was Havering and Jacko. The others had been told she had *female issues*. She really didn't want to cry in front of everyone. She was supposed to be the strong one in charge.

Ellen reached out and placed her hand over India's. India swallowed, fighting off the tears.

'I'm sorry you went through that. So you have some idea of what I'm feeling. Thank you for coming to see me,' Ellen said withdrawing her hand and wiping her tears. 'I guess I'd better get on with making the house more presentable for my parents. My mother is very particular. I have the bathroom to scrub yet.'

Ellen felt completely drained of energy when she finished the cleaning. She'd been tempted to leave some for her mother to do, but she knew her mother would have a fit if there was any mess and didn't want her parents' visit to start with a conflict. After a quick shower she sat on the bed in Josh's room and thought about all those vile articles in the paper. She needed to do something to stop them printing all those lies about her. But what? She looked over at Josh's little chest of drawers and thought she might have the answer. She'd have to write a letter first. She had just about enough time before her parents arrived. Her mother had phoned and said they were about an hour away. She'd persuaded Cheryl to leave once the policewoman had spoken to her mother to confirm they would soon be there. It had been long past the time that Cheryl should have gone off duty. Ellen felt sorry for her. She knew being at the house with them was all part of her job, but Cheryl and that other officer had spent long hours with them every day, with no time off. Now they could have a break.

When her phone had been partially charged she'd had had a quick look and seen that she had loads of messages she hadn't read from her mother, sister and friends. She hadn't had time to read them all yet, but it was comforting to know they had been there to support her. She'd look at them later and give her sister a call. She'd left her mobile charging in the living room.

She stood and walked into the spare room and sat down at Max's desk. She'd have to get a wriggle on.

32

Hayley and Neil Shaw, Ellen's parents, were sitting in their car at the side of a busy road waiting for the NRMA to come out and assist them. Their car had spluttered to a stop almost seventy minutes ago now and they'd been told it would be at least another thirty minutes before the breakdown vehicle arrived.

'I can't get any answer from Ellen's mobile and the land line is still engaged,' Hayley said. 'And she didn't reply to the message I sent after we first had to pull over.'

'You don't think she's sulking, do you?' Neil asked. 'You know what she can be like.'

'I don't think so Neil. I know she was looking forward to us coming and she might be upset that we're not there yet, but I doubt that would stop her from answering my calls. Do you think I should try and get a taxi to take me the rest of the way? I'm worried about her.'

'It would cost a bloody fortune from here. We're still at least forty minutes away. Try getting hold of Max.'

Hayley scrolled through her contacts and pressed the number for Max. He answered after a few rings.

'Hi Max, it's Hayley here, Ellen's Mum. We're still

about forty minutes from the house and we've broken down. We've been waiting for more than an hour for the NRMA and they say it will still be some time before they arrive. Is Ellen alright? We can't get through on the land line – it's giving off an engaged single. And Ellen's not answering her mobile.'

She listened to him for a moment and then said, 'I see. Well could you run over there and tell Ellen that we've been delayed? … right, but can't Pamela hold off serving it up for just a little while?'

'He's at his parents,' Hayley told Neil. 'Says his mother is just about to serve up a meal. He's going to ask her if she can wait while he drives home. He didn't sound too keen though. I don't think things are very good between them from what Ellen mentioned.'

'It doesn't surprise me. You know I've never been that keen on the bloke. He's always struck me as a bit of a mean, selfish bastard. Put two selfish people together and you have a disaster.'

'Neil!'

'Well, you know Ellen can be selfish.'

'Hello? He's back,' Hayley whispered to Neil.

'I see. Okay, well can you tell Ellen we'll be there as soon as we can?'

She disconnected the call. 'He said his mother has already plated the food. He's going to eat first then he'll go over there. I just hope Ellen's alright. Why won't she answer Neil?'

'She might be having a long leisurely bath or something and can't hear the phone. Who knows? I'm sure she'll be fine.'

Max disconnected the call to Hayley Shaw and sighed. The last thing he wanted to do was drive over to the house. He'd decided he wasn't going back there tonight and planned to stay at his parents. In fact while Ellen's parents were going to be at the house he didn't want to be there at all and he'd readily agreed to his mother's suggestion that he stay with them. He knew Ellen would start carping on at her parents about his attitude towards her and then he'd get into clashes with Ellen's father. They'd been down that road before.

His mother couldn't stand Hayley Shaw; she thought she was a snob and he thought her suggestion that he stay with them was so she wouldn't have to encounter Hayley and be forced to engage in polite conversation. Max didn't think Hayley was a snob – she was simply very different to his mother. Hayley considered herself a bit of an artist and worked part-time in an art gallery. The two women had very different outlooks on life, led different lifestyles and their tastes in décor and furniture were polar opposites. His mother's tastes left a lot to be desired. At best it could described as gaudy. Nothing she had in the house was cheap though – just a hodgepodge of clashing colours. But it made his mother happy, so he and his father never said a word about it.

Although he would've had to drive over to the house tomorrow for some clothes, he didn't see why he should have to go back tonight. There were police officers there. If the landline was engaged Ellen was probably talking to one of her friends.

Well he wasn't going to rush. He'd enjoy his meal first.

The house was all dark and quiet when Max arrived more than an hour later. There was no sign of either of the police officers who were normally there. He let himself in, turned on the lights and checked the land line. It wasn't sitting on the cradle properly and from the digital display he could see it had been connected to some number for more than two hours! He picked it up and listened. Nobody was there – just a long silence. Bloody Ellen! She hadn't hung it up properly after calling someone. That was going to cost a fortune, were his first thoughts, until he realised he had a fortune now. Still. It wasn't on. He slammed the phone down and called out to her. She didn't answer. He walked to the door of Josh's room and could see her lying on the bed. The bloody woman was asleep again – he'd bet she'd taken one of the tranquilisers the doctor had given her and she probably had her mobile on silent.

He pulled out his phone and tapped in a message to Hayley saying Ellen was asleep and that he would leave a note for her. He didn't want to speak to Hayley again. He grabbed some paper from his desk and wrote a quick note to Ellen, placing it on the dining room table. Before leaving he went into the spare bedroom and packed a small bag of clothes for himself. He left the door unlocked for the Shaw's and the hall light on this time. It wouldn't cost much.

Hayley and Neil Shaw finally arrived at the house at ten pm. There was no answer to their knocking, but the door was unlocked. They let themselves in calling out to Ellen. She didn't answer.

'Max said she was asleep in Josh's room – I'll go and wake her.'

Hayley walked through to their grandson's room and switched on the light. Ellen was still asleep. She walked over and nudged her.

'Ellen darling, we've arrived. I'm so sorry we took so long.'

There was no response. It was then Hayley noticed the pill packets and empty glass on the chest of drawers beside the bed and an envelope addressed to Max. Oh No! She shook Ellen but there was still no response.

'ELLEN,' she shouted. 'Ellen wake up! Oh Christ, Ellen what have you done!'

She rushed back out to the kitchen where Neil was unloading some beers into the fridge.

'Call an ambulance and the police Neil! I think Ellen's taken an overdose.'

33

When India arrived at the Gibson house there were several police cars and an ambulance parked outside. She'd received a call from comms saying there was an emergency at the house and asking her to go over. Rob had driven her because she'd had two glasses of wine whereas he'd only had one.

'Do you want me to come in with you?' Rob asked.

'No. There's no point in both of us losing sleep. I could be here for some time. I called Jacko on the way here; he said he'd make his way over so he can drop me back home.'

'Okay, if you're sure,' Rob said leaning over to kiss her before she climbed out of the car.

Sergeant Morrison met her at the front gate.

'What's happened?' she asked him.

'Ellen Gibson is dead.'

'What? How?' India couldn't believe it and stood shaking her head in shock. It only seemed like a few hours ago that she'd spoken to Ellen. When comms couldn't tell her anything, she imagined it was some sort of family dispute.

'It looks like she took an overdose. Her parents were due to arrive several hours ago, but they broke down. If they hadn't been delayed and if the husband had checked on her properly I'm sure we'd have a different outcome. The paramedics tried to revive her, but she was gone.'

'I can't believe she intended to kill herself,' India said still shaking her head. 'She seemed much better when I saw her this afternoon and was looking forward to her parents arriving. Wasn't Cheryl with her?'

'No. After the parents said they were less than an hour away, Cheryl left the house. I gave her permission to do so – she was already hours over her normal clocking off time. We had no idea this was going to happen.'

India nodded. It seemed fair enough, but really Cheryl should have stayed until the parents arrived – even if it meant putting in extra hours.

'Max Gibson wasn't here then?'

'No, he's over at his parents. He doesn't know yet. I've just despatched a patrol car to inform him and told them to wait there. Apparently, he drove over here after a frantic call from Hayley Shaw, Ellen's mother. She hadn't been able to get through to Ellen. He took his time coming. Had to eat his meal first. Then after he arrived at the house, he sent a message to Mrs. Shaw saying Ellen was asleep. Clearly he didn't check on her properly or notice the letter addressed to him. Or maybe he *did* notice it and pretended he didn't.'

'She left him a letter?'

'Yes.'

'Have you opened it?'

'No.'

'Well I think that's the first thing I need to do.'

India walked into the house and could see a distressed couple in the living room, who she surmised were Ellen's parents. Jun Li and Marlee had interviewed them after Joshua's disappearance, but she hadn't met them. There were a couple of uniformed officers with them now. She carried on to Joshua's room and could see the paramedics clearing up their equipment. Ellen was lying on the bed, a deathly pale colour; mouth open. India could see from the waxy texture of her skin that she was dead.

'If you had to take a guess, how long do you think she's been gone?' she asked the paramedics.

'A little over an hour I'd say. Too long to revive her. Sorry,' one of them said.

'Right.'

India waited for them to leave. A different type of ambulance would be calling to collect Ellen's body and take her to the morgue. She waited until they left the room, then donned a pair of gloves and walked over to the chest of drawers. There were three lots of pill packets there. The first one she picked up were Lorazepam. It was a recent prescription, no doubt issued by the doctor called to sedate Ellen after news of Joshua's death. The second pack she picked up was Oxycodone, which she knew was an opioid painkiller. She was surprised to see it had been prescribed to Ellen eight months ago. She'd have to find out why Ellen had been prescribed these. She knew it was usually only prescribed to people suffering from cancer or recovering from other conditions.

Had Ellen recovered from cancer? The third pack was Temazepam, which was similar to Lorazepam. It too was an older prescription but like the Lorazepam, each tablet was 20mg. Higher than the average dose doctors prescribed. All the packets were empty. How full had they been?

'Oh Ellen, you silly woman. Why did you do this?'

'From what I understand I don't think she'll be able to answer you,' Jacko said walking into the room. 'Another tragedy eh? What's she taken?'

'A mixture of opioids and benzodiazepines.'

'Bit of a mouthful. In English?'

'The equivalent of Valium and Morphine.'

'Ouch. Not a good mix. How did she get her hands on those?'

'All prescribed. I'm not sure why the opioid one was. Perhaps her parents or Max Gibson can tell us. I can't be sure but I suspect the overdose was a desperate attempt to stop the media attacks against her and turn them into articles of sympathy instead. I don't think she was meant to die. Her parents should have been here hours ago. If they had been, she would have survived I'm sure.'

'What about Max. Why isn't he here?'

'We'll have to ask him that, and exactly why he didn't look at his wife more closely when he saw her lying here earlier.'

'He saw her and left?'

'Apparently so. He also didn't pick up the letter she'd left for him. Shall we see what she's written to him?'

India opened the letter and read:

Dear Max,

    I know you blame me for what happened to Josh, but I am not the only one at fault. If we had moved into a luxury hotel as I'd asked, Josh would still be here. If you hadn't gone to work the morning Josh was taken I doubt the kidnappers would have had an opportunity to take him. You are just as much to blame as me. Then there was the checking of the ticket in the first place. If you had checked it, and dealt with it, I probably wouldn't have let everyone in that newsagent hear that we'd won the money and I wouldn't have done such a silly thing like calling the press conference. I know now it was a really stupid thing to do and since Josh was taken I have regretted it over and over again. I am so sorry for putting our child at risk like that. I was so excited at the newsagents when I saw we'd won and I just thought all big winners gave interviews with the press. You see it all the time.

    I would never have intentionally done anything to hurt Josh. The accusations that have been made against me by the press are so horrible. I had nothing to do with his kidnapping as you well know. It hurt me so much when you asked me if I had been involved. I was also really upset that you didn't seem to mind what the papers were saying about me and didn't want to do anything to defend me. If they had been saying similar things about you, I would have been right onto them defending you to the hilt. You told my parents not to come when I really needed them and yet you had the comfort of yours. We *should be comforting each other at this time. Not arguing and blaming each other. I have felt so alone. My heart breaks every moment I think about Josh being gone. I can't bear it and I don't think I'll ever recover from his loss. That's why I can't take any more. The pain is too great. Don't think too badly of me. Your loving wife Ellen.*

India passed the letter to Jacko who scanned through the contents. 'Notice she says, "we should be", rather than "we should have been". I think she was hoping that her overdose and this letter might bring them closer together,' she said.

'Mm. Do you think Gibson really believed his wife was involved in the kidnapping?' Jacko asked.

'I don't know but he asked her if she was. More than likely just to be cruel. It will be interesting to see what he has to say.'

Cheryl erupted into the room at that point. 'I've just heard the news. It's terrible. What happened? Ellen's parents should have been here about seven.'

'It seems their car broke down,' Jacko said.

'Oh shit. I should have stayed with her until her parents arrived.' She looked down at Ellen and put her hand over her mouth making groaning noises.

Yes, you should have. But India didn't have the heart to say so. She could tell Cheryl was devastated and was no doubt feeling guilty enough as it was.

Jacko pulled a sheet up over Ellen's body. They didn't need to keep looking at her.

'How was she when you left?'

'Really good. The best I've seen her since I've been coming here. She was looking forward to seeing her parents.'

'Yes, I had that impression when I saw her this afternoon.'

'I can't believe she's done this. Why would she?' Cheryl asked.

'I don't think she was meant to die. I think it was a desperate attempt to swing public opinion perhaps,' India said.

'Hm. She was pretty upset with what she read in the papers.'

'Any mother who had lost a child, like Ellen had, would have been. The media has levelled some pretty harsh accusations and judgements on her,' India commented.

'I know. And it's not just them. Social media has gone mad with it – there's comments coming in from all over the world!'

'That's why I don't look at it,' Jacko said. 'Who wants to read what every unpleasant bastard on the planet has to say. I'm not interested in those morons, but I imagine lots of people do read their comments – unfortunately.'

'Where was Max Gibson?' Cheryl asked. 'He was supposed to be home by about eight. That's what he told Ellen before he left.'

'Good question. We'll be going to see him soon, but first we need to go and speak to Ellen's parents. You too Cheryl – and don't show any guilt.'

'Are you aware of any reason why Ellen would have been prescribed strong painkillers?' she asked Hayley and Neil Shaw after introducing herself, Jacko and Cheryl.

They both started nodding.

'When Josh was about one, Ellen was involved in a nasty car accident,' Hayley said. 'She wasn't at fault, another driver went through a red light at speed, slamming into Ellen on the driver's side. Although Ellen was wearing a seatbelt, she suffered spinal, head and leg injuries. Not life threatening, but she was in hospital for several weeks recovering and had difficulty walking for quite a while. When she was ten years old Ellen had a serious leg injury that left her scarred and in terrible pain for years. It meant she had to give up dancing. She could have been a professional – she was a talented little dancer, wasn't she Neil?' Hayley said turning to her husband who nodded. 'The car accident caused a further injury in the same leg and for the pain to flare up again.'

This was all news to India and now she thought about it, she'd never seen Ellen's legs exposed. Ellen didn't wear short skirts; her dresses were always below the knee. For a moment she felt ashamed of the short skirt she'd bought when she was delivering the ransom money, pretending to be Ellen.

'Thankfully Josh wasn't with her when she had the accident. He was at home with Max because he had a cold. Ellen had gone to the supermarket to do their shopping.'

'Ellen, Max and Josh had to move after that,' Neil jumped in to say. 'Eventually anyway. Max didn't want to and made Ellen suffer unnecessarily for months climbing up and down the stairs to their flat on the second floor carrying Josh and the shopping. There was no lift in the block and Ellen just couldn't manage things with all the pain she was suffering. We had to intervene and persuade him to move into a ground floor flat in a different block to make things easier for Ellen.'

'I know that as well as pain in her leg, Ellen suffered neck, shoulder and back pain for ages afterwards. And she had terrible migraines. She was prescribed painkillers. It always worried me that she'd become addicted to them, she came pretty close to that when she was a child. I didn't know she was still having problems or on any medication. I saw the empty tablet packets in there. We had to tell the person on the phone what she'd taken,' Hayley said.

India nodded. 'If it's any consolation, I don't think Ellen intended to kill herself,' she told them. 'She expected you to be here by about seven. She expected Max to be home by eight. I think she thought she'd be discovered in plenty of time, rushed off to hospital, have her stomach pumped and then it would all be tea and sympathy.'

'Bloody stupid girl,' Neil Shaw mumbled, shaking his head as though to ward off tears that were threatening to slip from his watery eyes.

'It's because of everything the press has been saying isn't it?' Hayley asked. 'I saw an envelope addressed to Max. Has anyone read it?'

'Yes, we have,' she told Hayley.

'What did she say?'

'The gist of it was how upset she's been about

everything,' she said.

'Can we read it?'

'I don't think that would be appropriate – not at this time anyway.'

'I'm sorry I didn't stay with her until you arrived,' Cheryl said before India could stop her. 'Ellen encouraged me to go home after I spoke to you. I think by then she must have had this planned.'

'You don't think she invited us down here just to find her unconscious and near death, do you?' Hayley asked with a horrified look on her face.

'No Mrs. Shaw, I don't think that was Ellen's intentions,' India was quick to say. 'She was really looking forward to your visit and was cleaning the place up for you.'

'Yes, she was really excited about seeing you and was talking about having barbequed steaks for dinner,' Cheryl jumped in to say. 'She'd bought quite a few when I was out shopping with her this morning. She said she really needed her mum. That was before Inspector Hargreaves came to see her.'

India could have killed Cheryl right at that moment. She wished she'd kept her mouth shut.

'When I was talking to her this afternoon, she asked what *she* could do to stop the press printing these things about her. I'm sure the idea came to her after we'd gone. I suspect it was an impulsive, spur of the moment plan she devised.'

The horrified look on Hayley Shaw's face relaxed. Instead she looked distraught.

'We didn't expect to break down, and because it was

peak hours, we had to wait for *hours* for the NRMA,' Neil Shaw said. 'I should have let you catch that taxi over here like you wanted,' he said turning to his wife and taking her hand. 'I'm sorry love.'

'I heard about your breakdown. It was unfortunate. We've checked the landline here and this is the last number Ellen dialled,' India said passing them a slip of paper. 'I can see it's a Central Coast code, but as you were on the road, I don't imagine she would have been calling you. Do you recognise the number?'

The couple looked at it before Hayley shot back with, 'It's our daughter Alison's number, but she's away from home tonight. They've gone to Newcastle to collect Dylan, their young son. He's been up with his paternal grandparents because Alison thought she might need to come down here to see Ellen. She's been sending Ellen messages, and trying to reach her on her mobile for days without any response. I've been filling Alison in on what Max has told me.'

'Ellen's phone had been dead for days,' Cheryl said. 'I don't think she'd even thought about it since Joshua disappeared. She was charging it this afternoon. Perhaps she picked up some of the messages and then tried to get through to Alison. She told me she hardly ever used her mobile for calls as it was a basic pay-as-you-go. She only used it for messages or to receive calls.'

'Yes Max was too mean to allow her to have an account phone. One of the first things she said she was going to do with the money they won was to get an upgrade to the best phone she could. Now that will never happen,' Hayley Shaw said and promptly burst into tears.

They all stood awkwardly for a few moments before India said, 'We need to go and speak to Max now. I assume you'll be staying here tonight?'

'Yes,' Neil Shaw said.

'Once again I'm sorry for your loss. I will no doubt see you again soon,' she said turning and indicating that Jacko should follow her.

In the car she phoned Superintendent Havering to give him the news. He cursed and mumbled about 'the bloody press', before saying he'd already organised a press conference the following morning at 10 am. India had phoned Havering after leaving Ellen earlier that afternoon. After filling him in on the incident at the mall, she'd asked him if he could talk to the press again to ensure they knew Ellen wasn't a suspect.

34

India handed Ellen's letter to Max Gibson. When they'd arrived at the house, the two policemen who'd given him the news were still there. They'd been told to wait until the detectives arrived and had now gone. India asked Mr. and Mrs. Gibson senior to leave the room while they spoke to their son. Pamela Gibson had objected and insisted she had a right to stay, but her husband had grabbed her elbow and persuaded her to adjourn with him to the kitchen. India made sure the door from the living room into the dining room was shut.

'You've read this?' Max asked, looking at the letter which India had put into a clear plastic sleeve.

'Of course. We're investigating your wife's *death* Mr. Gibson,' Jacko said. India noticed Jacko had reverted to a formal use of Max Gibson's name.

'But it's addressed to me.'

'That's right. But you weren't there, were you? Did you see the letter and the empty tablet packs and decide to do nothing about it? Were you hoping she'd die? Had she become an embarrassment to you? An inconvenience you wanted to get rid of?' Jacko asked him.

'What? No. Of course not!' Gibson protested, turning bright red.

'Then why didn't you read it when you were at the house tonight?'

'I … I didn't see it. I swear. I didn't turn the light on in the room when I saw Ellen was asleep and didn't go into the room. She's been sleeping so much since Josh was taken. I thought it was just another example of her copping out of things.'

'Copping out?' India challenged him. 'What do you mean by that?'

'I thought she was sleeping all the time so she didn't have to think about her foolish actions. She's done it before.'

'Are you referring to the time when she suffered terrible injuries in a car accident some years ago?' Jacko asked him.

'You know about that?'

'Yes, Ellen's parents told us that was when she was prescribed strong painkillers and tablets to help her sleep.'

'It was, and she slept a lot of the time. She said she was only taking them when I was home to take care of Josh, claiming she was in a lot of pain after looking after him all day.'

'And judging by what we've learned about her injuries she probably was in a lot of pain, having to lift and carry everything up two storeys to your flat – including your son,' Jacko said.

Gibson at least had the decency to look embarrassed.

'I was never sure though. I suspected Ellen was

sleeping a lot during the day as well.'

'Did your son look neglected?'

'No … but Ellen … I thought she'd become addicted to the tablets and it was all in her head. That's why I wouldn't move at first. I wanted her to stop taking the tablets.'

'Even if it was in her head, and I'm not convinced it would have been, the pain would have been real to her. Did you talk to anyone about it?'

'Only mum. She … never mind,' he said shaking his head.

'So you didn't seek professional advice?' India asked cutting in.

'No. Ellen saw a specialist every so many months. And our local doctor. I never spoke to them.'

'Were you aware that she still had painkillers in her possession?'

'Yes. I knew she'd had to get a new prescription last year some time. She still had the odd problem she claimed – she spent a couple of days in bed just after Christmas. Anyway, why are you asking me about Ellen's accident? It has no relevance to what happened tonight.'

'I'd have to disagree with you there, *mate*,' Jacko said standing and moving in front of Gibson in a menacing manner. 'What happened back then is directly connected to your wife's death.'

'In what way?' Gibson asked, looking genuinely puzzled.

'Your wife was still using the medication she was prescribed back then. She's been going through a distressing and painful time recently, just like after the accident. And the most important thing of all is your *attitude* and *behaviour* towards her. The same old bullying approach.'

'I wasn't bullying her. I was worried about her after the accident.'

'And in recent weeks? We've heard some of the things you've said to her. I'd call that bullying.'

'I didn't intend to … I was upset and angry. I suppose I took it out on her,' he conceded.

'We've also been told that your wife was sleeping a lot. You must have realised from that that your wife was self-medicating.'

'She only started it after Josh was taken. I suspected she might be taking some of her old medication because she was sleeping a lot. In some ways it suited me because we just kept arguing when she was awake.'

'Because you kept reminding your wife that her actions had been foolish?'

'They *were* foolish. She should never have held that press conference. That's where all the problems stemmed from.'

India decided it was time to break up this little exchange. Jacko's behaviour was verging on bullying. And she was not going to let Gibson get away with that comment. Some of Ellen's actions might have been foolish, but his were not exactly saintly either.

'We don't believe the problems stemmed from the press conference, foolish as it may have been,' she said.

'Then where …?'

'We believe someone at the newsagent overheard Ellen discussing the win with the owner there. That person must have heard her giving him your home address. I suggest you read the letter now Mr. Gibson.'

Gibson blushed red again before turning his attention to the letter. After reading it his face turned pale and he looked like he was going to be sick.

'I ... I don't know what to say. I didn't really think she was involved in the kidnapping. I just said that to hurt her. I was so upset about Josh's death I wanted to hit out at her. Ellen's right. It was my fault as well.'

'It might have been good if you'd said that while she was still alive,' Jacko said.

'Were you aware of the incident that occurred at the shopping mall this morning?' India asked him.

'No.'

'Ellen was spat at and called names by a member of the public. It caused her considerable distress. Then she read everything the papers were saying about her.'

'I didn't know about the incident at the mall. She didn't say. What should I do?' Gibson asked tears beginning to slide down his face. It was the first time India had seen him cry.

'I think it would be a good idea if you made a statement to the press,' she said.

'And say what?'

'Something nice about your wife for a start and you could stress that she wasn't involved in your son's kidnapping. She was a mother who was heartbroken. Superintendent Havering will be giving a statement to the press at ten am tomorrow. You could stand up there beside him. We'll leave you now to work on what you're going to say and collect you at say, nine? That okay with you?' she asked him.

Max Gibson gulped and nodded. He still looked sick.

As they were driving away, Jacko said, 'you know, when I first met Max Gibson, I thought he was a pretty sound bloke, but now ...'

'Yes, I know what you mean. I wasn't sure about him, but he seemed okay. I thought Ellen was a bit of an air-head, who only thought of glamour and money. But I was wrong.'

'Well she *was* preoccupied with celebrity stuff. But that's not all there was to her obviously.'

'Gibson looked quite sick after reading Ellen's letter, didn't he?'

'Anyone would look sick if they sat on a pea green couch looking at a bright red carpet and that clashing large floral print wallpaper surrounded by high-gloss honey coloured furniture,' Jacko said in a bland voice.

India giggled. 'It was all pretty awful wasn't it? Not my taste, but each to their own I suppose. Pamela Gibson would probably think our places were horrendous.'

'She definitely would if she saw your stripped floor boards and would probably say something like, "Couldn't you afford to put down carpets dear?"'

'Stop it,' India laughed. 'I can't comment on your place because I've never seen it.'

'It's just a beige box.'

'What do you mean?'

'Oh, you know, beige walls, beige carpet, beige tiles, beige built-ins, beige bathroom suite, beige kitchen units.

My landlord is one of those people who clearly thinks beige is a good neutral colour for *everything*. He won't let me paint any of the walls. I've had to brighten it up with colourful rugs, and cushions, plus bright artwork and bedding.'

'It doesn't sound too bad to me. But why don't you buy your own place, then you could have it how you want.'

'I intend to. Maybe next year. Right here you are your highness. Safely delivered home.'

India looked up surprised. It was one of the first car journeys she'd had with Jacko where she hadn't been nervous about his driving. He'd actually driven like a *normal* motorist and not a policeman on his way to an emergency.

'Thanks, Jacko,' she said, climbing out of the car. 'I'll see you in the morning. Don't forget we have to pick up Gibson around nine.'

'I won't. I'll meet you at the station at shortly after eight-thirty. I don't want to be in before then after this late stint. You okay with that?'

'Absolutely, I don't intend to go in before then either.'

35

Thursday

Max Gibson stood between Superintendent Havering and India, with Jacko standing immediately behind him. She half suspected Jacko would start prodding Gibson if he said anything inappropriate.

'Once again I am sorry to say I am here to relay tragic news to you,' Havering began. 'Late last night twenty-nine-year-old Ellen Gibson, mother of five year old Joshua Gibson, died of an accidental overdose of her medication.' He paused for effect and India could hear murmuring among those gathered. 'A child's death is distressing enough for a young mother. But the suggestion that she was responsible for her son's death, and the personal attacks on her character caused her even greater distress. I hope you will all take a moment to reflect on this matter. Ellen Gibson was not involved in her son's kidnapping. Now Max Gibson would like to say a few words.'

Gibson cleared his throat and there was a few moments of silence before he started.

'From when she was a young girl my wife Ellen dreamed of being a famous dancer. It was one of those fantasies young girls have and she was very good I was told. She'd studied dancing since she was tiny. A serious injury to one of her legs, caused from a deliberate assault, meant she had to give up that dream. For years she watched reality shows seeing different men and women being propelled into stardom and wished she was one of them. When she discovered we'd won Powerball she saw it as an opportunity to be in the limelight. She thought all big winners gave interviews to the press. Now would be her chance of becoming famous. Very soon after doing the interview, Ellen regretted it. When our son was kidnapped, she blamed herself and thought it was because she'd done the interviews. It wasn't. And she wasn't to blame. I was just as much, if not more to blame. I didn't take the time to check our ticket. I left it all to Ellen and she had to go into a newsagent to do that. I had taken our laptop with me on a trip up north so she couldn't check the winning ticket number on-line. Then when she discovered we'd won, she wanted to go to a luxury hotel and live in style for a bit. I wouldn't. She asked me not to go into work the day after we learned of our win. I went to work. If I hadn't gone to work and if we had moved into a hotel, both our son Joshua and Ellen would still be alive today. I'll have to live with that knowledge for the rest of my life. My wife adored our son and was an excellent mother. She was very distressed that people would think she would do anything to harm Josh. She wouldn't. Yesterday my wife became very upset after she was assaulted by a member of the public.

She was also distraught about everything she read in the papers. She swallowed a load of prescribed tablets in desperation. Those tablets had been prescribed due to injuries she'd received in a car accident a few years back. An accident that wasn't her fault, but caused by a motorist who drove through a red light. If I had been home last night I would have been able to save her, but wallowing in my own grief I had left the house to seek comfort from my own parents. Ellen's parents were due to be at our house, but unfortunately their car broke down and by the time they received roadside assistance and arrived at the house it was too late for Ellen. My wife's death was a tragic accident. One thing everyone seems to have forgotten in this whole sad business is that the people who *kidnapped* Joshua are the real villains here. Not me, nor Ellen. One man with learning difficulties, it would appear, was duped into taking part in it and both my son and the man's dog tragically died in the process. That man buried our son in an unknown grave before taking his own life. But out there, there is another man, or woman, who was behind this, who knows where Joshua is. And who is sitting with a very large pot of money. I implore you, the press and public, to remain vigilant. If someone you know suddenly turns up with a *lot* of cash, and I am talking millions here, then please report them to the police. Thank you. That is all I have to say.'

'No questions,' India said. 'Please respect that.'

They turned and led Max Gibson into the station. He had shown them his speech and apart from the end where he'd wanted to add in a reward, India had approved it. Havering said it was okay for him to include the reward, but she had persuaded him to hold off on that for a while. It was alright for the Super, he wouldn't have to handle the hundreds of calls they would be receiving – mainly from crackpots.

'Well done,' she said to Gibson.

He nodded. She almost felt proud of him. Almost. He'd at least had the decency to clear Ellen's name and admit his culpability. The press would have a field day with all that. Now it would be his turn to be on the receiving end of their vitriol.

'I need to get back home and discuss funeral arrangements with Ellen's parents. When will you be releasing her?'

'I'm afraid it won't be for some days yet. A post-mortem will have to be completed.'

'I'll have to give them a timescale. Do you think it will be three days, four days or longer?'

'I couldn't tell you at the moment, I haven't had time to speak to the pathologist. I will contact her and then let you know.'

36

'Superintendent Havering pulled me aside just before we left to tell me Talbot and Penn are off the case. I kept my face a deadpan mask when he told me.'

'But I bet inside you were jumping for joy,' Jacko said.

'No. It was more relief, mixed with guilt. You know I went to the Super to put a stop to them bringing in Ellen for questioning again.'

'I kind of gathered that.'

'I wasn't happy about doing it, and in some ways, it might have been better if they had brought her in. Maybe she'd still be alive.'

'You don't know that. She might have found another time to take that desperate step. Or she might well have been committed. As you told Talbot, she seemed to be on the verge of a breakdown.'

'She rallied when she knew her parents were coming to stay. And it would be better for her to be in a psychiatric ward than dead though.'

When they arrived back at the station India and Jacko

found two uniformed constables waiting for them. They were to be part of their team in today's property search. Sergeant Morrison was leading one team, and Jun Li and Marlee another, each with uniformed officers who had been assigned to them. The other teams had set out at eight and each had a target of searching two properties today. So far, they'd excluded nine properties, including the Kurrajong and Agnes Banks ones. With the owner's co-operation, and sometimes participation, they would scour every part of the property, looking for signs of any recently disturbed soil. It was a time-consuming process, but one she was determined they would complete.

She needed to find where Joshua was buried and hoped it would provide other clues linked to his kidnapping. Forensics had come up with very little for them to work on. Every piece of evidence that was available to them, only led to Jimmy Lansford. Roger Lansford was still on their radar and they were keeping an eye on him, but so far, he looked squeaky clean.

Despite the early hour the teams must have met, it was clear that a plate of chocolate monte biscuits had been shared over the briefing. Two solitary biscuits remained on the plate surrounded by crumbs, evidence that they'd had earlier companions. India leaned over and scooped up one of the biscuits.

'You left these for us I assume?' she said, addressing the two constables. 'Jacko, take the last one before I do.'

'No, help yourself, I know how much you love them. It's a good thing you two didn't finish them off or you would have been in for a difficult time today,' Jacko said.

'We were tempted,' one of the men said.

India didn't recognise either of them.

'What are your names?'

'I'm Morgan,' the one who had spoken said.

'That's your first name?' she asked him, unsure whether he was quoting his surname at her.

'No my first name's Lyn,' he said. 'Welsh origins. I prefer to just be called Morgan.'

She could understand why, suspecting he would have received some ribbing about his first name. She turned with a questioning look to the other constable who had remained silent.

'Adrian Oliveira. It's Adriano really, but I've dropped the 'o'. I prefer just Oliveira as well.'

'Italian origins?'

'No Portuguese. Third generation.'

'Interesting.'

'What do we you call you Ma'am?' Morgan asked.

Jacko laughed.

'Certainly not "ma'am". Some people call me "boss". Jacko here is one of them. He calls me other things from time to time as well. Other people call me "inspector" or "Detective Hargreaves". I suppose we ought to introduce ourselves. I'm Detective Inspector Hargreaves, and this is Detective Senior Constable Jacko.'

'You can call me Detective Jacko or just plain old Jacko. I don't mind which.'

'Is Jacko your first name?' Oliveira asked.

'See I told you,' India said.

'No, my last name,' Jacko said through gritted teeth.

'I guess we'd better get started then. Have you two got your own vehicle?'

They nodded in unison.

'Good. We can travel in separate cars then. Jacko knows where we're going, so you can follow us.'

India had left it up to Jacko to choose the property they were targeting today. It was one of the larger ones in Castlereagh they'd picked up details of from Jimmy Lansford's tax records and would be the only one they could cover due to their late start and the size of it.

'What type of farm is it we're looking at?' she asked Jacko on the drive.

'Mainly vegetable. Although they grow some fruit as well. It's the Italian one Jimmy Lansford worked at.'

'Ah, so you're hoping to experience some of the famous food Jimmy talked to his cousin about,' she said turning to look at Jacko.

'You got me there,' he said sporting a cheeky grin. 'But there's another reason I chose this farm.'

'Oh, what was that?'

'The owner's name is Paramo. It's not a very common name and I wondered if they might have a connection to your old boss.'

Jacko was referring to Joe Paramo, her mentor, and a detective inspector she'd worked with almost thirteen years ago when she'd been stationed in Parramatta. He was murdered and an attempt had been made for it to look like suicide. She and Jacko had had a few conversations about Joe.

'I've no idea. I know some of his family were in the fruit and veg business, but from what I understood they owned a number of shops, not farms.'

'It wouldn't harm to ask them if they're related. If they are, it might help to melt the ice with them a little more.'

'We'll see. I'm not sure it's something that may be appropriate to raise, given that we're going to be trampling all over their property today.'

The property owner greeted them out at the front of the main house. India introduced the team, before he reciprocated.

'My name is Luca,' he said. 'This is my mother Gabriella and my son Joey. Joey, or Joe as he prefers to be called now, was named after my cousin. He was in the force as well, killed in the line of duty.'

She looked at Jacko. It sounded like the family *were* connected to her old boss. The boy must have been born many years before Joe's death as he looked to be in his mid-twenties. The cousins must have been close then. She had a vague recollection of Joe mentioning he was meeting up with a Luca once or twice.

'I worked with a Detective Inspector Joe Paramo in Parramatta,' she told them.

'Thatsa him,' Gabriella said enthusiastically. She was clearly the matriarch of the family. 'My husband's nephew. Lovely boy. They say terrible things abouta him when he first die. But we knew they not right.'

She suspected Gabriella, who looked to be in her late seventies or early eighties, had spent most of her life in Australia, but she still spoke with the accent of someone who was learning English. She probably was in a way, if she used her mother tongue most of the time.

'I had a lot of respect for DI Paramo. He was my boss.'

Gabriella nodded, shedding tears as though she'd just heard the news of his death. She used her apron to wipe her face and smiled. 'I make a nice meal for later. You come back to the house to have – in garden,' she said. 'Snacks for lunch as well.'

India could sense the smile she knew would be on Jacko's face.

'Thank you, but you shouldn't go to any trouble,' she said, thinking Gabriella's snacks would probably be far more appealing than the sandwich she had in the car.

'Is no trouble.'

'Righto mamma, we need to get on now.' Turning to India, Luca said, 'We have a couple of lemon and orange orchards, plus all the vegetable paddocks. Where would you like to start?'

Luca volunteered to accompany India so he could answer her questions about Jimmy.

'How often did Jimmy work for you?' she asked him

'A couple of times a year. He'd come and stay over for a few weeks at a time. We have accommodation quarters for workers not far from the house. He was a lovely young man. I can't imagine how he became involved in the kidnapping of a young child.'

'That's what everyone seems to say about him but someone, somehow, persuaded him to get involved.'

'Mamma adored him and spoiled him rotten because he loved her food and was such a good worker.'

She nodded.

The property was much larger than she had expected. It was hot and thirsty work trudging through paddock after paddock. She was impressed with the operation they had, which Luca explained serviced the three fruit and veg shops the family owned.

'Of course, we have to buy in produce as well,' he told her.

They broke for lunch after a couple of hours, with one of Luca's daughters driving down to collect them. If the cold spread they were greeted with was considered a snack, India dreaded to think what a meal would look like.

Towards the end of the day, Jacko and Joe joined India and Luca down in the far-left corner of the property where Joe had mentioned they'd spotted animal diggings recently. It was a shaded area surrounded by a clump of trees and it did look like someone or something had been digging near the trees.

'Rabbits, I'd say,' Luca said when he inspected it. 'Have you checked this out Joe?'

'Yeah, but we couldn't find any trace of them. They've probably moved out over the back.'

India thought the holes were too large to be potential rabbit burrows, which she mentioned to Luca.

'You'd be surprised,' he said. 'Some of the males we get around here are bloody enormous. Rabbits are a perennial problem for us as you can imagine. We have to go over the back here and clear them out all the time.'

India wandered over to the boundary fence and looked out across the back of the Paramo property. It looked like waste land that ended at the river. She couldn't see the river from here, but it must be nearby. She could see some kind of track.

'Where does that track lead to?' she asked.

'It runs right along the back of our properties eventually ending at a road.'

Just the kind of isolated spot Jimmy might choose to bury Joshua and his dog.

'Who owns the land?'

'All of us property owners along here. It's a fire break. As you can see there's lots of trees and bush around here – even though we don't have that many on the farm.'

'We need to check out every inch of that track,' she told Jacko. 'That can be tomorrow's task with everyone involved. And we need to look at every property that backs onto it. This needs to be our priority now. Let the other teams know.'

'On it,' Jacko said taking out his phone and moving away from them.

'It mustn't be far down to the river. Has your land ever been flooded?' she asked Luca.

'The river's not that close. There's the Cranebrook Creek first. In the fifty odd years we've been here we've never been flooded. Not on the farm itself anyway. The water levels have risen on the creek and there's been water almost up to this fence. But as you can see the land rises steeply here which keeps us safe. I couldn't tell you about before that. We didn't own all the land back here when my grandfather first settled it. He acquired more from the next-door neighbour as the businesses grew.'

'Who owns next door and what do they do there?'

'Old man Farrugia. He's Maltese. He raises some beef cattle for the market, but mainly breeds and rears cattle for the dairy industry. Although he keeps a couple for milking, he doesn't run a dairy himself, but sells the females on to dairy farms.'

'Do you know if Jimmy ever worked for him?'

'I doubt it. Jimmy always said he didn't work with animals. And I can't imagine Farrugia bringing in any outside casual labour. He mainly uses family members for all the work.'

'Are there ever cattle in the paddock adjoining yours here?'

'Sometimes. Not very often. As you can see most of it's pretty dry. He doesn't irrigate it. And I know he's had problems with cattle climbing over that outcrop of rocks there and injuring themselves. Apparently, there's pockets of grass growing in amongst them. Probably from seeds carried in by the wind.'

She looked across to where he was indicating. It was like a large mountain of rock exploding up from the land. They needed to search it. They needed to search everywhere.

Over the following week, every square inch of the track that ran along the back of properties, including the Paramo one, was searched, without any success. Every depression or looser soft soil was examined. They'd also looked through all the properties, including Farrugia's

– despite his protests. Jimmy could easily have accessed his land, or any of the other farms and smallholdings that ran along the track. India was disappointed. She'd had one of her "gut feelings", as Jacko put it, convinced it was the area Jimmy had dug the makeshift grave.

37

Hayley and Neil Shaw persuaded Max to hold Ellen's funeral up on the Central Coast to avoid members of the press and the public showing up. Max thought that Ellen might have quite liked the media at her funeral.

He had initially wanted Ellen to be buried near Windsor so that when they found Josh he could be buried with her.

'Joshua can still be buried with Ellen up at the Central Coast,' Hayley protested.

'But we can't visit him easily there,' his mother argued.

'It would be the same for us if Ellen and Josh were buried around Windsor,' Hayley reminded her.

Max could see it was going to turn into an all-out war, so he'd conceded. Hayley and Neil had told him their family members were all cremated. They'd shifted their position on that when he mentioned he wanted Josh buried with her. They were still hoping that Josh would be found in time for them to be laid to rest together. But as time dragged on it was obvious that was not going to happen.

He made an appointment to see Detective Inspector

Hargreaves. During their phone call he'd informed her of the funeral date, time and place. She'd told him a group of them would like to attend. But he wanted to discuss the option of offering a reward as he'd suggested weeks back.

'If you really want to offer a reward, then I think now would be the time,' Detective Hargreaves told Max when they met. 'We've had no luck with the searches as you know. We had quite a few calls came in following your statement and appeal, but nothing that has led us anywhere. I think offering a reward will bring much of the same, but in far higher numbers.'

'That can only be a good thing surely?'

'Not necessarily. We'll have every Tom, Dick and Harry phoning in to report a friend, neighbour or relative that has had a supposed big win on the pokies, lotto, horses – or something similar. We've had some of that already. They don't seem to get that we are talking about *millions*, not a few thousand.'

'Right. So you don't think it will be helpful?'

'It could be; the chances are slim, but money motivates people differently to heartfelt appeals.'

'I think I'd still like to do it,' he said. 'As you told me on the phone, you've exhausted all other lines of enquiry. So how can we go about doing this?'

Despite the details being cloaked in secrecy, members of the press did turn up at Ellen's funeral. Invitations had been limited to family members and a couple of Ellen's close friends. Plus, the police. India suspected someone at the funeral home or one of Ellen's friends had leaked it. They remained unobtrusive though, standing at a respectful distance and not approaching anyone.

She had attended Ellen's post-mortem with Marlee and had seen the scars on Ellen's right leg from her childhood accident. It had caused tears to form in her eyes when she thought about all the pain the young woman had suffered in her short life. Ellen's foolish attempts to stop the media from repeating lies about her had led to this tragic death. Just nine days after discovering they'd won fifty-five million dollars here she was lying dead on a stainless steel slab instead of living a life of luxury. And her son was also dead, buried god knows where.

India was attending the funeral with Jacko, Marlee, Cheryl and Rhona. If the funeral had been held in Windsor, she was sure a much larger number of the force would have turned out. Jun Li and Sergeant Morrison would have attended. Even the Super might have come. But they were all dealing with urgent matters in their line of work. Jun Li and Marlee had been recalled to Richmond. Superintendent Havering had scaled their team down, saying he could no longer justify so many people being involved. Not without any new leads. He was still going to allow them to continue enquiries and this reward business was going to keep them busy for some time.

38

Windsor November 2019

Detective Chief Inspector India Hargreaves was just about to lock her office up for the day when her phone rang. She sighed knowing it was too good to be true that she would manage an early night.

'DCI Hargreaves,' she said answering the phone.

'*Detective Hargreaves, some remains have been found and I know you are going to want to take this one,*' the familiar voice of the desk sergeant said.

'Why do you say that?'

'*It's a child and possibly a dog.*'

'Joshua,' she whispered.

'*It could be. The remains are pretty old and might fit the time frame for Joshua Gibson.*'

'Where were they found?'

'*On a property called 'Morningside' out in Castlereagh. The owner just phoned it in. He'd been working out on the north-western boundary where there is a large rock outcrop. It was while they were breaking it up when they uncovered the remains.*'

She recognised the site he was describing. Almost seven years ago when her team searched the area, she'd believed it was a possible location where Jimmy Lansford could have buried Joshua Gibson. Jimmy was familiar with Morningside which was next door to a property he knew well, and there was easy access from a dirt track behind that ran along the back of both farms.

'How many times did we search that property?'

She recalled that Sergeant Lucas, then a senior constable, had been part of Jacko's team on a second search of the place.

'A couple of times I believe. I remember the rock outcrop he's talking about. Some huge buggers if my memory serves me correctly. We couldn't shift them all, we just searched in all the crevices and where it was possible.'

Clearly not well enough. 'What's the name of the owner again?'

'Hawkins. Brian Hawkins. He'll meet you at the main gate and take you across. You'll need a four-wheel drive he said. I've alerted forensics and the pathologist.'

'Okay, thanks Sergeant Lucas.' Hawkins wasn't the name she remembered. There must have been a change in ownership.

She'd have to phone her mother and tell her that, once again, she'd be delayed. She'd also have to phone Rob and ask him to pick up Sam and Georgia from her parents' house.

After she'd given birth to their first child, Sam, In April 2015, India's parents had returned from Aberdeen, Scotland where her father had been working. He'd since retired and they both helped out with looking after the children. Rob's parents lived out in Bathurst and came to stay when India's parents were away on holiday, but they weren't able to help out with day to day care. Rob had suggested she give up work after having Georgia. But that had never been an option for her. She wasn't the stay-at-home mother type. She'd taken maternity leave with both children, but couldn't wait to return to work, sending them to full time kindergarten. They were lucky the one they used had a baby unit which would take children from the age of six months – around the time India returned to work after her leave. Her mother usually collected both children from the kindy – unless she was able to leave work early. Which didn't happen too often.

Rather than retiring from the force, she had finally accepted a promotion instead, following Georgia's birth. With two children to support the additional income she received as Detective Chief Inspector was useful and it meant she directed events more from the station. For years she'd been happy to remain a Detective Inspector. There'd always been a vacancy for the post of Detective Chief Inspector at the station, but she'd never sought it, and successive District Superintendents had made no effort to replace the previous title holder, who had been her husband Rob.

India hung up the phone after speaking to Rob and knocked on the glass partition to catch the attention of Jacko and Naomi, waving them in.

Jacko had been promoted to senior sergeant and was hoping to rise to a detective inspector. Naomi Partinger had joined them as a detective constable in 2014, and she'd risen through a few ranks to become a Detective Sergeant. Jacko and Partinger hadn't hit it off too well at the start, but now most people would be forgiven for thinking they were a couple. They were always clowning about and were quite tactile with each other. Only Naomi preferred women and had a live-in partner. Jacko was recovering from a recent marriage split that had lasted all of three years. He didn't seem too affected by the split and had a cheerful smile on his face as he entered her office. That would soon go.

'We're off to look at some remains that could prove to be Joshua Gibson,' she told them.

'Holy hell,' Jacko said and added a whistle. 'After all this time?'

'The Powerball winner's kid?' Partinger asked.

'That's the one. It may not be him, but from the report that's come in, I'd say it's pretty conclusive. It's the remains of a child and an animal. Grab your things. I'm taking the squad's 4 x 4. You follow in your car Jacko. This is the address. We'll meet just inside the main gates,' she said, handing Jacko the property details.

'Morningside?' he asked after looking at it. 'We searched that property a few times. Where on the property are you talking about?'

'Remember that large rock outcrop near the rear of the property?'

Jacko nodded.

'Well they've been moving rocks from there today and that's where they've discovered the remains.'

'We looked there, so it must have been some bloody big rock he put them under.'

'Apparently so. We'll soon see anyway.'

'Can I hitch a ride with you, boss?' Naomi asked not looking in Jacko's direction.

'Sure,' she said knowing exactly why Naomi preferred to travel with her.

'My driving isn't that bad!'

'We would beg to differ,' India mumbled walking out of the office.

'We'll see you there,' she called out to Jacko as she pulled out of the car park a few minutes later.

Unless it was an ancient burial, she suspected the remains were those of Joshua Gibson. She hoped so anyway and couldn't bear the idea of investigating the death of another child buried in suspicious circumstances. At least they knew Joshua was dead.

If these were Joshua's remains, it raised the question once again of who Jimmy Lansford was working with. Lansford was a big bear of a man who, they'd learned, lifted cars as a hobby to show his strength. It would have been possible for him to move large rocks to bury Joshua and his dog.

Despite offering a substantial reward they were never able to trace his accomplice – or most of the four million dollars that had been paid out in the ransom demand.

As though reading her mind Naomi said, 'you never found the money the parents paid out, did you?'

'No. We found five hundred thousand in a rucksack in Jimmy Lansford's room. We think Jimmy's accomplice kept the rest of the ransom money. Initially the kidnappers asked for two million, but when Ellen Gibson mentioned two million was a *small sacrifice* to pay out to get her son back, they increased it to four million.'

'A small sacrifice?'

'That's how she put it. She told the family liaison officer she was all flustered when the press questioned her and just said it without thinking and that it was a phrase her husband used all the time with her – telling her she had to make small sacrifices in her spending.'

'Hmm. I remember watching her give interviews after discovering her winnings. She seemed to lap up the publicity. I thought it was bloody stupid. Do you still think Roger Lansford had anything to do with it?'

'As you might have heard – with Jacko and me talking about it – we still keep tabs on him, checking his spending and lifestyle. There has never been anything to suggest he has any money other than his earnings. Roger Lansford had solid alibis for the time of the kidnapping, ransom demands and ransom pay-out.'

She filled Naomi in about Roger Lansford's pattern of behaviour and then went on to describe everything they knew about Jimmy Lansford.

Joshua Gibson's kidnapping was an unsolved crime that had haunted her for almost seven years. Having two children of her own now, she had a greater understanding of what Ellen and Max Gibson went through after the kidnapping. When she and Rob had learned that their daughter Georgia had been born with a hole in her heart, they'd been torn apart with anxiety until the surgeons had successfully operated on her. If it hadn't been successful then … she couldn't bear thinking about that.

'You still hear from Max Gibson don't you?'

'Yes, he was in touch back in January. He phones or

calls into the station every year on the anniversary of the kidnapping to see if there is any new information.'

His contact with them reminded her of Douglas Boyd who'd called into the station each year to see if there was any news on his daughter who'd disappeared more than thirty years before. At least Douglas's story had had a happy ending. He'd been re-united with his daughter and spent many years with her before his death last month. Max Gibson would not have the same happy outcome.

'If this does prove to be Joshua, at least it will give Max Gibson and Joshua's grandparents some closure. He might be able to move away then. Although he had a new house built – with additional security, he's never been able to face moving away – believing Joshua was buried nearby somewhere.'

'That's so sad,' Naomi said.

India turned into a driveway and announced, 'We're here.'

Jacko was standing talking to a man. 'That must be Brian Hawkins, the owner,' she said pulling into a spot next to where Jacko had parked. She'd seen Jacko overtaking her earlier and had chosen to ignore him.

She climbed out of the car to exchange brief greetings with Hawkins who suggested they all follow him. After a slow bumpy drive, they finally pulled up at the site. Some uniformed constables had already taped it off and it looked as though the pathologist was there with forensic technicians. She could see where the digger had been excavating some large pieces of rock.

'Can you wait here Mr. Hawkins? I'll be wanting a

word with you later. Did you touch anything around the remains?'

'I opened the blanket once it was exposed and saw what was underneath it. I didn't touch anything after that.'

'The blanket?'

'The remains were wrapped in a blanket.'

'I see. Thanks,' India said moving off to inspect the find.

39

'It's definitely a young boy around the height and size of a five-year-old,' Doctor Connors, the pathologist said.

India could see the forensics technicians had dug carefully around the body leaving it now fully exposed but had retreated when the pathologist arrived. They were setting up some equipment a short distance away.

'And I'd say the other remains are definitely those of a dog,' Doctor Connor continued. 'I can see no obvious signs of injuries on the child. But we'll have to wait and see what we find when we look at him back at the mortuary.'

'Okay. No obvious injuries would tie in with what Jimmy Lansford said about Joshua having a fit. We think he had an asthma attack.'

The pathologist nodded.

India had to look away quickly after glancing at the remains. They reminded her of photographs she'd seen of unwrapped Egyptian mummies.

'The clothes have rotted as I would expect, leaving just scraps and synthetic thread. The blanket wrapping hasn't deteriorated – neither has the toy bear. I believe we'll find they're both made of synthetic materials. Although the grave was relatively shallow, I think where he was buried, with a large boulder covering the grave site apparently, larger animals would have had difficulty gaining access to the bodies. However, there is evidence of the soft tissue being devoured by insects and some feeding on the skin and tendons. The soil here must be alkaline as the body hasn't reached the advanced drying decay stage. It is still exhibiting signs of black putrefaction. All this indicates alkaline soil – I would say with a lime content. The technicians could tell you more, but this looks like limestone to me.'

'Isn't this area mainly made up of sandstone?'

'Yes. All of the Hawkesbury region, Sydney and much of the Blue Mountains are. Around here I'm not so sure. I know there are limestone deposits out at Bathurst and of course it can be found in the Jenolan Caves. I'm just surprised to find it here. But the greyish colour of the rocks would seem to indicate that it is limestone.'

'So, you'd consider the site to be relatively intact?' India asked her.

'Correct. A cross was placed on top of the body – forensics have taken that and then there is the toy bear you can see tucked under his arm. He has a St. Christopher's medallion on a chain around his neck and he was then wrapped in this blanket,' the pathologist continued.

'Looks like Lansford made an effort to treat Joshua's burial with some respect,' Jacko said peering at the remains over India's shoulder. Naomi was standing beside her.

'We need everything bagged up and sent to the lab.

Can you two remain here with the techies? Get them to take close photographs of the cross and the medallion – once they've removed the St. Christopher from the remains and then ask them to send copies to us. I'm going to speak to Hawkins.'

'No worries boss,' Jacko said saluting her.

'How long since you've removed any rock and stone from this site Mr. Hawkins?' India asked him.

'I've never moved any rocks from here since we owned the property. It's just the missus wanted some for the garden near the house and I wanted some to put some around one of the dams so I decided to take it from here instead of buying any in.'

'How did the body come to be exposed?'

'I asked the man in charge of the digger to move a large boulder so that we could get at smaller rock surrounding it. When he started excavating the smaller stones quite a bit of the earth that was under the large boulder came away as well. I was standing up near it and noticed what looked like a cloth being exposed. I told the digger to stop and had a closer look. I dug around it a bit more and was able to pull the cloth back. I soon realised it was a blanket and when I saw what was inside it I dialled triple zero.'

'How long have you owned Morningside? You weren't here when we searched the property back in twenty thirteen.'

'No, we've only been here four years. We bought it after the previous owner, Farrugia died. His wife was long dead. Apparently the one son who was interested in carrying on with the farm had died in a farming accident the year before.'

She remembered that. The son had been moving some earth when the digger overturned, trapping him beneath it. He'd been working on an isolated part of the property at the time and hadn't been found for many hours.

'The selling agent told us one of his other sons had not long moved to Melbourne, a further son and one of his daughters were in Sydney and his eldest daughter had moved back to Malta so they all wanted to sell. We were based up near Casino before that, but my wife wanted to move down here to be closer to her family.'

Mr. Farrugia had been a memorable character. A grumpy old man who had not been happy about them searching his property back in 2013. He claimed he had never hired Jimmy Lansford. At the time of the kidnapping and their search, Farrugia had had one of his daughters and two sons working with him. All of whom claimed they'd never met Jimmy Lansford. Jimmy must have gained access to the burial site – either through the neighbouring property where he *had* worked or from a track along the rear of the property. Either that or members of the Farrugia family had lied.

After returning to the station, India and Naomi spent the next few hours going through the Joshua Gibson file. Her memory had been correct. There was no mention of a missing cross or a St. Christopher's medallion. They could have belonged to Jimmy Lansford and they'd have to check with Roger Lansford and Max Gibson to see if either of the men could identify them. She didn't think they were the kind of thing that Ellen and Max Gibson would have in their house, but she'd seen some religious statues at Pamela Gibson's house when they'd visited there.

'We need to dig into the Farrugia family's finances,' she said. 'To check and see if they show any signs of acquiring sudden wealth – apart from the money they might have received from the sale of the property. Can you start on that Naomi? I'm going to arrange a meeting with Max Gibson and see if the pathologist has been able to get hold of Professor Alexakis.'

'The remains are definitely Joshua Gibson,' Doctor Connors said. 'We have identified him through dental records and we expect a DNA match once our work here is complete. Professor Alexakis looked at the remains last night. I'm afraid she wasn't able to make it this morning as she was flying out to Melbourne.'

'Was she able to tell you anything new?'

'She confirmed that insects had devoured the tissues and have caused tendon deterioration as I told you at the site.'

'Were you able to establish a cause of death?'

'No. His lungs and muscles have all disintegrated so there is no evidence to suggest he might have died from an asthma attack. And of course there is no mucus, so it's not possible to give you a definitive answer. What I can tell you is we found no injuries on him so there are no obvious signs of trauma to the body. It's likely that we will have an indeterminate cause of death. That's all I can tell you at the moment – although at the burial site you mentioned the man who had been present at his death had said the boy had some kind of "fit".

'That's right.'

'It's possible that the child had a seizure, which led to a panic attack, causing breathing difficulties. One thing that can lead to seizure is dehydration. Are you aware whether the child was given sufficient fluids?'

'No,' India said, recalling details of what forensics had found at the cabin where Joshua had been kept. 'I can't give you an accurate answer regarding fluids. Some water bottles were found at the site where he had been held, but only a couple of small ones. You think that might have led to his death then? Because he was dehydrated?'

'I am only speculating. Like you, I am unable to give you a clear answer on that. We'll be taking hair samples plus bone and bone marrow samples for further screening – including a toxicology screen. They might tell us something although it will be several days before we obtain any results.'

India was disappointed to hear cause of death couldn't be determined. After all this time they would still be left with unanswered questions. Unless they learned to the contrary, they would have to assume his death *was* due to natural causes. If Joshua had been within reach of medical care though, it's likely he could have been saved if he'd had an asthma attack, or was dehydrated.

'His father may want to view the remains,' she said.

'I would advise against that; he is not going to recognise him as his son and he might find it quite traumatic.'

'That will be for him to decide.'

40

India had called Max Gibson the previous afternoon to inform him that they might have found Joshua's body. She hadn't wanted him to hear some remains had been discovered through a leak to the press. He'd asked her to come to his house as soon as she had confirmation. She took Naomi with her for support together with photographs of the cross and St. Christopher medallion and chain. This was not going to be an easy visit.

'I'd like you to keep Pamela Gibson out of the way while I talk to Max Gibson,' she told Naomi. 'She can be a bit controlling and tries to dominate conversations.'

Max Gibson and his parents, who she knew lived with him at the new house, were waiting outside after she'd announced their presence at the security gate. Max had bought the derelict house next door and added the grounds to his own property. The old house where he, Ellen and Joshua once lived was long gone.

'Is it him?' Max asked as soon as she stepped out of the car.

She nodded, but waited until she was standing in front of him to speak. 'Yes, it's Joshua. We have a positive identification from his dental records.'

She noticed him wobble a little and thought his legs might give way until his mother moved up to place her arm around him. 'At least we've finally got little Joshua back Max. He can have a proper burial now. We can put him in our family plot,' Pamela Gibson said.

'NO,' Max said, rather forcefully. 'Josh will be buried with Ellen.'

'But Max—'

'Mum, we've talked about this. I want Josh buried with his mother.'

Pamela Gibson nodded and didn't say another word.

'I want to see him,' he said turning to India.

'I wouldn't advise that Max. He's been in the ground for more than six years and no longer looks like Joshua.'

Over the years, and at Max Gibson's insistence, India had started calling him Max.

'I don't care. I still want to see him.'

India sighed, suspecting he might say this. Some family members needed to see the bodies or remains of their loved ones no matter what the condition. As though they couldn't believe they were gone until they were confronted with the final evidence.

'I'll arrange that for you as soon as possible.'

'Would you like to come in for some refreshments?' Pamela asked them. 'I'm sure Max has some more questions for you.'

'Yes, thank you. Detective Sergeant Partinger could help you,' she said and waited until the three family members turned back into the property before she and Naomi followed. She noticed that Pamela Gibson had said Max would have questions. India hoped that meant she'd stay out of the way.

'What happens next in your investigation?' Max asked her when they reached the lounge. She was pleased to note that Pamela Gibson had not influenced the décor and furnishings in the room, remembering what her house had been like. The room had minimal furnishings, but still had a cosy, warm feel about it.

'We have forensic technicians examining evidence found at the burial site.'

'What sort of evidence?'

'Things that were buried with Joshua, including his toy bear.'

'So they did take Ted,' Max said. 'Ellen said they must have.'

She pulled out the photographs she'd brought with her. 'Do you recognise any of these items?'

Max looked at the photos and shook his head. 'I can see that's a cross. What is this thing?' he asked pointing to the St. Christopher medallion and chain.

'It's a St. Christopher. We found this around Joshua's neck. He didn't wear one?'

'No, he didn't. We would have told you if he had. He was wearing this?'

'Yes.'

'That bastard who buried him must have put it on him then.'

'Quite possibly,' she agreed. 'Your mother wouldn't have given Joshua a St. Christopher without you knowing?'

'No, you can't think—'

'I'm only asking, wondering whether it was something she might have given him when you weren't around as you don't recognise it. Maybe when Ellen was with Joshua.' *Or when Joshua was alone with his grandparents, she didn't add.*

'My mother would never have given Josh anything religious. She'd know that neither Ellen, nor I, would have approved.'

'I did notice some religious ornaments in your mother's display cabinet at her old home.'

'Those were things I was given by my Sunday school teacher. My mother only kept them because they were mine – not because she's religious. My parents aren't religious but they allowed me to go to Sunday school because I asked them if I could. I wanted to go because my best friend went and he used to talk about all the wonderful outings they organised. Those ornaments are long gone now. I persuaded mum to donate them to Vinnie's when they moved into the house here with me.'

She talked to Max for a further fifteen minutes while they drank the glasses of homemade lemonade that Pamela Gibson had served. When she and Naomi left, India promised to contact Max soon about the viewing.

'We have partial fingerprints and a hit on the DNA base,' Naomi exclaimed excitedly to India two days later. She had just returned from Max Gibson's viewing of his son's body. As she'd suspected he'd found it very difficult and had collapsed sobbing into his parent's arms after they'd left the viewing room.

'Tell me,' India said.

'DNA the techies identified on the chain around Joshua's neck and the blanket matched one Gerard Coughlan, born on the twenty-eighth of July, nineteen sixty-eight. I've sent a picture of him through to your computer. They also picked up Jimmy Lansford's DNA. Partial fingerprints on the cross and the St. Christopher also match Coughlan and Lansford. Coughlan was arrested back in May twenty-twelve for his part in a drunken brawl outside a hotel in Penrith. The case proceeded to court but Coughlin was let off with a fine when the other party admitted extreme provocation and starting the fight. The good thing about it was that he gave a DNA sample, and of course, his fingerprints.'

'Do you have an address for him?'

'No. The last one recorded is no longer valid. Following his arrest he claimed a disability pension – supposedly for injuries he received in the brawl, but his claim ceased in December two thousand and twelve. The last payment made to him was on the twenty-seventh of December that year.'

'Mm. The timing just about fits. Coughlin sounds like an Irish name,' India said.

'It is. I've done a bit of digging into his background. His family immigrated to Australia when he was a teenager in eighty-three. He was born in Cork, Ireland. The family settled in Penrith and I've tracked down the address and phone number of his younger brother, Liam, who still lives there. He posted bail for Gerard Coughlin back in twenty twelve. I have a phone number, but I'm not sure if he'd be home at this time. Do you want me to phone him or should we go and see him?'

'I think we should pay him a visit. Good work Naomi.'

Liam Coughlin was not in, but his wife directed them to his place of employment. He managed a wholesale plumbing spares outlet situated on a trading estate. As she drove into the estate, India recognised it as one where a few of the businesses had employed Jimmy Lansford. Might there be a connection here?

She asked to speak to Liam Coughlin after showing their identities at the counter.

A sandy haired man whom she judged to be in his late forties came to meet them. He looked nothing like the image of his brother she'd seen on her computer screen. Gerard Coughlin was dark haired. They both had blue eyes though.

'I haven't seen Gerard since his trial in two thousand and twelve,' Coughlin told them. 'He contacted me just before Christmas that year, and told me he was moving to Queensland to run a bar. That was the last time I heard from him.'

'Which part of Queensland?'

'He didn't say and to be honest I wasn't interested enough to ask him. When he said he was going to be running a bar, I thought that would be the end of him and that he'd drink himself to death. Gerard has a problem with alcohol.'

'He hasn't been in touch with you or any other

members of the family since then?'

'I know he phones our mother back in Ireland a couple of times a year, on her birthday and at Christmas, but he's never mentioned where he lives, except to say he's in Queensland and near the sea. He talks about walking on the beach and going out to sea on his small boat. None of us has his address or a phone contact. Sorry I can't help you any more than that. Why are you asking about him? What's he done this time?'

'We're just making some enquiries Mr. Coughlin. I wonder if you could tell me if you recognise this man?' she asked showing him a photograph of Jimmy Lansford on her phone.

'Can't say that I do,' Coughlin said. 'Who is he?'

'A man called Jimmy Lansford.' She looked closely at Coughlin to see if the name meant anything to him. There was an obvious flicker of recognition. Fresh articles referring to Jimmy Lansford had appeared in the paper following the discovery of Joshua's body.

'Wasn't he the fella who took that little kid?'

'Yes. And we know Lansford did odd jobs for people on this trading estate over the years and that every business here was questioned about him. Did he ever work for you Mr. Coughlin?'

'I wasn't here back then,' he said shaking his head. 'Two thousand and thirteen, wasn't it? I only took over this business in two thousand and fourteen.'

'What did you do prior to that Mr. Coughlin?'

'I was a plumber, but after recovering from an injury I decided not to go back into the trade, and took over this franchise instead.'

'What about your brother Gerard? What did he do for a living?' Naomi asked.

'He was a qualified carpenter – and a good one when he was sober enough to take on work. And he could turn his hand to almost anything in the building trade, Gerard could. Brick work, plastering, and small electrical and plumbing jobs. You name it, he could do it. He just couldn't stay off the booze or out of the poker games. If he'd been able to, he'd be a wealthy man by now.'

'Your brother was a drinker and a gambler?'

'Yes. Once upon a time Gerard owned his own house – one that he built. But he was forced to sell it back in two thousand and five to pay off some gambling debts and rented after that.'

Someone who gambled and drank regularly could be just the type of character who would take a chance on kidnapping a small child, India thought.

'You both worked in the building trade. Did you ever come across Jimmy Lansford in your work?' she asked him.

'No. You found that kid's body, didn't you? You don't think Gerard had anything to do with it do you?'

'As I told you Mr. Coughlin, we are just making some general enquiries.'

'I'm sorry I can't help you any further.'

'Well thank you for your time then.'

It was disappointing to hear that Liam Coughlin had no knowledge of his brother's whereabouts and that there was no obvious connection to Lansford. Had Coughlin moved to Queensland before Joshua's kidnapping? Or, when he spoke to his brother, had he been talking about his intended plans to move the following year? And if he was a builder how could he have laid his hands on the type of drugs that were found in Joshua's remains? The tox screening had proved interesting. They'd been able to ascertain that Joshua had been drugged, presumably to knock him unconscious to make it easier to move him to the cabin.

'I was hoping we'd find a connection to Jimmy Lansford there,' India said after they climbed back into the car. 'I think it's strange that there are no records on Coughlin since December twenty twelve. I'll contact Queensland Police Headquarters when we get back to the station and see if they can trace him. If he was involved in the kidnapping and has the rest of the ransom money, he might be flying under the radar though, living off the cash somewhere.'

'Or he could be *working* in this so-called bar for cash and not declaring any of his earnings,' Naomi said.

Due to the serious nature of the crime Jacko's friendly tax officer had told them that Gerard Coughlin's records showed no declared income since 2012.

'I think we need to check out Liam Coughlin as well. See what the state of his finances are. You never know, his brother may have gifted him a large sum of money. But before we head back to the station, we need to pay a visit to Roger Lansford and see if he recognises Coughlin. And we could also try his next-door neighbour to see if she recognises him. You might have read about her in the files – she suffers from Parkinson's and arthritis. She saw a dark-haired man leaving the Lansford house shortly after the shot that killed Jimmy Lansford was fired.'

'I don't recognise him,' Roger Lansford told India. 'What's his name?'

They were interviewing Lansford at home. His business had not survived the onslaught of unfavourable publicity back in 2013 and he had sold the premises. From their tracking of him, they knew he now worked for another company. She'd decided not to approach him directly at work, but had phoned him to arrange this interview at home.

'Gerard Coughlin. Did Jimmy ever mention him?'

Lansford sat thinking for a minute, his face screwed up in concentration. 'When I returned from being away one weekend a few months before Jimmy died, the place was in the most terrible state. Jimmy told me he'd had his friend Gerry staying over. There were blankets left in a mess on the couch, bottles of beer, and an empty whisky bottle, so I knew he'd had someone here because Jimmy didn't drink alcohol. It was the first time I'd ever heard him mention the bloke. I was so angry about the mess, I made Jimmy help me clean it up and I didn't ask him any more questions. I was too focused on sorting the place out.'

'It might have been helpful if you'd mentioned this to us back then.'

'It didn't occur to me. Jimmy never mentioned his name again and I thought it was probably someone he'd met on a job who dropped him home. Do you think this is the man who pulled Jimmy into the kidnapping?'

'It might be. We're still making enquiries. You wouldn't still have those blankets you found on the couch that night would you?'

'They were Jimmy's. I had a clear out and threw them all away after he died. They weren't good enough to donate to Vinnies.'

India was disappointed to hear that. They might have found Coughlin's DNA on them.

'What about these items? Do you recognise either of them?'

India showed Lansford the photos of the cross and the St. Christopher medallion. With Coughlin's DNA on them it was unlikely they belonged to Jimmy Lansford but they needed to check.

'No sorry. You wouldn't find anything like those things in this house.'

'Well, thanks for your time Mr. Lansford.'

At the neighbour's house, a young woman holding a baby opened the door to them. 'I'm looking for Mrs. Kerr,' India said showing her identification.

'Mrs. Kerr died three years ago,' the woman said. 'We bought the house from Mr. Kerr last year. If you need to speak to him, he's living in the Anglican retirement home in Richmond.'

'Okay, thank you,' she said, further disappointment creeping in. This was one more set-back to their enquiries. There was no point in going to see Mr. Kerr; he hadn't seen the man they'd wanted to show Mrs. Kerr.

41

It was two days before India heard back from the Queensland authorities to say that they had no trace of a Gerard Coughlan. They had found a 'Bradan' Coughlin, born 18th December 1969, with a match to the partial fingerprints which had been found on the St. Christopher. Coughlin had been arrested for driving whilst intoxicated and injuring a third party. He was arrested in 2016 and served four months of a six-month sentence as well as losing his licence for a year. Queensland Police sent through a photograph of Bradan Coughlin. Although Bradan Coughlin had a beard, she was convinced he was the man on the New South Wales records called Gerard Coughlin. She'd passed the details onto Jacko to deal with, but he was out on a dental appointment that afternoon, so she sought Naomi out to see what he'd discovered.

'Jacko searched through records this morning and found Bradan Coughlin does exist. He's another brother, born between Gerard and Liam.'

'I think we need to visit to Liam Coughlin again,' she told her. 'See what he can tell us about Bradan. If the fingerprints match Gerard Coughlin's, either he's masquerading as his brother or Bradan Coughlin was the one arrested back in twenty twelve and gave us the wrong name. When Jacko comes back, can you two visit Coughlin while I make further enquiries with Queensland?'

'Bradan was killed in a motorcycle accident while he was on a trip back home,' Liam Coughlin told Jacko and Naomi.

'By home, I assume you mean Ireland?' Jacko asked him.

'Yes, mam moved back there in ninety-four after Dad died and she kept encouraging us to go back as well. Bradan did. I don't think he was intending to stay. It was during the winter months when he had his accident. He'd borrowed a cousin's motorbike that night and while driving home skidded on some black ice and crashed into a tree.'

'When was this?' Jacko asked thinking this would account for them having no records of his death.

'Early ninety-five. He was buried over there. Gerard and I went over for his funeral, but then returned here. We've made Australia our home now.'

'Why didn't you tell Detective Hargreaves about your brother Bradan? You failed to mention you had a second brother.'

'To start with she only asked me about Gerard. And he *is* the only brother I have left living. Why would I think Bradan was relevant to anything she was asking me? He's been dead for twenty-five years.'

That was fair enough, Jacko thought. 'So, if a Bradan Coughlin with fingerprints matching Gerard Coughlin was arrested in Queensland, it would be fair to say it was probably Gerard wouldn't it?'

Coughlin's eyes widened in surprise. 'Gerard's using Bradan's identification?'

'It would seem so.'

'But how could he do that? Bradan's dead.'

'Not according to our records. You wouldn't have a photograph of Bradan anywhere would you?'

Bradan Coughlan, Queensland police informed India, lived in Cooktown, a small coastal town in far north-east Queensland. He owned a hotel in the town and ran it with his wife. She'd heard of Cooktown, a place where Captain James Cook, the Englishman who claimed Australia for Britain, had landed and spent some days carrying out repairs on his ship.

'I've put in for Coughlan's extradition,' she told Jacko and Naomi at the briefing that afternoon. 'And I've asked Queensland Police to gather more information on the hotel. When it was purchased – who did the conveyancing – how much he paid for it. I'm sure we're going to discover that he bought the hotel some time in two thousand and thirteen – after receiving the ransom money.'

Jacko and Naomi filled her in on their visit to Liam Coughlin and what they'd discovered. Coughlin had contacted his wife and asked her to dig out a photograph of Bradan for them to collect. The one they were given showed the three brothers together at what looked like a barbecue. Gerard and Bradan looked alike.

'Liam Coughlin's wife told us that Liam took after his mother and his two brothers took after their father,' Jacko told her.

'How long will it take to extradite Coughlin?' Naomi asked.

'It could take months. The Queensland Police will be wanting to interview him with regard to charges of identity fraud, so they will get first shot at him unfortunately.'

'But ours is a much more serious crime!' Naomi said.

'I know. But there isn't much we can do about it. We'll just have to wait and see what happens.'

'Would they let you travel up to North Queensland to interview him?'

'I've asked them that. They said it would be fine as long as our Commander approved it.'

'When are you going? I wouldn't mind going with you,' Naomi said. 'The furthest I've ever been from New South Wales was a trip to Tasmania when I was eighteen, just before I joined the force. I've never been north. Not beyond Coffs Harbour anyway where I went on a couple holidays with my parents when I was a kid.'

'Well I wouldn't mind going to North Queensland either,' Jacko said.

'Perfect,' India said. 'You two can go together then.'

A further phone call from Queensland police put paid to

any visits up to the north of the state. They told India that when they went to pick Coughlin up, his wife claimed he'd gone back to Ireland suddenly.

'*Something to do with his mother,*' DS Ford told her. Ford, who worked in Brisbane's CIB, had been her main liaison contact.

'When did he go? Do you know?'

'*He flew out of Cairns on the twelfth November. We've ascertained that he left the country using a passport in the name of Bradan Coughlin'.*'

It looked like he'd taken off when the news of finding Joshua's body had been released to the press. He must have been seriously worried and known that something with the remains could implicate him.

'Did you find out where he flew to?'

'*Yes, Dublin, but his wife said his mother lives in Cork, so no doubt he'll be heading there.*'

'How long has Coughlin been married do you know?' Liam Coughlin hadn't mentioned a wife and they had nothing on their records about Gerard Coughlin being married.

'*I don't know. But I can find out and get back to you. I'll send you the information in an email. Is that Okay?*'

'Yes, fine, thanks DS Ford. What about the purchase of the hotel? Did you find out anything about that?' She listened and made notes while he reeled off the information, looking at the dates in puzzlement. Surely that couldn't be right?

'Your trip is off, I'm afraid,' India announced to Jacko and

Naomi. 'The bird has flown. He's in Ireland somewhere. He took off a couple of days ago.' She explained what the Queensland police had told her about Coughlin.

'He must have heard about Joshua being found then,' Jacko surmised.

'I'd say so.'

'Could we go to Ireland instead?' Naomi asked, looking more than a little excited about the idea.

'I have no interest in going to Ireland,' Jacko said wrinkling his nose up and turning his mouth down.

'No-one is going to Ireland. Well not at the moment anyway. I'll have to try to reach someone over there and see what they have to say. In the meantime, can you check marriage records in New South Wales and see if there's any information about either Gerard or Bradan Coughlin marrying. Also, can you contact Liam Coughlin and ask for contact details for his mother in Cork. It looks like Coughlin may be heading there.'

'After we've done that we could still go and question Coughlin's wife up in Cooktown, couldn't we?' Jacko asked. 'She might be able to tell us something interesting.'

'I think that might be a good idea. I've just received some information that has put paid to my theory about Coughlin buying his hotel with the ransom money. According to records, Coughlin has owned the hotel since November ninth, two thousand and twelve.'

'That's almost a couple of months before the kidnapping then,' Jacko said.

'And just a couple of weeks after his court case. So how did he pay for it, if he was broke?' Naomi asked.

'That's the interesting part. No money seems to have

changed hands when he took over the ownership.'

42

At Cairns airport, Naomi and Jacko had to transfer to another plane for the last leg of their flight to Cooktown. Jacko stopped as they followed a small number of people across the tarmac.

'What the hell is that? We're not flying in that thing are we?' he said pointing to a small plane ahead of them. He had expected to be travelling in another jet.

'That mate,' a man who had been following behind them said, 'is a Cessna single turboprop engine plane. It's the type used on regular flights from Cairns to Cooktown.'

'It looks like a toy plane – or one you see being used in the outback,' Jacko said. He wasn't keen on the idea of flying in this thing.

'Cooktown is not a very big place. The larger planes don't fly in there,' the man told him. 'Don't worry, I fly this route all the time. It's perfectly safe.'

At Cooktown, a shaky Jacko and Naomi took a cab for the fifteen-minute journey into town. After landing Jacko swore that he wasn't going to fly back to Cairns in such a small plane. He hoped he might be able to catch a train back to Cairns, but had learnt that there was no railway line in Cooktown and that plane or road journeys were the only options.

'It wasn't so bad,' Naomi said teasing him. 'I enjoyed the flight. The scenery out of the window was spectacular.'

He hadn't wanted to look at the scenery. He'd just wanted the damn flight to be over. He wasn't a keen flyer at the best of times, but he felt safe in the bigger jets. In that small aircraft, which had bounced about on much of the journey, he'd felt sick.

Coughlin's hotel, called *The Corkscrew* was a large sprawling Queenslander-style building which had had some obvious add-ons over the years. Naomi had read up about it before they'd left Windsor. As well as offering accommodation, they catered for special events, had a restaurant, a coffee lounge selling snacks, several bars and the standard swimming pool. It sat in spacious luscious grounds with views out to sea from the front. Knowing that Coughlin had originated from Cork in Ireland she suspected the hotel's name was linked to his past, using a play on words. The Australian wine industry no longer used corks for the majority of their stock, and hadn't for years. Would younger drinkers, who would be inclined to buy cheaper wines, even know what a corkscrew was?

Naomi and Jacko had booked into a different hotel, and had arranged to meet a Sergeant Devlin outside Coughlin's at 7 pm. She'd been expecting to meet an

Irish looking male, so was surprised to see Devlin was an indigenous mixed-race man. After introductions, Devlin took them through to an office near the reception.

'Tracey is expecting us,' Devlin said, tapping on the door before opening it. First name terms, Naomi noted. Was Devlin a friend of the couple?

'Good evening,' Tracey said standing and shaking their hands after Devlin introduced them.

Naomi judged the slim, short attractive blonde woman to be in her forties.

'How can I help you?' she asked them once they were all seated.

'We understand you and Mr. Coughlin have been married since December twenty-thirteen,' Jacko said. 'Can you tell us how and where you met your husband?'

Tracey looked nonplussed by the question.

'Why would you want to know that?'

'It's relevant to our enquiries,' Jacko said without explaining.

Tracey cleared her throat. 'I was working in an employment agency in Cairns in two thousand and thirteen. Bradan flew down in August looking to recruit a chef. He'd not long opened the hotel after carrying out major improvements and only had a couple of cooks offering simple meals. He wanted to open a proper restaurant. We hit it off and I ended up following him back here a fortnight later. That was in the September. At first, the intention was that I was going to help him develop the business, but one thing led to another and we were married a few months later.'

Tracey was still calling her husband Bradan, Naomi

noted, even though she'd been told his name was Gerard.

'Did you husband ever explain how he came to own the hotel and was able to pay for all the refurbishments?' Naomi asked her.

'He won the hotel in a game of poker. I know that because he allowed Roddy Mulligan, the previous owner, to stay on living here until his death three years ago. Roddy was an alcoholic and he'd let the place become really run down. He still had one of the bars going here which mainly drew in a local crowd. When Bradan took it over there was so much to do. He told me he'd sold a property he had down in Sydney to pay for the refurbishments. Plus savings he had from working in the building trade for years. He'd never married or had kids so he didn't have high outgoings.'

'I notice that you are still referring to your husband as Bradan. I understand, from Sergeant Devlin here, that you now know his name is actually Gerard?' Jacko asked her. 'Had he ever mentioned the name Gerard to you?'

'Yes, Bradan – I'm sorry, I've only ever known him by that name – he told me that he had two brothers, one called Gerard who had died in an accident in Ireland, and another one called Liam who lived near Sydney. He and Liam stopped speaking after some falling out he told me. Sergeant Devlin has told me that Bradan's real name is Gerard. I don't know why he adopted his brother's name – perhaps he didn't like the name Gerard. Was it Bradan who really died in the accident in Ireland?'

'Yes, it was. And I have to tell you that our enquiries have confirmed that your husband didn't own a property in Sydney at the time he took over the hotel.'

'Then how ... hang on, you said he didn't own a property *at the time*. Do you mean he'd sold one earlier and had the money left over from it?'

'No. That's not what I meant. I didn't phrase it very well,' Jacko said. 'Your husband was living in a rented property in Sydney and had been for some years. He was *broke*.'

'Bradan didn't ... you don't think he *stole* the money for the hotel work from someone do you? Is that what this is all about?'

'I'm afraid we're unable to tell you anything at the moment,' Jacko said shaking his head.

'If that's what you think then I'm sure you're wrong. Bradan probably won the money for the building work from gambling again. And he did a lot of the work himself. He confessed he used to be a terrible gambler and drinker, but he'd quit both by the time I met him. He had the odd relapses, like that time he knocked someone down a few years back. Thankfully they weren't badly injured otherwise he would have received a longer sentence. The person he hit only received a few grazes because Bradan had almost stopped in time. But he hasn't drunk since. Not like Roddy, who drank himself to death.'

Ignoring her protestations about her husband's innocence Jacko asked, 'Have you heard from your husband since he arrived in Ireland?'

They knew from their enquiries that Gerard Coughlin had not visited his mother and the police in Cork had not been able to find any trace of him.

'He phoned me to say he'd arrived in Dublin and was

spending the night there before heading down to Cork. I then received an email from him after that saying he was staying at his mother's. I don't have her details.'

'We *do* have your mother-in-law's details. She's not ill, and your husband is not staying with her,' Naomi told her. 'We're going to need the phone number he called you from and a copy of the email.'

'Then where … where is he? And why would he … that's why you're here isn't it? He's running away from something or someone. I don't know where he is then. I tried phoning him yesterday, but the phone wasn't switched on. Bradan did say he was going to buy an Irish mobile and would let me know the number, but he hasn't.'

'We have a search warrant Tracey. I'm afraid we're going to need to search the hotel,' Devlin told her.

'What are you looking for? Perhaps I can help you without disrupting the whole hotel.'

'We're looking for cash,' Jacko told her. 'Or items which hold a high value.'

They knew from Police Queensland enquiries that Coughlin hadn't paid out any money for the hotel. Only legal costs. It had been in a poor state of repair when he'd taken over ownership and he'd spent quite a bit on refurbishments. But it only accounted for a very small amount of the ransom money if you added in the money that had been paid to Jimmy Lansford. Coughlin would have taken some with him to Ireland, but he must have stashed the rest somewhere else. They were hoping to find it at the hotel.

'The only cash we have we keep in the safe here in our

offices. And we don't keep huge amounts here. We bank it. We don't have anything valuable on the premises. When you say "items of high value" what sort of thing are you looking for? We don't have anything valuable here.'

'We're not sure,' Devlin said. 'Do you own, or rent any other premises?'

'No. We live in the hotel. If Bradan has stolen some money, does that mean we're going to lose the hotel? Is my marriage to him even legal?' Tracey asked, with a look of panic on her face.

43

Sergeant Devlin drafted in a number of uniformed officers to help with the search. After removing the drawers from a fitted wardrobe in the couple's bedroom, which held Gerard Coughlin's clothes, they found documents taped to its underside, revealing Coughlin rented a post office box in Cairns and had another bank account Tracey hadn't known about down there. There were also documents relating to a rental property in Cairns, handled by an agency. That accounted for where some more of the money had gone. Apart from a few thousand in cash, no other money was found at the hotel. The hotel bank account showed a healthy turnover and income, but it did not contain millions. Neither did the couples personal accounts they held in Cooktown, or the one Coughlin had in Cairns. Jacko said they needed to look into the Cairns property and rental information on their way back to Windsor and asked Devlin to arrange with his colleagues in Cairns for another search warrant to be issued.

They left Tracey Coughlin looking distraught and worried. Naomi couldn't help but feel sorry for the woman. She still hadn't been told about the crime her husband was suspected of being involved in, but she had learned that her married life had been based on a lie and now her future was uncertain.

'Mr. Coughlin visits us once a year to go over the accounts,' the woman in the Cairns rental agency told them. 'We pay all proceeds from it into his account.'

'We're going to need to see all those records and we will need to search the property. Are there any tenants in there at the moment?' Detective Sergeant Moore asked her. Moore had met Jacko and Naomi at Cairns airport and was co-ordinating investigations in the city.

'Yes, it's a busy time of year for us. There's a family from England in there at the moment who have another three days to go and we have another couple booked in for a fortnight from next Sunday. Mr. Coughlin was staying in the property himself before this current family arrived. We had a gap in the bookings through a cancellation and he said he'd take advantage of it to check the place over.'

'You'll need to find the English family urgent alternative accommodation and I suggest you line up something else for the tenants due to stay there next week,' Moore said.

The rental property was a three bedroomed mid-century single storey house located close to a beach just north of the city. They found nothing after a thorough search inside the house, including the loft space

'We need to look outside and under the house,' Jacko said.

When they'd arrived, he'd noticed the house was built on brick pilings, with a generous crawl space underneath. Borrowing a torch from one of the officers helping in the search, he knelt on the ground and shone it under the house.

'What's that over there in the far-right corner?' he asked the constable who he'd sent crawling under the house to investigate. 'It's like some kind of brick enclosure.'

'It's probably something structural,' came the mumbled reply. The constable didn't want to look any further and kept going on about snakes.

'The bricks look different. Can you crawl over there further and have a better look?'

He heard a lot of complaining and swearing before words that were music to his ears. 'I've found something!' the constable yelled. 'It looks like some kind of metal safe chained to the brick wall built around it. We're going to need some bolt cutters.'

44

Jacko phoned India to fill her in on their findings.

'When the safe was finally opened, we found just under a million dollars in it,' Jacko told her.

'Do you think he's had the money there all the time?'

'I don't know, but I suspect so. He bought the house fairly soon after he arrived up this way.'

'Wouldn't that be risky? Might he have kept some hidden at the hotel in Cooktown and his wife is covering up for him?'

'Naomi and I don't think his wife knows anything. He mainly rented the house out to overseas visitors. I don't suppose they'd go crawling about under a house. There was a notice in the kitchen warning guests about spiders and snakes. Coughlin used to stay at the house on some of his visits to the area where he could've freely dipped in and out of the money.'

'Okay, makes sense I suppose.'

'He stayed there just before he left the country and so we think he cleared some of the money out of the safe then. He deposited a large sum into his Cairns bank account, telling them he'd just sold one of his properties for cash. He showed them some documentation, which was probably forged. He then

withdrew quite a large sum which they converted to Euros for him. Since he's been in Ireland he's been withdrawing money every day as well. From different banks in Dublin. Moore suggested we cut off his money supply and freeze his bank account, but I told him I thought it would be better to leave it open so we could keep tabs on him. What do you think?'

'I agree with you. We need to keep him thinking he's not come to anyone's attention. He might move on to Cork or somewhere else. In which case we'll know. But we need the bank to keep us informed. Can you arrange that with the manager directly or do we have to go through Moore? Find out and let me know. That was a great find by the way. Naomi said it was you who spotted the different bricks under the house,' she said. 'Well worth paying for the cost of you two to travel up there then.'

'I told you it'd be worth it. When I saw the bricks it made me think of what his brother had told you, that Coughlin had skills in all sorts of building work. I'll see what I can sort out with the bank. Anyway, we're on tomorrow morning's flight back to Sydney. Landing at three forty-five. We're going to take the rest of today off to look at some sights here.'

'Okay. Enjoy. I'll have someone pick you up from the airport,' she said, ringing off.

India had been talking to the Irish police – known as the Garda Siochana. When she'd told them Coughlan was a prime suspect in the kidnapping, ransom and death of a young child, they were willing to co-operate in a search for him and his mother. Enquiries with passport control in Ireland revealed that Coughlin had landed in Dublin on an Irish passport in his brother's name. That meant he had at least two passports on him. An Australian and Irish passport in the name of Bradan Coughlan. But they'd also discovered he held an Irish passport in the name of Gerard Coughlin. How had the Irish Passport Office not noticed they were the same man? There was no record of Gerard Coughlin holding an Australian passport.

She'd been making enquiries into the procedures they would have to follow when they located Coughlin in Ireland and had enough evidence to bring him to trial. She thought they now had enough. As an Australian resident, he had to be tried for the crime in Australia. But with Coughlin only having Irish citizenship, it complicated matters. Whatever happened they'd have to put in an extradition request to Ireland in order to bring him back for trial. She'd started the ball rolling on that matter this morning.

She'd been talking to a Sergeant O'Hare who was based in Cork, but after discovering Coughlin had not been in touch with his mother or any other members of the family, O'Hare said he'd get in touch with Dublin and find someone there to take over dealing with the matter for her. She was still waiting to hear from them. Looking at her watch, she decided it was time she left for the day. It was the middle of the night in Ireland. No-one would be calling now. It was an opportunity for her to pick up Sam and Georgia herself from kindy and save her mother the journey. Rob said he'd be home early today. She was looking forward to picking them up; it always made her heart melt to see their little faces light up with delight when she collected them. This evening they could spend some quality time together as a family.

'Our DCI doesn't want Coughlin's accounts frozen,' Jacko told Moore. 'We don't want to alert him to the fact that he is on our radar.'

'I'd say he already knows he'll be on your radar,' Moore said. 'Why not squeeze him financially. That might make him seek help from family members.'

'We suspect he took quite a bit of cash with him and he's been withdrawing money daily. We don't know how much he has on him. He's obviously building up his store of cash and it could be a couple of years before he runs short of money. If we let him keep drawing money out, we'll know where he is.'

'Fair enough.'

'But our DCI would like to be kept informed by the bank. Can we do that directly with the manager we saw today?'

'I don't see why not. I have your details. I'll ask him to set up an alert on the account and have the bank make contact with you every time Coughlin withdraws money. I said I'd get back to him with instructions anyway.'

'Okay great. Right. Well we're going to head off then. Thank you for all your help,' Jacko said standing and shaking Moore's hand. Moore also offered his hand to Naomi. She'd been a bit piqued that he'd studiously ignored her for much of the time they'd been in Cairns. Jacko watched her hesitate before reaching out and shaking his hand.

45

A few days later, the bank in Cairns informed India that Coughlin had withdrawn money from an ATM in Cork. The Dublin police had had no luck in tracking down where he was staying in the city and his withdrawals were spread out over a wide area. Excited by the news, which indicated Coughlin was likely to be heading to his mother's, she phoned O'Hare at Cork Police Headquarters asking him if they could place a watch on the mother's house.

The following day India received an email from O'Hare to tell her that they had picked up Coughlan and arrested him. After all these years they finally had the man who'd masterminded Joshua Gibson's kidnapping in custody. Now they needed someone to go over and question him and find out if anyone else had been involved and discover what went wrong.

The initial charge made against Coughlin was travelling on false documents. O'Hare asked her if anyone from the Australian police intended to come over and question Coughlin. When she approached Jacko, he reiterated that he didn't want to go. Naomi was keen to, but she hadn't been involved in the investigation from the outset. India wasn't sure what to do as she didn't really want to spend any time away from her family. She'd have to discuss it with Rob.

'Much as I hate to say it, it should be you who goes across and interviews him,' Rob said that night.

'I don't really want to, but I can't persuade Jacko to do it. He's adamant about it and I can't force him.'

'Then I think you have to go India. You shouldn't need more than a few days there to wrap things up surely?'

'I don't know. I submitted extradition papers once we knew he was in Ireland, but I don't know how long these things take. If extradition between states in Australia are anything to go by, it could take months, maybe even longer as we're talking about a foreign government. If I went, ideally, I'd like to bring Coughlin back with me, but I don't think that's going to be possible.'

'I think the best thing would be for you to go over now and interview him. Then a case for prosecution can be made and once the extradition papers are processed, someone else could escort him back to Australia. Maybe even someone from the Irish police.'

'I suppose so.'

'I could put in for some leave while you're away and I'm sure your parents would be willing to help more than usual.'

'Okay, I'll talk to the Super and see what he says.'

Superintendent Brocken, who had taken over from Havering when he retired, agreed that India should travel to Ireland to question Coughlan. He wasn't prepared to cover the cost of more than one member of the team, saying only she or Jacko could go.

'*Detective Sergeant Partinger hasn't been involved in the investigation from the start anyway,*' was his justification. She terminated their call and rose to go and break the news to Naomi, knowing she would be disappointed.

46

Cork, Ireland
November 2019

Two uniformed gardas welcomed India warmly when they met her at Cork Airport. The cold wind hit her as they exited the terminal and she hoped she'd brought enough warm clothes with her. They dropped her at Police Headquarters where she met up with Sergeant Rory O'Hare. He told her he'd organised an interview with Coughlin for the following morning at ten and suggested she go to her hotel to recover from her flight. She *was* feeling quite exhausted. The journey had taken thirty-one and a half hours with waiting times in Singapore and London. She'd flown into London as she'd done on a trip back in 2014 and then had to take a flight from there to Cork. She'd slept briefly on the long-haul flight, but was glad she would have this respite. She wasn't in a fit state to be starting any interviews today; she needed a hot shower and a long sleep.

At nine-thirty the following morning, feeling refreshed, India met with O'Hare who drove them to the new Cork City jail. He pointed out the old Victorian jail as they passed it, which O'Hare said was now a visitor's centre.

He told her that Coughlan had refused to speak to the Irish Garda except to acknowledge his name. She suspected she would receive the same treatment.

They were shown to an interview room where she and O'Hare waited while Coughlin was brought in with a solicitor. Coughlin didn't look much older than the photograph she'd seen of him. He must be in his early fifties, but he looked younger, which she thought was surprising for someone who had once been a serious drinker. His dark brown hair showed no signs of grey and there were few lines around his face. His blue eyes carried a look of sadness though.

Coughlin's solicitor had been informed about the nature of the questioning and charges. India suspected he would have advised Coughlin not to speak.

After O'Hare introduced them and read Coughlin his rights, she launched into her first question.

'Can you tell me how you and Jimmy Lansford came to be involved in the kidnapping of five-year-old Joshua Gibson?'

Coughlin didn't answer her, just as she expected. He kept his head down as though examining something interesting on the edge of the table. She tried another approach.

'I don't think you intended to harm Joshua did you?'

She was surprised when Coughlin raised his head, looked at her and responded.

'It was that bloody idiot Lansford. The boy was

supposed to be released unharmed. He messed everything up!' Coughlan shouted before settling back into his seat with a sulky look on his face.

'Can you tell us what happened?'

Coughlin shook his head. At least he'd admitted to his involvement. She needed more though. 'So tell me what happened Gerard. How did Jimmy mess everything up?'

Keeping his head down, Coughlin answered after a few seconds. 'He collected the money. That all went well. He was then supposed to drop the kid back in Windsor as I'd agreed with the boy's mother when it all went pear-shaped.'

She raised a hand up to stop him at this point.

'Can you explain what you mean when you say you were supposed to drop Joshua in Windsor as you'd agreed with the boy's mother?'

'Like I said, I'd agreed with the mother that I'd drop the kid in Windsor.'

'When did you agree to do this?'

'When we spoke about releasing the boy.'

She racked her brains to recall the details of the conversation that had been recorded from the phone call the kidnappers had made to the Gibson house. She couldn't remember any mention of a particular location where Joshua would be dropped. Was Coughlin lying or had Ellen Gibson been more involved all along as Talbot thought.

'When did you speak to Ellen Gibson about where you'd release her son?'

'I phoned her once Jimmy confirmed he had the money in a message. Only I didn't know what had happened at that point. The mother was back home by then.'

Coughlin thought Ellen Gibson had delivered the money. She wasn't about to enlighten him on that. There had been no mention, from Ellen or the duty officer about a further phone call from the kidnappers. Coughlin was lying, she was sure of it.

'This was on the night the money was delivered?'

'That's right. I had no idea at the time that the boy was dead.'

'What did you say to Mrs. Gibson in that phone conversation?'

'I told her we had the money and made some sarcastic comments about how it must have been hard for her to part with all that money, but that she'd done well lifting two heavy bags all alone. I said we'd keep our end of the bargain, dropping her boy somewhere in Windsor and that we'd phone the cops and let them know where, but she had to promise not to make any more stupid statements to the television cameras or newspapers.'

'Right.' So that was why Ellen didn't want to speak at the public appeal. Why hadn't she mentioned the phone call? But thinking back Ellen had asked her a couple of times if the police had received a call from the kidnappers. She had also mentioned that the kidnapper had talked about releasing Joshua when he'd spoken to her. *She* should have picked up on that and questioned Ellen further. Ellen was in no state to talk with any clarity about *another* phone call from the kidnappers. All she'd been focused on was whether her son had been released.

'When did you discover that Joshua Gibson was dead?'

'Not until after Jimmy arrived at my place. When he confirmed he had the money I sent him a message telling him to go ahead and leave the boy where we'd agreed. The plan was, he'd leave the boy tied to a post of the swings in a park in Windsor. I wanted Jimmy to tie him up so he didn't run off somewhere in fright. He could've been knocked down by a car or something. Anyway, Jimmy was supposed to send me a message saying he'd done it, so I could make the call to your lot about where he was, but I heard nothing further from him. When he turned up at my place, he didn't say anything at first but when I asked him why he hadn't sent me the confirmation message he started blubbering like a baby and said his dog, and the boy, were dead. I couldn't believe it.'

'Did he tell you what happened?'

Coughlin nodded but didn't speak for several seconds.

'Jimmy claimed he heard rustling in the bush and the boy started shouting out thinking it was his mammy coming to collect him. He put his hand over the boy's mouth to shut him up when a giant kangaroo appeared and attacked his dog. A giant kangaroo! I never wanted him to take the bloody dog with him, but Jimmy wouldn't do the job without it. He said he dropped the kid and ran over to his dog. He planned to carry his dog out and go and find help. He told the kid to get up, but Jimmy said he was making funny noises for a few minutes and shaking about and then stopped breathing. His dog died from its injuries. As well as being kicked by the roo, its head had been smashed against a rock.'

The dog's injuries he was describing tallied with their findings. The pathologist had found a fractured skull, one broken front leg and broken ribs on the dog's remains.

'What did Jimmy do then?' O'Hare asked.

'He started digging a grave for them, but then thought he heard something moving around in the bush. He was worried the kangaroo would come back so he shoved both the bodies in a spare duffle bag he had with him and carried them and the money out. After he told me, he started going on about how he couldn't live with himself. He had made some kind of connection with the kid – he'd told the boy his name was Billy because I said he couldn't tell him his real name. Jimmy wanted to bury the boy and his dog in a special place he knew on some property. I was worried then that he was going to hand himself in to the police, but he promised me he wasn't. He took the money – I gave him five hundred thousand, which was the sum we'd agreed at the beginning of the job when we were asking for two million and he went off to bury the kid and his dog. I tied one on a bit that night – drowning my sorrows in too much whiskey. I was really upset about the boy dying; it wasn't what was supposed to happen. I didn't get up until quite late and it was then I realised Jimmy had taken a blanket off my couch, my St. Christopher's chain that was sitting on the sideboard and a cross I had hanging on the wall.'

'What happened next?'

'I was worried about my things so went around to his house. I saw his cousin's car wasn't there, only the ute Jimmy had stolen. I was just about to get out of my car when I heard a gunshot blast. I rushed into the house and found Jimmy had blown his head off, the stupid bugger. He'd left a note saying what he'd done and where he'd buried the boy. Down the back of some property under a large rock next door to where he used to work. A family with some foreign sounding name. I ripped the bottom half of the note off and scarpered, leaving for Queensland that day. I couldn't take the chance of you finding the boy with my stuff on him.'

Coughlan went quiet at this point. India could see tears running down his face. Were they tears of shame or regret that he'd been caught?

'How did you know Jimmy?' she asked.

Coughlin sniffed and started talking again. 'I'd met him on a building job a few months before over near Grose Vale.'

'I thought you were claiming a disability pension?'

'I was, but I was a lot better by then and the work was for cash and I needed the money. It started in mid-November and only lasted for two weeks. A bunch of us stayed over at the place, sort of camping out, rather than driving backwards and forwards each day. I dropped Jimmy home the night we finished, buying a take away for us to eat when we got to his place. His cousin was away that weekend and I started drinking after we'd eaten. I'd had too much to drink to drive home so I crashed out there for the night. Jimmy and I got on well. He was a bit immature, but a nice fella.'

'How did you discover where the Gibson family lived?'

'I was in the newsagent in Penrith when that stupid woman told everyone she'd won. I overheard her giving her address to the owner and remembered it. I went to look at their place that evening and saw the woman drive off with her son. It was then the idea came to me about kidnapping her kid and demanding a load of money. They'd won fifty-five million for Christ's sake. What would a few million be to them?'

Interesting that both Coughlin and Lansford were in the newsagent at the same time. Were they together? Was Coughlin covering for Roger Lansford?

'Who were you with at the newsagent shop?'

'What do you mean who was I with? I was on my own. I'd just been in the supermarket to buy a few things.'

India nodded. So it had been a co-incidence. Maybe.

'Did you ever meet Roger Lansford, Jimmy's cousin?'

'No. He wasn't at the house the couple of times I went there.'

'You went into the Gibson house that night didn't you? Can you tell me what you did?'

'Yeah, after the woman drove off, I discovered she'd left the house unlocked. I went in and took some of the boy's things.'

'Can you tell me exactly what you took?'

'I can't remember,' he said shaking his head. 'I know I picked up a story book, his teddy bear and some clothes. Something like that.'

'What about magazines?'

'Oh yeah, I did take some magazines. That's what I made the ransom demand from.'

'And a phone bill with their number on it?'

'Yeah, that as well.'

'What did you do after you left the Gibson house?'

'I drove across to see Jimmy. I found him walking back from his local pub and we went into his place. I told him that the boy's mother wanted us to take him and make it look like a kidnapping. Jimmy was a good person and wouldn't have gone along with the kidnapping unless he thought we were doing it for someone like the mother. So I told him it was all her idea because she wanted the publicity.'

India stopped him there.

'I just want to clarify that you and Jimmy Lansford *were* the only two people involved in Joshua Gibson' kidnapping. You weren't working with Ellen Gibson or anyone else?'

'No. The mother had no idea, but that's what I told Jimmy. He thought it was a great idea and said he had a cabin in the middle of nowhere he could take the boy to. I think he saw it as a big adventure. He said he'd try and get a car from his cousin's repair shop and I went home to make up the ransom demand. It *was* a great idea except for the boy dying. Jimmy said he had some kind of fit. I was never sure if he told me the truth or whether he killed him accidentally and didn't want to own up to it.'

'The boy, Joshua, suffered from asthma. We believe he may have died from an attack. He might have also had a seizure due to lack of fluids. We didn't find much in the way of water at the cabin and he would have needed it after—'

'I gave Jimmy plenty of money to buy food and drink,' Coughlin said cutting her off. 'He never mentioned what he'd bought. Couldn't you tell how the kid died after you found him?'

'So tell me how you managed to take Joshua,' she

said, not answering his question.

'We went to her house a few mornings later, parked the ute Jimmy had stolen in the dilapidated garage next door and waited. She let the boy out to play on his own in the yard. Jimmy managed to grab him and we took off.'

'After injecting Joshua to knock him out.'

'Well yes. We couldn't leave the kid awake, could we? We had to keep him unconscious long enough to get him to Jimmy's cabin.'

'The drug you gave Joshua would have left him very thirsty. If Jimmy didn't give him much water he could have become severely dehydrated. How did you manage to acquire that particular drug?'

Coughlin looked surprised, then narrowed his eyes and scrutinised her. As though he wasn't sure how much more to admit.

'You know what I gave him then?'

'Yes.'

'Right. I got it from a vet I knew. I told him my mate's small dog needed some wounds tending to, but he was a savage little bugger and we couldn't do it unless the dog was knocked out. He gave me some ketamine in a needle when I said my mate couldn't afford to bring the dog into his surgery.'

'Can you tell me the name of this vet?'

Coughlin shook his head. 'I'm not going to get any mates into trouble. This was all my doing. I didn't know what the after effects of the drug would be. And he thought we were giving it to a dog.'

'Okay moving on. Did you ever go to the cabin where

Jimmy was holding Joshua?'

'No. That was all Jimmy. The bush is not my scene. I had no interest in going there. Jimmy assured me it was all great. He'd stayed there loads of times and never came across anyone.'

'A man like Jimmy Lansford, operating at the level of a twelve year old *would* think it was a great adventure. But it was very sparse and not an adequate place for holding a young child.'

'Well he told me it was fine. Jimmy spent most of the time there with the boy, although he had to leave him there a few times to travel to an area where he could get a signal on the mobile phone I'd given him to find out what was happening.'

'Leaving Joshua tied up and probably gagged.'

'Tied up yes, I don't know about him being gagged. But Jimmy told me he fed the boy, gave him drinks and brought him water to wash with from the stream nearby after he'd wet himself. Jimmy said they talked a lot and he really liked him. He didn't think he deserved to live after his dog and the boy died which is why, I guess, he killed himself.'

'What was your intention when you made the ransom demand?'

'What do you mean?'

'Why did you want the money?'

She knew he needed money for renovating his hotel, but she wondered if he had another motive for the kidnapping.

'I wanted to use part of it to do some work on the hotel in Cooktown. I hadn't been there, but Mulligan had shown me photos of it. I knew it needed a lot of work.'

'How did you, a man who lived in Sydney, come to own a hotel in Cooktown?'

'I flew up to Cairns for a short holiday after my court case – as a kind of celebration. I got involved in a poker game where a bloke called Roddy was playing. I won it off him.'

India nodded. She knew all this through the interviews with Coughlin's wife, but wanted to hear how he explained it to see if he gave a different version. She found it interesting that he said he only needed *part* of the money for the hotel. What else had he wanted money for?

'But the hotel didn't need millions of pounds spending on it. You increased the ransom from two million to four million. Why did you do that?'

'After that stupid woman made that statement to the press about two million being a small sacrifice, I thought she could pay double. Share it around a bit more.'

'Share it around? What do you mean by that? Besides Jimmy, who else did you give money to?'

Coughlin shook his head and went quiet.

'We've managed to recover the money you still had at the house in Cairns. We know you bought the house and also paid out for repairs and improvements on the hotel you owned in Cooktown, but adding that money to the sum you gave Jimmy, plus what the police here found on you, it still leaves well over a million missing. What did you do with the rest of the money Gerard?'

'I gave it away – well sort of. The whole idea of getting my hands on that much money was to help people – but I also wanted to make sure I had a decent place and home for myself.'

'Gave it away to whom?'

'Homeless people in the main. When I was up in Cairns for my holiday, I noticed there were a lot of homeless people there. Drunks who were living rough and others just down on their luck for other reasons. I bought the house in Cairns and started to go down there regularly after I got the repairs underway in Cooktown. I'd go in search of people, clean them up with a shower in my house, feed them and give them new clothes. I'd help them find a new place to live, pay their bond and the first couple of month's rent. It was up to them then to find a job. Some had just fallen on hard times, but there were some who needed to go into rehab. If they completed the rehab, I set them up in a rental unit after they came out – like I did with the others. I foolishly gave Roddy Mulligan a chunk of money. He was the fella I won my hotel off in Cooktown. I won it fair and square, but always felt a bit guilty about it. I gave him money to set himself up somewhere else, but he just gambled and drank it away and never moved out.'

His revelations were a surprise. She thought he was going to say he'd given money to friends or family members who had withheld information about Coughlin.

'I know you used to have a problem yourself – is that why you helped these people?'

'Yes,' he nodded. 'I know how bad it is when you sink that low. A friend of mine helped me out years back when I lost my house and everything I owned. My bastard brother Liam wouldn't take me in. Said he couldn't have me around his kids, who were only little at the time. I was homeless for a few weeks myself back then, sleeping rough, until my friend stepped in. It made a hell of a difference in my life and so I wanted to do the same for others. I've been helping out a few people in Dublin since I've been here.'

That was why he was withdrawing so much money every day.

'We're going to need the name of the centre in Cairns you booked people into to verify what you've told us.'

'Sure, no problem. Only Roddy can't verify how much I gave him because he died some years back.'

'We know about his death. Was your wife aware of all these people you helped?'

'No. I used to tell her I was going off to Cairns to meet up with mates. Obviously I took money with me from profits we'd made at the hotel on these trips, but she didn't know about the extra money I had – or the rental property. I'm not sure that Tracey would have approved. Besides she'd start asking me questions and I couldn't tell her about the kidnapping, could I?'

'What brought you back to Ireland?' O'Hare asked.

'I'd always planned to come back to see mam and the old country once I got the hotel up and running successfully. It just took longer than I thought. When I read that you'd found the boy's body, I decided it was time to do it. I don't want to go back to Australia. I've decided I'd rather sell the hotel in Cooktown and split the proceeds with Tracey. I can stay here, can't I? Serve whatever time I have to do in Ireland?'

'That won't be up to us or you,' O'Hare said. 'The

Australian Government has requested your extradition.'

'They can't do that can they?'

'Yes, they can, and I suspect our government will agree to it,' O'Hare said.

'But I'm an Irish citizen!'

'You have also been a resident of Australia for more than thirty years. And have committed crimes there that you have to answer for,' O'Hare reminded him.

'You masterminded the kidnapping of a five-year-old boy, who subsequently died,' India pointed out.

'But I had nothing to do with his death. The plan was always to release him.'

'Was it though? You threatened the family saying if they didn't pay the ransom they wouldn't see their son again. That was a serious threat and shows an intent—'

'I only said that to scare them into paying the money. I was always going to release him.'

'That might have been your intention, but Joshua Gibson still died. Your defence can argue your case in court.'

'If you take me back to Australia, I will never see the outside of a prison again. You know how harsh their sentences are. I don't want to die in an Australian prison. Couldn't I serve my time here? I'd rather die in my own country.'

'I understand what you're saying but we cannot prosecute you for the crimes you committed in Australia. And you have to answer for them,' O'Hare said. 'You could only serve time here in Ireland for a crime you committed in another EU country. I'm sorry, but that doesn't apply in this case.'

India could see that O'Hare sympathised with Coughlan.

'When you're convicted in Australia you can apply to return to Ireland under the International Transfer of Prisoners Scheme. I am sure Ireland would be a participant in that scheme,' she said.

O'Hare nodded.

'In that case I'd rather return to Australia with you now. Get this over and done with. Then I can apply for this transfer. Would that be possible?'

India looked at O'Hare, not sure whether Coughlan could be released to return to Australia with her. Coughlin had charges to face in Ireland as well.

'I don't know. I suggest you talk to your solicitor about it and I'll see what I can do for you,' O'Hare said.

47

India was looking into making arrangements for Coughlin's return with her when O'Hare rang and asked her to pop in to see him. When she arrived at his headquarters, she could tell by the look on his face that something was wrong.

'I'm afraid I have some bad news – bad news for you anyway. Coughlin was found dead in his cell this morning.'

'What? How? Was he murdered?'

'We don't know – we'll have to wait on the post-mortem to find out the cause of death. Coughlan's cell mate claimed he was fine when he left him there this morning. Coughlin said he didn't want any breakfast so remained in the cell. When his cell mate returned some hours later, because he went off to work in the laundry after breakfast, he found Coughlin sprawled out on the floor with blood trickling from his head. Prison Officers said it looked like he'd hit his head on the sink.'

'Wow. That was unexpected.' She started pacing around the room trying to take it all in. It was very convenient that Coughlin had died, and highly suspicious. She stopped and turned to O'Hare.

'Surely his death should be considered suspicious?'

'All deaths in prison are treated as suspicious until we know otherwise.'

'I assume there will be an investigation?'

'Ah for sure, but it's always difficult to discover the truth in these type of deaths.'

'There would be cameras around his cell wouldn't there?'

'Yes, I would imagine so.'

'Was Coughlin in the general prison population?'

'Yes.'

'Could word have got out about him being involved in the death of a young boy because prison inmates generally don't take kindly to prisoners whose crimes involve young children?'

O'Hare shrugged. 'I don't know the answer to that, but you're right. Prisoners like Coughlin are usually placed in a special unit, but when we arrested him it was for identity fraud and he was placed in the general population. He was due to be transferred after the new charges, but that hadn't happened yet.'

'Who will be investigating his death?'

'Given the seriousness of Coughlin's Crimes, Inspector O'Connell will become involved in the investigation with me.'

India nodded. She wondered whether they would make any serious effort to investigate Coughlin's death. It would be very convenient for everyone if his death was ruled accidental.

'Well at least Coughlin achieved his heart's desire to

die in his home country,' O'Hare said.

'I suppose.'

'And it will save the Australian authorities a lot of taxpayer's money.'

'There's that as well. I don't think Joshua Gibson's family will be too pleased to hear that Joshua's kidnapper won't be brought to trial though.'

'At least you'll be able to tell them that he didn't want the money entirely for himself, that he used it to help others.'

'I don't think Max Gibson was ever worried about the money. It was his son he cared about. He would have happily parted with all the money to have his son back.'

O'Hare invited India to attend the post-mortem that afternoon which revealed that Coughlin had died from an open skull fracture to the prefrontal cortex.

'An injury of this sort can cause the circulation of blood and oxygen to be cut off causing bleeding and brain swelling – which is what happened to your man here,' the forensic pathologist told them.

'Would he have died straight away?' she asked.

'I doubt death would have been instantaneous. He could have been lying there for a while before expiration of life. Maybe thirty minutes or so.'

'Are you able to tell whether his death was accidental or caused by someone else?' She noticed Coughlin had bruises on his upper arms – someone could have gripped him tightly causing his head to collide with the sink.

'There are some bruises on both arms, but I'm told

that these could have occurred when he was arrested, or once he was taken to the jail.'

She nodded. These were all feasible scenarios, but the bruises looked fresh to her. Coughlin had been in jail for some days.

As they were leaving the morgue O'Hare told her Coughlin's mother had been informed of her son's death.

'What did you tell her?'

'That we'd be able to tell her more once the post-mortem was completed. I'll go around and see her this afternoon. By the way, the cameras on Coughlin's block malfunctioned yesterday morning. They were out for about four hours before they were fixed. Due to that, we weren't able to discover whether anyone went into his cell after his cellmate left for the dining room. Guards on duty at the time didn't see anyone go in there.'

All mighty convenient. It looked like Coughlin's death would record an open-ended verdict and remain a mystery.

O'Hare suggested they find somewhere to eat after leaving the post-mortem, but she couldn't face it and agreed to meet up with him the following morning.

India contacted Jacko late that night to make sure the news was delivered to Tracey Coughlin in Cooktown. They'd spoken the previous day where she'd filled him in on what she knew at that point. With the up to date information she related to Jacko, he agreed with her that it looked like Coughlin had been murdered, but she stressed no matter what they personally thought, they could only give out the official version.

She also asked Jacko and Naomi to call on Max Gibson and deliver the news.

'Tell Max I'll call on him when I return to Sydney. I'm hoping to catch a flight out tomorrow night if all the paperwork is completed. I'll confirm it with you tomorrow morning,' she told him.

'Out of interest, what will happen to Coughlin's hotel and his house in Cairns?' O'Hare asked her when they met the following day. O'Hare had organised a copy of Coughlin's death certificate for her to take back to Sydney with her. He'd also made a copy of Coughlin's interview which he'd put on a USB stick for her.

'I don't know about the hotel. The house in Cairns will definitely be sold and the money from that, plus the cash found at the house will no doubt be paid back to Max Gibson. What he does with it will be up to him. The hotel is a tricky one. Coughlin used ransom money to pay for the repairs. I guess if Coughlin's wife Tracey raises a mortgage to pay that money back, she might be allowed to keep it. I'm not sure where the law would stand in situations like these where he owned the property in the first place.'

'With any luck the widow will be allowed to keep it. From what you've told me they built it up into a really successful business. I looked it up on-line and was very impressed with what I saw. I wouldn't mind a holiday there myself.'

'Hm. I've only seen it on-line as well. It was two members of my team who visited the place. The local policeman told them the Coughlin couple had really worked hard to turn the place around.'

'It wouldn't seem fair to throw the widow out then.'

'Thankfully it won't be me who will be making those decisions.'

Unlike O'Hare, she felt little sympathy for Coughlin. He had committed a serious crime involving a young child and a man with learning difficulties, which had tragic consequences and resulted in two deaths. Then there was Ellen Gibson's death. Coughlin might have used a substantial amount of the money to help people down on their luck – Jacko had confirmed that Coughlin had paid for several people to attend the rehabilitation clinic in Cairns. She wasn't sure that Max Gibson would find any comfort in that piece of information. Coughlin might have used some of the money for good causes, but it didn't excuse or justify the original crime. Although Joshua was to be laid to rest with his mother and they now knew who had masterminded his kidnapping, India was unhappy that elements of Joshua's and Coughlin's death would remain a mystery. At least now though, she could move on without the haunting guilt that had plagued her for the past six plus years. Joshua's funeral had been postponed Jacko had told her, as Ellen's parents had wanted the information to be made public. Max Gibson had agreed to it. With Coughlin's premature death, she should make it back in time for the funeral.

48

Central Coast, New South Wales
November 2019

A small crowd gathered around the open grave where Joshua Gibson's remains were being laid to rest above his mother's. Word had been leaked on social media and the funeral announced in the press. Crowds had lined the streets leading to the cemetery to pay their respects as the funeral cortege made their way there after the church service. Large crowds had also gathered outside the church. The predicted rain had held off and it turned out to be a beautiful warm sunny day.

Police had been called in to prevent members of the public from entering both the church and the cemetery grounds. The press, with Max Gibson's permission, were allowed to film the internment at a respectful distance.

India stood with Jacko, Naomi and other police who had been involved with the initial enquiry back in 2013. Marlee and Cheryl had joined them, both travelling from their current postings. Retired Superintendent Havering was also there.

When India returned to Windsor, she'd paid a visit to

Max Gibson to tell him everything she'd learned from Coughlin. The following day he'd contacted her and said he didn't want the widow in Cooktown to be forced to return any money. He also didn't want the cash they retrieved from Coughlin or any money that would be raised from the sale of the house in Cairns.

'I want the money to be donated to charities,' he said. When India asked him if he had any particular charities in mind, he said, 'I really don't care. Why don't you suggest some?' She said she'd get back to him on that. He gave her the details of the funeral, asking if she planned to attend. Of course she would be going.

At the end of the service she walked over to say goodbye to Ellen's parents, Max's parents and finally Max.

'Ellen would have loved all this,' Max said as she turned to leave. She stopped and turned back to him with a quizzical look. She wasn't sure if he was having one last dig at his wife. If so she didn't want to hear it.

'All the cameras,' he said sweeping his hand towards the press. 'And all the people who came out to say goodbye to Josh. We found it very moving and Ellen would have been happy to know that people cared enough about Josh to come and pay their respects,' he added waving his hand towards the crowds in the distance.

India heaved a sigh of relief and nodded. 'Yes, I'm sure Ellen would have found it very moving,' she said before turning and walking away.

Acknowledgements

Thanks to Judy who is always the first person to read my draft manuscripts. Thanks for your scribbles over my mistakes and feedback. Thanks to Heather, who first read the final section in its first draft as a short story back in 2018. Thanks to Heather's friend Carol, a retired police officer, who added comments for me to take on board. Thanks to Laura for taking the time to discuss and analyse characters and the plot with me. Thanks to Bianca in Italy – a professional beta reader whose feedback is invaluable. Thanks to Rachel of Rachel's Random Resources for organising my Blog Tour. Thanks to Sandra from Set-to-print for your patient and accommodating typesetting services. Thanks to Bojan from Pixel Studios for your cover work and thanks to all my other friends who have encouraged me to carry on writing and offered feedback on my previous work.

About the Author

L.E. Luttrell was born in Sydney, Australia and spent the first 21 years of her life there before moving to the UK. After working in publishing (in the UK) for a few years she went on to study and trained as a teacher. From the 90s she spent many years working in secondary education, although she's also had numerous other part time jobs. A frustrated architect/builder, L.E. Luttrell has spent much of her adult life moving house and wielding various tools while renovating properties. Although she has written many 'books' now, Small Sacrifices is only the third book she has published. More will follow. L.E. Luttrell lives in Liverpool, Merseyside.

Follow on 🐦 : @LLuttrellauthor

🅕 : L.E. Luttrell – Author

leluttrell.com 📖 : and sign up to L.E. Luttrell's VIP list to receive your **free book**.